THE ARROWS OF THE HEART

UNCHARTED REALMS – BOOK 4

by

Jeffe Kennedy

Thank you for reading!

<u>Credits</u>
Content Editor: Peter Senftleben
Line and Copy Editor: Rebecca Cremonese
Back Cover Copy: Erin Nelsen Parekh
Cover Design: Ravven ravven.com

A STRANGER'S FAITH

As the Twelve Kingdoms and their allies are drawn toward war, a princess cast aside must discover a purpose she never dreamed of…

Karyn af Hardie behaved like a proper Dasnarian wife. She acquiesced, she accepted, she submitted. Until her husband gave her a choice: their loveless, unconsummated royal marriage—or her freedom. Karyn chose freedom. But with nowhere to run except into the arms of Dasnaria's enemies, she wonders if she's made a mistake. She wants love, security, a family. She can't imagine finding any of it among the mercurial Tala.

Worst of all is Zyr. The uninhibited shapeshifter is everywhere she looks. He's magnetic, relentless, teasing and tempting as if she's free to take her pleasure where she wishes. As if there isn't a war rising before them, against a vile and demanding force far stronger than they. But with Karyn's loyalty far from certain, Zyr offers her only chance to aid the defense—a dangerous gambit to seek out a land not seen in centuries, using clues no one can decipher. Together, they'll have every opportunity to fail—and one chance to steal something truly precious…

Dedication

For Carien, because Zyr likes you best, too.

Acknowledgements

Thanks to all of my wonderful writer friends who ask me how I'm doing and then listen to the answer: Grace Draven, Kelly Robson, Darynda Jones, Megan Hart, Katie Lane, Jennifer Estep, Minerva Spencer, and many others. Special thanks to Grace for the beta read, and Kelly for the daily sunshine and for always knowing which book I'm working on.

Love to Terri Beth Chenault and Rachel Cox, for tea and prosecco.

A grateful shout-out, too, to all the denizens of Jeffe's Closet for cheering every time I post an excerpt. To them and all the faithful readers of this series, many thanks for your patience during the extended wait.

Thanks to Peter Senftleben for his excellent developmental editing and to Rebecca Cremonese for her stellar production editing skills.

Much appreciation to my Santa Fe critique group for wine and conversation: Edward Khmara, M.T. Reiten, Jim Sorenson, Sage Walker, and Eric Wolf.

I'm giving yet another special prostration of awe and gratitude to Ravven for the absolutely incredible cover. I've been looking at it for the best part of a year for inspiration while writing, and I'm still not tired of it.

Many thanks to my family, especially to my mom, who told me she loved Zynda.

Love to David, first, last, and always.

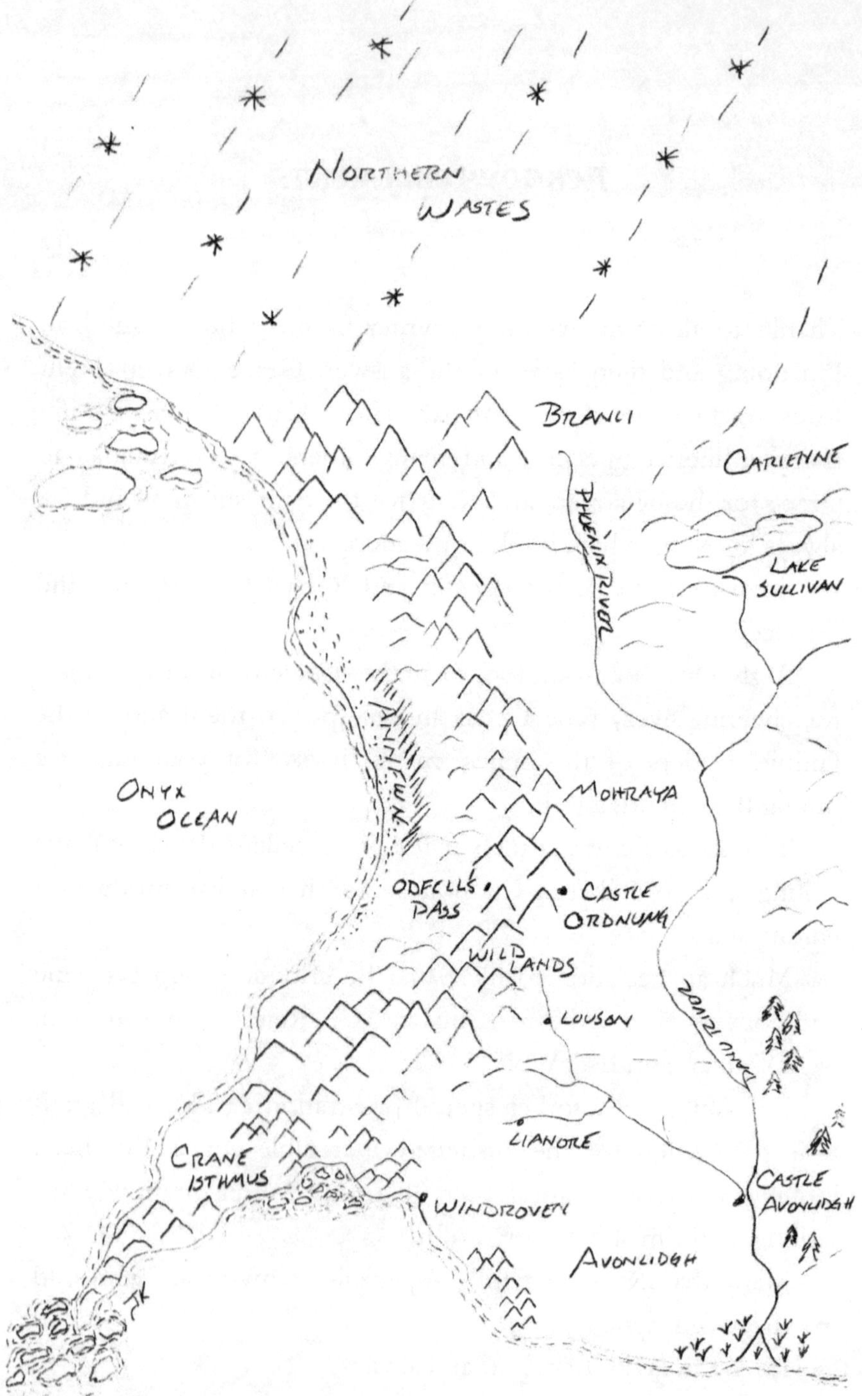

NORTHERN WASTES
BRANLI
CATRIENNE
PHOENIX RIVER
LAKE SULLIVAN
ONYX OCEAN
ANNHEUN
MOHRAYA
ODFELL'S PASS
CASTLE ORDNUMH
WILD LANDS
LOUSON
LIANORE
CRANE ISTHMUS
WINDROVEN
CASTLE AVONLIDGH
AVONLIDGH

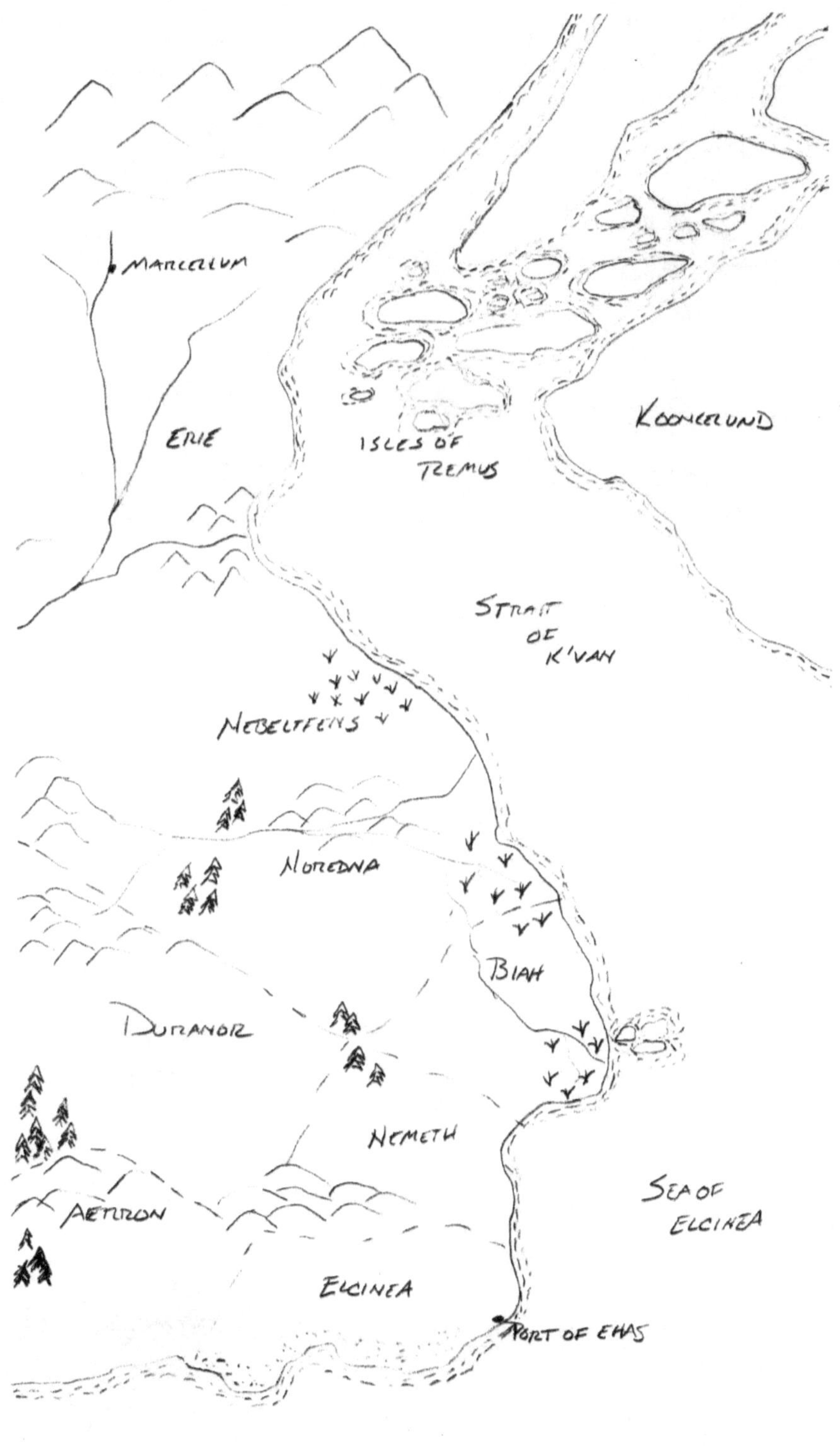

MARCELLUM
ERIE
ISLES OF TREMUS
KOONCELUND
STRAIT OF K'VAN
NEBELTFENS
NOREDNA
BIAH
DURANOR
NEMETH
SEA OF ELCINEA
AETIRON
ELCINEA
PORT OF EHAS

DASNARIA
TO JOFARSTYRR
THE SENTINELS

NORTHERN WASTES
THEORETICAL PAST BARRIER PERIMETER
BRANLI
CATIENNE
LAKE SULLIVAN
PHOENIX RIVER
ORIGINAL BARRIER PERIMETER
ONYX OCEAN
ANNFERN
MOHRAYA
ODFELL'S PASS
CASTLE ORDNUM
WILDLANDS
LOUSON
NAHANAU
LIANORE
CRANE ISTHMUS
WINDROVER
AVONLIDGH
CASTLE AVONLIDGH
WITH ADDITIONS BY DAFNE MAILLOUR KRUPO

The Arrows of the Heart

by Jeffe Kennedy

~ **1** ~

A S SOON AS the sky lightened with the promise of dawn, I dressed and went out.

Better than staring at the empty foreign sky outside the unglazed windows, waiting until it was time to meet the Hawks for training. I'd walk down to the market stalls and get breakfast and hot floral tea, then sit and watch the sea, try to pretend I fit in. That way I could at least be around other people.

Walking out of the little apartment they'd assigned to me in the cliff city of Annfwn, capital of the Tala homeland, I took a deep breath, hoping it looked like I only admired the view, instead of needing a moment to steady myself. It was a spectacular one, to be sure. Only a broad path separated my front door from a stone balustrade and then a sheer drop to the beach below. The gentle, tropically warm sea lay in shadow still, with the sun yet to break over the mountain behind me. Farther out, though, the sun's rays hit the water, turning it an astonishing shade of aqua.

If I had to be stranded in a foreign land, forever exiled from my family and the future that had once shone so bright, at least I'd ended up in a pretty place. Until they kicked me out for being at best useless and at worst an enemy.

For the moment, however, I had coin—actual money, for the first time in my life—and I could buy some food to assuage my empty belly. One aching hole in myself that could be easily filled.

Resolutely straightening my spine—after all, I'd been the fourth highest ranked woman in the Dasnarian Empire, until I threw it all away—I turned my feet downhill, walking on the public path down the cliff face to the market level.

I hadn't gotten more than one level down when I came around a bend and saw the child. Like all Tala, she had long, dark hair, hers in elaborate ringlets. She perched, weeping piteously, and squatting on a low wall that bordered the road—with a sheer drop beneath. My heart skipped into a panicked beat. The Tala were casual about such things, but I couldn't understand how. I wanted to seize her and sweep her off the ledge, then lecture her furiously.

Though I'd be speaking in Common Tongue, which I understood reasonably well now from my friend Jepp's thorough—and occasionally pointed—tutelage on board the *Hákyrling*. The warrior woman hadn't taught me any of the liquid Tala language. The Tala didn't seem to have rules for me to cite, regardless.

Still, I'd never forgive myself if the child fell and I'd done nothing. Moving swiftly, I put my hands on her shoulders. "Careful," I said in Common Tongue. Or rather, started to say.

Beneath my touch, the girl vanished, a pretty songbird exploding to wing in her place. I shrieked in reflexive shock, clasping my hands over my mouth. The bird returned to circle my head, then became the little girl again. If she were a Dasnarian child, I'd guess her to be about eight, as I had several nieces that age. The Tala didn't age the same as normal people, though, so I couldn't be sure. She stared at me owlishly, eyes a light shade of blue, and she said something in her language.

I held up my palms in ignorance. "I'm sorry, I don't understand."

"I speak Common Tongue," she said, with a better accent than mine. "You scared me."

"*You* scared *me*," I said sternly. "It's not safe to be…" I trailed off, realizing that a child who could become a bird at a moment's notice would hardly be vulnerable to a fall. What a fool I was, in this strange place where nothing made sense. "I heard you weeping," I finished instead. "Are you all right?"

Her smooth face crumpled, tears welling up again and magnifying the pretty blue. "My aunt is dead, and my mother is sad all the time."

Oh. How terrible. "I'm so sorry," I said, wanting to cuddle her. I didn't know the customs for dealing with children here, though.

"Why are you sorry?" She asked, cocking her head, much as the bright-eyed bird would've done. "It was the Deyrr sleeper-spies. She was out swimming as a fish and an undead shark ate her."

I wondered how they knew what happened to the aunt, if she'd been eaten, not that I'd be so rude as to ask. The magically animated corpses that the Tala called sleeper spies didn't eat, so probably the thing had just chewed her up. Did the Tala revert to human form after death? A daunting thought. I shuddered. "I'm sorry. That sounds very hard."

"You shouldn't be sorry. I know you didn't kill her. And even though you're Dasnarian, you're not *them*." She said it with such scorn and disgust that she sounded very nearly adult.

I didn't know what to say. The practitioners of Deyrr came from Dasnaria, but no right-thinking people had anything to do with the cult and their black magic. Still, I felt some responsibility, that such a dark thing had come from my homeland to hers. Not that I could affect anything in this ongoing war. I was only a woman, not a warrior. I was also a refugee and dependent on their tolerance. How to explain that to an eight-year-old girl?

"You seem to know a lot about the war," I ventured. No girl child in Dasnaria would know so much.

"I have a very good teacher," she explained. "Zyr teaches us about shapeshifting, and we've been practicing how to fight the sleeper spies. I jump on them from above and make them confused by flying around their heads really fast. I can only be a songbird, so I'm not much other use in a fight." She made a face, clearly disappointed with that.

Privately I thought Zyr shouldn't be teaching the girls to fight anyway—and who knew the flirtatious, changeable man who plagued me at every turn was a teacher? "That's more than I can do," I said.

"Yes, all Dasnarians are mossbacks," she replied with authority. "Zyr said. But you can shoot a bow really well, he said, too. You're Karyn and a nice person. You won't hurt us. I'm Thalia," she added, almost as an afterthought.

I curtseyed, lowering my gaze. Zyr had talked about me? How…disconcerting. "It's a privilege to make your acquaintance, Thalia."

She laughed. "You're funny."

It just figured that a Tala child would find good manners laughable.

"I'd better practice some more," she said, then nodded solemnly. "I'm going to avenge my aunt and protect Annfwn."

"It was lovely to meet you, Thalia."

The child grinned, waved, and ran to the stone wall. "Die, Deyrr sleeper monsters!" she yelled, and jumped off. Unable to help myself, I ran to the wall and looked over the dizzying drop. The little bird swooped in circles, joined by several others. Real birds or other shapeshifter children, I had no idea.

I withdrew to the safety of the road and continued on, thinking about young Thalia, her tears, and her determination to fight. And about Zyr who talked about me to his students. The people I passed nodded and smiled. Some called out greetings in their own language, others in Common Tongue. I didn't have to wonder how they or Thalia knew who I was. They all recognized me easily as I was pretty much the only blonde in all of Annfwn.

I fiddled with my braid, pulling it over my shoulder to run my fingers along the smooth bumps. That, at least, had stayed the same, a comforting anchor to my past, much as I hated the way I stood out in Annfwn, in a sea of the dark-haired Tala who wore their hair loose and wild as their manners. I wouldn't ever cut mine for exactly this reason—I couldn't lose that last tie to who I'd always been. Dasnaria had birthed me and her daughter I'd remain to my dying day.

I had, however, strongly considered coloring my hair dark. Until the shapeshifting sorceress Zynda had advised me not to only the day before, even though she'd agreed it made me exceptional. "In an interesting way," she'd said, which didn't quite make sense to me. I wasn't interesting. Not anymore.

I might have been somebody, if I'd held on to being Kral's wife. He'd been an Imperial Prince, in line for the throne, and I could've been Empress of the Dasnarian Empire. That would have been something. But I'd given that up. So had Kral for that matter, and for love of the mannish Jepp, of all things. I didn't understand it. Most days I didn't understand what in Sól *I* had been thinking.

Except that I'd wanted more. Stupid, because I'd ended up with less than I'd had.

The loneliness was getting to me. That's what had made me babble the way I had with Zynda. I'd been so happy to have someone to have an actual conversation with and then I'd blundered so badly that it made me wince to think of it. What had possessed me to blurt out that I wanted to change my hair so Zyr would lose interest and stop his flirting—and then he turned out to be her *brother!* I groaned at myself, tugging hard on my braid so my scalp ached. *Stupid stupid stupid.*

The gorgeous Tala woman had discomfited me, that was all. I'd seen her shapeshift into countless different animals and work actual magic, and she'd chatted with me, kindly offering advice. She'd even told me just to tell Zyr "in no uncertain terms" to leave me alone. As if a woman could order a man about.

Then I'd dissolved into a spate of apologies—even after she'd chided me for it—and embarrassed myself beyond recovery. Something about her brash confidence and those deep blue eyes that seemed to see inside my head… she flustered me utterly. Just as Zyr did.

Zyr. First Thalia mentioned the troublesome man and then he appeared, walking right toward me.

I'd reached a narrow portion of the road with a flower-draped wall on one side and the balustrade on the other, with the sheer drop below. No awnings or houses, nothing to duck behind. He hadn't seen me yet, as he seemed to be studying a large wooden box he carried, so maybe I could run back the way I came, then slip behind that sculpture back there and—

"Karyn!" Zyr. Looking right at me.

I jerked my gaze from his piercing blue one. A man's eyes shouldn't be so noticeable from that distance. I halted, dropping the skirts I'd immodestly gathered to free my feet for the run, sincerely regretting that I hadn't bolted when I had the chance. To duck him now would be unforgivably rude.

I curtseyed a little, eyes politely averted. "Lord Zyr. Good morning."

"I've told you nine thousand times that I don't have a title." He sounded irritated, his voice rough as if he hadn't been awake very long.

I studied him surreptitiously. He looked like it, too—rumpled, barefoot, and wearing knee-length pants with a big shirt over them, his long hair loose and tangled. The shirt hung open and wrinkled, and he hadn't bothered with the ties. I hadn't thought he was an early riser and his dishevelment seemed to bear that out. What had he been up to so early?

"I apologize," I replied. These Tala with their lack of rank and titles—how did anyone know how to address anyone? I knew I'd never be able to call him baldly by his name. It also seemed equally impolite to just truncate my apology like that. I truly longed for Dasnaria's clear rules for behavior.

"Don't apologize so much either," he bit out, and I swallowed a sigh. Zynda had said the same. Even Thalia had remarked on it. I couldn't say anything without apologizing again, so I stood there, waiting for him to lose his patience with me entirely, which usually didn't take long—I couldn't imagine how he could be a teacher—so he'd quit blocking my path and let me go have my breakfast. "Where are you going so early anyway?" he asked, when the silence stretched out too long.

I could ask him the same. "I'm going down to the market to buy tea and a sweet roll," I replied, adding a silent *Lord Zyr* to make myself feel better and satisfy the voice of my etiquette tutor in my head.

"I'm hungry, too. I'll join you."

I would have liked to protest, but I could hardly contradict the command. So I glumly followed along when he turned and headed back the way he'd come. He slowed, so I slowed, too. When he stopped, I stopped, peering at him peripherally to determine what the problem might be.

"Why are you trailing along behind me—something wrong with your feet?" he asked, looking me up and down.

"In Dasnaria, it's proper for a woman to—"

"Well, you're not in Dasnaria, are you? I don't see any hulking brutes in armor like giant beetles anywhere around here, stinking up the place, do you?"

I had to suppress a giggle at the image, it shocked me so. "No," I replied carefully. "We are in Annfwn."

"Then walk beside me already. I feel like a fucking idiot leading a parade with you dragging your feet behind me. I'm buying you breakfast, not taking you to be punished."

Obediently, I moved up to walk next to him. It felt wrenchingly wrong to walk so boldly next to a man, and one I wasn't even related to, but it would be far worse to disobey. Musing over his comment about taking me to be punished, I dearly wanted to ask about that. So far as I'd been able to tell, the Tala were an exceptionally undisciplined people. Children like Thalia ran wild all over the cliff city, climbing vines and sliding down tunnels—often changing form as they did. I could never be sure which were people as animals and which were the actual animals that flocked to the fruit trees and warm alcoves of the area. Then there were the *staymachs,* which seemed to be some sort of magical animal that could shapeshift into different animals. So confusing.

Sometimes I suspected even the Tala couldn't tell which was what. The difference between us was that they didn't care, whereas not having that certainty made me profoundly uncomfortable.

"I just said goodbye to Zynda and Marskal," Zyr told me, sounding less annoyed now. Maybe even kind of sad and weary.

I nodded, covering my surprise. I'd known Lieutenant Marskal hadn't planned to stay long. All of the leaders had been in strategy meetings the last couple of days and were dispersing to handle their missions to prepare for war. I supposed I'd thought Lieutenant Marskal would take the Hawks with him. Which kind of included me. No one had made that clear, of course. For all that the folks of the Thirteen Kingdoms at least observed some kinds of military and royal rank, they still had a casual attitude toward assigning people responsibility. They seemed to think I'd go and do whatever I wanted to. Utterly bewildering.

Oh. With a sinking stomach, I realized what must've happened. Lieutenant Marskal *had* taken the Hawks with him, and because I wasn't really one of them I'd been abandoned in Annfwn.

The lieutenant had given me coin, those precious wages, so I could buy food, but now he'd left me here without a word. Kral and Jepp had sailed the *Hákyrling* back to the magical barrier protecting the realm, watching for more attacks by Deyrr. They had to be delighted to be rid of me. Jepp had suffered my company far too long—and had been much kinder to me than any Dasnarian would have been to her deposed rival. Not that I wished to be married to Kral still, but I'd at least been sure that he wouldn't let me starve. Now I had no protector, no way to earn more wages. I'd already spent so much of them and now I would starve. Alone in a foreign land. Why had I been so *stupid?* Panic stole my breath.

How much coin did I have left? I shouldn't squander it on breakfast. I needed to hoard it, make a plan. But what? I couldn't think.

"What in Moranu is wrong with you?" Zyr had gone back to impatient, and I realized he'd been talking to me. He'd even set down the wooden chest and taken me by the shoulders. "Talk to me—are you ill?"

"Lieutenant Marskal left," I managed to reply, the command spurring me to answer.

"Yes, that's what I said." Zyr sounded puzzled, ducking his head to try to look into my face. "Explain why that has you looking like you'll faint."

I had to catch my breath, my lungs too tight to draw air. "He… didn't take me… along and now… I'm all alone… in this place…and I'll starve… and die!" I finished on a wail that robbed me of the last of my breath and would've had me melting in embarrassed horror if I didn't feel like I might fall into a puddle of faint instead.

Zyr cursed in his language, which would have sounded pretty if he weren't so annoyed. He backed me up to the balustrade and made me sit, forcing my head down almost to the ground. "Deep breaths. Slow and even." He spoke slowly and gently, rubbing a hand down my back. Far too familiar a touch, but it felt good and I could hardly throw him off. "That's it, gréine. Calm and easy. Breathe."

And I found I could. Being upside-down made my head feel funny, but I no longer felt like I'd fall the dizzying drop to the beach.

"You're not all alone," Zyr said, spacing out his words as if talking to a child. Which, I supposed was fair, as I was acting like one. "Only Zynda and Marskal left, on a private, stupidly heroic mission. The rest of the Hawks are still here, and you'll keep training with them. My cousin Ursula, her royal high whatever, is sending more Hawks and troops here to Annfwn, to reinforce defenses in case there are more Deyrr attacks—remember? No one is going to let you starve. All right?"

I nodded.

"An actual verbal reply would be helpful, so I know you're with me." A hint of his usual teasing in there, but he still sounded gentle. Soothing. Totally unlike the Zyr I knew.

"All right," I answered.

"Better now?"

"Yes."

"Can you sit up?" He helped me straighten, and I caught a glimpse of his concerned expression before I averted my gaze. "Also, you wouldn't starve anyway. Watch this."

I did as he told me, watching as he reached up a long arm to an overhanging tree limb, plucked a fruit and handed it to me. Bemused, I held it, the smooth globe cool from the night, the sweet scent almost like flowers.

"No one starves here." Zyr tapped the fruit, then put a finger under my chin, lifting my face so that keeping my eyes averted became more difficult. "Your cheeks are all pink now," he noted.

"From being upside down," I pointed out, more tartly than I would've if I'd been feeling fully myself. *Your impulsive tongue will get you in trouble someday.* My mother's words echoed in my mind as if she stood right there. By now she would've heard that my impulsive tongue had made me ask His Imperial Majesty, the Emperor of Dasnaria for an annulment of my marriage with Kral. She likely believed me dead. Just as well, as I'd never see any of my family again.

Zyr broke into my mournful thoughts, his fingertips feathering over my cheek, as if testing the color, sending a shivery sensation through me I didn't know how to handle. "Your skin is so pale and clear all the blood shows through."

"That's disgusting!" I yanked away from his touch, shocked by his words and mortified that I'd let a strange man touch me. Even if it had felt nice for a moment. And not lonely.

"How is that disgusting?" he asked, laughing and not caring at all. "People have blood in them and have skin to hold it in. This is true of animals, too. The Tala understand this—don't Dasnarians?"

"Yes, but we don't discuss such things in public." I smoothed my braid, refusing to look at him, no matter his antics. "It's not an appropriate topic for mixed company."

"Mixed, as in Dasnarians and Tala?" His tone held plenty of mischief.

"Mixed as in men and women."

"So, are only conversations about blood not allowed, or all bodily fluids?"

I nearly choked, so I stood, straightening my skirts.

"I guess that's all bodily fluids," Zyr observed, uncoiling to his feet with that odd animal grace. "You come from a very strange people."

"At least my people keep one body," I replied, annoyed enough to be outright rude.

"There, you sound better now. Your usual prim and offended self." He retrieved the wooden box and started walking, so I had to go along. "And you're blushing even more now, by the way. Is that what bothers you about me—that I'm a shapeshifter?"

"It doesn't bother me." I looked out over the sea, bluer now with the rising sun that hadn't yet tipped over the rim of the towering cliff above. "Zynda is a shapeshifter and I like her."

"Then you don't like me personally."

"I don't have an opinion about you one way or the other." I kept my tone as neutral as I could manage. This man made it impossible to be polite.

"But you won't consider taking me as a lover," he replied with that easy openness of his people.

I pressed my lips together, mortified to be in this conversation, my face burning hot.

"I'm an excellent lover," Zyr continued, uncaring of the group of Tala girls who passed us carrying baskets. They giggled, several of them calling out what sounded like agreement. Zyr replied in their language, obviously flirting with them.

I considered simply leaping over the balustrade and ending this. Instead, I quickened my pace, striding ahead while he dallied. Perhaps he'd forget about me and run after them.

But no, he immediately caught up. "I'm not bragging," he insisted, ducking his head to catch my eye. "Well, I'm bragging a little, but I can back it up. You'd enjoy yourself in my bed."

I stopped so fast he went a step past me, before whipping around. That was uncanny, too. These shapeshifters moved so fast they almost blurred, back in front of you before you realized they'd changed position. "Your *bed?*" I squeaked out, astonished and horrified enough to look him directly in his eyes.

They widened, searching my face, his expression abruptly serious. "Why do you say it that way—is that an insult?"

No. No, it couldn't mean the same thing in Common Tongue. "It's nothing."

"I don't think so. We must talk about this," he said.

"Nooo." I shook my head emphatically, drawing out the word so he'd hear it. "We will *not* discuss this. In fact, this whole conversation is over. I never should have talked with you in the first place. I'm going for my breakfast now."

Head held high with all the dignity of the Hardie family, I walked on.

There, Zynda. I'd told him.

~ 2 ~

"Y OU'RE PAYING TOO much." Zyr's voice came so close to my ear that I jumped and dropped the change the Tala merchant had handed me. The coins clattered to the stones, making a merry racket.

Zyr swiftly gathered them up, speaking rapidly in Tala. The woman behind the counter grinned and shrugged elaborately. The Tala had a way of doing that, shrugging with their whole bodies, kind of rippling in a way that made it clear they didn't care at all about your opinion. Or for anything like an objective standard of law.

Zyr pointed a finger at her, going on at length, his words severe enough to make her pout—though that didn't stop her from replying in rising tones as she waved her hands at me in implicit accusation. A group of Tala sitting at a nearby table watched with great interest, murmuring to each other as they stared at me with animal bright eyes. I wanted to shrink inside my skin.

"Zyr—please," I begged, weakly, and far too quietly for either of them to hear me over their escalating argument.

Then they were done. The Tala woman grudgingly gave me my original coin back and Zyr handed her one of the smaller ones. She set out my tray with a pot of tea, two mugs, and two sweet rolls, giving me a brilliant smile as she had the morning before, and as if nothing had occurred. Zyr took the tray before I could, and I realized he didn't have his box. He carried the tray over to a table on the edge of the balcony, forcing me to follow, where—mystery solved—the box sat.

"Here," he said after setting down the tray. He held out a hand and I cupped my palms so he could pour the coins into it. He pointed to one. "That's how much your half of breakfast is worth. Don't ever pay more than that."

"The gold coin is what I paid her before," I grumbled.

"What?" Zyr paused in mid-pour, blue eyes blazing as if on fire. I quickly looked away. "How many times?"

"Just yesterday," I managed, the intensity of his anger making me timid.

He growled—actually growled, like a wolf—and was gone. From where I sat, I could hear him loudly berating the merchant woman, who argued back at the same volume. I sipped my tea, grateful for both its sweet warmth and for something to do while I pretended I didn't know him.

When he came back, he slid into the chair in a flurry of tossing hair and bright silk then settled immediately into a pose as languid as if he'd never argued with anyone a day in his life. He placed another gold coin on the table, tapping it. "See this one, with my cousin's unbeautiful face?"

She did have a sharp profile, with a strong nose and chin. But I'd seen the High Queen of the Thirteen Kingdoms in person and I'd never call her "unbeautiful." Definitely not pretty, like a milk-bathed Dasnarian girl. Still, she had a force of personality that made such considerations irrelevant, as if a woman like that couldn't be defined by something as frivolous as physical beauty. "Her Majesty High Queen Ursula," I said, hoping he'd take the hint and use her proper title.

"Yes, yes." He waved that off. "These coins are shiny and

new, which are both things Tala like."

I laughed and coughed it back. "You make your people sound like magpies."

"Some of us are," he replied in utter seriousness. "Remember that. You are also new—and shiny, though in a different way—so you won't know that we haven't had foreign coin, or foreign goods, or delightfully beautiful foreign women, here in Annfwn for very long at all. We lived for centuries in isolation, and it hasn't even been two years since that changed. These merchants aren't even trying to cheat you, exactly. They just want to collect these coins because Ursula is half Tala and she's Queen Andromeda's sister and they see her as heroic and I don't know what all. The point is, Marskal and Ursula had bags of these things and they handed them out like love potions at summer festival. But they're worth a lot. You can get a hundred days of breakfast for one. Another reason you won't starve. Understand?"

I covered the coin with my hand and slid it into my little pouch, deciding not to try to explain that I still wasn't sure how to handle money in general. I'd recognized the smaller coin he'd pointed to as being the price of breakfast, though, so I could remember that. Unlike most Dasnarian women—and thanks to an indulgent father—I could at least count. But he wasn't so indulgent that he'd violate the law that Dasnarian women couldn't handle money. So I'd never used coins before, or purchased anything, as everything I needed had been given to me.

"May I ask you a question?" I ventured, since he seemed to have wound down, and he also didn't seem to mind me questioning him.

"You just did." He grinned when I flicked a glance at him. "Oh, come on—Dasnarians don't have a sense of humor?"

"No," I replied primly. "But we do answer questions when asked."

"Seems I've asked you a few questions you've declined to answer." He plucked his roll from his plate, unwinding it and licking the sweet icing from it as he exposed each new bit, lolling back in his chair, long legs outstretched.

I wanted to tell him that wasn't the proper way to eat it, but even I could recognize that particular trap from a distance. So I quietly ate my roll in polite fashion, cutting neat pieces from it with my eating knife, hoping to set a good example for this wild man.

He eyed me. Licked off the last bit of icing. Then sighed dramatically. "Ask your question already, gréine. And for future reference—just ask, don't beg for permission." He had the roll entirely unwound and licked clean. Now he tipped his head back and fed the long rope of it into his mouth, bite by bite. His lips closed over it in a way that made me think of kissing, and his graceful throat… What was I thinking, staring this way?

I decided to pour more tea, keeping my gaze firmly on my cup, and mentally scrambled for my question, which no longer felt relevant at all. "Why do you refer to Her Highness Queen Andromeda by her title, but Her Majesty High Queen Ursula you call by any number of irreverent nicknames?"

"Irreverent nicknames," he echoed, sounding vastly amused. "Because, my sweet Dasnarian, Queen Andromeda is *my* queen, Queen of the Tala. No matter how many documents my mossback cousin might draft declaring her majestyness, Annfwn and the Tala don't belong to her and her cluster of acquired realms."

"But Annfwn is the thirteenth kingdom of the Thirteen Kingdoms," I pointed out. "That's the law. Doesn't such irreverence make you a—" I glanced about, to be sure no eager ears lurked nearby to overhear. "A traitor," I whispered.

"A traitor?" Zyr shrieked, clutching his hands to his heart. He'd popped his chair up onto its two hind legs, so it wobbled wildly with his gesticulations, threatening to pitch him over the edge. "Oh, no! Save me, someone—the big, bad mossbacks are coming to get me!"

"Shh!" I hushed him, though no one seemed to be paying attention, despite his loud calls for help. "It's not a joke."

He let the front legs of his chair smack down. Quick as a snake he reached across the table and grabbed my hand, eyes dancing with mischief. "Call me irreverent again—it makes me feel so naughty."

"Absolutely not." I extracted my hand pointedly but he seemed unbothered. "And you wouldn't find being in prison so amusing, should it truly happen to you."

Abruptly he sobered, as if a shadow passed over the sun. I even glanced at the sky, but it remained clear, the first rays of full day shooting over the sharp edge of the cliff. "You're right," he replied, easily enough, but with something under it. "I have been, and amusing it wasn't."

"You've been in prison?" I was aghast, and—though I kicked myself for my imprudent curiosity—dying to know more. I'd never known anyone who'd been imprisoned. "What happened?"

"Nothing much," he retorted. "Prisons are notoriously boring. Fortunately, shapeshifters are notoriously difficult to keep in prison." He shot me a smile, but he wasn't as cavalier as he wanted me to think. "Answer my question about the bed thing."

"What?"

"Why did you have a fit when I said you'd enjoy being in my bed?"

My face went hot, and I picked at some crumbs, wishing I

hadn't eaten my breakfast already so I'd have something to do. "Because I don't want to be your lover," I said quietly, desperately hoping no one was listening.

"No, I know you say *that*." He waved that off as easily as he did formalities. "I don't believe you, by the way. This was different than your usual virginal protestations. You were shocked by my saying that exact phrase. Why?"

Unspoken words tumbled in my mouth, fighting each other to be first. "You don't get to not believe me," I told him, finding myself furious. "I am a virgin and will remain untouched until I marry."

"You were married to Kral and stayed a virgin." He'd gone back to sprawling in his tipped-back chair, but something in his relaxed posture reminded me of the big cats that liked to lie on wide tree limbs in the older orchards back home. Still in the shadows, apparently asleep, they pounced without a sound on the unwary that passed beneath. Could Zyr shapeshift into that kind of cat? The thought made me shiver and Zyr seemed to note it. Those blue eyes—almost feline, now that I thought of it, with that same uncanny illusion of seeming to glow—keen on me. "I bring that up to point out the flaw in your logic," he added, as if being helpful. "That virginity and marriage aren't necessarily equivalent."

I curled my hands together in my lap. "That was a different situation, and this topic is not appropriate—"

"For mixed company," he cut in. "Right. I feel like I'm chasing my tail with you."

"Easily solved. Stop chasing me."

"I was going to." He said it musingly. "I told Zynda not an hour ago that I was done trying to seduce you."

Hearing those words made me oddly flustered, though I'd of course known his intentions. Knowing he'd discussed as much with Zynda made it more…pointed. "And what did she say?" I asked, though I should have refused to participate in this conversation any further. He kept enticing me back into it.

"She said that was too bad, as you might be good enough for me."

Oh.

Not what I expected. And I didn't know what to say to that. Zynda had been kind to me—but what an extraordinary thing for her to tell him. "So that's why you asked me to breakfast?"

He shrugged, looking out at the water. "Eh. Not really. Mostly I was tired of carrying this *thing* she gave me." He kicked his heel against the box. "And feeling sad and worried, which I don't enjoy. Then I saw you and thought, some flirtation with a beautiful woman is just the thing to cure my sad and worried."

"And yet I make you feel like you're chasing your, er, tail."

His chair thumped down as he leaned his forearms on the table again. Did the man ever sit still? "I'll tell you a secret, gréine," he said in a conspiratorial tone. "I kind of like feeling that way." He shook his head. "I don't know what's wrong with me."

I didn't either.

"But if you truly want me to leave you alone, I will." His playfulness had fled again. "I don't wish you unhappy."

I should've said it then. *No uncertain terms.* But I couldn't quite make myself. Maybe because telling a man "no" in any terms isn't something a Dasnarian woman does, so the words didn't leap to my lips. Also… though talking with him could be aggravating and infuriating, it was far better than being alone.

"Why were you feeling sad and worried?" I asked instead. He *had* looked unhappy. Certainly not his usual mien.

If he noticed my equivocation, he didn't say. "It's a long story. War, death, the end of the world. The usual." Sitting up, he raked his hands through his hair, hitting tangles. "No wonder I'm getting nowhere with you," he commented. "I'm all scruffy. Comes of being muzzy headed from getting up so early, curse my crazy, obsessed sister."

He blurred, like he did when moving fast, then a big black cat was sitting in his chair. Before I could react—at least mentally, because my heart jumped immediately, my fingers twitching for the bow I'd left in my rooms—he was him again. Human him. But now his hair flowed smoothly, neatly tied back, his shirt a deeper blue than his eyes, laced and unwrinkled.

I knew I was gaping at him, my default reaction it seemed, but I couldn't gather my wits.

"Did I scare you?" he asked, frowning.

"A little," I allowed. "In my world, when a big predator shows up in front of you, it's a bad thing and you'd better react fast before you get dead."

"I wouldn't hurt you as a panther any more than I would as a man. I'm still me."

"Exactly the same?" I asked, unable to squelch my curiosity, as it was something I'd been burning to know for a while.

"Not exactly." He looked thoughtful. "It's kind of like when you're dreaming, how you're you but also other things. With more control, though, like when a dream isn't going the way you want it to and you can turn it and guide it in a new direction."

I gazed back, aware I kept forgetting myself by looking right into his eyes. "No," I said slowly. "I've never heard of anyone being able to guide a dream. And I don't dream at all."

"Nonsense. Everyone dreams. Even animals dream. Surely Dasnarians do, too."

"So they say," I replied with some tartness, "but not me. I never have."

"Never? Not once in your entire life?"

"No." I shook my head to emphasize it. "That's just how I am."

"And you've never had sex of any kind, with anyone at all."

I would not clap my hands to my hot cheeks, no matter how much I wished to. "The two are hardly related."

"I don't know," he mused, a wicked turn to his mouth. "Maybe you should experiment."

"With you?" I retorted, which was hardly wise.

"You know the offer is open."

"Is this an offer of marriage then?" This I asked deliberately, to snap him out of his determined flirtation, and it worked. He blinked and sat back.

"Ah… the Tala don't really marry," he said, looking uncomfortable. "For most of us, our animal natures aren't really suited for monogamy."

"Their Highnesses King Rayfe and Queen Andromeda are married," I pointed out, because I'd asked about that and knew it to be true. A fixed point in the otherwise chaotic lawlessness of Annfwn.

"That's different," Zyr replied, with that wave of his hand.

I really wanted to ask why, but couldn't think of a way that didn't sound like a challenge.

"Is that truly the only way a Dasnarian woman can enjoy sex, is if she's married?" Zyr asked, seeming to be sincerely trying to understand, though the concept clearly made him incredulous.

"An honorable, high-station woman, yes."

"And the dishonorable types?" His eyes glinted again, lips shaping the question with a hint of sensuality that shouldn't be there at all.

"They have options, to some extent, from decent to terrible." I hesitated briefly, then figured I might as well explain. "A man might offer a woman his bed, which means he'll provide for her—food, shelter, all her needs—and protect her. For the rest of her life," I added with some zest, delighted to find myself enjoying the play of astonishment, shock, and maybe even a brief hint of terror flying over his expressive face. It felt good to have a step up on him for once. A Dasnarian man would never reveal so much of his thoughts, so that came as an unexpected pleasure. One thing to be said for the crazy Tala culture—their openness made conversations more fun. I put some effort into schooling my expression into polite lines, rather than grinning at my bullseye hit.

"I...ah. Oh." Zyr started to rake his fingers through his hair, found he'd tied it back in his shapeshifting tidying up, and irritably flung the tie away so he could shake his hair out. It flowed around his shoulders like a mane, paradoxically adding to the sense of him as some great feline predator. Especially as he worried his lip with his rounded human teeth in a distinctly unpredatory way. "See, ah, Karyn. I hope you know there's a translation problem there and... Um."

I nodded in understanding, adding a woeful smile. "Unfortunately, according to Dasnarian law, once the offer is made, it cannot be retracted. In fact, because Dasnarian women don't participate in the drafting and signing of contracts, making the offer is as good as sealing it. So." I lifted a shoulder and let it fall in a decidedly not elaborate, but quite fatalistic Dasnarian shrug. "What's done is done. I greatly appreciate that you'll care for me for the rest of my life."

He actually spluttered, casting his gaze from side to side, seeking escape. "Oh, see. Um. But you were worried about starving and that was after—" He broke off, narrowing his eyes at me and I let go the laughter I couldn't restrain any longer.

I convulsed with belly laughs, unable to stop, particularly when Zyr folded his arms and scowled at me in decided disgruntlement. If anyone had told me days or even an hour before that I'd ever enjoy a joke at a man's expense, I'd have said they were crazy. As it was… oh, what a fine thing to laugh like this!

"Are you done?" Zyr asked with injured dignity as I subsided, wiping away the tears the deep laughter had squeezed from my eyes.

I nodded. But an unladylike snort-giggle escaped me. I took a breath and calmed myself, at last meeting his gaze calmly—although my mouth kept twitching into a smile.

He broke into a grin. "It's good to hear you laugh, even if the joke was on me." He held up his hands when I began to protest. "No, no—I deserved that. I had it coming."

"You did," I replied. "That's what you get for your flirtatious ways."

"Now, hold on a moment." He frowned at me, not playing this time. "I'd argue that flirtation is one of the joys of being alive. So is sex. I'll bow my head to running afoul of your customs, but I won't agree that I deserve to be punished for wanting to share a goddess-given pleasure with you. *Or*," he said meaningfully, when I opened my mouth to argue, "for thinking we should be able to enjoy that together without rules. It seems to me that your laws have brought you more misery than joy."

That arrow hit home, striking the deep bruise in my heart. All those years of a marriage in name only, with no material change in my circumstances. I'd begun to long for a normal life like my sisters had, with a husband present in it, and children to warm my heart. To keep me from dying alone as the withered branch of my family tree that never bore fruit. By giving up my marriage with Kral for the possibility of a real marriage, with children, had I taken too much of a gamble?

"Karyn?" Zyr stroked quick fingers over the back of my

hand. "I didn't mean to make you sad. Laugh again."

A command I couldn't obey, as laughter is not so easily summoned. But I stretched my mouth in an obedient smile. "Regardless of all that, they are my laws and I will follow them," I told him. There. My no uncertain terms.

He inclined his head in sober acknowledgement. "I suppose we shall have to be friends only, in that case."

"Friends?" I tasted the word, though it was a familiar one. A deeper shading on ally, which was the sense most commonly used in Dasnaria. It would be unheard of for a woman and a man to be friends there, so much so that we didn't have a word for it. We had ways to describe men who took each other's part and supported one another. And unrelated women could be friends in ways that made them like family. Men and women, though… "What would that mean?" I asked, in all sincerity. "So we won't run afoul of translation problems," I clarified when he smirked at me.

"We spend time together that isn't sex," Zyr replied, looking thoughtful, like maybe he didn't know either. Then he grinned. "It will be interesting. Fun! We can learn about each other."

"All right. So I explained about the bed thing. Will you tell me why you were sad and worried?" That was something I'd discuss with a friend.

"Yes. I meant to tell you before but you distracted me. I'm tired of sitting, though—shall we walk?"

I'd long since finished eating, so I agreed. We both stood and he started to go.

"You forgot your box," I pointed out.

He turned and scowled at it, as if it had personally offended him. "Zynda's *thing*. I need to take it to my rooms, so we'll have to walk there first." He hefted it easily, though it looked quite heavy, then shook his head at me. "Don't look all suspicious.

We're just dropping it off. You don't want me to have to carry this *thing* all day, do you?"

The way he said "thing" made me want to laugh at him, he sounded so put upon. So I agreed. I'd just wait outside his rooms. I didn't have to go in. And my etiquette teacher would never know, no matter how she whispered her cautions in my mind.

~ 3 ~

Z YR KNEW EVERYONE we passed. No surprise since he'd lived in Annfwn his whole life and it's not a big place. Probably their whole country would fit inside just the city of Jofarrstyr, which is part of why I doubted the Thirteen Kingdoms could withstand the empire, should His Imperial Majesty be serious about acquiring them. The magic barrier protected them, yes, but obviously Deyrr had found ways through the barrier—and had been planting sleeper spies for some time that way—so that might not last long.

The Dasnarian Temple of Deyrr wasn't the same as the emperor, but from what Jepp had uncovered in her spying, the followers of the dark god might be His Imperial Majesty's tools in expanding his empire.

Even so, *everyone* said hello to Zyr. He might have been king the way each person took pains to greet him. Walking with him was like being in a bright circle of light. Even if only reflected, it still warmed me.

"You were going to tell me about Zynda," I prompted him, a little tired of him talking to everyone but me.

He slid me a glance. "I will, but it's something of a secret, though a poorly kept one. I'd like to wait until there are fewer people around to hear." Indeed, the road had grown quite busy while we ate, so I nodded agreement. "Sorry about that," Zyr added. "If Zynda hadn't given me this *thing*, we could've gone straight down to the beach."

I focused on his aggrieved tone rather than on the surprise that a man had apologized to me, and for something as trivial as inconveniencing me. "If you don't like it or want it, why are you keeping it?"

"Besides the fact that my sister made me take it and I'm afraid of her?" He flashed me a cheeky grin when I laughed. "No, I do like and want it; I just don't like *things*, you know."

"*Things?*" I repeated in the same tone. The Common Tongue word meant any physical object, I thought, but maybe I misunderstood.

"Yeah." He shrugged, the elaborateness hampered by the wooden box. "Most shapeshifters don't. You understand."

"No, I don't."

"Oh. Hmm." He considered. "Well, I guess it's that you can't take much with you when you shapeshift. Some Tala get really good at it and can keep special, small mementos that come back with them to human form, but mostly, why bother? You either leave it behind or lose it forever."

"You came back with clothes on just now," I pointed out.

"Yeah, but very simple ones. Nothing special. If I shifted and took this box with me, it would be gone. And my sister would kill me," he added as an afterthought.

"Where would it go?" I asked, completely perplexed.

"A question for the ages," Zyr agreed.

"You don't know?"

"Why would I?"

"Because…" I floundered. "You go there, when you're in between one thing and another."

He flashed me a smile. "It doesn't work that way."

Oh. I really wanted to ask how it did work, but that seemed

to be rudely pressing for an answer to a question I'd already asked and he'd ducked answering. And he called me evasive.

"Why is the wooden box important?" I asked instead, as that seemed safe.

"Here." He stopped and turned toward me. "Open it."

Delighted to satisfy at least this itch of curiosity, I undid the latch and lifted the lid. It was filled with pieces of wood in varying sizes. "Oh," I said, disappointed. How dull.

"That's what I said to Zynda," Zyr confided with a grin. "Take one. Doesn't matter which."

I plucked one out at random and Zyr nudged the lid with his chin, making it drop with a clang, then started walking again. I hastened to catch up. His rooms must be near the top of the cliff.

"What do you think?" he asked.

Turning the stick over in my hands, I studied it. It had been more deliberately formed than I'd thought on first inspection. Not round, but flat, it had irregular indentations all along two sides. And it felt smooth, polished by the maker, yes, but also by the action of many hands touching it over time.

"I think it's very old," I said.

"You can sense that?" Zyr's eyebrows winged up.

"Sense? No, I mean, it feels old, like a staircase where the passage of feet from generations of family have made indentations in the middle of the steps."

"I've never seen a place like that."

"Dasnaria is a very old civilization," I informed him with pride. "The Hardies have held our lands for a long time."

"How long?"

"Eight hundred and twenty-seven years." Unlike most Dasnarian women, I also knew how to read and write, and the history of the Hardies. "Long enough for the stone steps in the original hall in Castle Hardie to have big scoops in the middle." I drew it for him in the air.

"Ah, well, Annfwn is a child in comparison then," Zyr replied, seeming not at all upset to come in junior. "Current guesses are we've only been living here for a few centuries."

"You don't know?"

"The Tala aren't much for writing stuff down. Goes with not liking *things* maybe." He shrugged that off as unimportant, pointing his chin at my stick. "But that's where that comes in."

I gazed at it, perplexed. "I don't understand."

"It's a map!" He grinned in excitement. "See?"

"Ah." I nodded, totally not understanding at all.

"Look." Zyr set the box down on the low wall. We'd climbed quite high by then, but he seemed not to notice the precipitous drop. I stayed well back from the edge. He took the stick from me, holding it so we looked down on it. "Imagine you're looking at it like this as you fly along a coastline."

Oh, right.

"Got the image in your head?"

"No," I burst out, more than a little annoyed. "I've never flown, Zyr!"

"Oh." His face wrinkled in chagrin. "I forgot. Wow. I'm sorry."

Abruptly I realized he wasn't apologizing, but feeling sorry for me. "People aren't meant to fly," I informed him crisply. "That's not the way of things."

"Good thing I'm not a people then," he retorted, "because flying is the best feeling in the world, a goddess-given joy beyond compare."

"I thought that was sex," I shot back, realizing too late I shouldn't have let that particular arrow fly, because his smile went salacious.

He leaned in. "They're a lot alike," he confided, his tone velvety.

"I wouldn't know," I replied stiffly, looking away, wishing I could control my stupid blushing.

"Never mind." He sounded conciliatory. "That was unfair of me. I'll do better. Don't be sad."

"I'm not," I said, meeting his gaze with some surprise.

"But you are," he insisted softly. "You're one of the saddest people I've ever met."

Our gazes locked and held for an endless moment before I wrenched mine away. "Explain this stick. I'm flying over a coastline."

"And these ridges are how it looks from above." His long finger traced the uneven edge on one side. "These are bays, inlets, rock outcroppings, river deltas."

He seemed so concerned I understand that I nodded. "And the other side?"

"That's the best part—those are islands!"

I gazed in incomprehension, not getting his excitement. "Islands," I repeated. There were a lot of islands out there. We'd sailed around them for weeks in the Nahaunan Archipelago.

"See." He was losing patience now. "I can shapeshift into a bird and carry this stick in my talons. If I can match this side to a known coastline, like somewhere in Annfwn, then I can find the islands represented on the other side."

"Because you want to find more islands?" I ventured.

"Because we can find n'Andana!" He said it with such explosive excitement that I smiled and nodded. Hopefully that would be enough. But it wasn't. He frowned at me. "Haven't you been paying attention to *anything*?" he asked, with enough preemptory dismissiveness that it put my back up. In my realm, a man of his rank wouldn't dare speak to me that way, even though I was a woman.

"Which things?" I asked icily. "The war-planning sessions I'm not admitted to? The conversations in Tala I can't understand? Oh! Maybe you mean all the secret meetings I'm not privy to? You're right—I really need to make up for my lack of attention."

I must've surprised him—either with my vehemence or the different perspective—because he stared, as if seeing something new in me. We stood in front of a rambling set of apartments near the top of the cliff that must have been his, because he started in. When I didn't follow, he looked back, cocked his head at the open doorway. "Come on in."

"I'll wait out here."

"Karyn." He narrowed his eyes at me. "How can we be friends if you don't trust me?"

So much for that. I followed him into the bright interior. Much of the ceiling was open to the sky, making me wonder what he did when it rained.

"Zyr?" A naked Tala woman emerged from the next room, her long hair falling around her like a cape, hiding very little. Her heavy-lidded eyes looked sleepy as she spoke to him in their language, glancing at me with a warm smile. She came up to me and—before I realized her intention—gave me a lingering kiss on the mouth. Stroking my braid, she said something, including Zyr in it.

For his part, Zyr looked…chagrined? Embarrassed as I'd never seen him. He set down the box, speaking rapidly in their language, then took her hand and led her away from me, explaining all the while. The woman pouted, shaking back her hair, then leaning into him. Setting her firmly away, he said something that seriously annoyed her. With a last sharp set of words, she condensed into a crow, flapping mid-air, cawed at him a final time, and flew out the open ceiling.

Zyr slid me an assessing look. "Sorry about that. I forgot Sey was here or…"

"Or what?" I asked, genuinely curious, and not at all sure what he was apologizing for.

"Well, I wouldn't have brought you here," he replied defensively. "I had no intention of throwing another lover in your face or for her to…" He trailed off again, watching me warily.

"For her to assume you'd brought me here to join you in bed play?" I was developing an affection for watching the confident Zyr flounder when I put him off his game. "It seemed a natural assumption for her. Likely you've done so before."

He cocked his head, no ready words for that. "You know…about…"

Heavens. The man couldn't finish a sentence. "I'm a virgin, not ignorant," I replied, quite tartly. "The women of Dasnaria receive extensive training in bed play, which includes satisfying multiple partners. Men very often like to enjoy several women at once, isn't that so?" I gestured to him and the next room.

Zyr regained some of his composure, regarding me narrowly. "I'm surprised you consider *this* a proper topic for mixed company," he retorted.

"Yes, well." He had a point, but never mind that. "You've made it clear you have no respect for such conversational boundaries."

He grimaced ruefully. "I deserve that. But I'm surprised you're not angry."

I considered him. "Why would I be?"

"Because I've been courting you but obviously just had sex with another woman."

"Isn't that the Tala way? Very little monogamy. Much free trading of partners?"

He actually looked uncomfortable. "Yes, but…"

I waited and he didn't finish. "It's much the same in Dasnaria," I explained gently. "Men rarely confine themselves to one woman. It's not their nature. Everyone understands this."

His arched brows drew together, a vertical line between them. "Then why wait for marriage—what's the point if you all sleep around anyway?"

"The men do," I clarified. "The women are monogamous. At least, wives are."

"How is that even fair?" he burst out.

I lifted my shoulder and let it fall. The word "fair" always struck me oddly in Common Tongue. The closest translation to Dasnarian that I knew was a legal concept that explained the equal division of property among a man's sons. "That is the way of things," I told him.

"That's fucked up," Zyr replied with some bite, a bit of that predator behind it.

"Is it?" I gestured to the inner room where Sey had been waiting in his bed for his return. "Isn't that what you do?"

"Yes, but—" He flung up his hands. "Sey does it, too. It's fair when everyone gets to."

"Though 'everyone' doesn't want to," I pointed out.

He fumed at me, momentarily wordless. "You," he finally said, pointing an accusing finger at me, "make rational argument impossible."

The words hit me hard, thudding into me like so many well-aimed shafts. What in Sól's name was I thinking? Arguing like this with a man—even one not of my rank and culture—*not* at all who my parents had raised me to be. Abject shame seized me and I fell to my knees, putting my forehead to the stones.

"I apologize most sincerely," I babbled. Then realized I'd spoken in Dasnarian and had to search through my frantic thoughts for the right Common Tongue words. "I'm so very wretchedly sorry. I've shamed myself and my family in offending you."

I had my eyes tightly squinched shut against the onslaught of shame and guilt, so I only realized Zyr had fallen to his own knees before me when he ran a hesitant hand over my hair.

"Karyn," he said quietly, voice breaking a little on my name. "Don't do that. Sit up. Look at me."

Knowing I must obey but reluctant to, I sat up, finding a balance between looking at him without meeting his direct gaze. He didn't say anything for a moment or two, the silence of our mutual chagrin settling around us like dust motes from a scuffle soon ended.

"I'm discovering," he said finally, and wryly, "that I must watch my words with you very carefully, which anyone can tell you is not my strength. Will you forgive me?"

Nonplussed, I flicked a glanced at his eyes, finding them full of remorse. I had no idea what to make of this beautiful, feral man, kneeling on the floor, his hair spilling around him, gilded by the morning light flowing in from above as if the sun himself caressed him.

"I wonder what you are thinking," Zyr murmured, searching my own eyes. I seemed to be unable to look away, much as I knew I should. Applying force of will, I lowered my gaze, staring fixedly at his wickedly curved lips, which didn't do anything to restore my poise. "If you were any other woman, I'd kiss you right now," he said, his sensuous mouth shaping the words.

I stared at them helplessly. "Zyr," I breathed. "I can't."

"No, I know." He shook himself, took my hands and drew us both to our feet. "I shall have to find my way with you through a maze of words, it seems."

With nothing to say to that, I stepped back, the sunlight

warm on my head. Which finally penetrated my brain. I glanced up at the sun, now completely risen over the cliff's edge. "I'm late," I gasped. "I should've been down to the beach by now." Now maybe I *would* get thrown out of the Hawks.

Zyr strode to the window, looked out, then shook his head. "Just a few of them there. You have time."

I moved beside him, this window part of an outthrust of rock that overhung the path and afforded a dizzying view straight down to the beach. The people there looked like ants to me. "How can you possibly see who is who?"

Zyr turned sideways, cocking his hip to lean against the window ledge, saucy grin on his face. "Trade secret."

Fine. "Well, regardless, I'll be late because I have to stop by my rooms and get my bow, then walk all the way down there again." I'd forgotten more than my manners on this strange morning.

"Really, there is no 'late' in Annfwn. The Tala don't care for such things."

"I, however, am not Tala—and neither are most of the Hawks." In fact, I wasn't even one of the Hawks. They tolerated my presence, but barely. "I have to go, Zyr. Right away."

"But we never finished our talk," Zyr protested.

"We can finish it later?" I said, desperate enough for him to let me go that I made such a wild proposition.

He studied me, thinking. "I want to share something with you. Something special, as friends, to make up for before. If I give you a ride, we can stop at your rooms, get your bow, and get to the beach in time for me to explain a few things and you'll still be on time."

"A…ride?"

"Yes!" He grabbed my hand and pulled me back through the room, then out the door to the path. "Time for your first flight."

And he shapeshifted.

~ 4 ~

I STARED IN shock—and not a little fear, my fingers itching for my bow—at the beautiful and terrifying creature before me.

As black as Zyr's shimmering hair, gleaming with glints of blue, like nothing I'd ever seen or imagined, it towered over me half again as tall, immense wings half furled. Beneath the feathered wings—streaked with blue and gray underneath, revealed as he idly stretched them—his long body looked like the panther's, complete with curved claws. A long whiplike and tufted tail snaked in the air, waving like a pleased and proud feline's.

The head, however, that was all raptor, with a large beak as wickedly curved as Zyr's lips. A plume of feathers rippled arrogantly in the ocean breeze as he arched his neck. And the creature had Zyr's sharp blue eyes, dancing with mischief. He actually preened, then lifted a wing and pointed his beak significantly at his back.

I folded my arms. "Absolutely not."

He ducked his head and leveled a glare straight into my face. Oddly enough, I returned it without qualm. In this form, he wasn't a man so much, so I found it much easier to defy him. I turned my back and started walking. "Goodbye, Lord Monster. I have somewhere to be."

Zyr caught up with me in human form again, the blue shirt fresh and unwrinkled, laced, his hair once again tidily tied back. Interesting.

"Oh, come on—it'll be fun!" He tugged on my braid and I snatched it out of his hand, snorting.

"I have no wish to die a virgin."

"Well, we could take care of that, too."

"I thought you promised to stop flirting with me," I pointed out. Going downhill was at least faster than the climb up had been.

"No," Zyr drew the word out, shaking his head. "I agreed to friendship without sex. Friends can flirt."

Impossible man.

"Karyn, wait. Stop."

Unable to disobey the direct order, I dragged my feet to a halt. But I wouldn't look at him. I folded my arms again and stared steadfastly at the sea. "I am not getting on that *creature*, whatever it was."

"It was me." Zyr moved around in front of me, full of disingenuous charm.

"I know that," I snapped. Then threw up my hands in the air, waving them in my frustration, realizing I imitated his gesture. "How can you become things that aren't even real?"

"Aha!" He held up a correcting finger. "In point of fact, the gríobhth must be real or I wouldn't be able to turn into one."

I narrowed my eyes at him. "Is that an actual rule of shapeshifting or did you make it up?"

He laid his hands over his heart. "An actual rule—and you know it must be one, because the Tala are not so much for rules."

"So… you've actually seen one of these greepthva." I mangled the Tala word, but he didn't laugh at me.

"No." He shook his head very seriously. "We don't have to see an animal to become it, it just has to have been real at some point in time. It's like it exists out there, in the in-between place—"

"The place that doesn't exist, but where you can still lose things," I cut in, surprising myself that I'd dared interrupt him. But something had changed between us in that moment on his floor. I didn't know what. Maybe that he hadn't reprimanded me. Or that he hadn't even understood my apology. We both knew something had happened, though, because he'd said he wanted to make it up to me. Some men would give you jewelry. Zyr wanted me to risk my neck riding a mythical creature.

"Exactly," he agreed, ignoring my sarcastic tone.

"Jepp said she saw Zynda become a mermaid," I offered. I hadn't been sure if the warrior woman was teasing me at the time. She had an odd sense of humor. But it had made me curious.

Zyr rolled his eyes. "Yes, my sister thinks she's so special that she can do that form. But she can't do a gríobhth, so we're even."

"If they're all in this in-between place, why can't you do them equally well?" I thought of Thalia telling me she could 'only' become a songbird.

He shrugged elaborately, holding up his empty palms. "No one knows. Some of us who can do multiple forms keep adding to them over time. Some can only ever do one form, the same way some have a gift for painting or music and others don't." A shadow of his earlier sadness crossed his face. "Some reach for the impossible, at great risk to themselves, like Zynda."

I stilled. I really needed to go, but he looked so distracted, even worried. "Is this the secret you were going to tell me?"

"Yes. I'll tell you now. We're nice and private up here, and

I'd love to confide in a friend. But then you'll be really late." He cocked an eyebrow. "Especially if you insist on walking the whole way."

Torn, I glanced down at the beach far below. More ants. I couldn't afford to be seen as less than useful, not with my few friends disappearing one by one, off doing actually important things. On the other hand, Zyr had piqued my curiosity with this secret. Also, it bothered me to see him grieved, about Zynda, who I liked. I shouldn't worry, as a trickster like him hardly needed sympathy, but if it was a secret, perhaps no one else knew to give him the support.

"Did you tell Sey about this?" I found myself asking, then cringed at how it sounded.

But Zyr snorted, wrinkling his nose in a way that oddly reminded me of the gríobhth's sharp, curving beak. "Her? No way. She'd blab it all over Annfwn."

Arrested, I considered him. "Why do you think I won't?"

"You're not like that," he replied easily. "I think you're someone who would never betray a confidence. Even if you could speak Tala," he added with a wink.

I let that go by, mulling. Flying. I'd never really conceived a wish to do so, but… it might be incredible. "Do you promise I'll be safe on your back—what if I fall off?"

"I'm very good at balance in that form," he answered in all seriousness. "I would never let you fall, Karyn. If for some reason you did fall, I'd always catch you. Trust me in that."

"If nothing else?" I replied, full of sass all of a sudden.

He grinned back. "In all things. I'm resolved to be trustworthy."

"So full of resolutions this morning."

"I know. Very strange." His brow wrinkled, then cleared. "Comes of getting up so early, no doubt. I shall have to watch that in the future."

I laughed. "All right, I'll ride the grevepth—"

"Try this. Gah-reeb-vha-tha," he coached, and I repeated the syllables slowly. "Yes, now slide them all together. Gríobhth."

I couldn't manage his lyrical pitching and liquid ease, and I ended up laughing.

"You'll get it," he told me, smiling back, all sorrow forgotten.

"So many things to learn." It felt like a confession. I hated being this person who understood so little, who had no real place in the world.

He didn't answer immediately, pressing his lips together, eyes focused on some distant thought. "I think," he finally said slowly, "that maybe we all have many things to learn, only we pretend to ourselves that we don't. It's only when we finally figure out how much we don't know that we can start learning."

I regarded him in some surprise. The playful, irreverent Zyr, waxing philosophical?

As if reading my mind, he gave me a rueful smile. "The thing is, my sister has gone off to take Final Form. That's if she survives liberating the dragon under Windroven, which is nearly as insane. And which means that she may never return. Or if she does return, she will not be…recognizable to me. It hurts my heart."

I held still, recognizing the depth of his feeling, if not the sense of what he'd said. "Is 'Final Form' a kind of death?" I asked, hesitant to apply that hard-edged word, but not knowing any more pleasant euphemisms in Common Tongue.

"No," he replied immediately, then considered. "Eh, what is death? I don't know if Final Form is even real—and neither does Zynda, so she should know better than to chase her tail after a myth. It's that cursed priest who's filled her head with nonsense.

'Sacrifice yourself to save the Tala.' Well, what good is that, I ask you?"

I shook my head, a bit bemused by the vehemence of his outburst. A good listener listens, which means getting the other person to talk. "So Final Form is a myth?"

"It comes back to n'Andana. The short version is that the Tala come from the n'Andanans, who were shapeshifters, but also practiced far more powerful magics than we—their pitifully attenuated and inbred descendants—are capable of. The goal of the most proficient and talented shapeshifters was, so some Tala believe, to take Final Form. Which is a dragon. Immortal, impervious to damage or disease, still able to retain human intelligence *and* the ability to wield magic. But final is *final*, right? You can't come back from it. And dragons basically *are* magic, so when magic disappeared from the world, *pffftttt*."

The sound he made became nearly rude in his scorn and disgust, all but spitting it out. He had gotten that wild look in his eye and I half expected him to shift into some restless creature as he paced, waving his hands.

"So," I said carefully, testing the waters, though he seemed to have wound down, "when Zynda returns, it will be as a dragon, and she'll never be human again?"

"*If* she comes back," he bit out. "She has to ask that cursed dragon Kiraka on Nahanau to teach her. The first time Zynda asked her, Kiraka burned her to death! How can she survive that a second time?" he demanded, stopping in front of me, as if I'd know the answer.

Maybe it was my misapprehension of the language, but… "How did she survive the first time?" I asked tentatively.

Zyr rolled his eyes in elaborate disgust, though not for my ignorance, I thought. "Because she's so super talented she managed to shapeshift into her First Form—a hummingbird—

and that mossback Marskal nursed her back to life. And then he capitalized on her gratitude, persuading her to be his lover."

That explained so many of the various dropped comments I'd overheard. I wanted to ask what he meant by First Form, but didn't want to divert him from the story. "So, she didn't die after all," I clarified.

"Oh no, Karyn. You don't know my sister. She says she absolutely died, went to the afterworld, had a cozy chat with Moranu, and the goddess Herself sent her back. My sister Zynda, the reincarnated saint, now running off to do it all over again."

He was fuming. Furious, but also already grieving her loss. *It hurts my heart.* Such a simple thing to say, and yet so potent. "Why is this so important to her?" I asked, for surely Zynda had good reasons. She had never struck me as foolish. Or as a martyr.

"Eh," Zyr snorted. "Babies. All you women ever think about is babies."

"I wouldn't say *all*," I retorted dryly, a bit stung because of how many of my own choices had been driven by the desire to have children of my own. "But you have to admit our bodies are geared to want to conceive—just as men's bodies are driven to scatter their seed widely."

He stopped, hands on hips, staring at me in mock astonishment. "An insult. Really? And one not appropriate for mixed company."

"I apologize," I replied instantly, "I don't know what—oh." He'd broken into a wide grin. "Ha ha. Very funny."

"I thought so."

"What do dragons have to do with babies?" I asked, with considerable patience, I thought, resisting the urge to glance at the beach.

"It's a long tale, and one we don't have time for if you're to go meet with your dear hawkish mossbacks. I'll tell you over dinner."

"Zyr," I started, as repressively as I could, but he held up his hands in sunny innocence.

"As friends! Friends have dinner." He leaned in. "But be careful of using that stern tone with me—it makes me want to do irreverent things to you."

Flustered, I stepped back, not at all sure how to chastise him without sounding stern. He watched me flounder with wicked glee, then glanced significantly at the beach. "Ready to go?"

"I should maybe just walk." Being late would be better than plummeting to my death.

His face fell in what looked to be genuine disappointment. "But you promised."

Had I? I hadn't sworn, but… "Why does it matter so much to you?"

He considered me, choosing his words, I thought. "You're the first mossback I've shown that form to, did you know that?"

"No," I answered, somewhat taken aback. How would I have known that?

He shrugged a little, a small one that didn't bump his hands off his hips. "It's special. My best, most powerful form. I wanted to share it with you. I want to show you what it's like to fly." Despite his insouciant pose, he watched me closely, something hopeful and vulnerable in his spectacular eyes.

My mouth had gone dry. Not from fear of flying, but from some acute emotion I couldn't identify. "Why, Zyr?" I asked, before I realized I was only repeating myself.

"I don't know." He broke into a cheerful grin. "One of those things I'm accepting that I don't know and thus need to learn. How about you?"

The challenge in his taunt couldn't have been clearer. All right, fine. I could do this. I nodded, and his grin widened. "But if you let me fall and don't catch me, I'll get your Moranu to send me back from the dead, too, so I can haunt you the rest of your life."

"Fair enough," he agreed. "Though Moranu is yours, too."

I shook my head. "She is only a minor deity in the Dasnarian Empire."

"I'd say She'd be disappointed that you think so, but Moranu is happy to keep to the shadows and dark of night."

I didn't know what to say to that. What good was a goddess who kept to the shadows?

"Ready?" Zyr repeated, arching his brows, eyes bright with excitement. He seemed to have entirely forgotten his distress over Zynda's fate. Or…did he just want to appear that way? In the past couple of hours I'd glimpsed far more of a serious aspect to his nature than I had in all of our previous encounters.

"Ready," I replied, fervently hoping it was the truth.

At least I'd braced for it, so the manifestation of the creature several times Zyr's size didn't startle me quite so much. I had no idea how he could make something so much bigger out of his slim body. But then he'd said Zynda's First Form was a hummingbird—and Sey had become a crow much smaller than her human form. What happened to their actual bodies? Magic made no sense at all.

Zyr ruffled his feathers, spreading his wings as if displaying them for me, turning to preen one with that lethally edged hooked beak, and I did have to admire his spectacular, other-worldly beauty. He'd made a couple of references to what his mind was—and wasn't—like in animal form. So in some ways, despite his argument that it was still him, the gríobhth must embody a slightly different nature. Like a person who behaved one way in public and another way in the privacy of home.

He lifted his head, cocking it at me, and in those large raptor's eyes I caught a hint of Zyr's impudent challenge. Angling a wing and crouching, he turned pointedly, inviting—or commanding—me to mount.

Taking my heart in hand and closing it tight away, I bellied onto his back, taking a moment to get a feel for the balance, then swung a leg over and sat up. Much like mounting a horse bareback—which I'd thankfully done enough times to be practiced at it. Plus, the layered petticoats and skirts of my simple gown had enough give to allow me to sit astride easily, without fuss and adjustment as I would've had to do with the klúts I'd always worn back home. I missed my klúts, but I'd escaped with only the one on my back—and that one a formal, embroidered court garment I'd folded away. A memento of my visit to the Imperial Palace, and of who I'd been then. And would never be again.

Jepp had loaned me fighting leathers on the *Hákyrling*, but I could never become accustomed to dressing like a man. It always felt obscene to me. And the barely there clothing the Tala liked were far too immodest. So I'd adopted some of the simpler gowns the women of the other twelve kingdoms wore, with a few more layers beneath until I felt sufficiently covered. I sometimes got overwarm in the tropical humidity of Annfwn, but mostly it worked.

Especially for activities like riding, though this was like no riding I'd ever done before. Zyr's feline body had an entirely different feel. His shoulders sat more square and less bony than a horse's, and the massive musculature that supported the vast wings made his front body large, the attachment points flexing under my knees. Tentatively, I sank my hands into the rippling blue-black mane, a curious mix of silky fur, soft down, and the stiff vanes of the sleek feathers.

He adjusted his feet, furling and unfurling his wings, as if getting a feel for me, too. And it occurred to me that I hadn't asked if he'd carried anyone this way before. But before I could, he sprang, leaping over the low wall, and plummeting to the drop below.

~ 5 ~

MY SCREAM FELL out of me, as if left behind on the ledge above. Along with my heart and stomach. We were falling, falling, falling. My eyes squinched closed, my hands fisted the mane, I screamed in a long, unstoppable wail of sheer terror, expecting the imminent thud of death.

The great wings pumped. Muscles flexed under my squeezing thighs. Then again, almost lazily.

I cracked one eye open and saw ocean spread below us, so clear that I could look through it and see the white sand beneath, then the reefs of coral and the darker abysses between. Beautiful—so different than how it looked from a boat—and so far below. Dizzy, I swayed, and Zyr compensated, tilting one way, then another.

Then he zoomed straight for the beach, dropping in a diagonal. My breakfast rose from a gut roiling with terror, and I swallowed it back, though saliva filled my mouth in dire warning. Zyr landed in a plume of sand and I flung myself off his back, on my hands and knees, puking, no longer caring that I humiliated myself.

Human hands held my shoulders, drawing my braid back, and I became aware that Zyr crooned some sort of song. Soft and liquid, the words made no sense, but they spoke to something deep in me, the childish part that woke in the night, afraid and full of dread.

I wiped my mouth with the back of my hand—not easy because I was shaking so hard. I sat back on my heels and drew a deep breath.

"Karyn, I'm so sorry!" Zyr sounded genuinely stricken.

"No, it's fine." I couldn't look at him. I shoved sand over my sick and pushed to my feet, both embarrassed and grateful that Zyr steadied me when I staggered. Escaping his entangling hands, I scuffed through the thick sand to the water, bent to cup some of the salty sweet stuff into my mouth, so I could rinse and spit. The gentle surf lapped around my bare feet, wetting my hem, but I'd grown accustomed to that. The Tala seemed to spend as much time in the water as out of it, and no one looked sideways at anyone for being disheveled.

When I turned to find Zyr watching me, worry on his face, I noted that he'd gone back to his cleaned-up look: hair sleek and neatly tied back, clothes pristine. It irritated me, foolishly perhaps, to be so utterly discomposed compared to him.

"Why do you always look exactly like that when you shapeshift back to human form?" I demanded, sounding angrier than I thought I'd felt.

He blinked, reconsidering what he'd been about to say, surprised by my question. "Habit," he replied. "We drill in it, so we have a form and appearance—clothed, just in case—that we can return to without thought."

That made sense, I supposed, but it also made me uncomfortable. Shapeshifting. Flying. All of that was just unnatural. Certainly for me. Imagining otherwise had been a grave mistake. *Friends.* Zyr and I had nothing in common.

I looked up the beach to where the Hawks had assembled, then to the cliff where my rooms sat halfway up. I still didn't have my bow, or even my daggers. If only I'd stuck to my resolve and not let Zyr distract me. That would be the challenge for me. Bereft of the clear laws of behavior I'd grown up with, I'd behaved like an undisciplined child. Better to recognize the error of my ways and correct them. Starting now.

"I really thought you'd like flying," Zyr said, sounding contrite and humble. "Maybe if you…"

He trailed off as I started walking. The morning's drills would have to be without my weapons. Perhaps I could borrow some.

"When I teach the kids shapeshifting, and they mess up a form, I encourage them to try again," Zyr said hopefully, catching up. "That way fear doesn't set in. I can still take you up—"

"No." I said it with all the certainty Zynda could have wished for.

"I think if you—"

"Zyr, please." The shaking had stopped and my stomach had settled, but my heart still pounded and the whole incident had left me inexpressibly weary. I turned to face him, and his expression went from boyishly hopeful to wary at whatever he saw in mine. "Leave me alone. I don't want to have anything to do with you."

He didn't say anything. Did I imagine hurt in his eyes? I turned my back on it, on him. Resumed walking.

Then a bird shot past me into the sky, and Zyr was gone.

Good. Maybe now I could think straight.

As I headed up the beach, I passed some of the other Tala shapeshifters I'd worked with the day before, exchanging polite greetings with them—and wondering why they weren't with the Hawks.

Indeed, the group was all Hawks, with no shapeshifters present. One of the older male Hawks, a man named Tays, with a silver beard and a hard face, was addressing the others as I walked up. He frowned at me as I joined the group, and I cringed a little at the implicit censure. The walk hadn't taken long, but the combination of shuddering weakness and my water-weighted skirts had made me work up a sweat. I was no doubt red-faced and shiny on top of my general dishevelment. How easy to simply pop into animal form and come back all clean and fancy.

"You're late, Karyn," Tays informed me. "You've missed half the briefing."

"I apologize, sir," I told him, feeling my face grow even hotter, ducking it in submission, but locking my knees so as not to shame myself by falling to them again. Curse Zyr for all his bad influence.

"Address me as Lieutenant Tays, now," he said.

"Yes, sir, Lieutenant Tays." The other Hawks shifted around me. The worn boots of one of the female Hawks—Wren, I thought—edged into my field of vision.

"As I was *saying*," Tays drawled, "before Lady Hardie decided to grace us with her assistance in the urgent business of creating a defense of the Thirteen Kingdoms, Lieutenant Marskal departed this morning and left me in command."

"Glorianna preserve us," Wren muttered beside me.

"You have something to say, Karyn?" Tays demanded.

"No, sir, Lieutenant Tays," I hastily assured him, having no intention of correcting him on his error.

"Eyes up on me." He waited until I complied, and I found his expression stern, even mean. "You all know we face a dire threat. Deyrr and their creatures could launch an attack on Annfwn without warning." He paused significantly, and I kept my face composed, though his mispronunciation of the Dasnarian word put my teeth on edge. "Lieutenant Marskal authorized me to share some details that have been only rumor for most of you thus far."

"Five gets you ten that *he* didn't know until Marskal told him either," Wren said from the side of her mouth. Fortunately Tays was still talking and didn't hear this time.

"There have been *incidents* of animal attacks that seem to be reanimated by *Deyrr* magic much as happened to many of our unfortunate comrades at Ordnung, wrought by the evil Dasnarian sorceress." Tays frowned at me, as if I'd been personally responsible, even though I hadn't even been there. The Hawks cursed or made signs to their goddesses, murmuring to each other. They sometimes told tales of those dark days, and it seemed all had lost at least one friend or relative. It surprised me that I'd known this much, from Thalia, but also from being on the *Hákyrling* with Jepp and Kral.

Tays scanned the group, nodding. "The current theory is that these creatures are a sort of sleeper spy planted by the practitioners of *Deyrr* to undermine our defenses."

"Why isn't the magic barrier keeping them out?" one of the Hawks asked.

"Apparently it's not all that the Tala made it out to be," Tays bit out, sounding personally aggrieved. "Regardless, we can't trust in that. We have to be braced for attack, which it's believed will most likely come from the sea. Right here." He swept a hand at the peaceful and pristine beach. "Her Majesty High Queen Ursula will be sending reinforcements, but until then, it's up to the Hawks to stop any attack."

"And the Tala," one of the Hawks pointed out.

"And the Vervaldr," another chimed in. "Harlan left a crew of his mercenaries behind."

"They are not *us*," Tays emphasized. "They are not Hawks! They don't have our discipline and training."

"I thought Lieutenant Marskal wanted us to continue drilling with the shapeshifters like we did yesterday." Wren nudged me with an elbow. "Right? You came up with that fun game of tagging the shapeshifters with dye from your arrows and—"

"We are not here to have *fun*," Tays cut Wren off. "The Hawks operate best as an independent group. We know each other and those skills pay off in the crisis of combat. On my watch, we drill alone."

"Lieutenant Marskal said we have to change our old ways, that—"

"This is not a democracy. I know you've become accustomed to Lieutenant Marskal's lax mode of leadership, but I'm the one he promoted, knowing full well what I'd bring to the table. We are at war, soldiers." Tays glared at Wren. And me, though I'd said nothing. "Time to start behaving like it. Are we Hawks?"

The warriors all snapped to attention at that, clapping their fists over their hearts in their Hawks salute. Imitating them, I did the same, only to find Tays' outraged scrutiny on me.

"Lady Hardie," he snapped. "What in Glorianna's name do you think you're doing?"

Desperately trying to blend in and failing. "Lieutenant Tays, sir?" I asked.

"You are not one of the Hawks," he enunciated clearly, as if I might be deaf or stupid. "You haven't earned the right to that salute. This is an elite fighting group, hand-picked by Her Majesty High Queen Ursula herself—have you the least clue what that means?"

Probably not. I certainly didn't have the least clue how to answer that. "No, sir, Lieutenant Tays," I replied, as deferentially as I could.

"Oh, come on, Tays," Wren protested. "Karyn is a foreigner here. Cut her some slack."

The wrong thing to say. "An excellent point," Tays agreed, jumping on that. "Lady Hardie is Dasnarian, in fact, from the empire which happens to be plotting to attack us. Seems like a thrice-cursed coincidence in timing to me. Are you a spy, Lady Hardie?"

The improper address grated on me, and only the tireless instruction of my etiquette tutor kept me from correcting him. But I worked so hard to repress an imperious reply that I couldn't find another.

"No answer to that?" Tays asked, with considerable menace. "Perhaps we—"

"Hey!" Wren cut in. "Jepp personally vouched for Karyn, and Marskal wanted her to train with us. You have no business—"

"*You* have no business, Wren!" Tays rounded on her. "How dare you break discipline."

"Oh, knock it off, Tays," another Hawk drawled, as if everyone hadn't gone tense. "You know perfectly well we operate best as a team, which Her Majesty herself encouraged when she was still a scrawny teenage princess and we only called her captain. We'll follow your lead, as Marskal directed, but don't be letting the power go to your head."

Tays pointed a crooked finger at the Hawk who'd spoken. "You'll follow my lead, Issop, because I outrank you. And because I'll drum you out of the Hawks for disobedience."

They fell into a sullen silence, which seemed to satisfy Tays. "Good. Now, today we'll drill basics of hand-to-hand. If the enemy land on this beach, I want us ready to drive them back into the sea. Work in the surf, one-on-one, with that objective."

They all saluted and I carefully kept my hands by my side.

"Come on, Karyn," Wren said, "you can work with me." I smiled back at her. Older than I, but not by a lot, I thought, Wren was named for a Thirteen Kingdoms bird I'd never seen. *Plain, but with a lovely song,* she'd told me once, which fit the freckle-faced woman who fought with the grace of a bird in flight.

"Lady Hardie will work with me," Tays interrupted.

"She doesn't have much hand-to-hand," Wren protested.

"All the more reason for her to learn."

"Jepp taught her some knifework, but Karyn's proficiency is with a bow and …" Wren trailed off at Tays' baleful glare.

"Are you done?" he asked softly.

Wren lifted her chin, glaring back. A head shorter than Tays and she didn't look the least bit intimidated. Remarkable. And dangerous. "I cannot wait until Marskal returns," she bit out.

Tays' lip curled in a sneer. "The lieutenant is besotted with his unnatural shapeshifting lover. I doubt we'll see him again, so better get used to my command."

Wren threw up her hands in disgust, tossed me an encouraging smile, and stalked off. Tays sized me up and smiled, not at all nicely. "All right. Let's find out what you've got, Lady Hardie."

"I apologize, Lieutenant Tays, sir," I said, cursing Zyr with every word, "but I'm afraid I don't have my weapons this morning."

"I didn't imagine you did, unless you'd had them stuffed up under all those skirts." His smile took on a taunting edge. "Guess you'll learn how to defend yourself when unarmed. Over here."

I had no desire to be a hand-to-hand fighter—even Jepp had

suggested it wasn't my strength and she'd been surprisingly patient with me—but I also had no wish to be useless. Zyr might joke about living on plucked fruit, but I knew what happened to women who didn't make themselves useful. Especially those without a father and brothers to protect and feed them. Not a fate I wished on anyone.

But I was a Hardie till the day I died, and a Hardie doesn't back down from challenges.

Tays had me wade thigh deep into the cool water, refreshing after my overheating. That small relief didn't last long. Though I'd learned to swim in my country youth, that had been in still lakes and slow-moving rivers. Swimming in the ocean with its swells, even these gentle ones, seemed to require a new set of skills.

Going deeper, Tays crouched down in the waves as if swimming in. "Stop me from reaching shore," he ordered, and came at me. He didn't seem as hindered by the drag of resistance, surging out of the water with swift strength. Though I'd been braced, he tumbled me easily, dunking me and holding me under for a long, panicked time.

Sea water ran from my mouth and nose when he dragged me up by way of a bruising grip on my arm. "Worthless," he sneered. "Are you a rug? You just stood there and didn't even try to stop me. Again."

My dress hung on me as if made of wet sand, but I squared myself, doing my best to obey. Tays came at me and I swung at him with my fist, the way Jepp had taught me. Though weaponless in deference to my own empty hands, he easily batted my hand away and punched my cheek. The pain startled me, flashing hot and bright. Then I went down, choking on the salt water as he held me there. Sputtering as he dragged me up again.

"What's the matter?" he demanded. "I barely tagged you.

You're no fighter. Toughen up. Again."

Tears sprang to my eyes, and I only hoped he'd confuse them with the salt water, for surely he'd mock me for that, too. I tried to sink into my legs as I would when shooting targets, weighting myself against the surge of the swells. Tays crouched, a grin of ferocious glee on his face. When he came at me, I barely managed to swing at him before his fist plowed into my gut, sending me underwater again.

He held me under and I tried not to panic and sob in the water.

Then, miraculously, Tays was gone. I struggled up, gulping air, my head swimming with humiliation and frustration.

I blinked my stinging eyes at the extraordinary sight of Zyr holding Tays clean out of the water. Zyr's hands locked around Tays' throat, while the lieutenant struggled weakly, kicking his feet in the air. Zyr seemed to spark with feral magic, like a panther in human form.

"Tell me, mossback," he hissed, and I swore his teeth looked like fangs, "what's it like to be at the mercy of someone stronger than you, hmm?" Almost playfully, he shook the bigger man, wading onto the sand, but still holding Tays high off the ground with laughable ease. I'd thought I'd understood shapeshifter strength, but this…

Tays gargled, plucking wildly at Zyr's hands. And I was petty enough to enjoy the sight. For a moment. Then I waded out of the water, too, my skirts dragging. "Zyr, no!" I called. "Stop. Put him down."

Zyr barely glanced at me, wild blue eyes taking on that glow in a face subtly altered. The cheekbones broader and the teeth definitely sharp as a cat's. "I'm practicing fighting mossbacks, Karyn," he said in a deceptively cheerful tone. "Isn't that what we're doing here?" Tays flailed, face going a darker red.

Wren came running, sword unsheathed, mouth set. "Put him down, shapeshifter!"

Zyr only smiled, lazy as a mountain cat on a ledge, and just as lethal, I felt sure. "Oh goody. More mossbacks to practice on."

"Zyr." I pulled on his upraised arm, his muscles an iron bulge beneath. "Please. It was an exercise. He didn't hurt me."

"Lies," Zyr ground out, his gaze flicking over my throbbing cheek. "He hurt you. I saw."

"All right, he hurt me, but it was to teach me."

"And what did you learn, hmm? I'm a teacher," he said to Tays conversationally, as if the other man's eyes weren't bulging out of his head. "I know the difference between teaching and bullying."

"Zyr, please," I begged him, acutely aware that the Hawks had encircled us, and all had blades drawn. "We're all supposed to be on the same side."

"Is that so?" Abruptly Zyr released Tays, dropping him to the sand where the man crumpled into a gasping heap. Zyr bent the arm I held, trapping my hands in the fold between biceps and forearm, reaching over with his other hand to pat me soothingly, eyes on my throbbing cheek. None of the other Hawks advanced. Zyr swept a glare as slicing as any blade around the circle. "Let me remind you stinking mossbacks that this is *our* realm. If you're too stupid to know it, let me explain: you are sheep surrounded by wolves. We have chosen not to eat you, so far, but if we change our minds, your flimsy blades won't save you. You're in Annfwn on our sufferance, and don't forget it."

A huge black raptor plunged to the sand, immediately becoming His Highness King Rayfe, raven hair rippling around him like a cape. He fastened unamused dark blue eyes on Zyr.

"Funny," he said mildly, as everyone but Zyr bowed deeply. "I thought, since I'm king here, that it's on my sufferance."

~ 6 ~

I N MY GREATLY reduced circumstances, I'd of course not met Their Highnesses King Rayfe and Queen Andromeda. I'd seen them, from a fairly close distance at the welcome celebration when we'd arrived. Still I'd been circumspect in not gawking at them, which would be unforgivably rude. Certainly I'd avoided doing anything to draw their attention. Until now.

Everyone bowed to His Highness, or gave him the Hawks salute. Everyone but Zyr and me. I still wasn't at all sure what the correct salutation would be, so I managed a sort of curtsey as best I could with Zyr still holding my hands on his arm and kept my gaze humbly lowered. Zyr... Well, Zyr practically vibrated with challenge. He faced his king down with no sign of submission, no hint of apology.

His Highness King Rayfe studied Zyr thoughtfully but didn't deliver the punishment I expected on the heels of that implicit reprimand when he reminded Zyr who was king. He held a hand down to Tays, helping him to his feet, keen gaze sweeping over the rest of the Hawks.

"Would someone care to explain?" he asked the Hawks, pointedly ignoring Zyr and me.

"I'm in command here, Your Highness," Tays bit out. "I was attempting to teach Lady Hardie some hand-to-hand skills when—"

His Highness King Rayfe held up a hand to stop him, his deep blue gaze fastening on me. I watched the king surreptitiously, alert for cues. He looked like Zyr in the way all Tala looked similar to me, with their long, rangy bodies, dark hair, and blue or gray eyes. Where Zyr—normally, at least—had a mischievous mien and easy smile, His Highness possessed all the hard edged ruthlessness in his face I'd expect of a king. He wore all black, more formally fitted than Zyr's bright and flowing clothing. His strong nose, cut jaw, and narrow lips gave him a slightly cruel aspect, but when he spoke to me, he did so with a gentleness I didn't expect.

"Lady Hardie? I don't believe we've been introduced."

"No, Your Highness." I managed to tear away from Zyr's grip, though he gave me a furious glare for doing so. What in Sól's name had gotten into him? I curtseyed again, deeply and properly this time. "I'm Karyn af Hardie, no honorific, as I left my rank behind in Dasnaria."

He nodded. "Your sacrifice to rescue Jepp, a great favorite of my heart-sister, has not gone unnoticed and is greatly appreciated." Flicking an assessing glance at Zyr, who had not relaxed his aggressive stance a whit, His Highness considered me. "I'd thought you were an archer—one of considerable accomplishment, from what I'd heard."

I swallowed my surprise that he knew anything about me, though I had to remember I stood out with my fair coloring in this land of dark-haired people. "Your Highness flatters me. The bow is my preferred weapon, yes."

"I doubt it's flattery as I've yet to hear Jepp exaggerate anyone's weapons skills. But you were working hand-to-hand?" His Highness switched the question to Tays, waiting expectantly.

"Your Highness." Tays drew himself up. "Lady—Karyn is under my command. I simply sought to toughen her up as she has no combat training."

"Toughen her up?" His Highness returned mildly, with a sharpness beneath that breathed warning.

"Begging your pardon, Your Highness," Tays explained, seeming unaware of the quiet menace in the king's manner, "I don't know how it works with the Tala, but with our kind, green recruits need to get the snot beat out of them, so they understand the reality of battle."

His Highness regarded him with a coolly remote expression, which Tays seemed to take as approval, because he leaned in, speaking almost confidentially. "Especially privileged females, princesses, and ladies—they think they get a pass and it's up to us to make sure they come up to standard or they become a liability to us all."

His Highness raised a dark eyebrow in supercilious question. "Much like my honored wife, formerly a princess of your land, and at least half 'your kind'? I'm sure Andromeda would be fascinated to hear this theory."

Too late Tays realized his error. He started to backpedal, but His Highness cut off the explanation. "The Hawks are Ursula's, so I won't interfere with your training for the moment. I'm giving you notice, however, that we are involved in planning an overall defense of Annfwn, with this place the logical point of probable massive attack. The Hawks will be under Tala command, barring my heart-sister's return, or any designee of hers. Understood?"

Wren flashed me a grin, though I kept my own expression carefully schooled. It was never wise to antagonize a man of any rank.

"As for you…" His Highness cast Zyr an oblique look. Zyr had relaxed fractionally, but clearly still seethed with the desire to finish throttling Tays, as betrayed by his spasmodically twitching fingers. "I have need of you, Zyr," the Tala king seemed to decide on the spot. "Karyn, if you would be willing to join us?"

I could hardly refuse, though it wouldn't endear me to Lieutenant Tays. I curtseyed. "As Your Highness commands," I said, hoping that would remind Tays of my obligation to obey higher rank. I included the leader of the Hawks in the curtsey, inclining my head. "If I may be excused, Lieutenant Tays, sir?"

A grating sound came from Zyr's direction and I dared not look at him. Tays agreed, gruffly. Then, in an astonishing—at least to me—display of rudeness, turned his back on His Highness and strode off, calling the Hawks to attend him. The King of the Tala gazed after Tays, expression cold as the glint of wolf's eyes on a winter's night. His face chilled even further when he returned his gaze to Zyr.

"Do you have control of yourself, cousin—or do I need to do it for you?" he inquired.

Zyr seemed to visibly master himself, a muscle flexing in his jaw. Very carefully, he looked at me. "Are you all right?"

"I'm fine," I assured him.

Zyr jerked his chin in an approximation of a nod, his eyes hot blue on mine. "Why did you participate in that…what I witnessed?"

"I may be only a woman," I answered him, pride stiffening my spine, "but I was not raised to back down from a challenge."

Zyr's jaw clenched. "You…" he ground out, seeming unable to complete the thought. Then he walked a few paces, bent to the sand to pick something up, then returned to me. My bow and quiver. "I brought these for you," he informed me, somewhat unnecessarily.

"Thank you," I replied carefully, restraining my irritation at the presumption that led him to go through my private things. "But you didn't have—"

"You're welcome," he interrupted in a savage tone that implied anything but.

"Walk with me," King Rayfe cut through, an order, not a suggestion.

Though Zyr moved rigidly, with none of his usual languid and restless ease, he obeyed, falling into step beside the king. I slipped the quiver strap over my shoulder, hooked the bow in place with it, and started to follow behind. Until Zyr leveled a melting glare on me, pointing to the ground at his side. Unwilling to risk his temper further, I obeyed the implicit command, walking beside him. I had no idea what had gotten into him to make him so ferociously protective all of a sudden, nor how I'd ended up walking along the beach with the King of Annfwn. With some bemusement, I noted we were all three barefoot. The Tala often went without shoes, and I'd grown up running barefoot in the summers—easier to climb trees—so I appreciated the custom. It struck me as odd, however, that a king would do so.

"Several people reported seeing you as the gríobhth this morning," His Highness noted in that same conversational tone. "Unusual for you, with foreigners in Annfwn."

Zyr swallowed something down. "It seems to me that having foreigners in Annfwn is the new normal."

"Hmm. Beginning with me bringing Andromeda here, my half-foreign wife?" the king inquired almost idly.

I wanted to warn Zyr to tread carefully, but he seemed to shake himself, shedding more of the fierce aggression. "No, my king," he replied, almost with courtesy. "If you'll recall, I went with you to Ordnung to retrieve Queen Andromeda. I volunteered readily."

"And were taken prisoner," His Highness observed, gaze trained on some distant point. "You have more reason to hate the mossbacks than most. Personal reasons. Especially the warriors of Ordnung."

If I'd felt out of place before, my discomfort deepened. I should not be part of this conversation, and had no idea why the king had so deliberately included me.

"Are you one of those," His Highness continued, as Zyr had not replied, "who agitates against our alliance with the other twelve kingdoms—who resents Ursula's reign over us?"

"I don't like it," Zyr replied shortly, "but I understand the reasons for it. And I'm loyal to you and Queen Andromeda. And my cousin, Ursula," he added. "I have no quarrel with her."

"Good to know." The king sounded dryly amused. "I would've been disappointed to hear otherwise. I'm aware that many of the Tala would follow your lead, Zyr, were you to differ from the directions Andromeda and I have settled upon."

That sounded terribly alarming. In Dasnaria, such an accusation would be followed by an order of execution, but Zyr simply shook his head. "I have no wish to lead anyone, King Rayfe. I never have. You should know that. I follow you and Queen Andromeda."

The king nodded, accepting that at face value. "We appreciate your loyalty. So, you two are lovers then."

Not a question, and I'd been better trained than to speak to a king without being asked a direct question, but I choked a little, my face going hot. Zyr glanced down at me, an inscrutable expression on his face. Still, I thought he enjoyed my embarrassment, so I narrowed my eyes at him.

"We are not lovers," he said in a neutral tone that carried a hiss of frustration beneath, "nor ever will be, so I'm reliably informed."

"Ah." The king seemed to mull that over. "Not that I don't believe Zyr, but Karyn, would you verify?"

"Your Highness, we are not lovers, it's true. Nor ever can be." I wished I'd planned that statement better, because with that phrasing it sounded like I would've liked it to be otherwise.

"Call me Rayfe," he told me, leaning around Zyr to study me with an intense gaze that belied his casual tone. "That's a command, by the way. I understand Dasnarians pay a great deal of attention to commands and etiquette." He paused expectantly. "Is that so?"

"I suppose so," I replied, not quite able to bring myself to call him by his given name aloud.

"Harlan, my heart-sister's consort, is Dasnarian," Rayfe continued. "But he and his Vervaldr have relaxed their rigidity on such things considerably from being forced into company with us." He looked amused. "Such is the influence of Tala informality. Ah, here comes Andromeda."

Indeed, Her Highness Queen Andromeda emerged from a shaded stair that led from one of the first level balconies of the cliff city. She slowed as she spotted us, but she'd clearly been hurrying. Rayfe said nothing more until she reached us.

"I never thought I'd complain about not being able to shapeshift," she commented, smiling generously, though her gaze remained sharp on Zyr, then moved in a thorough assessment of me. "But it takes *forever* to get down to the beach walking on human feet. Hello, I'm Andi." She held out a hand in the Thirteen Kingdoms greeting.

No amount of etiquette training could have prepared me for *this*. I ended up taking her hand and kind of awkwardly bowing over it, like I might be intending to kiss it, then I jumped back in case I'd given offense. "Your Highness," I mumbled, hoping to just get through this… whatever it was. What *was* going on?

"Oh, please," Queen Andromeda rolled her eyes. "We're not in court. Everyone calls me Andi."

"Except Rayfe," Zyr spoke up, showing a bare hint of his usual mischievousness for the first time since his wild rage.

"Yes." The queen gave her husband a long look. "Because he's unreasonably stubborn on the topic."

"Andromeda is a beautiful name," he retorted.

"It sounds like something you'd name a star, not a person," she shot back with a saucy smile, one he returned. Though they didn't touch, I felt as if I'd witnessed something intimate. Maybe even wonderful—and what I'd been longing for ever since I found out my marriage would never be that. "Now, 'Karyn,'" she continued, "that's a lovely, simple name. And we haven't gotten to talk yet. Walk with me?" An echo of Rayfe's earlier command, and no more optional for being phrased as a question.

With easy camaraderie, the Queen of the Tala looped her arm through mine and guided me into a stroll. Making me realize that both Zyr and I had been deftly managed. By the King and Queen of Annfwn no less, who surely must have more important concerns. With a glance over my shoulder, I noted that Rayfe had indeed put a hand on Zyr's shoulder and bent his head close, obviously in intense conversation.

"He'll be all right," Queen Andromeda patted my hand. "Rayfe is adept at managing our wilder citizens. Tell me about yourself."

I had no idea what to say, or how to process that statement. "There's not a lot to tell."

The sideways look she gave me implied she didn't believe that. "I imagine it's hard, being in a foreign land, surrounded by new customs, new languages. I've been that person."

"You have, Your Highness?"

"Andi," she replied firmly. "Save the titles for formal occasions, of which there are vanishingly few in Annfwn. One of its many charms. You'll grow to appreciate that about it, once you settle in."

"Thank you… Andi, but I don't plan to stay in Annfwn."

"Don't you? Well, you're a free woman, obviously, so you may do as you wish. And yes—when I came here, no one who wasn't Tala born and bred had even been inside the magic barrier that sealed Annfwn off from the world. Rayfe was my enemy, and I only married him to stop a war."

I'd had no idea. "But you're happy with him?"

"Oh, yes—now. Even early on." She frowned a little, thinking. "It's hard to explain, but even as I fought the attraction, though I knew in my head that agreeing to marry him would be betraying my family, my realm, somewhere deep inside I …felt it would all work out as it should. Does that make any sense?"

"Of course," I replied.

"You don't have to lie." She laughed, shaking back her dark hair, the curling waves glinting with bloodred highlights in the sun. "Half the time I can't explain it to myself. But there's something you should know about the Tala—and I'm speaking as a partblood who grew up in a decidedly nonmagical realm— though the Tala seem as human as you or I, they're not, entirely."

"Not human?" I echoed.

She made a sound of frustration. "There's not a good word to describe it. Yes, they're human and we can make babies together, so we have a great deal in common, but they're also… other. Do you know about First Form?"

"I've heard it mentioned," I said, unwilling to commit to more.

"The Tala will tell you—and the Tala are a cagey lot, so they don't explain much—that their human personality tends to be influenced by their First Form. That's the animal they shift into intuitively for the first time, often as infants."

I tried to absorb that, unable to imagine what that would be like for a mother to deal with. Regular babies were difficult enough. Andi nodded at me, and I realized I must've made a face. She squeezed my arm in sisterly commiseration.

"That was my reaction, too," she said. "So, what the Tala *don't* tell you—and sometimes I think they're so close to it that they don't understand this about themselves—is that it's more than that they're influenced by that animal First Form. It's almost as if they're as much the personality of that animal as the person. And the shapeshifters who can take multiple forms, well, they all have their favorites, and extensive time spent as *those* animals influences them, as well. So, under stress, they tend to revert to the instinctive responses of those animal beings."

Ah. I suddenly understood the purpose of this cozy conversation. I stopped, slipping my arm from the queen's and faced her. We'd come a ways down the beach, and many people now teemed in various activities. I couldn't make out whether Zyr remained where he'd been. Not close enough to overhear, regardless.

"Excuse me for my bluntness, Your Highness. Are you telling me that Zyr acting so wild just now came from some sort of animal reaction?"

A hint of amusement quirked her mouth, though it didn't reach her eyes, dark gray and stormy as summer thunderheads. I could almost imagine flickers of lightning in the threatening cloud bank, making the small hairs stand up on my arms, though the day continued in its balmy warmth.

"What happened today is somewhat unprecedented, but it matches what I sensed and is essentially how Rayfe assessed it. We didn't have a lot of time to discuss before Rayfe shifted to intervene," she added drily.

"So the king is talking Zyr down and your job is to handle me?" I hadn't meant to be so terse—not to mention rude—but the emotional turmoil of the morning was getting to me. I had sand in my drenched clothes, my cheek throbbed, I'd failed utterly in any number of ways. If I hadn't left Dasnaria, I could be still living on the family estates. Forever a virgin and never realizing more of a life than that, yes, but not dealing with so much chaos and strangeness. At least there I hadn't worried about my next meal or why some half-wild shapeshifter lost his mind. If I'd remained Kral's wife, I would've outranked this barefoot queen.

The queen cocked her head, studying me. "You're no fool, Karyn. I understand you could have become Empress of Dasnaria, that but for a moment that went one way instead of another, you would have been."

For a moment I thought she'd read my mind—but of course she would know that about me. She would have discussed me with her sister queens. She said I wasn't a fool, but perhaps I had been, thinking that I'd been forgotten and ignored.

"I have no rank now," I replied. "I am no one."

Her mouth quirked and I almost imagined her hair rustled, as if stirred by a breeze—though the day had gone still. "You will never be no one," she said, and it had a final feel to it, as if she knew more than I did. "I know something of Dasnaria, and quite a bit more than that about how future rulers are raised, even those of us one or two down from inheriting a throne. Do you expect to fool me into thinking you understand nothing of delicate political situation we're in?"

I closed my lips carefully over several replies to that. "It's none of my concern," I finally offered, hedging. "I'm not here as a political actor, only as myself."

She nodded, considering that, the look in her eye saying she didn't believe me. "Why *are* you here then?"

$$\sim 7 \sim$$

"I'M NOT A spy." I bit out the defense, not having meant to. Something about the way she made my skin crawl had me speaking more than I'd intended. Could she be working an enchantment to force truth-telling? Zynda had some skills as a sorceress, which she'd called small ones. A statement like that indicated a scale on which someone else possessed much greater talents. The practitioners of Deyrr were said to be able to influence minds—why not the Sorceress Queen of the Tala? Who watched me with stormy eyes, waiting me out, wanting an answer to a question for which I had nothing substantial to offer. "I had nowhere else to go," I said, stiff in my admission.

"Oh, I know that part," she replied. "After all, I'm the one who told Ursula you could stay here." She smiled at my consternation. "You'd hardly expect her to take you to Ordnung, seat of the High Throne of the Thirteen Kingdoms. We are in your debt for saving Jepp—make no mistake but that we deeply appreciate it—but we've had experience with a priestess of Dasnaria and little enthusiasm to go through that again."

"I have no affiliation with Deyrr," I said with as much dignity as I could muster, given the implied insult.

"Good to know. So, what *is* your plan? You said you have no intention of staying in Annfwn, but that you also have nowhere else to go."

"My only plan is to find a husband," I explained, feeling foolish and exposed. "I gave up a slim chance at being Empress for the possibility of having a normal life, with a family."

"Meaning children," she inserted leadingly.

"Children would be nice, but mainly…" I felt like a silly girl saying it aloud. "Love."

"Love," she echoed, sounding genuinely astonished. Probably few things surprised a mind reader.

"I would like to find someone who will love me." I tried to make it sound logical, but it came out wistful. "You've never been married to a man who didn't love you," I explained in a rush. "You can't know what that's like. I've had my fill of it. I did my duty to my family, emperor and empire; I remained a chaste virgin in a loveless marriage so my husband wouldn't threaten the stability of the empire. Now I'm a free woman, as you say, and my husband loves another. I am determined to find someone for me this time. So, you see, you can keep your politics, and your war, and your suspicions. I don't want any of it."

"And yet you train with the Hawks."

"To earn my keep. I don't have any protector, and no other skills to offer."

"I doubt that."

"Have you need of fine embroidery then?" I retorted, feeling quite bruised by this point.

A slow smile spread across her face, a true one that made her eyes lighten and sparkle. "Ah, I feel I'm at last meeting the woman I see in my visions. So, this search for true love—that's why you won't be lovers with Zyr?"

I struggled past my confused startlement over her reference to seeing me in visions, then slammed into more of it. She hadn't been there yet when Rayfe asked Zyr and me about our status.

More sorcery?

"I was listening," she confirmed, reading that in me, too. "I can't shapeshift and risk jeopardizing this pregnancy, but I have other tricks for keeping up with what's going on."

I hadn't realized, and had to work not to stare at her belly, looking for the evidence. The stark envy was almost more than I could bear. "It's not the way of things," I explained, sounding stiff, but better that than full of raw envy. "A woman of my rank who gives herself to a man not her husband can expect to suffer terrible consequences."

"But you are no longer in Dasnaria," she said, with a gentleness I hadn't expected.

"No, but I am still Dasnarian and I won't bring shame on my family. Certainly not for a fling with flirtatious shapeshifter."

She went utterly serious, that earlier menace returning to glint sparks from her eyes, the crackle of warning thickening the air around us. I had to steel myself not to step back. Or run. "Do the Tala revolt you then?"

"The Tala are not my people," I pointed out diplomatically.

"But neither are you likely to find a Dasnarian husband now."

"Surely there is something between," I argued.

"Because Zyr is beneath your notice."

"No," I replied carefully. "Zyr hasn't made an offer of marriage, nor will he ever. He's made that clear. *And*," I inserted as I saw she was about to argue, "we don't love each other and I have no intention of settling for another sham marriage."

She considered me a moment longer, then lifted a hand, waving all of that away, along with the sense of the threatening storm. "All of this is moot, and perhaps I've gone about this the wrong way. Allow me to explain."

That would be helpful, I thought—and by the twitch of her

generous mouth I thought she'd read the sentiment in me.

"Zyr's First Form is the gríobhth," she said bluntly, and with great significance.

"All right," I answered, then waited.

She sighed out an impatient puff. "Have you ever *seen* a gríobhth before today?"

"No, but Annfwn is full of things I've never seen before," I snapped back in the same tone.

To my surprise she laughed, rolling her eyes. "Fair enough. I once felt the same. We have a lot in common, I suspect."

I doubted that, but didn't want to say so.

"It's highly unusual for a shapeshifter's First Form to be a mythical creature. Usually they have to work at those forms," she explained.

"Zyr said it's not mythical, that the creature had to exist at some point in time for him to become it."

"Did he now?" She studied me, that uncomfortable gaze seeming to look through me. "Zyr confided a great deal in you— talking about intimate Tala topics, showing you his gríobhth form, then giving you a ride. I said you're not a fool, and I stand by that—you seem observant enough—but you are a foreigner to more than Annfwn. I'm wondering if you understand the extremity of the situation. How very unprecedented this is."

I must not, because I felt as if I must be drowning in the surf still. It said something, that I felt a twinge of preference for being held under water by Tays and his casually brutal strength over writhing under the too-prescient gaze of the Tala's sorceress queen. My parents hadn't raised me to capitulate to intimidation by foreign royalty any more than they'd have wanted me to back down before a challenge. And yet, I had trouble stiffening my spine.

"I'm afraid I must plead ignorance, at best," I replied to her with as much dignity as I could muster, "and lack of intelligence at worst."

She shook her head slightly, as if impatient—with me or herself, I wasn't sure. "Suffice to say that Zyr revealing himself to you this way means he's…Well, you have influence over him that we'd rather you didn't."

"I didn't conspire for this outcome. Nor did I even ask for it," I returned, much of my heat coming from embarrassment at the insinuation that I'd deliberately attempted to seduce my way into Zyr's bed. And maybe a bit for the heady sensation of having power over Zyr's attention.

"Sometimes—even very often—what we receive is not what we ask for. Or what we thought we asked for." The queen *looked* through me again. Then her gaze focused, crystal bright. "They return to us now, so the time for our confidences is over for the moment. Rayfe will have a proposition for you. I'm advising you to accept it, for all our sakes."

"Oh, that doesn't sound ominous," I muttered, turning with her to see the two men advancing toward us down the beach. They might have been brothers, in their similar build, the same arrogant tilt to their heads.

"And here Zynda told me that you apologize too much," Andi muttered back, in exactly the same tone. "I don't find you overly humble in the least."

I couldn't account for that, except that it had been an exceptionally long morning. "I apologize, Your Highness Queen Andromeda."

She snorted out a laugh and—absurdly—I had to fight down my own smile. Bizarrely, I felt as if we almost had become friends over the course of the uncomfortable conversation. I knew better than to pretend any such thing to myself, but it made me feel marginally less alone that this foreign queen and I at least understood one another. To some extent.

Zyr's predatory gaze fastened on me, the blue intense enough to cross the distance between us, and I shivered despite myself.

"Steady. He needs your spine, not your spleen," Andi murmured under her breath, making me wonder how she knew.

The men came up to us, Rayfe and Andi seeming to exchange a long and wordless communication of some sort. For all I knew, they *could* speak mind-to-mind.

"I have a proposition for the pair of you," Rayfe announced, as if he'd just thought of it. Only long training kept me from snickering, but Zyr seemed to sense it in me, a hint of amusement sparking in his otherwise turbulent gaze. "A special mission, as it were. I understand Zynda passed off the chest of map-sticks to you, Zyr, along with the charge to look for n'Andana."

"I'd been planning to," Zyr pointed out, somewhat surly.

"And yet you wasted time taunting our allies this morning," Rayfe returned icily, staring Zyr down.

Zyr's attitude didn't change dramatically, but something about his stance seemed to fold ever so slightly. If he'd had pointed ears, they would've flattened. "It was ill-considered, my king," he offered. Not an apology, but likely a considerable confession for the arrogant Zyr.

"Oh, are you implying you considered anything at all before throttling the leader of the Hawks and threatening to chase them out of *my* kingdom?"

"Yes," Zyr ground out, far less chastened than he should have been. "I considered that another of our allies was being throttled by an oaf."

"I didn't need to be rescued," I inserted, hoping for quiet dignity and coming up with frustration. "It was training, nothing more."

"He attacked you."

"I need to be useful," I shot back.

"And so you shall be," Rayfe smoothly resumed control of the conversation. "Karyn, I'd like you to assist Zyr in this quest. You've already demonstrated you can keep your seat on his gríobhth form; Zyr, you obviously are willing to carry her as a passenger." He held Zyr's gaze at that, some significance behind it.

"She didn't care for the experience," Zyr replied, a bitter tinge to his voice and the betrayed look he threw in my direction.

Oh, so it was all my fault, then? I suppose I was to have gleefully taken to such an alien experience. Well, it wasn't in me to back down. "I can learn," I said, aware by Andi's rustle beside me that I'd pleased at least her.

"Don't do me any favors." Zyr still had that wounded gaze on me.

"Actually, yes, do us the favor," Rayfe corrected, glaring at Zyr, who showed no submissiveness this time. "We need all the allies we can get. This conflict with Deyrr started in n'Andana. We need to know where it is and if any of our ancestors yet live and can give us answers."

"But n'Andana is hidden from us," Zyr protested. "They hid themselves on purpose."

"They hid themselves from the Tala by being outside the barrier," Andi corrected with some acerbity, speaking up for the first time since her husband had taken control of the conversation. So her silence hadn't been deference, but waiting. Interesting, their customs. "Since then they may have lived quietly, avoiding the rest of the world. It could be that there's some magical misdirection involved, that's guided ships away from them, but nothing that your innate magic, Zyr, shouldn't be able to overcome."

"If we're to go to war with Deyrr and possibly the entire Dasnarian Empire," Rayfe added, with an oblique glance at me, "we could use more dragons than Dafne's Kiraka."

"And if n'Andana is a denuded landscape littered with dragon skeletons?" Zyr inquired in a playful tone that barely concealed his scorn.

"Then we need to know that," Andi replied. "Remember that Kiraka herself advised us to use these mapsticks to find the place."

"I don't know why we listen to Dafne's ancient dragon." Zyr made a face. "The poor thing is likely dotty with senile dementia and delusions of grandeur."

"Dafne?" Andi inquired silkily. "Or the dragon?"

"Both," he shot back. Then grinned at her groan of frustration and held up his hands in surrender. "Fine, fine—I'll get out of your hair and start matching the coastline with the mapsticks. They might not correspond to anything around here, you know. But I can do it by myself."

"You'll take Karyn's help," Rayfe commanded.

"They're meant to be used by shapeshifters," Zyr argued with his king, most unwisely, I thought. "Why should I be burdened with a mossback afraid to fly?"

He had a point, and I stewed in my embarrassed uselessness. They clearly wanted him to babysit me, to keep me out of trouble, and to keep him from whatever animal urges drove him to be watching out for me even when I'd definitively told him to leave me alone.

"You need another set of eyes," Andi put in. "Karyn is strange to this land, so she'll see what you do not. We also need to keep records, which she can do."

"In Dasnarian," I put in. "Not in Tala."

"The Tala are not known for meticulous record-keeping," Andi told me with an enigmatic smile. "What matters is that the map-sticks are matched to known coastlines and categorized, so that we can begin to search for unknown coastlines. I have a feeling you're uniquely well-suited to this mission."

"Someone else can help with—" Zyr started.

"It has to be Karyn," Andi interrupted him. "I'm saying so."

Rayfe regarded his queen with a considering gaze, though only for a moment. "That makes it a royal command from both your king and queen, Zyr. Better start sooner rather than later."

"As you desire, Your Highnesses," Zyr inclined his head, barely a hint of annoyed sarcasm in it, gaze flicking to me and then away again. "You have but to command me and I obey."

"That would be refreshing," Rayfe returned in a dry tone. "Then let's—"

He broke off, every line of his body going alert, head lifting like a hound's to the scent, but eyes fixed on Andi. Beside me, the atmosphere around her thickened. I braced against the need to throw myself to the sand, instinctively hunching against the lightning that seemed sure to strike.

"Trouble," Andi said, terse and tense. Shouts of alarm wafted up the beach. "There."

I hadn't blinked, but Rayfe had become a huge black horse so fast it felt as if time had skipped a beat. Andi vaulted on his back and they took off in a cloud of sand.

"Can you ride?" Zyr demanded.

"What?" I couldn't parse the words in my shock at the abrupt turn of events.

Zyr's hand shot out, clasped my wrist. "Wake up! Can you ride a horse?"

"Yes, but…"

He'd become one too, tossing his head impatiently at me. I clambered onto his saddleless back quite a bit less gracefully than Andi had, remembering how earlier this morning I'd mentally compared mounting the gríobhth to this. That had been easier, as the Zyr-horse stood quite a bit taller and pranced fitfully in his impatience.

As soon as I had my seat, he took off like an arrow from a crossbow. If I hadn't had the reflexes of many summers racing my brothers through the meadows of the vast Hardie estates, I'd have precipitously tumbled to the sand. But my habits kicked in there, too, my knees clamping tight to his sides, holding me in place as I pulled the bow from my back, stringing it, and setting an arrow at the ready.

Down the beach, a furious battle took place. Some sort of creatures churned in the surf, the Hawks' swords glinting in the sun as they surged and struggled. Blood flew in the air, mixed with the brighter seawater, discernable as different because of its oily, black denseness.

The signature of Deyrr's creatures.

Zyr galloped at a furious pace, faster than any horse I'd ever ridden, without sign that he might ever tire. In the still distant fight, Andi swung off Rayfe's back fairly short of the actual conflict. He went straight from horse to wolf, bolting into the fray, while she stood back. Though she stood in broad daylight, it seemed as if shadows streamed to her. All around her, the air darkened, that thunderstorm I'd glimpsed in her eyes manifesting in a vast cloud shot through with blue lightning.

A bird dove at her, something large and unlike any that I'd seen before. Andi ducked, but it raked her face, catching her hair in its talons. Reflexively, I shot an arrow through it. Definitely of Deyrr, because the creature barely staggered in the air, the arrow making its flight unwieldy, but it gave no cry of pain or even acknowledged the hit. I nocked another arrow, tracking the thing as it wheeled around for another attack. For the precision I needed, however, I couldn't be rollicking at this speed.

"Zyr, stop!" I cried, not really expecting him to hear me, much less obey with such alacrity that I nearly went over his head this time. But my wild childhood served me well and I kept my seat. I followed the undead bird as it stooped… and I released a breath with my arrow. Sending it straight through the thing's skull. Headless, it dropped to the sand, where it flapped and floundered, still trying to reach the queen.

"Go," I yelled, and Zyr leapt into the gallop. Riding an intelligent horse was like nothing I'd experienced. He circled around Andi's cloud. With her hands upraised, she stood in the center of the storm of her own making, unseen winds tossing her long locks as if in a gale that touched no one else.

A great creature rose in the waves. A many-tentacled monster, thrashing and lashing at the Hawks who danced in and around its strikes like small birds harrying an eagle. As I watched, a tentacle wrapped around a smaller figure, yanking her off her feet. She screamed and I knew it was Wren. I sent an arrow into the tentacle holding her, knowing it to be futile even as I did it. With a normal animal, the pain might cause it to flinch. But Deyrr's creatures, fueled by foul magic and no motivation of their own, never showed care for their safety or wellbeing, never even felt pain, so far as I could tell.

Zyr skidded to a stop, dumping me to the sand as he melted into the panther I'd seen across the breakfast table. He must've shifted more slowly than usual, because I hit the ground gently, still on my feet and never dropping the arrow I had nocked at the ready. Scanning the area for a target while Zyr raced into the fray, I spotted more birds diving down. As they headed toward Andi, and with monotonously steady intent, I figured them for the enemy and began picking them off with arrows to the head.

They fell, to the sea or to the sand, still struggling to reach their target: Andi. Which made me wonder how they knew to look for her and why.

No time to think about that, however. Archery requires a peacefulness of mind and spirit, so I concentrated on that, mindful of how swiftly I emptied my quiver. More animals—Tala, I knew, by their growls and roars of aggression—streamed past me, some plunging into the foaming surf to assist, others setting up a perimeter around the area. Other birds joined in the aerial battle, attacking the Deyrr birds so that I dared not shoot, for fear of hitting one of ours. I should save my last few arrows regardless.

Seven wolfhounds ringed the queen, setting up a circle of protection, so I looked to the fight.

The black panther clawing its way up the spine of the sea monster had to be Zyr. Even in feline form, soaked with seawater, fur slicked with blood both Deyrr and human, he had a careless grace I recognized. He buried his jaws where the creature's body narrowed to its head, jerking back and then spitting out chunks of putrid flesh and bone. It made my stomach heave, but he did it again. A tentacle plunged at him, trying to knock the cat aside, and he howled a feline ululation that made my hairs stand up. I sighted an arrow on the monster's eye, now visible above the water as it reared up. I could at least blind the thing.

A man moved into my line of sight, and I aborted the pull. He climbed up the monster's head, using knives I realized, as he had no claws, planting one over the other for purchase, booted feet bracing. Tays. No one else had that beard. He came up just ahead of the Zyr-panther, sawing at the other side.

Suddenly, the monster convulsed. People variously screamed, shouted, roared and screeched.

And the tentacles went limp, dropping people in the water.

~ 8 ~

LIKE A DOLL dropped by a careless girl, Queen Andromeda fell to her knees.

I ran to her, then skidded to a stop when a wolfhound wheeled on me, fangs bared and dripping a warning growl. "I'm an ally," I yelled at it, to no avail as it didn't back off in the slightest. Maybe it was an actual animal and couldn't understand me. Or it could be one of those *staymach* creatures in different form. Ridiculous that I couldn't tell the difference. I couldn't even shoot the thing because it might be someone important. Such was the chaos the Tala brought to everything they touched.

"Let her through." The queen sounded terribly weary. The hound obeyed immediately, giving me the impression of a sweeping, even gallant bow as it stepped out of my way. I sank down in the sand next to Andi. Her cheek dripped blood, but I saw no other injury. Nothing to account for her extreme lassitude. Ripping a piece of cloth from one of my underskirts—still damp but at least rinsed clean—I dabbed at the blood on her cheek. No sign of poison. "What can I do for you?" I asked.

"Is the attack over?" she asked in turn.

I scanned the scene—the tentacles still limp, even the birds I'd shot had stopped their lifeless flapping. "It looks like it," I assured her. Though very odd that the creatures had all stopped. Usually the Deyrr-animated creatures had to be chopped up and burned. The only exception had been when Zynda used her sorcery out on the *Hákyrling* to zap the flock of undead fish-birds with a blue light that…Oh. Foolish me. "Did you magic them dead?" I had no idea how to phrase that better.

Andi smiled slightly, likely for my neophyte phrasing. "I tried something, though I wasn't sure it would work."

"Well, they're all unanimated again, so it must have."

"Time will tell," she replied enigmatically.

A huge wolf came bounding at us at top speed. Though I knew it had to be Rayfe—and the way the guardian wolfhounds all immediately deferred to him confirmed it—I very much wanted to run away as fast as I could. Andi held up her hands and began speaking before he finished shifting to human form.

"I'm fine. The baby is fine. Relax."

Rayfe scowled, the expression uncannily like the wrinkled muzzle of the snarling wolf. "What did you do?" he demanded, running his hands over her, checking for injury as if she hadn't spoken.

"My job," she snapped. "Isn't that the first thing you said to me—that Annfwn needs me? I did what needs to be done to protect our realm."

He gave her a long look, then sat back on the sand, a collapse as equally weary as hers. "As I recall, the first thing I asked you was whether you should risk moving after falling off your horse."

"I didn't fall off," she replied with coolly injured dignity. "Fiona fell—entirely your fault—and I perforce went with her."

"Perforce," he echoed, mouth twitching.

"Perforce!" she insisted.

I felt as if I'd witnessed an argument in code.

Rayfe raked a hand through his hair, then leaned an elbow on his upraised knee. "Andromeda. You cannot jeopardize yourself or the child."

I really wished I could excuse myself, but I couldn't with-draw politely without interrupting, so I made myself as small as possible, looking studiously away as if observing the clean-up. They were pulling bodies out of the surf and onto the sand. I couldn't tell who, however. The beach was otherwise empty. Just our circle, still guarded by wolfhounds, and the group dealing with the aftermath of battle. Everyone else seemed to have retreated to the cliff city, where people thronged on the balconies and overlooks. I wondered if Thalia was up there watching. If so, then at least her parents had restrained her from divebombing the fight.

"I want this baby as much as you do," Andi was saying, "but for you and I, being parents will always come second to our duties to Annfwn. You know that."

"Still—"

"*And* I have my duties to the Thirteen. I didn't relinquish my birthright or my loyalty when I married you. Annfwn now stands as the gate to bar Deyrr and Dasnaria from overtaking all the original twelve, as well."

"Yes, but—"

"There is no 'but.' Besides, we don't even know this child will survive to be born, much less any time beyond. I refuse to base every decision on something so far out of our control."

"If Zynda returns as the dragon, that could change."

"*If* she does, *if* the dragon magic dampening works as you all hope, and *if* we haven't fallen to Deyrr's undead attacks by then." She listed the points crisply and I listened in fascination despite myself. Zyr never had gotten to the part about what Final Form had to do with babies. "I'm prioritizing. There's no sense in ensuring the future generations of Annfwn if there's no Annfwn to leave to them."

He visibly clenched his jaw. "Sometimes you are so unrelentingly mossback that I regret more than usual that you were raised among them."

"You make it sound like I was raised by wolves," she shot back, clearly stung.

"No, because that would've been preferable," he ground out. "Then you wouldn't talk about our unborn child as simply another data point in a spectrum of priorities."

I really should have excused myself by now. Had I ever heard a husband and wife argue? No, I surely hadn't because a Dasnarian woman doesn't argue with any man, let alone her husband. Still, though Rayfe clearly seethed with anger and frustration, he showed no inclination to beat his wife. Possibly that was due to her delicate pregnancy, but I rather thought he wouldn't regardless. An odd opinion to have about a man with so much beast in him. Strange, too, that Dasnarian men were much more domineering and demanding—and inclined to easy violence to subdue the weak—with no animal nature influencing them.

Perhaps the answer lay in exactly that: a man who knows his animal nature also knows he must strive to control it.

Though I was an unwelcome bystander to the royal marital conflict, my observations gave me a bit more insight into their concern over Zyr's earlier aggression. They clearly feared he could lose control of his inner beast. Because of me? But in that case it made no sense to saddle him—literally!—with me. Ah, well. I hadn't been raised to question the decisions of those in authority over me. They held my continued wellbeing in their hands, so I would serve as they required of me.

Zyr prowled up the beach, still in the form of the massive black panther. As I watched, he shapeshifted midstep, continuing forward in the same liquid gliding motion, but as a man.

Uncanny.

"The Deyrr creatures are all truly dead," he reported, dropping bonelessly to the sand beside me, giving me a casual glance that didn't fool me—he made sure I remained unharmed in that quick assessment. He also seemed oblivious to the tension between his king and queen. Or didn't care. "Three injured, two dead—all Hawks."

"Who?" I asked, though it wouldn't change their fate for me to know it.

Zyr gave me a regretful look. "Not that Tays bastard, unfortunately. I didn't recognize their faces."

"We'll find out, as soon as Andromeda is recovered, and pay our respects," Rayfe said, regret in his face, too.

"I'll have to inform Ursula." Andi gazed at the recovery efforts as if she could see that far. "At least I can tell her the Deyrr sleepers are neutralized."

"And they're decomposing already," Zyr said. "Fast. Like they've been dead a while. I don't know if that's their nature or something else at work."

"Andromeda performed a sorcery," Rayfe told him, his gaze darkening again on his wife.

"Aha!" Zyr sat up straighter. "Then you *can* defeat them. What did you do?"

"Since you *asked*," Andi replied sweetly, giving her husband a vicious glare that bounced right off of him, for all the interest he showed. "I've been studying the creatures Deyrr has been sneaking through the magic barrier and—"

"When have you been doing this?" Rayfe demanded.

"Constantly," she bit out, then softened. She held out a hand and her husband took it, lacing their fingers together, more like a reflex than anything. It told me a great deal, however, that even though they fought and were angry with one another, under it all they remained connected. Kral and I had enjoyed all the perfect civility of our emotionless marriage, and absolutely nothing of this kind of connection. Suddenly I understood a great deal more of why he'd fallen in love with Jepp instead of with me. Even if I'd had the temerity—or bad manners—to disagree with Kral, I wouldn't have because I'd never cared enough.

"You have to understand, my wolf," Andi was saying. "The barrier is so much a part of my mind that I'm always aware of it. I think the n'Andanans designed it that way, to be an extension of the queen's magic. Once Ursula asked me to pay special attention to the portion of the barrier where it crosses that spur of Dasnaria, where Zynda theorized the barrier is permeable, I became sensitive to the feel of the Deyrr creatures as they tested it. I found I could explore something of their natures even at this distance."

"You didn't tell me this," Rayfe said quietly.

"I didn't want you to worry. It's…incredibly distasteful, I won't lie. Also, I wasn't sure if what I sensed would translate to anything useful. I didn't want to raise false hopes, especially if I couldn't do anything with the knowledge."

"But you did," Zyr put in. "You killed these sleepers."

Andi shook her head and tucked a long strand of hair behind her ear with one hand, her other still firmly in Rayfe's grasp. "No, they were already dead. It's more like I cut their strings, separating them from the magic that animated them. I could do that much."

Zyr and Rayfe exchanged a frown. "I don't understand," Rayfe told her.

"I'm not sure I do either, entirely." She slid me a glance. "Perhaps our Dasnarian guest can illuminate some for us."

They all looked at me—though with expectation rather than suspicion. Oh wonderful.

"I don't think I can." I ventured. "The Temple of Deyrr and its practitioners are not an above-board group in the empire. Not a topic of polite conversation at all. Certainly no honorable families associate with them, or even acknowledge their existence." I ignored Zyr's snicker at that. "I know mostly what you do, that Deyrr is an old god—no longer worshipped as all right thinking Dasnarians acknowledge Sól as the one true god and the emperor his divine avatar."

"You really believe your emperor is divine?" Zyr scoffed.

I met his scorn with a level stare. "That is the way of things in Dasnaria. Did I scoff at you when you told me your sister died and spoke to a goddess of yours?"

He opened his mouth to retort, then closed it again. "You're right. Go on."

Rayfe and Andi seemed surprised but said nothing, nodding at me encouragingly. "There's not much more to say. Deyrr is an old god worshipped by one of the tribes in the lands that eventually formed Dasnaria, before it conquered its neighbors and became the empire. Those people lived in warring nomadic tribes and worshipped Deyrr as the god of the hunt, but also of hunger through starvation. They saw him as ruling over the transmutation of the living animal into death and death cycling back into life through consumption of the meat. That's all I know of fact—the rest is all stories."

"Would you tell us one?" Though Andi posed it as a question, it felt like a command, her gaze intense and expectant.

I stumbled a bit mentally. "They're merely tales meant to frighten children."

"Nevertheless." She softened the demand with a smile. "Please. Sometimes stories hold the purest truth."

"All right. This is the best-known story." And my favorite since I was a girl. "Once there were three princesses, each more beautiful than the last, daughters of the king of all the lands. One day, as the eldest walked in her garden, a witch approached her. The princess couldn't know the woman for a witch, because the witch had disguised herself as a young maiden, with hair straight and brilliant as spun gold, and a face as lovely as morning. Only her eyes showed her true nature, for they were windows to the empty pit where her soul had been, filled with blackness. The witch greeted the princess and said it was a beautiful day. The princess agreed it was. And she forgot to ask how the witch had entered her garden.

"The witch offered the princess a kitten, soft and purring, and the princess gathered it to her bosom, delighted with her new pet. The witch asked the princess if it wasn't the loveliest, softest, most loving and adorable kitten she'd ever beheld, and the princess agreed it was. Then the witch took it back, saying the princess could only have the kitten if the princess came to live with her, and wouldn't she like that better than her father's castle, where her sisters were only jealous of her, and no one loved her anyway? The princess agreed that was true, and off she went to live with the witch.

"The middle princess began to miss her older sister, wondering where she'd gone. So one day she set out on her horse to search the forest where no one ever went, and where her father had forbidden her to go. Something spooked her horse and they fell. The witch appeared and helped her to her feet. Being raised to be polite, the princess thanked her, and the witch smiled to have her gratitude.

"The witch observed that the princess must be a wonderful horsewoman, to have such a well-trained horse that hadn't run off. Flattered, the princess agreed that she was. Then the witch offered the princess a puppy, warm and wriggly, and the princess gathered it to her bosom, delighted with her new pet. The witch asked the princess if it wasn't the noblest, strongest, most loyal and adorable puppy she'd ever beheld, and the princess agreed it was. Then the witch took it back, saying the princess could only have the puppy if the princess came to live with her older sister and the witch, and wouldn't she like that better than her father's castle where her younger and most beautiful sister got all of the attention? The princess agreed that was true, and off she went to live with the witch."

Andi had a very odd expression on her face, so I paused in my story. "Should I stop?"

"No…" She sounded thoughtful. "Tell us the third piece."

"Well, it goes as you might imagine. The youngest and most beautiful princess, while vain and sometimes shallow, was also pure of heart and loved her sisters truly and missed them terribly. She ventured out, over the mountains, and traveled to the witch's palace, so high on a mountain peak that it could see in every direction. Though the journey was arduous, the youngest princess persevered. By the time she reached the top of the mountain, her rich gown was in rags and her soft feet bled, leaving red footprints in the snow.

"She knocked on the door and the witch answered, smiling at the princess. 'I know you,' said the witch. 'You are the most beautiful of all your sisters.' 'No,' replied the youngest princess, 'for beauty can be measured in many ways and no kind is better than any other.'

"The witch didn't like this, because she had no power over those who didn't agree with her. 'Come in then,' the witch said, 'and warm yourself, eat at my table, drink of my wine.' 'I will come in,' said the youngest princess, stepping inside, 'for that is why I journeyed here. But I won't eat at your table or drink of your wine. I want nothing of yours.' The witch didn't like this, because she had no power over those who wouldn't accept her gifts.

"'Then why have you journeyed all this way?' the witch asked. 'I've come for my sisters, whom you stole from me,' the princess replied. The witch smiled at this because now she had the key to the youngest princess's heart, for the witch could use her heart's desire to bind her will. The witch summoned the other two princesses. When they arrived, the youngest princess saw that though years had passed, her sisters looked exactly the same as the day they'd disappeared. Except that their eyes had gone as dark as banked coals, and though they recognized her, they did not embrace her as they once would have.

"'Release my sisters from your chains,' the youngest princess commanded the witch. But the witch only smiled. 'They are free to leave. Freer than they were when they arrived,' the witch said. So the youngest princess said to her sisters, 'Come home with me.' At first the older two princesses didn't wish to leave their new home, but the witch gave them leave. 'Take your pets with you,' the witch told them, 'and you will always be able to return to me.' So the oldest princess beckoned, and a giant tiger wearing a collar strolled into the room and sat by her side. The middle princess whistled, and an enormous wolf wearing a collar strolled into the room and sat by her side. 'We are all ready,' the older princesses told the younger.

"'Aren't you going to thank me for my generosity in giving your sisters back to you?' the witch asked the youngest princess. 'No, I won't thank you because you've taken my sisters' hearts and turned them against those who truly love them,' the princess said, and the witch didn't like this, because she had no power over those who wouldn't express gratitude to her.

"The three princesses, the tiger, and the wolf journeyed home. When they reached their father's castle, the eldest princess commanded the tiger to slay the king, and she took his throne. The middle princess commanded the wolf to slay her younger sister, and took her pure heart to sacrifice to their god, who was pleased with them."

A thick silence fell while they all waited expectantly, Andi with a most peculiar expression on her face—and Rayfe watching her with an odd intensity.

"That's it?" Zyr demanded with hot indignation. "You can't tell me that's how the story ends."

"How else should it end?" I asked him, perplexed.

"Happily," he declared. "Stories should end happily. That's a horrible tale."

I lifted a shoulder and let it fall. "Most Dasnarian stories end tragically. That's the way of things."

"I'll regret hearing that tale for the rest of my life," Zyr muttered. "What does it have to do with Deyrr anyway?"

"The eyes," Andi put in, still sounding thoughtful. "Illyria had eyes like that. I'd never seen anything like it. So that's a sign of possession by Deyrr."

"So we learned nothing new from that terrible story," Zyr complained.

"That's not true," Andi countered. "We learned many interesting rules for dealing with the practitioners of Deyrr. The witch bound the will of the elder two princesses by getting them to agree with her and to be beholden to her. She gave them pets—which could correspond to the sleepers, possibly shapeshifters—and those animals followed their bidding. I can match that to what I've sensed from the sleepers we've encountered. I think the Deyrr magic animates them through their own spirits which maintain channels to their previous bodies. The bodies have died, then were pulled back from death and transmuted, with the spirits held prisoner with magical bonds."

"What are you saying?" Zyr asked, sounding horrified. I

squelched the impulse to reach out and take his hand, to offer him the same comfort our companions shared.

Andi sighed. "I'm guessing—and some of this is from what Zynda was able to tell me—but it seems likely that it goes this way with the sleepers: a person with the ability to shapeshift is forced to shift into a form, dies as that animal, and their living essence captured and attached to a well of magic. Let's call it the god Deyrr for simplicity's sake. Employing that enslaved spirit's connection to its body, the practitioners of Deyrr can then direct the actions of that body, making it appear animated. They're working from some distance, so the creatures tend to be dull and equipped with simple missions."

"So you deanimated these sleepers by liberating the captive spirits?" Rayfe asked, though I could tell he only hoped for that truth. Indeed, his queen shook her head, misty regret in her eyes.

"I severed the connection from the practitioner animating them to the bodies. It's similar to how my connection to the barrier works, so I thought I might be able to do that much."

"Then the spirits of those shapeshifters..." Zyr trailed off, unable to voice it.

"They remain with the followers of the dark god. I can sense them. And I've seen them in visions, not knowing what I saw." She sounded deeply unsettled, even horrified, and Rayfe edged closer to her, putting an arm around her. She leaned into him.

"Can you describe it?" he asked softly.

She nodded. "It's... horrible, though."

"Then better to share," Zyr spoke up. "Things always seem worse in our heads than in the bright light of day."

I glanced at him curiously, wondering if he meant his imprisonment. Which, I'd point out to him, he hadn't wanted to talk about. Indeed, he avoided my gaze.

Andi had closed her eyes, lines crumpling her high forehead, and showing strain around her mouth. "I've seen a vast globe, colorful but wrong in a way I can't explain. It's full of people, though they're somewhat formless, some more clear than others. I think the globe is formed of *them*. There are…extrusions coming from the people, extending like stems from a flower to the globe, but working in reverse. They don't draw nutrients, they feed the globe. The glow of their life energies flows up the tether, running into the sphere, which spins with thousands of the threads. Another connection, like a great rope—or umbilical cord—flows into the distance."

Silence fell over us. I rubbed the chill off my arms, one that had nothing to do with the balmy weather.

~ 9 ~

"YOU CAN'T RELEASE them?" Rayfe asked, though we all knew the answer.

Andi opened her eyes, cloudy with her vision. "If I do, I think they will cease to be entirely. I can only cut them off from their old bodies. The globe holds them captive."

"Then we have to make sure Deyrr doesn't take any more of us," Rayfe said with grim determination.

"Where is Deyrr obtaining these people with the ability to shapeshift?" I asked, and they all turned to me with bemused frowns. "There are no shapeshifters in the Dasnarian Empire," I pointed out. "Of that much I'm certain."

"Shapeshifting can be a latent ability," Rayfe explained, though thoughtfully, still thinking through the ramifications. "Theoretically, anyone with some Tala blood carries that potential. Back when Salena was queen, and before that, the Tala came and went more or less freely through the barrier. In those days no one worried about leaving partblood children in the greater world. Add that to the fact that those with Tala blood seem to be deeply attracted to one another on a subconscious level." He slanted a wicked grin at the queen, who unaccountably blushed. "You end up with families consolidating and concentrating those latent abilities outside Annfwn."

"Like Uorsin," Andi mused. I'd noticed they all had the habit of speaking of the former High King by name only, no honorifics, not even that of 'father," from his daughters. "Driven by Tala blood he never knew he had."

"I'm sorry to disrupt this theory," I said, feeling that I should point out the fallacy in their logic. "But Dasnarians know very little of your people. I don't think this is just me. How could the practitioners of Deyrr possibly know about these partbloods in order to target them?"

"Kir." The queen said the word with peculiar emphasis and particular distaste. Rayfe's expression hardened, but Zyr seemed as perplexed as I. "He used to be the high priest of the Church of Glorianna under Uorsin's reign," she explained to me. "And had been long involved in tracking down Tala partbloods, like Ash's father, who was burned at the stake at the priests' hands."

I hadn't met Ash, or Queen Amelia, who'd taken the commoner as a lover—quite scandalous to my mind—but Zynda and Jepp had discussed the pair quite a bit. Queen Amelia had taken her twin toddlers, one heir to Andi in Annfwn and the other heir to the High Throne of the Thirteen, to Castle Windroven in Avonlidgh. Coincidentally—or not?—where Zynda and Marskal planned to travel, to liberate a dragon. All very muddled to me. The apportionment of heirs most of all, including why the heirs weren't near the thrones they were meant to inherit, in case of sudden death. If the Emperor knew, he'd surely take advantage of that choice information.

Which meant I would make a good spy, if I had the inclination. Not that I did.

"Salena's dolls that she left you three," Rayfe was saying, as if just remembering. "The one she left Amelia changed color in the presence of Tala blood. But I thought she got it back from Kir."

"She did—right at the same time he disappeared. Presumably to work with Deyrr, as Jepp saw him in the entertainment salons at the Imperial Palace in Dasnaria with the High Priestess of Deyrr."

Again, they all looked at me. "How does that fit with your assertion that no honorable family would have dealings with Deyrr?" Rayfe asked me.

I didn't know. Covering my shock, I held up my hands in Zyr's gesture of innocent ignorance. "I was only at the Imperial Palace twice," I told them. "And when I wasn't in the Imperial Seraglio, I was at formal events and occupied with matters of my marriage or lack thereof." Or in my cell, waiting to be burned for having the gall to request an annulment. Where that courage had come from, I had no idea. It would be nice to have some of it now. "I wasn't in Jepp's confidence, nor would a woman of my station and status have been allowed into the entertainment salons. I only ever saw the High Priestess when she attacked High Queen Ursula on the *Hákyrling*. I didn't know she had any association with His Imperial Majesty."

Rather than satisfied, they seemed disappointed. Rather, the queen and king did. Zyr watched me contemplatively.

Andi sighed, sitting up straight again. "Well, in the absence of more information—and as Ursula is unlikely to send anyone back to Dasnaria to spy again—we have to assume that Kir somehow taught the practitioners of Deyrr how to detect Tala partbloods."

"Ash has been concerned for some time that the partblood ex-convicts he'd been working to succor in hiding and repatriate to Annfwn were disappearing suspiciously," Rayfe put in.

Andi frowned at him. "I thought you held the opinion that they didn't trust us as king and queen, and me in particular as holder of the barrier. That they'd simply gone deeper into hiding—something made easier since Ursula gave them legal status and eliminated the hunting of them."

"A logical conclusion, and that could account for some of it—but that was before I knew all of this."

"Glorianna curse Kir if this is so," Andi growled, the air stirring around her once more. She must have been regaining her strength. "Even in his misguided zeal to eliminate the Tala, how could he stomach betraying us to attack by the Dasnarians?"

I understood her sense of betrayal. That sort of thing would be an immediate death sentence in Dasnaria. It should've been here, too. Impatience gathered in me for their naiveté. "But so many of these sleepers," I put in, judicious in my phrasing. "How many dead here today? And in the fish-bird attack, there were dozens and dozens of them."

Zyr frowned at me—at first I thought for my temerity, but I realized he was nodding thoughtfully. "And how are they subdued, transported with no one knowing, in such great numbers? It makes no sense to squander so many here today simply as a test..."

"Unless they have many more in reserve," Rayfe finished. "I don't see what they gained today, however. Especially since we defeated them handily."

"Did you?" I'd spoken too sharply, even contemptuously, my question too preemptory, given their expressions. I heard my father, my brothers, even Kral in my tone. Unforgivable to have forgotten myself in such a way. Sitting on the sand on a lovely beach, one forgets that one is with royalty. "I apologize," I said, ducking my gaze, my face hot.

"Don't," Zyr said.

"I agree," Rayfe put in. "Explain."

Andi touched my arm, her fingers soft, her eyes hard. "We value your insights. You know how your people view wars of this kind. We've been so long fighting each other in close quarters over mostly irrelevant, endlessly shifting borders that our strategy is not the same."

I hadn't thought of it that way. She—they—had a generosity and flexibility in their willingness to entertain new ideas. I'd have to mull that over.

"Yes, you won today," I said. Zyr raised a brow at me, and I started over. "We won—if you want to call repelling a very small force at great cost a victory. Queen Andromeda, you cut the ties to their magic, and now the practitioners of Deyrr know you can. The Emperor has had little intelligence about your realms before this. No matter what you believe about his divinity, he is a great strategist who's added many kingdoms and protectorates to his empire. His Imperial Majesty will see it as critical to assess your abilities to defend yourselves, so he can determine what an overwhelming force will be. You suspect the Emperor is working hand-in-hand with Deyrr? If so, then they could've had people observing this attack. They'd know it exhausted Queen Andromeda to defeat just this many."

Andi's gaze sharpened. "Can they do that—observe from a distance?"

"I don't know—but why not? You can, as you've told us. I never knew people could magically detach souls from their bodies or shapeshift into mythical creatures. My not knowing didn't make it impossible."

"Point taken," Rayfe said dryly.

"But if they observed this battle—and if I were you I'd assume as much—then they'll know that your, I mean, our defense is disorganized."

"What?" Zyr sat up from his languid pose, offended. "The Hawks responded immediately. And we arrived to help within moments. We worked together, just like you mossbacks were bitching at us to do! What?" he demanded again, this time of

Rayfe, who'd clapped a hand over his face.

I gave Zyr a cool stare. "The Hawks responded immediately because they happened to be right there, which might not have been a coincidence. And we still sustained at least two fatalities and many injuries. You—we—were far from ready. And yes, *we* ran to help, but what about the rest of the Tala?" I waved a hand at the cliff city. "People *watched*, like they found it entertaining."

"Things like this don't happen much," Zyr grumbled, sounding sheepish now. "Besides, it was only a little attack."

"That's my point!" I stabbed a finger at him, aware that Rayfe and Andi listened intently. "There is no such thing as a little attack. They'll consider the numbers. I've heard them. How many of them they can afford to lose to take the critical percentage of yours. You all are arrogant and complacent here. Had there been the slightest threat to my family home, it would have been *crushed* with massive and decisive force."

"You Dasnarians live constantly at war," he sneered. "That's hardly any way to live."

"Perhaps so," I shot back, "but when it comes to war, guess who'll have more practice."

Rayfe nodded and stood, uncoiling rapidly enough that I momentarily perceived him as shapeshifting, even though he remained a man. "This is my fault," he announced. "And my responsibility to repair."

Andi made a sound of impatience, fluidly rising to her own feet and ignoring her husband's move to help her. "Don't be ridiculous," she started, but he cut her off with a fierce look.

"Karyn is right. *Arrogant and complacent.* We've been so long accustomed to our insularity, the protection of the barrier, happy to be ignored, forgotten, even reviled for the privacy it afforded us. So focused on protecting our backs from Uorsin that we sit here and treat an attack on our soil as entertainment. Allowing the Hawks to do the lion's share of the work." He focused on Zyr. "You say we worked with them, but not really. We need to drill together, to coordinate our forces."

"In all fairness," I put in, "Lieutenant Tays made the decision for the Hawks to train alone this morning."

He looked slightly less fierce when he nodded thanks to me, but his jaw remained tightly set. "I am king here. I lead the forces of Annfwn, not him. From now on, I decide how our forces work and train together. I should've been out here this morning."

"We had strategy to determine. Ursula's plans to set in motion," Andi reminded him. "Contingency plans. Unexpected developments." Her eyes flicked to Zyr and away.

"Nevertheless." Rayfe brushed all that off like a wolf shedding water. "I'm calling a Gathering."

Zyr's brows rose, but Andi looked confused. "What's that?"

Rayfe laughed, without humor, and shook his head. "How far we've descended that the Queen of the Tala doesn't know what a Gathering is."

"I'll remind you that I didn't grow up in Annfwn," she said tartly.

"This is on me, not you," he replied, taking her hand and giving her a fierce smile. "Let me put it this way: the last Gathering was when I called all the Tala together to recruit a fighting force to come after you, when we defeated Ordnung and laid siege to Windroven."

"Oh," she murmured. "I've never seen so many Tala since then. I've wondered if I misremembered or if you made your army look bigger with illusion and supplementing with *staymachs*."

Rayfe's grin went wolfish, mirrored by Zyr. "Oh, we have all sorts of tricks, my queen. You will see."

"And I have tricks of my own this time," she returned.

He sobered. "I know I can't tell you not to risk yourself, but Karyn saw that clearly, too. Defeating this small force knocked you to your knees."

"I was learning, and unprepared. I'll do better next time."

"It's more than you and the child," he said, with some layered meaning beneath. "We know what they're after. It must be kept safe."

Andi cut her gaze to me and away again. "It will be," she replied shortly. "I'm working on it."

Ah. Something they didn't trust me knowing. Another woman might've been hurt by their distrust, but it reassured me that they weren't being completely stupid. A true Dasnarian spy would love to unearth a secret of that apparent magnitude. If I obtained enough useful information, took advantage of their confidences, I could likely parlay my way back into His Imperial Majesty's good graces. The unexpected possibility took my breath away. I could be forgiven, perhaps even rewarded with rank, even a true marriage. I could go home, marry a Dasnarian man and raise my children as I'd been raised.

I could have certainty again, not this strange friendship with a half-wild man. Studying Zyr from the corner of my eye, I suddenly felt terribly confused. I'd always known where my loyalties lay. Now I wasn't at all sure.

"How soon will you call the Gathering, King Rayfe?" Zyr was asking with unusual gravity and courtesy.

"Tomorrow morning should give everyone who can time to arrive," Rayfe replied. "But you will not be here. You and Karyn have your mission."

"Silly mapsticks, imaginary dragons, and unfindable n'Andana aren't important now," Zyr protested. "Not if you're calling a Gathering."

"Your mission is still critical," Rayfe replied implacably. He slid a glance at me. "We learned from today, too. And we know now that need help more than ever."

"But n'Andana? It's dead and gone."

"We once thought that about Annfwn," Andi pointed out. "Entire realms don't disappear. They're simply forgotten—sometimes through deliberate action. Moranu only knows what we might find there."

"Probably a landscape full of giant skeletons since the dragons all died!" Zyr waved his hands in the air.

"Not all of them," Rayfe answered. "Kiraka lives. There's one under Windroven that Marskal and Zynda will hopefully recruit for us. But if today was simply a test, we'll need more allies than that."

"Besides, not all of the n'Andanans shapeshifted into dragon form. It sounds like very few achieved that level. It doesn't follow that all the people died. Only those that needed magic to survive," Andi replied.

"Then where have they been?" Zyr demanded, sounding as if he thought he'd scored a point.

"Hiding," she replied crisply. "Just like the Tala used to do."

Rayfe snorted. "We weren't *hiding*, we kept to ourselves for good reason."

Andi rolled her eyes. "Whatever you want to call it. The n'Andanans are the ancient enemy of Deyrr. They'll have a stake in this war, perhaps critical information and assistance to offer."

"Oh, right." Zyr curled up a lip. "They're just weak moss-backs that rolled over and gave up their magic rather than fight Deyrr long ago. Now we're going to ask them to help *us*?"

"First we need to find them," Rayfe said. "They left the mapsticks in the library at Nahanau so n'Andana could be found."

Zyr snorted. "Pure speculation."

"Maybe you're not capable," Rayfe countered. "If so, tell me now."

"I'm capable," Zyr ground out. "I'm fine."

"Karyn?" he asked me, more gently.

"I stand ready to assist, Your Highness." I bowed a little, feeling I needed to, if only to compensate for Zyr's lack of courtesy. At least I'd already decided to do this quest. It would give me time to think.

"Good. I expect you both to start immediately. Check in every couple of days."

Every couple of *days*? Wait. I couldn't go off unchaperoned with a man—especially one of Zyr's lascivious nature. We'd have to spend nights together. I had to refuse. I'd take any other assignment…

Andi caught my eye, that seeing-through-me expression in her gray gaze, reading my refusal clearly. Her expression reminding me of our conversation. I understood. All too clearly. They'd assigned Zyr to get me out of there. This time the mistrust did wound me, perhaps all the more because I knew I deserved it. Worse, I hated that Zyr had been made my keeper.

I supposed, however, that I'd brought this on myself. I'd known that by leaving Dasnaria I'd be turning myself over to the whims of hlyti, perhaps to my own destruction.

Rayfe and Andi watched me closely, seeming to be waiting for my concession. Gracious of them, as they could simply command me. I curtseyed, this time deeply, as much to hlyti as to their willful goddesses. "As you command," I said, hearing the bitter edge to my own voice and hoping no one else did.

It must've been everything that had happened so far, but only then did it occur to me that I'd have to try flying again.

"Maybe if we didn't have to start by plummeting off a cliff," I suggested to Zyr, who only raised that raptorish brow at me.

"We didn't *plummet* off a cliff before," he explained slowly, as if I might be dense. "A controlled drop is necessary for some kinds of animals to fly. Those too heavy to launch from the ground on wing power alone."

"Like the gríobhth."

"Like the gríobhth, yes—especially with the extra weight of you on my back." He had that tone of exaggerated patience that made me want to kick him. "Now, if you're ready, I'll shift and we'll go."

We stood outside his apartments where I'd met him after changing clothes and gathering supplies. He'd selected a dozen or so mapsticks he thought mostly likely represented the coast of Annfwn and nearby islands and packed the rest in saddle bags. I'd wanted to catalog all the map-sticks first, mark them somehow. Zyr nixed that idea, too. To appease Rayfe he'd wanted to get at least one or two flights in before sunset and insisted we could start with the "low-hanging fruit." If he had to miss the Gathering, he wanted to be *doing* something. He also insisted that my procrastinating on flying again would only allow my fear to entrench.

It seemed pretty well entrenched to me already. My gut had gone to water at the sight of the drop below. "Maybe a different form then," I suggested. "One that does have the wing power to—"

"That's the only form I have that can carry a grown person," he cut me off, clearly irritated with my balking. "Most shapeshifters don't even have that. My sister can't, for all her other skills, so you should appreciate me. Why do you think I even shared the gríobhth form with you?"

"I don't know. I didn't ask you to, nor did I ask for this assignment."

"That makes two of us," he snapped. In my mind, I saw him as the gríobhth with its sharply curved beak taking a piece out of me.

"Don't be mean to me," I warned him. I meant to sound sharp, to vent my own fear and frustration—and, yes, hurt that no one here trusted me. I shouldn't have left home. All the turbulent emotions undermined my determination, and the words came out more like a plea, all watery and sad.

Wren had died in the attack. Though I didn't know her well, her death dug at me. She'd been kind. Maybe she could've been a friend, if I'd known how to accept her overtures and small kindnesses. Only the fact that I knew she'd have been the first to tell me to get busy and do what I could to stop other deaths had me still going.

Zyr's fierce glare melted into remorse. He took a step toward me, hands out as if to embrace me, then curled his fingers into impotent fists he dropped to his sides. "*Nothing* is going right today," he hissed.

"Tell that to the people who died down there," I flung at him, pointing at the beach where teams of Hawks and shapeshifters worked to remove the nastily melting carcasses of the Deyrr creatures.

To my astonishment, Zyr laughed. Not his big-bellied joyful one, but in quiet chagrin. "You would bring that up. And before you yell at me again, you're right. I'm being an ass."

"I didn't yell at you." Had I? My mother would be horrified at such a lapse. "Today is a terrible day," I agreed. "So much has happened—and I know you're worried about Zynda on top of it all."

"See? This is what comes of getting up early." He nodded at me, probably in an attempt to look wise, but his irreverent humor leaked through. Then he sighed. "I'm sorry for it, but we have to do this. I have to fly you out of here and this is the only way I can do it."

I'd noticed that more Tala than usual already teemed around the cliff city. "Has the Gathering call gone out already then?"

"Yes." He considered. "Before you ask, you wouldn't have heard anything. It's Tala magic."

Wonderful. "All right. Let's just do this. I know the king and queen want me out of here before I witness anything important."

He blinked at me, a slow smile spreading over his lean face. "Figured that out, did you?"

$$\sim 10 \sim$$

"I COULD BE a spy." I shrugged. "And there's a reason the attacks are focused here."

"You don't have magic, so you couldn't have signaled anyone," Zyr assured me. "And you don't have any way to send messages."

"Is that what they think?"

He winced. "I'm terrible at this. Forget I said anything."

"Fine." My turn to sigh. "Let's get going. Which mapstick do you want to start with?" I held out the handful and he picked one out.

"Hold that for me," he instructed while I put the others away in a pouch over my free shoulder, as my quiver and bow hung over the other. "I'm pretty sure that's for the Annfwn coastline. Once I shift I'll hold it in my front claws. We'll do a nice easy flight—I'll stay high, so no *plummeting*." He grinned at me and I found myself smiling back, a bit shy now at how acerbic I'd been. "If that's correct, I'll follow the coast to the end of a part represented by the mapstick, then I'll hand that one back to you with my beak, you give me another, and we can see if we can figure out the next one down."

"How will I know which next one to hand you?"

"You have eyes. See if you can compare the features of the coast to the bumps and hollows of the stick."

"It's not that easy."

"Hey—an animal can do it."

"A shapeshifter. You said you're still you inside."

"Mostly me." His smile sharpened to that predatory edge and he winked at me.

"Maybe you should land, shift back to human, and *you* pick out the next one to try."

He was already shaking his head. "I can't be guaranteed a high place to launch from. Besides, I've already shifted a lot today. With the energy demand of flying—including your weight—I'd do better not to keep shifting back and forth."

"I'm not over heavy." The constant mentions were getting to be a little much.

"No, but you're tall." He tugged on my braid, seeming as if he settled for that kind of touching when he really wanted more. He was being careful to observe my requests that he not touch me more than that, though, so I had to credit him with that much circumspection. "Which I love about you—that you're tall—but I have to consider my endurance. Plus I need to keep some energy in reserve as there's the possibility of sleeper attacks."

"Oh." I felt myself pale. "What should I do if so?"

"You're good with the bow. Do what you did today. I'll evade and try to get you open angles. Good shooting there, taking the heads off those undead birds," he added, the nonchalance of the compliment making it all that much more meant.

Still, I didn't like it all being up to me. "You can't fight as the gríobhth?"

He cocked his head. "Beak, claws, even my tail—sure I can. Having you on my back, though, I'd rather evade and strike at a distance. Unless you have a better strategy?"

I flushed, though he hadn't meant it sarcastically, I thought. I didn't know what had come over me, that I'd been handing out advice on strategy and battles when I'd only ever been a dinner-table bystander to such discussions. I could shoot an apple off a tree or the head off an undead bird—very similar challenges—but I didn't know how to fight. So, I shook my head, averting my gaze and hoping to restore myself as properly humble.

"Tonight, wherever we end up camping, and after I've rested," he continued thoughtfully, "we might practice some maneuvers. I'd rather you didn't accidentally put an arrow through my wing. Or on purpose because you're vexed with me."

"Oh, I never would!" I'd gasped it out, horrified he'd think it, before I realized he was teasing me.

"I don't know." He frowned dubiously. "You have quite the temper when vexed."

"Weren't you anxious to get going?" I asked with pointed dignity.

"Yes." He grinned, and I realized also that I'd forgotten to be afraid for a little while. "Once I shift, put the packs over my haunches, and you sit in front of them. Got it?"

I nodded, watching closely as the man became the gríobhth. His body didn't distort or stretch; he seemed to simply trade places with the other. The transition went too fast for my eye— or maybe my mind—to follow. As if the change happened outside a place my brain understood to be real. And though I'd seen the gríobhth before, the sight of him as the mythical beast astonished me all over again. Perhaps even more so for my being braced for it.

How could the man who laughed so easily and teased me relentlessly become this…truly magnificent creature? He cocked his head at me, spreading enormous wings, feathers clicking as he did. The black plume on his head ruffled in the breeze, and his eye, deep black and sparkling, fixed on me in a mischievously pleased way that was all Zyr.

I must never let him know how compelling I found him.

"Move your wings out of the way and crouch down so I can lift these packs on," I told him, finding it far easier to order the gríobhth about than the man.

He complied, and I hefted the two packs, joined by a strap, over the furred black haunches. Wide and muscular, with the fur sleek and gleaming, his back end looked like a lion's—complete with a long tail. But, unlike a cat's, his gríobhth tail was as thick as my upper arm at its base narrowing as it reached the tufted ebony tip. He whipped the tail in the air, snapping it with a crack, as if demonstrating for me. Oh, that would hurt connecting with flesh all right. I'd assiduously avoided whippings myself, but they were commonly employed as a punishment in Dasnaria, so I'd witnessed plenty.

"Yes, I see," I told him. "A most formidable weapon. How are the packs—does that feel good?"

He pranced and wriggled, the muscles under the sleek fur rippling, then ducked his head under a wing to snag the strap with his beak and tug it forward.

"I'll do it." I nudged his head away and he rubbed the upper curve of his beak against my hand. Reflexively, I petted him where the small blue-black feathers fringed over the enamel-hard ochre of his beak. And he purred.

I almost didn't place the rumbling sound at first, glancing at the sky for clouds to go with the low thunder. But it was him, a sleepy pleased expression in his eagle eyes.

"Just a big pussy cat," I murmured. "I knew it. Now quit messing around." I adjusted the packs. "How's that?"

He bobbed his beak in a nod, so I ducked under his belly as

he straightened to allow me to buckle the straps. Of course, I'd done the same with horses and saddles, never thinking about what I moved in proximity to. Not at all the same when you knew the animal was truly a man. I sent a fervent prayer of thanks that that part of his body bore more resemblance to a discreetly hidden cat's than a flamboyant horse's.

Still, my face must be bright red judging by the hot, tight feel of it, so I kept it carefully averted as I tightened the straps. Then I crouched by his front paw. Again, like a big, black lion's, but the curved talon-like claws didn't retract like the cats I'd known. They looked almost reptilian, like they belonged on a giant lizard, gleaming polished marble smooth, the lethal edge evident. I held out the first mapstick. "Can you hold it?"

With surprising dexterity, he took the stick from me, the claws flexible as fingers. So very strange. I repositioned it slightly, so the mapstick lay horizontal in the obsidian cage of the claws. "Better?"

He bobbed his beak, holding the paw upraised and steady on the other three legs. "All right," I told him. "Climbing on."

He crouched slightly, thoughtfully making the mounting much easier this time. I situated myself—and arranged my skirts so cloth lay between the bare skin of my upper thighs and the sleekly hot fur of his back. I didn't know how much sensation he had there, but no sense encouraging him with intimate contact.

Canting his head back, he gave me a look both inquiring and challenging—and somehow entirely *him*.

"Yes, yes. I'm ready." I clenched my teeth and steeled my stomach. And closed my eyes. "Go." A scream ripped out of me, despite my resolve, the force of it wrenching my eyes open. Better that way, even though the rushing air tore moisture from them. Having my eyes closed made the drop feel worse. Zyr's great wings worked furiously around me, a cloud of glittering blue and black, the massive muscles bunching under my clenched thighs. The feeling of falling lessened. We leveled out.

And we began to climb.

Without the stomach-hollowing sensation of falling all the way to the beach, I did better. Maybe I could handle flying. I just hated the taking off and landing parts. I steadied myself, taking a moment to look around this time. Sitting on Zyr's solid gríobhth body, shielded from the wind of our passage by his arched neck and with the billowing curtains of his wings on either side, I felt remarkably safe. I released my death grip on his black mane, realizing how the silky strands had cut into my fingers deep enough to turn my fingertips bloodless. Feeling the change somehow, Zyr craned his neck around to glance back at me and I smiled, giving him a thumbs up to show I was all right.

If a beak could grin, he did. Circling over the water, he came around to align with the beach. Circled back again. Then, his body gathered under me, wings pumping to take us higher, and realigning. Flying forward slowly along the line of the beach, he held the mapstick in his claws, looking from it to the ground below.

Feeling quite useless—a burden in a literal sense more than ever—I surveyed the landscape, accustoming myself to seeing it from this very new perspective. For the first time I glimpsed the land beyond the high cliffs of Annfwn. The dense shrubs and short coastal trees on the flat top of the cliff rose quickly into forested hills. Those mounded on each other until they grew into high peaks, white with snow, their tops lost in a fog of blizzarding storms. How odd that winter blew so near the bubble of tropical warmth surrounding us. Though I knew the cliff city shouldn't have changed, I leaned back for a clear view of it, unobscured by Zyr's dense wings. Who knew? Perhaps it shapeshifted, too.

But no—the cliff city remained verdant and calm as ever. Flowering vines and fruit-laden trees gleamed in contrast to the white walls. The jewel-bright sea lapped against the crystalline sands in warm serenity. Looking back to the winter-tossed peaks, I glimpsed a vast flock of birds rising from the forested foothills. It swirled, gathered, then arrowed in our direction. Rather, in the direction of the heart of Annfwn, where Tala teemed over the beach and crowded the cliff road in greater numbers than I might've imagined.

The Gathering.

Zyr must have found his bearings because he flew faster with steady strokes of his wings, a ground-eating pattern that soon left the cliff city behind. The peaks remained on my left, the open sea on my right, but the expansive beach below dwindled, in places giving way entirely to spurs and falls of rock. In others, sheer cliffs appeared to drop straight to the water, which flung itself against them in foamy churning, no longer the gentle surf as at the city. In the distance ahead of us, more and higher mountains disappeared into storming clouds.

Tala lived here, too, because I saw them flying, leaping, climbing and running—sometimes in human form, but most often as animals—and all heading the opposite direction from us, answering the summons of their king and queen.

Zyr had to have noted them, too, and I wondered if it rankled in him to be moving away from, rather than with his brethren. And weighted down with someone at best worthless, and at worst the enemy.

After a while, Zyr's steady pace eased off, and he began to circle. Taking the mapstick from his claws with his beak, he handed it back over his shoulder to me. Unprepared, I began rummaging in the pouch for another. He clacked his beak impatiently, so I gave him the first one at hand. He took it, aligned it to the coast, then gave it back with a toss of his head. Fine then.

If I'd been thinking, I'd have been sorting through them as we flew, teaching myself to see the coast in the stick's geometry. They still looked like wood sticks to me. Prettily carved, but with no more significance than that. Zyr clacked his beak at me.

"Just wait!" I raised my voice so he'd hear, though the gentle circle made it easier to be heard than it would have in the rushing wind of full-out flight, so it sounded like I was yelling. "I wasn't ready," I added at a more modulated volume.

He sighed dramatically, his chest expanding then deflating under my thighs. In retribution, I tugged sharply at his mane, rewarded by a chuckling purr. Straddling him bareback as I was, with his exertion-heated body pressing into my open crotch, the purr vibrated through me in a delicious—and startling—way. I sincerely hoped he couldn't sense how that affected me. I would have to fashion some sort of blanket to put between us to prevent further impropriety.

"Here." I thrust a mapstick at him, uncaring if it might be the right one, so long as it distracted him—and me. "Try this one."

Taking it from me, he kept it a bit longer, climbing higher for a better perspective, then giving it back with a rueful shake of his head that had his plume ruffling. The reprieve had given me time to study the rest of the ones we'd pulled out for the possible second leg. Truly, Zyr's discernment in getting the first one correct impressed me. I'd kept that in another pocket until I could figure a way to code it as the coastline at the cliff city and south. Zyr continued in lazy circles. The sun declined over the water, and he didn't seem to be working as hard, even gliding now and then as he caught some air current off the land. Playing a little as he waited, a peaceful feeling that allowed me to soothe my mind and even enjoy the scenery as I tried to match it to the wooden sticks.

We moved over a spectacular cliff with a high waterfall that thundered into the sea—and off to my right I caught sight of a substantial, very nearly round island. Something about it...

In a burst of inspiration, I sorted through the mapsticks and found the one I recalled. As if my vision had come suddenly into focus in a different way, it made sense to me. A perfectly round indentation on the right side of the flat stick matched the circular island. If I saw the wood as representing the water, that sharp point exactly opposite could be the cleft of the waterfall.

Excited, I handed it up to Zyr. He took it, purred approval, which sent that shiver of delight through me—I definitely needed to put a pad between us—and set out straight down the coastline again. The approval and sense of pride warmed me also. I'd always done reasonably well with the lessons my tutors set me, those subjects my father thought might be useful to me as a candidate for empress. Certainly I hadn't learned everything my brothers were taught, but far more than my sisters did.

I'd been betrothed to Kral in early adolescence, and my father had reasoned that as empress someday, I'd need to know more than the average wife. And if, as it had seemed likely back then, I ended up spending the rest of my days as sacrificial virgin to Hestar's reign and heirs, living celibate on the Hardie estates, then I might as well know enough of the family accounts to provide continuity. I, of all his children, was the least likely to ever leave.

A fine game hlyti had played on us all there. I'd not only left, I'd gone so irrevocably that I'd never see any of them again. No matter how this war turned out, I could never return to Dasnaria, unless I wanted to die. Unless I wanted to change sides. I shouldn't feel so traitorous contemplating it. I was a daughter of Dasnaria, after all, and though these people had all been reasonably kind to me, I owed them nothing.

Truly, whether I assisted the Tala and the folk of the Thirteen Kingdoms, or returned to Dasnaria, I'd be betraying the trust of the other side. I couldn't win.

Gloom settled over me along with the cooler air of twilight. It might be my imagination, but it seemed cooler here than back at the cliff city. My bare arms grew chilled, and my body ached with exhaustion—both physical from the long ride and lessons from Tays, and emotional from the grueling day. Perhaps the tiredness accounted for the downward turn in my mood, not actual depression.

Still, as much as I looked forward to getting off the gríobhth's wide back and letting my stiffened hips relax into a more usual position, I found myself dreading what the evening would bring. I understood perfectly well now why it wasn't practical for us to return to the cliff city for the night. We hadn't finished traveling the entire map of only two sticks and we'd spent the entire afternoon on it. If we went back, it would be well into full night and we'd have to start over again in the morning. I supposed we could go the other direction, but then we'd face the same problem.

And none of that took into consideration that they very obviously didn't want me there. Who could blame them? I was fortunate they hadn't decided on the simple expedient of executing me.

Camping made sense—and I'd certainly slept under the stars before, both in my youth and on this journey—but I really feared what Zyr might expect of me. We'd agreed to being friends. No sex, he'd said. But that had been before the odd incident on the beach, when he'd succumbed to his animal self. Plus we'd be alone, with no other females available to ease his appetites. Men had strong sexual urges, I understood. I'd overheard enough talk among my brothers and other men to know they craved release often. Because of that, I'd never begrudged Kral his dallying with other women. Not that it had been my place to begrudge him anything. Besides, he'd faced no consequences of conceiving a child that would have to be executed at birth.

It would be a great twist on my life's story if I ended up losing my so carefully guarded virginity in some remote place, weeping and protesting as the virile shapeshifter had his way with me. I didn't think Zyr would be cruel, but I also didn't think he understood our Dasnarian ways. He saw sex as a fun recreation, not what would determine my identity and fate for the rest of my life.

Even if I managed to hold him off, it would anger him and he could strand me forever in this increasingly remote wilderness. The Tala didn't want me in Annfwn. Jepp and Kral had to have been relieved to be rid of me without effort or shame on their part. My family already considered me dead.

Absolutely no one would come look for me. No wonder I felt so gloomy. Without realizing it, I'd stumbled to the precipice of my life. Tonight would change me irrevocably. I faced either death—fast or slow—or my final fall from grace as an honorable woman. That was the way of things, so I must prepare myself for either eventuality.

As if in sync with my thoughts, Zyr slowed, then handed the mapstick back to me. I'd had another possibility ready, but he refused it and began a gentle circling descent. I put the stick with the first, carefully apart from the untested ones, and braced myself for landing—and the night ahead that would set the course of the rest of my life, however long that ended up being.

Instead of landing immediately, however, he flew inland a

ways. Seeking higher ground to launch from in the morning, I realized. Oh, and fresh water it occurred to me, as he headed for a pretty rise above a small lake. I'd been so preoccupied choosing between death or loss of honor that I hadn't thought about basic needs. Now that I glimpsed the water, though, I became aware of my thirst. And my hunger, as I'd eaten nothing since breakfast. Neither had Zyr, and he'd been the one doing all the work.

He brought us in so gradually, that I barely felt a jolt as we landed on soft grass under a gracefully branching tree. Nothing like that morning's precipitous landing in the surf. Zyr crouched for me to dismount, then simply lay down with a heavy sigh, his head drooping. Poor exhausted thing. I scrambled down, suppressing my own groan at my body's protesting, locking my knees against the wobble in my legs. *You're not the one who's been flying nonstop for hours,* I scolded myself. Working quickly, I unfastened the packs, pulling them off him.

Unburdened, he stood again, shook himself. Then he hopped off the rise, flew up—and dove into the lake. I gasped as he went under, putting a hand over my startled heart when he popped to the surface again as a man. A naked man this time, by the look of his bare shoulders as he tossed back his long, water-slick hair and grinned at me.

"Moranu, that feels good!" he called to me. "Come join me."

I waved in lieu of answering, able to ignore that command, couched in such friendly terms, and set about unpacking our things. We'd need to build a fire for warmth as the evening continued to cool, and to heat our food. My thirst could wait and I hardly needed to bathe again, as I had just before we left and had barely exerted myself since then. This night might see the end of my virtue, if I couldn't resolve myself to fight him off and face final abandonment. No need, however, to hasten the event.

By the time he climbed the rise—once again as his post-shift, cleaned-up self in the blue shirt with his dry hair tied back—I'd made a tidy ring of stones around a dip in the ground for a firepit and had a decent pile of logs assembled, with kindling set.

"You've been busy," he said by way of greeting, smiling at me easily. "But you should've come swimming. Aren't you thirsty?"

"I had some water in the packs. I'll go refill the flasks in a moment. But we have a problem—there's nothing to start the fire with. I hope you know the trick of starting one with two sticks, because I don't and it will be a cold supper for us."

"I don't know such a trick but it sounds dreadfully tedious." He glanced at my little pile of kindling and it burst into flame. Astonished, I jumped back, and he grinned wider. "So much easier," he told me.

"You did that… with magic?"

He crouched by the little fire and added a log. "It's one of the simplest magics. Even those of us without much sorcery can usually do that much, make a little flame."

"It seems like a major magic to me—few elements are as powerful as fire."

He lifted his gaze from the fire, regarding me thoughtfully, his eyes very nearly the same color as the purpling sky behind him. "I never thought about it that way. I suppose I call it 'simple' because it comes so easily in childhood. And even our elderly who've declined enough to lose most of their magic can still call a flame. First to come and last to leave, we say of it."

"Useful, too," I commented, gathering my supplies to make our meal. "It won't take long before supper is ready."

"I'll cook. You go have a swim and relax."

I glanced up, ready to laugh at his joke, only to find him

perfectly serious. "I couldn't possibly allow you to wait on me," I ventured.

He cocked his head, as if he hadn't heard me quite right. "I wasn't offering to *wait* on you. We can share the chores. You did some; I'll do some."

"You did all the flying," I pointed out. "You have to be exhausted."

"Some." He shrugged cheerfully. "But cooking dinner doesn't require a lot of effort—especially since you already assembled everything—and when I shapeshift back, it restores my body quite a bit. Something *you* can't take advantage of, and I know riding that many hours has to be hard on you. Go swim. Work out the kinks. I won't peek." He winked at me with jaunty lasciviousness, taking the food from my hands.

"I can't just play while you're working," I tried a final time, truly torn between obeying the direct command and allowing a man to serve me.

"Truly?" He raised a brow as he added another log, distributing the flame better for cooking. "I thought you're some sort of Dasnarian Imperial Princess destined to be empress. Don't you sorts have armies of servants to do everything for you?"

He wasn't wrong there, though something in his tone made me feel less than admirable about that aspect of my upbringing. "Of course," I replied stiffly, "but female servants. A man never waits on a woman. It's unthinkable."

He gave me a slanted grin, indicating the pot in his hands. "But not undoable."

"Please let me do that," I held out my hands, wishing I had the temerity to wrench the pot from his grip.

"No." He held it away from me, making it clear he wouldn't relinquish it easily. "You have weird ideas about men and women."

"I do not. That's just the way of things."

"It's the way of things," he mimicked me—not well, in a voice much too high to be mine—eyes sparkling at my indignation. "I'm thinking Dasnarians have buried themselves under that saying. You people are the mossbackiest of mossbacks."

"We are not!" I protested, stung into indignation before I considered exactly what I argued for. "I don't think that's even a real word: mossbackiest."

"I've been speaking Common Tongue much longer than you have. Besides, it has to be real, because I used it." He added the rest of the water to the pan and set it in the ashes next the flame, then handed me the flask. "Go make yourself useful and refill this. You're losing swimming time with this silly argument."

Affronted—and worn down by all the commands I found it so difficult to disobey—I took the flask and stood. I'd get a drink, refill, and be back directly.

"Take your bow," he directed me. "Animals come to water in the evening like this. Yell if anything happens, but be ready to hold something off, just in case." His face had an uncharacteristically serious cast, and I knew he thought of the battle with the sleeper spies that morning.

"I won't swim then," I told him, relieved to have that excuse.

"It's an enclosed body of water," he pointed out. "One I chose pretty much at random. I seriously doubt a sleeper spy is lurking in it. Besides, I shifted into a fish and checked it pretty thoroughly. If an attack comes, it'll be from land or air. Get cleaned up, Karyn," he said, with a certain gentleness. "You'll feel better for it."

I realized his intent then. He wanted me clean for him. No jasmine-scented baths and elaborate cosmetics for my loss of virginity then. No fasting to make me clean inside as well as out. Just lake water and inevitability. Because I would give in. A stronger woman than I might choose death over dishonor, but I'd already given up so much in order to live.

I would choose life.

~ 11 ~

I RESTRUNG MY bow as I walked down the little hill, the act so practiced it required no thought, leaving my mind free to assimilate what would happen between Zyr and me. What I knew of the actual act.

Because I'd been betrothed to Kral so young—and the guarantee of my celibacy clearly spelled out from the initial proposal to my father—I hadn't had the education in pleasing a man that my sisters received. My mother, showing rare initiative and her innate compassion, decided I'd be happier not knowing of those intimacies, to spare me wanting what I might never have. Should Hestar—Sól forbid—have passed away and his sons with him, allowing Kral to ascend to the Imperial Throne, she reasoned I'd have time to be taught what I needed to know. Likewise, if Hestar had lifted his ban on Kral siring children, my admission to my husband's bed would not have occurred without due warning. And extensive preparation.

In retrospect, my father likely never knew of my mother's deliberate omission in this part of her daughter's training to be a woman. We may not have had as cloistered a seraglio as some, but women still took care of female concerns, just as men took care of the male ones. It seemed my father must have known about Kral's ambitions to supplant Hestar. Kral had confessed them to me, out of an odd integrity that had encouraged my affection for him, young as I was. He'd wanted me to know his hopes. More likely he told me to test my loyalty to him. If I'd blabbed his secret, he could've had me killed easily enough.

At the time, however, I'd been proud that he'd trusted me. Proud that *I* had been selected, of all the potential brides, to be his first wife. And thrilled to be part of such a potent political secret, admitted to such a rarified society. When Kral asked how I'd feel about being empress—and if I thought I could stand the trials and keep his secrets—I'd answered that I'd be honored to reign at his side.

I'd been such a naïve girl, full of vanity and ambition. Despite having the conditions of my marriage-in-name-only explained to me, I'd nurtured girlish fantasies that it wouldn't stay that way. Imperial Prince Kral—so handsome, ambitious, general of the Dasnarian armies, so dashingly older than I, and brother of the emperor!—had dazzled me. My father had been so proud and pleased. I couldn't have climbed any higher in Dasnarian society than that.

And now I'd fallen out of existence entirely, about to lose my safeguarded virginity at last, as a wild shapeshifter's rekjabrel. Punishment for that girlish hubris, perhaps.

Or for being a traitor. I'd betrayed my emperor by agreeing to keep Kral's secrets. Not even eighteen and I'd established myself a person of no honor. No wonder no one could trust me. I had no loyalty to anything. How loathsome a creature I was.

The urge to wash myself clean at least on the outside became unbearable.

Carefully studying the landscape for movement first, I laid my bow and quiver on a dry rock at water's edge, then filled the flask and drank from it. I'd been thirstier than I thought, drinking it all down with gratitude before refilling it again and setting it beside my bow. Glancing up the hill, I spotted our campfire easily—the evening had grown quite dark—and Zyr silhouetted beside it, his back to me as promised. Perhaps his kind didn't require their women to undress completely. Though Sey had been naked that morning. Still, I might be able to convince him to take his pleasure of me by simply lifting my skirts. I might not know all the sensual tricks, but I understood enough of the mechanics to know he could take me that way.

Regardless, I had no plans of stripping completely now—perhaps ever, if I could avoid it. I took off my overdress, and the underpart, along with a couple of the petticoats, leaving on just two layers of shifts. Wading into the water, I found it delightfully cool and refreshing, the mud squishing between my bare toes. Zyr had been right to recommend this, as self-serving as his motives might have been. I struck out swimming, my body lengthening and loosening with the different exercise.

I stopped to tread water and unbind my long braid. Sea water makes for stiff hair and I'd take advantage of this opportunity to rinse it with fresh. Tying the ribbon from my braid around my wrist, I let my hair float free, combing it loose with my fingers. I had no soaps, no scented oils, but I used my undershifts to scrub at my skin. Then I swam a bit more, letting the cool water glide over my skin, rinsing me clean.

Swimming at night wasn't something I'd ever done. Even rambunctious country girls came inside before dark, dressing for dinner, and keeping to the safety of the seraglio. Being suspended in the lake, the darkness of evening blurring the difference between air and water, I felt my own edges soften.

Maybe it didn't matter who I'd been. I'd chosen life, which meant I could become anyone now.

I struck back for shore, orienting myself by the firelight. Back on dry land, I wrung out the shifts as best I could, then pulled on the layers of dress over them. The underthings clung clammily to my skin, but nothing to be done for it. If Zyr required me to strip, I'd lay them out to dry by the fire. A compensation of sorts. The night was warm, so I dried my hair more carefully, wringing out all the dampness, fluffing and finger-combing it, encouraging it to be dry enough to braid again.

"You all right?" Zyr called from above.

"Yes!" I shouted back, chagrined that he'd had to summon me. "Be right there."

Hurrying, I let my hair fall as it would and I climbed up the hill to the fire.

"Feel good?" Zyr inquired, then stared at me, an arrested expression on his face.

"What—do I have mud on me?" I swiped a hand over my face and examined it in the firelight for evidence of smudging.

"No." He breathed a laugh and stood, approaching me slowly, like he thought I might startle and run. I made myself stay still, wanting to flee, knowing that he could easily catch me and I had nowhere to go.

Picking up a long lock of my hair where it streamed damp over my bosom—carefully, so his fingers didn't brush me—he rubbed it between thumb and forefinger. "I've never seen you with your hair loose," he mused, eyes wandering over my face. "You look different. Wilder. Like a Tala woman but painted in gold."

Why that made me flush, I didn't know. Something about the way he looked at me... I shifted, uncomfortable, and stepped out of his reach despite my resolve to endure his attentions. Perhaps I'd do better with it once I ate. "I'm famished," I told him, making my movement seem as if I intended to check the food. "Shall I finish the cooking?"

"There's nothing to finish." He waited, head tilted a little as if listening to something beyond my ken. "It's done," he clarified, likely because I seemed confused.

Oh. What next? "I'll dish it up then."

"No, no. Allow me. If I'm going to serve, I might as well complete the job." He smiled, sly and close-lipped, clearly enjoying my discomfiture.

Gathering my poise around me, I sank to the grass and accepted the bowl full of meat stew. The dried meat had softened nicely and Zyr had put some sort of crunchy root in it that I didn't recognize, but that leant a fresh, bright taste. I was hungrier than I'd thought, the food hitting my empty belly and my body responding with greed. I tried to observe good manners, but in my haste I smeared some of the rich gravy on my upper lip. Casting about for the napkins we didn't have, I instead surreptitiously lifted the hem, ducking my face to dab at my mouth.

I'd thought Zyr was occupied with consuming his own meal—much delayed by my dallying—but when I peeked at him, I found him watching me with that wicked amusement in his eyes. "Taste good?" he asked, somewhat pointedly.

"It's excellent. Thank you." I held my head high with dignity, though I kept my gaze demurely lowered.

He didn't reply immediately. The only sounds were the crackle of the fire and the sound of him scraping the bowl clean. "There's more," he said.

I realized I'd emptied my bowl. Why hadn't I eaten more slowly? Though delaying wouldn't change much. "You have more. I can have whatever you don't finish."

With a gruff sound of annoyance, he dumped more stew into my bowl, then into his own. "Why do you do that?" he asked conversationally, though still with the edge of irritation in his voice.

I glanced up from the bowl cautiously, not sure what I'd done wrong. "Why do I do what?" *Lord Zyr*, I added mentally. I still felt… impudent, even asking as deferentially as I could.

"That. Exactly that." He pointed his eating knife at me. "*Defer*," he added, loading the word with scorn.

I blinked at him, then realized I was staring in confusion and consternation, so I looked down again. My stomach growled, demanding more food, so I took a bite and chewed slowly, hoping that would allow me some time to think of a reply.

"See? You're still hungry. I can hear your stomach growling and it's obvious you wanted more. So why did you say, 'Oh, Zyr, you go ahead and eat it all. I'll just sit here and be meek and hungry?'" He used that falsetto voice that he liked to mock me with.

My head snapped up of its own accord. "I did not say that and I do *not* sound like that."

He grinned at me, clearly delighted to have tweaked my nose. He sprawled on the grass like a big cat soaking up the warmth of the flames, leaning on one elbow and taking up the entire other side of the campfire. "Gotcha," he purred.

I nearly flung my bowl at him. But it would be a waste of the excellent stew, and I *was* still hungry, curse the man. So, I ate, biting down on the meat and chewing savagely.

"It's not good for you to keep all that anger bottled up," Zyr observed. "Bad for your health."

"I am not angry," I replied evenly, even sweetly, to prove I could.

He barked out a laugh. "Yes, you are, gréine. You have lots of anger that you like to pretend away."

"I thought I was the saddest person you ever met," I reminded him, setting down my empty bowl.

"That too. They probably go hand in hand." He was watching me, his intent gaze hotter than the fire.

I shifted restlessly, wishing he would just finish eating and move on to sating his other appetites. Did prey feel this way, longing for the stalking to be over with already, even if it meant they'd be devoured in the end?

"Sometimes I really wish for my cousin's ability to read thoughts," he observed in a wry tone.

"Ursula?" I asked, surprised enough to forget her title, then jolting a little when he burst out laughing.

"Moranu spare us, no!" He laughed more, then caught his breath. "That's all we'd need—her high majestyness able to read our minds on top of ruling everything in sight. No, I meant Queen Andromeda. She's also my cousin, as she is Ursula's sister. Also Ami. All three are Salena's daughters. Salena was my aunt," he added, with a slight frown, though I didn't know what for.

I kept quiet, heartily grateful that he couldn't read my thoughts.

"So, you'll have to tell. What makes you sad and angry?" he asked, setting his bowl aside, too.

"I never said I was."

"Karyn." He sounded disappointed in me, and when I peeked through my lashes at him, he had a determined look on his face.

"My life hasn't gone according to plan," I bit out. "Isn't that enough?"

"It's a start. What was your plan that things didn't go according to?"

He had such a twisty way of phrasing things sometimes. "It's a long story."

"We have time." He waved a languid hand at the campfire.

"I should clean up the dishes."

"Leave it," he ordered, sounding annoyed again. "Quit fabricating chores to avoid dealing with me."

I glared at him in rising and impotent fury, frustrated enough to stare him down. "Can we just get this over with?" I demanded.

He didn't move, instead blinking long and slow, realigning his thoughts. The way cats do when foiled in an ambush. I almost expected him to nonchalantly lick a paw. So odd how I could see the animal forms in him, the same way I could see his man self when he was the gríobhth or the panther.

"What, exactly, are we talking about?" he finally asked.

"Sex!" I huffed at him.

He cocked his head in that way of his, interest sparking, but also as if sifting through an unfamiliar scent in the air. "I thought we agreed to be friends only. No sex."

"But here we are." I gestured to the night hemming us in. "Stop toying with me. I'm not an idiot, Zyr."

"Of course you aren't, but you *are* a strange and confusing woman. What happened to clinging to your rules and virginity?" He still sneered the word, as if it tasted foul.

"I may be a virgin but I know what happens when men and women are alone together," I said, very reasonably, considering.

He looked around our little camp. "Swimming, cooking stew, and eating?"

"Oh, for Sól's sake," I snapped, jerking myself to my feet, unable to take the suspense any longer. I pulled my dress off over my head, the upper layer of my hair snapping and crackling from drying by the fire, the underneath snagging in still-damp snarls. It would be completely unmanageable, but that was the least of what I'd have to face in the morning. I struggled with the next layers, finally tossing them aside, too. The final two shifts were horribly damp and stuck to my skin. I tugged at them and found them all twisted up. Yanking harder, something ripped and a sob of frustration broke out of me.

Zyr was there—startling me, he'd moved so silently—hands gripping my shoulders, sternly enough to quell my struggles. "Karyn." He said my name in that same tone, maybe not annoyed so much as voicing his determination not to be annoyed. "I think I need for you to explain exactly what's going on."

I couldn't meet his gaze, but so close like this, very nearly embracing, we stood almost the same height. So I looked at his nose. Not a handsome nose, by any stretch, too big, arched like a beak. Like his cousin Ursula, I realized. I shouldn't find him so beautiful when he had such an unlovely nose. "Sex," I got out.

"So you said before, but I'm still confused by this change. Why are you suddenly eager to get naked with me?"

I felt like an idiot after all and on top of everything. If only I'd waited patiently for him to make the first move, the way a proper woman should. Perhaps I'd offended him by appearing eager.

"Karyn," he said, squeezing my shoulders a little, prodding me to reply.

"I thought if I undressed, you'd be aroused enough to stop your games and take me already. I can't—" To my horror, I sobbed again, a wrenching sound of grief this time. "I can't—" I tried again and couldn't breathe. Tears clogged my throat and filled my eyes. I choked them back, mortified to be weeping, and started coughing on the phlegm.

"None of that now. Calm down." Zyr sounded surprisingly kind. He wrapped his arms around me and pulled me against him. Good. At least this would be over with. I let him hold me, but he didn't do anything else, just held me, patting, then stroking my back when the coughing subsided, sliding his fingers through my hair, and murmuring something in Tala, something low and rumbly that reminded me of his purr in gríobhth form. He swayed a little, too, his unintelligible words almost musical. After a while, my tears stopped trying so hard to escape. He felt warm and strong, and I realized I'd kind of melted into him.

When had someone last held me like this? My mother, when I was a girl. I couldn't remember a time since. I'd grown up, too big for such coddling. And Kral, of course, had never touched me beyond a kiss on the hand, or at most putting my arm through his—and even then he maintained a formal distance, making it clear that we enjoyed no intimacy of any kind. Only wise, in Emperor Hestar's dangerous court.

Never by a man. It felt … remarkable. The long, lean lines of his body somehow fit into mine like a missing puzzle piece. As if I belonged there. The thought made the too-easy tears rise again. I didn't belong anywhere and I needed to get that through my thick head.

"Your clothes are wet," Zyr murmured.

"Sorry," I mumbled, trying to pull away. He let me, but only far enough so that he took my shoulders again, keeping me there.

"Don't be sorry. Why are you wearing wet clothes under dry ones? Let's start there."

He had a point that it was a simpler question to answer. "Because I swam in them, of course."

"You swam… in your clothes?"

"Yes, but they hadn't dried yet when you summoned me, so I put my dry clothes back on top."

"When I summoned…" He trailed off, frowning. Then let go of me to scrub hands over his forehead as if he had a headache. "I think we have a communication problem."

"It's true I'm not yet fluent in Common Tongue."

He laughed, but in exasperation, blue eyes full of some emotion I couldn't interpret. Remembering, I averted my gaze, and he growled, very softly. "For a start, stop doing that—averting your gaze and being all submissive."

"I'm sorry, I—"

"Don't apologize," he snapped.

I glared at him, angry enough to at least obey him by looking him in the eye. "Perhaps you'd prefer to issue me a list of rules that I can memorize so I won't offend you."

"Better." He did look relieved, as if some tension had been removed. "Let's sit, so I can explain something to you. And so your clothes and hair can dry. Sit with your back to the fire."

I obediently sat, staying still while he arranged my shifts around me, then spread out my hair, to maximize exposure to the heat. That meant I stared off into the night, which frankly came as a relief.

"Your hair is so soft," he remarked, combing his fingers through it. "Like silk. And so pretty. It catches all the different colors of the firelight, red-gold here, almost white there. I had no idea that it's so curly, the way you have it in a braid all the time."

I relaxed a little, his touch—and flattery—warming me. "That's why I braid it," I offered, "because the curls and waves make it unmanageable."

"There. That wasn't so hard, was it?" He came to sit in front of me, cross-legged on the grass in easy flexibility. "Offering me a bit of personal information," he clarified when I frowned at him.

When I didn't say anything—what was I supposed to say to that?—he sighed and took both of my hands in his. "I don't mean to give you rules," he said. "In fact, I'm finally figuring out something about you. If I say anything that sounds remotely like an order, you think you have to obey me. Is that right?"

This felt like a trick, but I played along. "Of course."

"Of course," he echoed with a pained look. "And why?"

"Because that's the way of things," I replied, puzzled.

"I'm really getting so I hate that phrase. No, don't apologize. Eh—it's really hard for me not to phrase things as orders. I'm not your superior, not a *lieutenant* of the Hawks." He sneered that and I smiled a little. "I'm not royalty," he continued. "Why is it the way of things that you think you have to obey me?"

"Because you're a man and I'm a woman," I answered slowly, still looking for the trick.

He squeezed my hands, dipping his chin in a sharp nod. "Aha! We're getting somewhere, even if it *is* a really stupid, ridiculous place."

~ 12 ~

I TRIED TO pull my hands away, but he hung on. "I'm not criticizing you," he said. "I'm saying it's ridiculous and stupid that you think—that is, that your culture makes you think … Eh! I'm not saying this well." He paused for a deep breath. "You don't have to obey me, Karyn. We're partners in this mission. I'll try not to phrase things as orders—which is an unfortunate habit of mine, apparently—and you'll try not to take what I say as a command that must be obeyed, no matter how I phrase it."

"Is that an order?" I replied dryly.

He laughed and I found myself smiling back. He had a wonderful laugh, uninhibited and musical—when he wasn't being exasperated with me. "Well played, gréine. Well played. See? I think you have it in you. When you forget to be all submissive— when I make you mad enough to fight back—you do just fine."

I hitched a little at that. I didn't think of myself as a submissive person, but Zyr did bring out an unusual defiance in me, which he said he wanted. "So, no averting my eyes, deferring, being submissive—and you want me to fight with you."

"It sounds odd summarized that way, but yes." His thumbs rubbed over the backs of my hands and he studied them. "It's also strange to try to explain something that's second nature to me—"

"Exactly," I inserted in a wry tone, and he smiled briefly,

meeting my gaze and sobering again. The firelight played on his face and his remarkable eyes caught the dancing flames, making them seem to glitter.

"The thing is, Karyn," he said slowly, "the thing to understand about us Tala is that our animal forms … inform our personalities in certain ways."

Just as Andi had tried to explain, but I kept silent, thinking he might not like it that I'd discussed his nature with his queen.

"Most of my forms are predators," he continued. "Not that I can't take other kinds, but those are the ones that fit me best. Does that make sense?"

I nodded, my throat dry for no good reason. Something about the intensity of his gaze made me aware that the firelight probably also silhouetted my body, the light cotton shifts drying and no longer clammily sticking to my skin. My nipples tightened with awareness and I only hoped he couldn't see.

"For a predator…" he trailed off, searching for words. "When you act submissive, it… it excites that part of me."

My heart picked up pace, the cotton of the shifts scraping my sensitive nipples. He spoke so simply of that excitement that it roused something in me, too. "I sometimes feel like prey around you," I confessed, my voice coming out throaty. "When you look at me a certain way."

His gaze sharpened, that feral hunger in it. "Like this?"

"Yes." I could only whisper that, suddenly certain that I played with fire.

"Karyn…" This time he said my name on a groan of need, that blazing gaze roaming over me, making me suddenly and absolutely certain he could see—perhaps sense—my arousal. "This is what I mean," he said, setting his jaw, gaze resolutely meeting mine. "If you want me to respect your wishes, then you must be firm with me. No acting soft and submissive, because it only whets my hunger for you—do you understand?"

I did, but only just then. "You mean, you don't plan to take your pleasure of me tonight?"

At least his bewilderment acted to diffuse the tension building between us. "This is what you kept anticipating—that I'd, what, rape you?"

Ah, not just surprise but growing anger. "We're alone out here," I explained. "And I know men have needs. There's no one else, so…"

Abruptly he dropped my hands, on his feet before I saw him move. He paced a tight circle, and I could almost see a long tail, lashing with a whiplike crack. "So." He rounded on me, fury crackling in the air. "So this is what you think of me. Or is it how you view all Tala? I'm just some animal who can't control himself. That the moment we're alone, I'll just force myself upon you, willing or not."

I decided not to point out that his whole "I'm a predator and you act like prey" talk didn't exactly contradict that impression. "I don't know, do I?" I said through gritted teeth as I stood again, watching him warily. "You Tala have no rules, no laws, no etiquette at all that I can see. How am I supposed to know what you think is allowable?"

"We don't rape people!" he nearly shouted at me.

"No, you just warn them not to 'excite' you too much!" I yelled back.

He stopped. Stared. Then grinned. "Moranu, how I love it when you yell at me," he said, almost reflectively. "What is wrong with me?"

"I'll make a list," I shot back, which only made his grin widen.

Then he sobered, coming toward me, slowly. "You should sit," he told me, very gently.

"Why?" I sounded suspicious but his quicksilver changes of mood confounded me.

"Karyn, gréine, with the fire behind you, I can see every detail of your gorgeous figure. I would never force you—I promised to abide by your rules, and I will—but it's no secret that I want you, rather dreadfully. I'm not above trying to seduce you, you know," he almost purred it, so close to me that it would take only a breath for us to touch. "And now that I know you're inclined to obey commands…" His tongue darted out, wetting his lip, and I watched in helpless fascination.

"That's what a Dasnarian man would do," I whispered. "He wouldn't have to force me. Just order me to submit."

"What?" Shock had Zyr gasping the word.

"It's the way of—"

"Don't say it." Zyr blinked, revulsion crossing his face, and he stepped back. His turn to avert his gaze. "Excellent way to douse my arousal. Well done. Ouch."

"I'm sorry, I—"

"*Don't apologize*," he snarled, then jerked his gaze away and stared into the night. "And for the love of Moranu, would you please *sit down*?"

Hastily, I sat. For good measure, and since my shifts had thoroughly dried, I grabbed my overdress and tugged that on, too. Zyr glanced over and smiled without amusement.

"Wise," he observed. Then sat, heavily for his lithe grace, and put his chin in his hands, propping his elbows on his knees. "So, tell me about this person you plan to marry."

"Who?" I asked, confused by the sudden change of topic.

"This mystery *man*." The way Zyr said it made that sound questionable. "The one you're saving your virginity for."

"Oh." I busied myself lacing up my dress over my bosom, reasoning that the more barriers between us, the better. But when I looked up, Zyr yanked his gaze away, staring over my shoulder. Probably I should try not to draw his attention to such places. "I don't know who it is. I have to find him."

"You sound like Dafne," Zyr observed. When I raised my brows, he waved a hand. "I tried to seduce her, too, you know. Another professional virgin," he added, with a note of disgust.

I hadn't known that, of course, but I didn't say so. I'd seen Queen Dafne Nakoa KauPo when we stopped at Nahanau. She seemed very happily married to the king—and anything but virginal, judging by the way they touched each other. "I don't think she is anymore," I said judiciously.

And he laughed, ruefully. "No. She found him. She felt she was waiting for someone special—her whole life, she'd waited—and boom! Off she goes to Nahanau and there he is. It wasn't me."

"Did you love her?" I ventured.

"Don't be silly. Most of us don't have to love people to want to take them to bed."

Ah. Point taken.

"Did you love Kral?" Zyr asked suddenly, straightening. "Or, do you?"

"No!" I burst out, then realized how it sounded. "I mean, I admired him. I was very young when we wed and I was so flattered…" I shook my head. "My family and the emperor arranged the marriage for us. No one meant for it to be about love."

"So that's what you're holding out for in your second marriage."

I drew up my knees under my gown and wrapped my arms around them. "My second marriage—that sounds so bad. I just wanted… a *real* marriage."

"With sex," Zyr clarified, eyes glinting. "You're not looking for love, but sex."

I didn't take his bait. "Children. No sex means no children. Didn't you say Zynda wants to take Final Form in order to have babies?"

"Not her. The rest of the Tala. Obviously if she's a dragon, she won't be having little Tala babies. And the Tala are obsessed with our declining fecundity. We're dying off as a race—I know you were listening when Queen Andromeda mentioned it—and having a dragon in Annfwn might make all the difference between babies being born dead or too twisted to live, and surviving to become healthy adults."

"Oh," I breathed and Zyr waved that off as negligible, eyes fixed on me.

"But what about you? Sounds like Dasnaria isn't hurting for population. Why did you risk everything just to have babies? Why not have Kral's babies, if you wanted them so badly? I don't understand this marriage of yours at all."

"It's not easy to explain," I temporized. "And it's getting late."

"Are you sleepy?" He gave me a canny look. "Because I'm a long way from being able to sleep, if you understand me."

I did. My body still sang with the need he'd roused in me, without even a kiss or caress. "I'm not sleepy," I said. When he smiled in commiseration, I felt I'd confessed too much, so I hurried on. "Kral is younger than Emperor Hestar, but not by much—and he was born to their father's first wife, which in some interpretations gives Kral the greater right to the throne."

Zyr made a face, but nodded at me to continue.

"But their father chose Emperor Hestar as his heir, and until His Imperial Majesty married and sired sons, Kral was *his* heir."

"I think I follow that."

"Emperor Hestar arranged a marriage for Kral, but on the

condition that the marriage remain celibate. His Imperial Majesty didn't want to run the risk that Kral might sire sons with a greater claim to the throne than his own sons."

"Then why arrange a marriage for his brother at all?"

"It was the best way to secure an alliance with my family. Very rich lands with orchards."

Zyr considered me with that slow feline blink. "Your family exchanged your life for *food?*"

"It was a good alliance," I replied defensively. "I was proud to do it. My marriage to Kral made me the fourth highest ranked woman in Dasnaria. I had a chance at being Empress, after all."

"Hmm. Did those things make you happy?"

No. No, they hadn't. As the years rolled on and I stayed on my family estates, watching my siblings wed and have children, my own life seemed to grow correspondingly emptier. "I wasn't unhappy," I said.

"But you had to remain a virgin. No sex, with men, ever."

I felt myself blushing. "Those were the terms, yes. Any pregnancy would've meant my death and Kral's too."

"What about women? You could've enjoyed sex with them."

My face burned. "That would've been frowned upon. My family had no wish to anger the Imperial Palace. They kept close watch on me—and they took care of me. I lived on my family estates and had a good life. Luxurious, even. Better than most."

"But you gave it up," Zyr pointed out.

"Arguably the stupidest decision I ever made," I agreed. A bizarre impulse of the moment. As if I'd become someone else entirely.

"How did that happen?" Zyr asked.

"Don't you know?" When he shook his head, I considered that. I supposed that made sense. Jepp would've reported the details to her queen, but she wouldn't have spread the information like gossip to anyone else. She said all sorts of things with astonishing frankness, but she wouldn't want me to be shamed. Or Kral, for that matter. "Jepp had been Kral's lover for some time when she found out about me and—"

"Wait." Zyr held up a hand. "Why didn't Kral have to be celibate, too?"

I frowned. "He's a man."

"Right—so he could be siring babies all over the place."

"Well, yes, but they wouldn't be legitimate heirs and besides, he was always very careful as he had no wish to see a child of his put to death."

"How noble of him," Zyr murmured, sounding as if he thought anything but.

"It's not reasonable to expect a man to be celibate," I explained, unfolding my arms and sitting up cross-legged, a mirror of him. "You understand this. Men have needs. That's the—"

"—way of things," he finished with me. "I begin to understand how you think."

I wasn't sure if that was a good thing. "Jepp thinks much like you do. She was upset to discover that Kral had a wife—she thought my life sounded terrible, just like you do—and she made a bet with Kral that if he offered me an annulment, I'd take it. So he summoned me to the Imperial Palace."

I'd been so excited, in such a flurry to pack my best *klúts* and jewelry, to travel in such haste to answer my husband's summons. I hadn't known what to think, but I'd hoped... Oh, how I'd hoped for *something*.

"There it is," Zyr said quietly. "The sadness."

I lifted a shoulder and let it fall. "I was foolish. I don't know what I thought he'd summoned me for. Maybe I thought I'd get to be his wife in truth, have babies."

"Because you wanted him that badly?"

"He's a handsome man, sure, though he never made me feel like—" I hastily corrected what I'd been about to say, *like I felt when you said I excited you.* "—like I wanted him *badly*. No, I don't know if I can explain what I wanted." I found I'd leaned forward, earnestly, as if trying to reach Zyr.

"Try," he urged, gaze fastened on me, giving me his full attention. A heady experience, to be listened to this way.

"I wanted… I wanted my life to start. I mean I was alive in body, but the rest of me…"

"You weren't really living," he said. "You were forever waiting."

"Yes." I sat back, savoring that realization, small as it was. "Forever waiting. In that moment, in the emperor's court, when His Imperial Majesty asked if I wanted the annulment, even though I'd been certain I'd say no—I glimpsed a possibility. Kral obviously loved Jepp. The way he looked at her… he never once looked at me that way. I'd never seen him like that, so part of me knew he wouldn't stay without her. And Jepp is not a woman who'd thrive in Dasnaria."

Zyr laughed with me and I shook my head. "So I blurted it out, said I wanted the marriage dissolved, hoping that I could have this *life* that… I don't know." Would be something more than being some frozen image of a person.

"What happened then?"

"Oh." I laughed, hearing the bitter edge in it. "His Imperial Majesty granted the annulment, then sentenced me to burn to death for my impudence."

Zyr straightened, lips parting over teeth gone sharp. The hairs rose on my neck, even though I knew his anger was on my behalf. "Excuse me?" he asked softly.

"The emperor felt he needed to set an example. Imagine how many wives would make similar requests, after all."

"Imagine," Zyr echoed, not sounding any less dangerous.

"It didn't happen," I told him firmly. "So put your fangs back in the in-between place and settle down."

He looked bemused, rubbing a hand over his mouth. "What did happen?"

"Jepp rescued me." I still couldn't believe it. "Then she was captured, but Kral intervened and smuggled me out of the Imperial Palace. He went back for her and we escaped." It hadn't been quite that simple, but the rest of the adventures weren't all that relevant. "I owe Jepp a great debt," I added. "My life twice over, and beyond. She taught me Common Tongue and how to use a knife. She..." I faltered. "She understood about me wanting a life—she called it freedom, though I never felt not free—before I knew to want it."

"And here you are, still waiting for your life to start," Zyr said.

I opened my mouth to retort, but the words died on their way up my throat, forcing me to swallow them. Zyr watched me with knowing eyes. "I wouldn't have put it that way," I said, finally.

"Am I wrong?"

No. No, he wasn't at all wrong, and I felt it in the fierce, sudden ache of uncertainty. "I have no idea what I'm doing, Zyr," I told him, saying it very quietly, as if someone might overhear and call me to task for it. "For a while everything was so crazy—running for our lives, escaping on the *Hákyrling*, fighting off the High Priestess when she came after us and Her Majesty High Queen Ursula nearly dying... And everything is so beautiful! I loved sailing around the islands, seeing Nahanau, coming to Annfwn. It was easy to forget, for a while, that I needed to be thinking of next steps."

"And now you're on this mission with me."

"Yes." I nodded, picked at the skirt spread across my knees, then made myself look at him, in case I looked too gaze-averted. "I'm glad to do this. I'm glad to be useful. I know you think I'm silly, getting all hysterical this morning—" Had it really been only this morning? "—about not having a place with the Hawks or being able to feed myself, but that's the kind of life I come from. Somebody has *always* taken care of me. Dasnarian women don't just go off in the world and be … free." I lost my argument at the end, because I suddenly remembered Inga and Helva's stories about Kral's older sister, Jenna.

The story had shocked me at the time, when Inga and Helva told me about their sister, when I visited the seraglio at the Imperial Palace. Even though I'd only been there a short time, the two sisters had cornered me, forcing me to politely listen to the tale.

They'd already told Jepp, they said, and insisted that I hear it, too. I didn't understand why at the time. Or rather, I'd thought they sought to manipulate me into thinking Kral a bad man—or give me a cautionary tale on what happened to women who left their marriages. By the end, I'd been terribly confused about their true agenda. As the oldest sister, Jenna had married first, apparently to everyone's joy at an excellent alliance with Arynherk, but the husband had beaten her and worse. When she left on her wedding journey, their baby brother Harlan—the same man now Her Majesty High Queen Ursula's consort—went along and helped her to escape.

Unthinkable. Even more shocking, they'd succeeded. I'd been a toddler when it happened, and I remember hearing whispers about the lost princess as I was growing up. Nobody ever called her by name and somehow in my child's head I'd conflated that tale with other colorful and romantic Dasnarian tragedies of runaway lovers and lost children.

Kral had tried to bring her back, but failed. Also unthinkable, knowing him as I did. And he'd never told me, during those years of our marriage. Not that we'd ever confided secrets to each other, beyond his designs on the throne. Hearing the truth, though, several bits of information fell into place. Kral had always carried some guilt in him, a deep remorse and anger that spurred him to travel. Oh, he'd always claimed that he sought treasure to finance his bid to be emperor, but once I heard the story…

It all made me wonder. I especially wondered what had happened to Jenna. Kral did, too—and he'd asked Harlan. But Harlan's vows kept him from saying. Jepp had told me that Harlan implied Dafne might be of help, but that was the last I'd heard of it.

I'd been certain Jenna had perished or been enslaved, as happened to women out in the world on their own, but Jepp saw things differently. For all her cynicism, Jepp possessed a huge streak of idealism. So I'd gone along with the idea that we could search for the lost princess.

Now I wondered if Inga and Helva had other reasons for telling me the tale.

"But you are free." Zyr interrupted my thoughts, cocking his head. "Look at you. A trailblazer. That means you're setting an example. Other Dasnarian women will tell tales of you. You'll be their hero."

"I don't think I make a very good hero." The concept appalled me, in truth. So much pressure. I'd just wanted to have a normal life. Though I was rapidly realizing I had no idea what that looked like.

"Guess you'll have to work on that," Zyr informed me cheerfully. "Fortunately, you're with me and I'm dazzlingly heroic already. I can give you tips."

"Oh, hooray," I replied dryly, but he'd made me smile.

"First tip?" He grinned at me. "Heroes don't follow other people's rules. They make up their own. You already defied an emperor and escaped execution. What else can they do to you?"

I gazed at him, sure his logic was flawed.

"Something to think about, anyway," he said, "when you're ready to."

"Why are you being so nice to me now?"

"Wasn't I nice before?" He frowned at me.

"Yes, but in a flirtatious way. Not… listening to my troubles."

"I like you, Karyn," he said simply. "That shouldn't be difficult to understand."

"Because I have yellow hair and you want to have sex with me," I clarified. I really did want to understand, but I had no experience with this.

Zyr cocked his head, and his unseen tail flicked in irritation. "First of all, your hair is like sunlight and firelight spun together. Calling it 'yellow' is a tragedy. Second, while I obviously would love to seduce you—and I admit to being generous in enjoying a variety of lovers—I find *you* interesting. I liked hearing about your life. Tell me more, anytime."

I smiled tentatively. I'd never really tried to create a friendship with someone I hadn't known all my life. Kral didn't count, as we'd really never been friends—just sort of coolly congenial allies. I supposed Jepp had been a friend to me, though I'd spent so much time being jealous of her, wondering why Kral loved her so passionately when he'd given me up without a qualm, and also wondering why she'd tolerated me around her man. Wren had offered friendship and now she was gone. "I'd like to hear more about your life," I offered.

"Done. But not tonight." He yawned hugely. "Let's get some

sleep. More mapping tomorrow—heroically accomplished, of course."

"Of course." I laughed. "Shall I take first watch?"

"Not necessary." His eyes gleamed, reflecting the light in that feline way. "I'll sleep as the panther. I hear everything in that form. Want to sleep against me?"

I couldn't tell if he was teasing. "No," I replied slowly, "but thank you for the offer."

"I won't bite. Or scratch." He was definitely teasing.

"But I might," I replied primly.

He laughed and the sound made me happy.

~ 13 ~

I WOKE FROM a dead sleep to the sight of a black panther, chin on its paws, whiskered muzzle inches from my face, bright blue eyes staring at me.

I screamed and somehow had jumped several feet backward before I knew it, flailing about for my bow. The big cat became Zyr—laced blue shirt, hair neatly tied back—laughing at me.

"That was *not* funny," I growled at him.

"Oh, you are so wrong, gréine. From this side, it was hysterical. If you'd seen yourself, you'd be laughing, too."

I finally spotted my bow and my daggers on the other side of the crackling campfire. Zyr followed my gaze and raised his brows. "It seemed wise, in case you're the sort who strikes first and asks questions later."

"If you hadn't been intent on scaring me out of my wits, you wouldn't have had to worry about it."

"True. But what's the fun in that?" He grinned at me, full of merriment, completely unapologetic. "Good snake jump, though. Better than Zynda's—and I used to do that to her all the time."

Poor Zynda. At least my prankster brothers hadn't been able to shapeshift into terrifying predators. I took a deep breath and let it out, willing my heart to stop its frantic hammering. "What in Sól is a snake jump, anyway?"

"It's a feline thing. Something surprises you and you jump back out of snake-striking distance. You did it from a sound sleep. Very impressive."

He clearly meant it as a compliment, so I took it as one. Strangest compliment I'd ever received. And now I'd become the new plaything for the cat. Wonderful. I looked around, seeing that the sky had lightened with approaching dawn, though the sun hadn't yet risen. "What happened to your aversion to getting up early?"

He grimaced. "Downside of sleeping in panther form. They're crepuscular, so I wake up well before dawn feeling the urge to hunt."

"I don't know that word—crepuscular."

"Active at dawn and dusk. Most felines sleep all day, hunt for a while in the late afternoon and evening, nap a while in the middle of the night, then wake early to do it all again. It works out well now, because the sooner we get going, the more coastline we can map." He dipped his chin at something roasting over the fire. "The upside of the panther wanting to hunt early is I caught some breakfast for us. I even waited for you to wake up, and didn't eat any raw."

"Thank you," I said, struggling not to make a disgusted face, but he caught it.

"As the panther," he clarified. "I don't eat raw food in human form, but as an animal, I tend to want to eat what those instincts dictate. It takes some effort not to give in."

"I wouldn't have minded."

"It's not good for me. Besides, *you* don't mind anything. I could eat all the food and not give you any and you wouldn't protest." His eyes gleamed with challenge. "Or would you?"

"I would say something." Eventually.

"As you lay dying of starvation? 'Oh, Zyr...'" He pitched his voice high in his imitation of me, making it all weak and whispery, too. "'I'm dying. Could I have a crust of bread, please?'" He held up a clawed hand, as if grasping for a crumb. "But… not… if… *you*… are… hungry."

I shouldn't laugh at him, as it only encouraged his mischief, but I had to look away to completely hide the smile. Retorting that I didn't sound like that only seemed to please him that he'd gotten to me, so I decided to try ignoring his bad behavior. Maybe if he couldn't get a rise out of me, he'd give up. Good luck with that. Still, once I had my composure, I gave him a cool look. "I'll visit the woods. Then perhaps we should eat, so we can get that early start you wanted."

He grinned at me, and I got the impression I hadn't fooled him at all. "I'll divvy it up while you 'visit the woods.'" He didn't do the falsetto mimic, but his tone still conveyed that he found my euphemism amusing.

When I returned, he handed me a bowl. He must've cleaned them at some point since last night, and I tried not to feel guilty for not doing it. The bowl held a pile of meat, some of it still on little bones. All right then. "What kind of animal is this?" I asked, not really wanting to know. Really it would be nicer if it didn't look like an animal at all.

"Rabbit." Zyr chewed his enthusiastically. "Nice fat one, too."

Oh. What had he done with the rest of it? No, strike that question. I didn't want to know.

"I'd give you crusts of bread, but we don't have any," Zyr commented while I stalled.

"If I'd known about this, I'd have brought more food," I retorted.

"We need to save what we have, in case the hunting isn't so easy next time."

Steeling myself, I closed my eyes and plucked up a piece of it and chewed. It tasted quite good. Bright like sunshine and fresh like clover. If you forgot it had been a rabbit.

"It's still a rabbit even if you don't look at it," Zyr observed.

"Yes, but I can pretend it's roast something else."

"Which was an animal first, too," he pointed out with remorseless logic.

I opened my eyes to glare at him. "Why doesn't it bother *you*? You've lived as animals like fish and rabbits—it seems like you'd be even more sympathetic."

He shook his head, looking thoughtful. "Predator at heart, remember? And animals, herbivore or whatever, aren't much given to sympathy. Eat or be eaten, so it's better to eat."

"Oh." I chewed some more and swallowed. "What does the gríobhth eat?"

His eyes glinted and his face took on a sharper cant. "Anything I want to," he said, and his voice almost hissed.

"Because that's not terrifying," I muttered, hastily looking at my bowl, which seemed much more soothing in contrast.

"I didn't mean to scare you." Zyr sounded contrite—and a little alarmed. "Did I scare you—really? Karyn?"

"Not like waking up with a panther in my face did, but it's… unsettling when you start to look and sound like the gríobhth when you're still a person."

He stilled. "Did I do that?"

"Don't you know?"

He shook his head. Then shrugged elaborately, as if shaking it off, but his eyes looked troubled. "It's not always clear, from this side, no. Especially with the gríobhth. That form has a brain big enough that I still think like I do in human form. I don't feel all that different between the two. Except for certain… instincts."

I suppressed a shiver, remembering Andi's cautions. Maybe this was part of what had them worried.

"That's part of why I don't eat as an animal, unless I'm desperate," he added in a more conversational tone. "And why I teach the kids that. The more you give over to the animal form's instincts—and eating is a core instinct—the more you think like the animal instead of a person."

"Aren't things like breathing, sleeping, and flying core instincts, too?"

"Aha." He waggled a bone at me, then stripped meat off of it with teeth still too sharp to be human. "Yes, but those are necessary. Or you'd die."

"If you don't eat, you'd die, too. As you keep bothering me about."

"True, but that's why we don't stay in animal form too long. Like with Zynda—she shifted into the hummingbird to live, but she stayed in that form too long. She slept and ate and healed as the bird for days. No one around her understood shapeshifters. That mossback lover of hers didn't know better. We're lucky she came back at all." He sounded uncharacteristically bleak, a glimpse of those melancholy shadows under the trickster nature.

"You don't like him?"

Zyr shrugged, staring at his bowl of little bones as if he'd like to eat those, too. "He's all right for a mossback."

"Which doesn't mean much, since 'mossback' is an insult."

He glanced up at me, a little surprised. "No, not really."

But he didn't sound certain, so I knew I had him. "And you called me 'mossbackiest of mossbacks,' so that was extra insulting."

"I didn't mean it like that," he protested.

"When you call someone a 'mossback,' it's because they're so rooted to one form that moss could grow on them, like a rock, right?" I pressed on when he didn't have an immediate reply. "So you meant that I'm rigid and unchanging, even more than a rock."

He smiled weakly. "I meant Dasnarians, not you."

"I am Dasnarian!" I flung out my hands, exasperated with him now.

"Aren't Dasnarians people who live in Dasnaria?" he asked, cocking his head a little.

"Of course," I snapped, not seeing the trap until too late.

"But *you* don't live in Dasnaria," he crowed in triumph. "Thus you are not Dasnarian. You are another thing entirely. You shapeshifted!"

I shook my head at his antics and handed him my bowl. "You can have the rest—really. I'm full."

I watched him eat, wondering if I dared ask him what I wanted to. "Do you hate mossbacks because they imprisoned you?"

He looked up from the bowl, eyes dark, face set. "It didn't help my opinion of the breed, no. And before you chastise me, as my king did, I'm well aware that *those* mossbacks—the ones led by mad tyrant Uorsin, murderer of Salena—are not the same as all mossbacks."

"Your cousins' father killed their mother?" I clarified.

Looking bemused, chewing his meat, he nodded, then swallowed. "You don't sound shocked."

I lifted a shoulder and let it fall. "It's not that unusual for kings to murder their queens, especially the tyrants."

"Dasnaria," he muttered, "what a place it must be."

"I'll point out that *your* tale of murderous marriage does not take place in Dasnaria."

"True. But Ordnung is just as bad. Or was," he amended. "My cousin may be many things, but she's not a half bad high queen. I imagine she's cleaned up the place. She eliminated the dungeon, so that's a start."

A dungeon. "Was it terrible?" I ventured to ask.

He set the bowl down, still with a few pieces of meat in it, and contemplated me. "You look so sweet and innocent, asking me that with your pretty blue eyes wide. So extraordinary."

"Almost all the Tala have blue eyes, or gray-blue," I replied, feeling myself color self-consciously.

"Yes and no. Not your shade of blue, like the sky in the morning, all fresh and dewy, before it gets hot. Soft and deep, rich and full of innocent promise."

"I'm hardly innocent."

"You're a virgin," he reminded me, picking up the bowl again.

I set my teeth. "Yes, but you called me innocent twice, and not about that."

He sighed and stared into the bowl. "No and yes, gréine. The dungeon itself wasn't pleasant, but neither was it terrible. Being imprisoned though…" He lifted his head, and when he met my eyes, his had gone stark and haunted. "I hated it," he said quietly. "Being trapped. Stuck. If I'd had to spend more than a day or so, I think I'd have gone mad."

I gazed back at him, uncertain what to say to that, how to comfort him for something that happened long before I met him. But he shook himself before I could think of what to say, giving me a crooked smile that did little to cover the raw pain he clearly still felt.

"But that's in the past," he said, speaking my own thoughts, but not meaning them sincerely, I sensed. "We should get going."

"All right." Finger-combing the mess of my hair, I separated it into three sections behind my head and swiftly braided it. At least I'd done that so many times I could do it in the dark.

Zyr eyed me dolefully, finishing the meat in my bowl. "Do you have to? It's so pretty loose. I love how wildly it tumbles, like ocean waves and eddies."

I didn't know how to take that. "It gets in the way of my bow."

"Ah. Well, that is important." He considered me. "We forgot to drill you in shooting from my back last night. We should do that before we go."

The sun tipped over the horizon, spilling light over the verdant, apparently uninhabited landscape. "I thought you wanted to get going, to map more coastline."

"I do." He finished the last of the meat. "But this is important. I have a feeling we'll meet trouble today." He frowned into the distance, as if he saw something.

I shivered a second time. "Can you see the future?" I asked tentatively.

His eyes came back to mine and focused, a deeper blue. Then he shrugged—extra elaborately, to my eye—and grinned. "Not really."

Somehow, I didn't believe him.

"Besides, we might as well take advantage of having a peaceful place to practice, with this nice hill for taking off and landing." He uncoiled to his feet and pulled me to mine. "Come on, it'll be fun!"

IT WAS NOT fun.

Once we'd cleaned up the campsite, doused the fire and packed up our things, Zyr shifted into gríobhth form. I must have been getting accustomed to my highly strange life, because the sight didn't unsettle me.

Or maybe waking to a black panther breathing in my face had set a new standard for strange.

I strapped our packs onto his back, feeling more practiced at it this time, then made sure I had my bow, quiver, and daggers easily accessible before I mounted. I'd stowed the mapsticks we'd already categorized in a separate bag in our packs and had the next batch of most-likelies in a pocket of my skirt. Zyr wanted me to practice exactly as I'd be midair. He'd been unusually insistent—even serious, but clearly being careful not to give me orders—so I went along.

Not that I'd mustered the spine to outright defy him yet, or even argue all that convincingly.

Once on his back, I practiced as we'd agreed, with him on the ground and me pulling an arrow from my quiver, drawing and shooting at whatever target I picked as Zyr pivoted and ran about. That was relatively easy, not so different from archery on horseback, and I'd pinned any number of apples—and apple-eating birds—that way.

I retrieved my second-best arrows, that I'd used for practice, and remounted. Then Zyr spread his wings, and I began shooting. Every arrow went wild. I didn't hit one target. Finally Zyr turned his head around—almost completely reversed, like an owl looking backwards, which was creepy—and gave me a hot glare. He didn't even need to speak.

"I *am* trying," I protested. "I don't want to hit your wings."

Abruptly, Zyr shifted back to human form, dumping me on the ground in a pile of upended skirts and our packs. He, of course, looked all neat and tidy—but the hot blue glare hadn't changed from one form to the next. "There's no point in you shooting at all, if you're so afraid of hitting me that you can't hit anything else."

I scrambled to my feet, embarrassed enough to return the glare. If nothing else, I'd at least had my skill with the bow and arrow. Now I'd lost even that. "Then there's no point in my shooting from your back. We're agreed."

"So you're just going to sit like a lump on my back if we're attacked? You'd be dead weight, making it difficult for me to fight back and you not helping at all!" He waved his hands as if fending off hoards of imaginary attackers.

"I never wanted to come along on this mission," I retorted. "You and I both know I'm only here to keep me from spying on anything important, because you people are too kind to simply kill or imprison me."

He leaned in, eyes sparking with predatory glitter, face sharp. "The Tala are many things, gréine, but we are not kind. You're along because Queen Andromeda saw that you'd play a role. So, pony up and get better at it."

"This isn't even my war!" I protested. "I don't want a role. I only ever wanted a normal life."

"Don't be a fool," he hissed, sounding very like the gríobhth if he could speak in that form. "This war will engulf us all. All the people who just want normal, peaceful lives will have to fight anyway. The point is to act despite that, to fight instead of cringing and hiding. After it's done, we can think about having normal lives. Let's try again. Do better this time."

"It's hard with your wings in the way," I complained.

"Of course it's hard." He rolled his eyes at me, reminding me of Andi. "We wouldn't be practicing if it wasn't difficult."

"If you talk to your students this way, I'm surprised they learn anything," I spat.

Unexpectedly, he grinned. "Then you'd be surprised. Besides, you're not a child, are you?" He nodded when I didn't reply. "Don't expect me to treat you like one."

"Fine," I bit out.

"Karyn," he said, more gently. "We're all afraid. Don't let the fear win. You're giving up before you've even started."

That took me aback. I hadn't though of how I felt as fear, exactly. But it explained that hollow loneliness inside, the perpetual sensation of being unprotected, unable to feed myself, to be useful in the smallest ways. I'd always thought I'd have a man to take care of me—my father and brothers, my husband—and now I had no one. Not even this mercurial shapeshifter who yelled at me to do better. Had Jenna felt like this on her escape? Surely she had. I only wished I knew if things had turned out well or badly for her.

"Are you really afraid?" I asked tentatively, more than half expecting his scorn.

But he only cocked his head. "Of course. There's no shame in it. Only idiots and crazy people aren't afraid when faced with an enemy like Deyrr. They're a plague upon the world—and particularly upon my people—for hundreds of years, maybe thousands. My race faces final extinction, either fast from the enemy or slow because we can't breed viable children. One of my sisters is pregnant yet again and this one is likely to kill her, as close as she came to dying with the last several she tried to birth. My other sister has gone to take Final Form so she might be lost to me forever. None of us have progeny, so our branch of the family line will be gone soon regardless. And if I don't get killed in this war outright, I face the enticing possibility of final imprisonment where my very spirit will be trapped and bled forever. How under Moranu's bright gaze could I not be afraid?"

I suddenly did feel like a child, selfish and self-absorbed. None of that had occurred to me. Zyr always seemed so playful, carefree and as if he took nothing seriously. Clearly what he showed on the surface covered a great deal of pain beneath.

"I'm sorry," I offered.

"Don't apologize," he snarled.

"I wasn't apologizing," I snarled right back. "I was offering sympathy. It's not my fault that your stupid Common Tongue uses the same words for different things!"

He blinked at me, slow and steady, losing some of the wildness. Maybe that signaled a kind of recentering in him, that long blink. "You're right. But it's not *my* stupid language. In Tala you could separate the feelings." He smiled a little. "Your sympathy is appreciated. I should've said so right off. This… isn't stuff I normally talk about."

No, I could see that. "Why did you?"

Cocking his head, he looked at me thoughtfully. "I don't know. You get under my skin, making cracks so things I keep inside spill out."

A strange energy zinged between us, like fire and ice at once, singing in my ears. I felt like touching him, holding him like he'd embraced me the night before, or weeping or laughing. Too many feelings all at once. I didn't know what to do with it all.

So, I made a face, wrinkling my nose. "That's a disgusting analogy."

"Ah, but you didn't say it was inappropriate for mixed company." He waggled a finger at me, apparently happy also to let the tension of the moment dissolve. "Progress!"

It hadn't occurred to me to say so, which probably meant further moral degradation on my part. Ah well—the least of my worries at the moment. "All right, let's try again."

"If you do hit my wing, I can shapeshift back and heal that way, so it's not the end of the world. Not yet."

I huffed at him in exasperation. "Why didn't you tell me that before?"

"Because I'd rather you *didn't* hit my wing, thank you. It will still hurt. And blood lost is blood lost. And it takes energy to shift. No sense squandering it when I don't need to."

"Fine," I grumbled, and he shifted, his sharp grin replaced by the wicked curve of the gríobhth's beak. Picking up the packs, I began strapping them on him again. "It seems to me that if you can shapeshift into a man and drop the packs, then you could become the gríobhth with them *on* and save me some work."

He curved his neck and caught my braid in his beak, tugging at it playfully. I swatted at him and he ducked. "Quit that, bird. Some of us are working here."

Only then did I spot my ribbon dangling from his beak. The ribbon I'd used to tie off my braid. With a groan of exasperation, I grabbed a hold of my already fraying braid, fixed it, and held out my hand for the stolen ribbon. He carefully laid the ribbon over my palm, then ruffled his crest playfully.

"Yes, yes. You're very funny."

A rumbling purr rose up, making me smile.

~ 14 ~

W E DRILLED FOR another hour or so. I got better, though I had nothing like my usual level of marksmanship. After a while I could hit what I aimed at by shooting over or under his steady wing, but my aim deteriorated completely when his wings moved. I'd freeze, or yank my arrow off so wild that it became a menace.

Zyr didn't scold me again. He didn't need to, I felt so glum at the failure. When he jerked his beak at the sky in a clear signal that we should go, I slipped the arrows I'd retrieved from hither and yon back into the quiver with relief and mounted.

He galloped to the edge of the hill, leaping off and plunging perilously near the ground before his laboring wings caught the air and lifted us up. One benefit of his relentless drilling—and mischievous prancing and twisting to challenge me—my seat had gotten better. In worrying about trying to aim around his wings, I'd forgotten to be self-conscious about gripping him with my inner thighs, so now I sat deeper and tighter against his back. Which hurt like the devil, from chafing and riding so long yesterday, but I ignored that pain, along with the sting on my forearm from snapping the bowstring on the tender skin there. It had been a long time since I'd been careless enough to do that, but then all my technique had dissolved with the new challenges.

I sighed, rubbing my arm as Zyr flew to the coast. It would be nice if I had one of my old vambraces, especially if I was going to keep making that mistake as I tried to learn this new skill. Those were, of course, back home on the Hardie estates with virtually everything else I'd owned—and the rest in the seraglio at the Imperial Palace. Even this bow wasn't mine, but one Kral had grabbed off a guard for me. The draw was more than I could comfortably pull for long periods, which meant my shoulder and arms ached from the intensive practice, too.

It would be nice to find a bow with a sweet draw like I'd had back home. More arrows, too. Maybe a second quiver, so I could keep my best and second-best arrows separate. A crossbow would really be ideal for shooting from Zyr's back, especially in a fight. With a mental start, I realized I'd started planning for an extended fighting partnership with Zyr.

No doubt a result of his trickery and browbeating.

The first stint of mapping went easily as I only had to hand Zyr the mapstick we hadn't quite finished following the night before. As he flew, I smoothed my skirt into a basin of cloth over my stretched thighs, laying out the most likely next sticks in one row and pulling out the three already identified mapsticks to sit in another. If I were making something like mapsticks for other people to use, I'd have a way to indicate which came next.

Before I expected, Zyr swooped into a circle, handing the mapstick back to me and I gave him another. He quickly gave it back. Curse it. This part of the coastline didn't have much in the way of nearby islands or distinctive features. I put another in his impatiently clacking beak. Another dud. Picking one at random, I tried another. Which he gave back immediately with a heavy sigh.

I didn't know how he could see it so quickly and easily— they all looked much the same to me. Giving him another, I held my breath, hoping. He grunted in approval and struck out. That should give me a couple of hours to figure out the next one.

I knew the order of the identified mapsticks, but putting them end to end didn't lock them together like a puzzle piece. That annoyed me, as it seemed like the most logical thing to do. If these map makers were so clever, why didn't they think of this?

Pulling out the mapstick Zynda had identified as being for Nahanau, I examined it, too. Dafne had marked it on the flat side, scratching on the name of the island in three different scripts—none of which I could read—and inking in the characters. A good system, I supposed, though I only knew which it was because it was the only one marked like that. The limitations of language, that you can write stuff down, but if people can't read it, that does only so much good. And even the scratches would smooth out over time, long after the ink wore off. Careful as Zyr was with his claws, he still marked the ones he'd held. Only the fact that the mapsticks were made of such hard wood kept him from knocking chips off the sharper spurs.

Maybe the puzzle-piece idea wouldn't work well because the ends of the sticks frayed too much, being cut across the wood grain. Though polished smooth as the rest, the ends had become rounded over time.

Frustrated, I tried placing two mapsticks end to end that I *knew* were a mismatch. And they clearly didn't align. So, that was something. I put two together again that should align. They didn't lock together like I wanted, but... they were more congruent. The coastline obviously followed from one to the next, even if the ends didn't match.

Maybe that's how Zyr could see so quickly when one wasn't right. Maybe his shapeshifter eyes gave him an advantage. Raptors could see really far, after all, like the falcons my brothers used for hunting, who could fly so high that they looked like dots in the sky, but could spot a hare on the ground and dive for it with perfect accuracy.

Struck by a thought, I looked at the end of the mapstick, holding it up to the bright sunlight to help me see better. Several pinprick holes penetrated the wood. I'd taken them for part of the aging of the wood, but now I wondered. Examining the mapstick I knew was its sequel, I found the same pinpricks, in the same pattern. Excited by my discovery, I checked the other identified mapsticks, finding similar matching patterns of tiny holes, bored so deep that wear wouldn't rub them out until the stick itself had disintegrated.

I laid out my candidate mapsticks for the next leg, I needed to see the one Zyr held before I could pick the next. When he circled and handed the mapstick back to me, I examined the pattern of holes. Though I felt I had them all memorized from the wait, it took me a moment to be sure of the next one. Those tiny holes weren't easy to see.

Zyr clacked his beak at the delay.

"Be patient, you daft bird," I snapped. "I'm testing a theory."

He subsided with a very human-sounding snort. I rolled my eyes at him. He couldn't see it, but it made me feel better. "Here," I said, giving him what had to be the right one.

He took it, surveyed, and zoomed out of the circle to fly along the coast.

I allowed myself a congratulatory wiggle, pleased and proud that I'd intuited the correct choice. A purr welled up through him in response, sending that shiver of delight through me. Curse it—I'd forgotten to find a pad to put between us, and my deeper, firmer seating only meant I felt the vibration better than before. Longing pulsed through me, and I had to take a breath against it, cooling and settling the urges that rose in me with fierce and unaccustomed hunger.

It made no sense that I'd be feeling these sexual cravings now. I'd never really missed that aspect of my marriage with Kral. While I'd found him so handsome, powerful, and dashing—as any girl would—I'd also been a little frightened at the prospect of bedding him.

There it was again: fear. Not unreasonable, as tales like Jenna's circulated in the gossip of the seraglios when the women retired for the evening. Some men were cruel in their lust and women must learn to bear it.

Thus, when my father had explained the emperor's edict that I would remain a virgin, the news came as a relief. Only later did I really mind what I missed—mainly that I'd never have children or that normal life Zyr had scoffed at. Never had that longing manifested this way, as a physical craving, like hunger.

You'd enjoy yourself in my bed. Zyr's sensual promise echoed in my head with tantalizing images. Now I knew how it felt to have him hold me, his body so warm and strong, his scent both wild and comforting, I wanted to know what else there could be.

I needed to take a big mental and emotional step back, though, because as offensive as that offer had been to a woman of my station—even if it had been a miscommunication—it still had spoken to that frightened core of me. That word again. Deep down, I *wanted* a man to take care of me. There. I'd admitted it to myself. And I wanted that because I was afraid to be on my own.

Even if Zyr would be willing to take care of me, to feed and protect me—which he'd been very clear that he wouldn't—I'd still be acting out of fear.

Don't let the fear win. You're giving up before you've even started.

Resolved, I cleared my mind of the erotic haze and focused

again on the mapsticks. I discovered some I'd set aside as too featureless to be of much use—pretty much just straight sticks with no bumps or grooves—had pinprick holes on the sides, too. By matching several of those together, I ended up with a series of sticks, finishing with one flat on one side—and carved with a deep curve on the other.

My heart pounding with the thrill of discovery, I found another stick to match to the end of the one with the big curve. It had bigger notches and a jutting thumb that could be a peninsula.

Had I found a lost continent, out across the vast stretch of open water?

I bounced a little in my excitement, unable to contain myself, and Zyr glanced back, giving me a jaundiced stare. "I think I've made a discovery!" I shouted over the rush of wind.

The fierce blue eye of the gríobhth took on an interested gleam and I could imagine Zyr raising an eyebrow.

"Maybe when we finish this mapstick, we could land and I'll explain," I yelled.

But he turned inland immediately, striking for a set of high cliffs that dropped sheer into the water, where the sea dashed itself in foaming waves against the rock. I sighed to myself, knowing that soon we'd be doing the drop of doom off of them again. I put my mapsticks back in their bags. It would be nice if I could keep them in order, but so it went.

Zyr came in fast, running as he slowed, wings arched high against a buffeting wind that yanked at tendrils of my hair that escaped the braid, lashing them against my face. When he came to a stop I slid off, surprised at the stiffness and aching in my joints. The sun tipped a fair amount past midday. It was late spring here, so the days would be getting longer. Even so, we'd been flying for hours. No wonder I ached. How could Zyr sustain that?

I turned to unbuckle the packs and found Zyr had already shifted back to human form. As always when he did that, he looked as fresh and neat as if he'd stepped out of the bathing chamber. But he sat on the sparse grass of the rocky ground, so heavily that he almost collapsed. Then he fell back with a groan, dramatically splaying his arms wide, staring up at the sky.

"Zyr?" I asked cautiously. His eyes were open, so he shouldn't be sleeping. Had something struck him down—maybe some kind of magic I couldn't see? I moved over to him, but he didn't seem to see me, staring glassily past me at nothing. "Zyr?" I asked again, louder, but he still didn't stir.

So I knelt down beside him and placed careful fingers on the pulse at his throat. It leapt fast and strong, his skin hot and slightly slick with sweat. Velvety, too. Unable to resist, I stroked him a little, fascinated by the play of muscle and sinew under his skin.

His eyes rolled over to my face, brows drawing together. "I'm not dead."

I snatched my fingers away, tempted to shake them to sluice off the tingle of temptation. "I didn't think you were," I replied, sounding prim. My cheeks burned and I knew I blushed.

"Do you always check the pulse of people you're sure aren't dead?" he inquired, sounding politely interested, but I didn't mistake the teasing sparkle in his eyes.

"I wasn't sure what was wrong with you. I'm sorry I bothered now." I drew back, but his hand snagged my braid where it had fallen on his chest, keeping me there.

"I'm just tired," he replied, sounding weary indeed. "That was a lot of sustained flying. More than I've done in a long time. I need a few moments to rest."

"Oh." Chagrined that I hadn't been solicitous of his health

and strength, I glanced to the packs. "Shall I fetch you some food and water?"

"*My Lord*," he said, chuckling a little. "Even when you don't say it, you say it."

"You can't fault me for what I don't say."

"I suppose not." His gaze went to my mouth. "How about a kiss? That would make me feel better."

"I seriously doubt that," I replied as crisply as I could, though the suggestion made me breathless, the need surging again as if it hadn't ever receded.

"Oh, I seriously disagree." He smiled, that sensual curve, and I couldn't pull my gaze from his mouth. "I like the way you feel on my back," he continued, his voice an echo of the purr. "The clasp of your thighs, your scent. I can feel your sex, hot and wet through—"

I clapped a hand over that wicked mouth, silencing his salacious words, my face burning hot. "You mustn't say such things," I hissed, utterly mortified.

His eyes gleamed over my hand—and he licked my palm, a slow, erotic caress.

I snatched my hand back, holding it against my breast as if he'd burned me. "Zyr!"

"Don't be embarrassed," he murmured, winding my braid around his hand so it tightened a bit. "There's only you and me here. I love that my purr arouses you. It drove me wild with wanting you."

I narrowed my eyes at him, remembering all those cautions. He'd been the panther all night, and the gríobhth most of the day. Animal passions rode strong in him at the moment. The problem was, I didn't know what to do about it.

"One kiss." Zyr wound another loop of my braid around his hand. I braced a hand on his chest with half an idea of using it to lever myself away—but the enticing flex of his muscles under the fine silk arrested me, and I curled my fingers into the sensation instead. His heart thumped under my palm, which seemed sensitized to him now, my heart an echo of his.

"It's a not a good idea." I sounded far too breathless, felt much too tempted.

"Why not—what can one kiss hurt? Surely even Dasnarian virgins get to have kisses."

I had a hard time remembering how to talk. "Not so much."

"No?"

"No, because kisses lead to … other things."

"Oh, do tell." His voice caressed me, strumming my nerves as his purring had vibrated against my sex—which had indeed gone hot and wet again with wanting. If mere words, a purr, a stroke of his tongue on my palm, had me so full of this new craving, how would it feel if I kissed him?

If he touched me elsewhere? Just the idea scattered my thoughts to the wind.

"What other things do kisses lead to?" he coaxed, then licked his lips, unbearably enticing.

"You know perfectly well," I breathed.

"Yes, but do you?"

I couldn't reply. My head swam and I could only think about how badly I wanted this. One kiss. What could it hurt?

"Gréine, have you ever kissed a man at all?"

Mutely I shook my head. I licked my own lips and he groaned, clearly as affected by the sight as I was.

"I want to be the one," he murmured. "Your first kiss. Will you at least give me that?"

"Do you promise to stop there?" I asked.

His eyes, always so full of light, flared with the ferocity of desire. "Yes."

"I mean it," I cautioned him. His answer had been so easy and immediate that I didn't trust it.

"I promise, sweet Karyn. For one kiss with you, I'd promise much more than that."

I laughed, but he remained perfectly serious, expression fierce, reflecting my own longing. "Don't tease me," I said, my mouth dry.

"I wouldn't and I'm not. I don't think I've ever wanted anything more in my life."

"One kiss," I repeated, attempting to sound firm.

"Yes." He drew me down and I let him, my eyes drifting closed. But he stopped, our lips a breath apart. After a long, heart-stopping moment, I opened my eyes. He was so near, those bright eyes filling all my world. "I should be honest with you, gréine," he said, so quietly, and his breath moved over my lips, tingling. "I can make one kiss last a very long time."

That should've alarmed me, but I couldn't muster the outrage. All those years of the rules safeguarding my virginity, never being allowed in the company of a man not my brothers or father, of being so careful every moment… All of that seemed to have happened to someone else. *This*, this was real. And I was brilliantly alive.

I closed that last whisper of distance, and his lips brushed mine.

Shocking and delightful. The sensation rolled through me, making me moan, and he seemed to drink in the sound, turning it into a hmm of answering harmony. The light, almost butterfly wing caress deepened, with his lips moving against mine, drawing me in. His hands moved to cup my head, changing the angle of our mouths so they fit even more precisely, sealing us together. He tasted … like nothing I'd ever known. Hot and spicy like his scent, but richer, like a draught of excellent liquor. I could get drunk on his flavor, on his kisses.

Already lost in the drugging kiss, I opened my mouth for more, and he made a sound like a soft growl, his tongue sliding to touch mine. Startled, I shuddered, and his arms slid to my back, stroking and soothing, the other hand threading fingers into my hair. Vaguely some part of me registered that my braid had somehow come loose—the heavy weight of my hair an unaccustomed sensation on my back and arms—but I lost the thought in the ongoing kiss. His tongue traced the tender inside of my upper lip, and I dissolved, melting into him, so I draped over him like a blanket, the sun hot on my hair, the scent of sea grass, ocean salt, and Zyr filling my senses.

Then he tore his mouth from mine with a groan, closing his eyes and setting his jaw. "We should stop there."

Bleary, dazed, I nearly asked why. Then remembered I'd made him promise. Hastily I sat up, disentangling myself from him, and he turned his head to watch me. He looked different. More sensual than ever, with his lips parted, gleaming from our kiss, the blue of his eyes like the dusk of the sky just after sunset. Still lying on his back, he seemed like a feast laid out entirely for me.

One I didn't dare indulge in. More than I already had.

"I think that was more than one kiss," I asserted, shakily, combing my fingers through my tangled hair. The ocean humidity plus Zyr's attentions had it curling in wild abandon. I looked around for the ribbon for my braid, and Zyr held it out, dangling from his long fingers as his lips quirked in mischief. I yanked it away, scowling at him.

"Technically, no," Zyr said, and it took me a moment to realize he was replying to me. "Once we started kissing, our lips never lost contact, thus it was one kiss and one kiss only, as promised. Just a very long one. I did warn you," he added, his expression full of masculine pride.

I might've said something to set him back on his heels, but the tension of desire obviously rode him, his body tense with it, his cock hard and ready, clearly delineated by his pants. "Thank you for stopping," I said.

He held out a hand and, after a moment of hesitation, I put mine in his. Sitting up, he turned our hands and laced our fingers together, intently holding my gaze. "I keep my promises," he said softly. "Will you trust me now?"

I laughed a little, uneven, revealing how shaken I was. "More than I trust myself, I think." No wonder they'd hemmed me in with so many rules. One taste of this forbidden fruit and I'd been ready to throw everything away, just to keep feeding that insatiable craving.

He brushed a wayward spiraling lock of hair from my forehead, tucking it behind my ear, then traced his fingers down my cheek. "I think you have to know yourself to trust yourself."

I frowned. "What does that even mean?"

"Trusting yourself is about knowing what you want, what you need, and staying true to that. You've been following what other people say you want and need."

Oh.

He smiled at my bemusement. "When you decide you want more from me, be sure to let me know as soon as possible."

When. "You're so sure I will."

"Gréine…" He stopped and shook his head. "No, any words I could put to this wouldn't sound right. I can be patient."

"Are you sure?" I asked archly. "Patient is not a word I'd use to describe you."

"No? Tell me—what words *would* you use to describe me?"

"I have no intention of telling you that. You're proud of yourself enough as it is." Too late, I caught myself.

"Aha! Then they're all good words." He grinned at how neatly he'd trapped and flustered me. "Maybe you could toss one or two my way, now and then, like crusts of bread thrown to a starving man."

I rolled my eyes at him, tying off my braid. "Impatient. There's one."

He laughed. "I shall prove myself to you, fair maiden. You'll see how patient I can be. Now tell me, what did you discover?"

"I can't believe I forgot!" I scowled at him. "You distracted me."

"You distracted me," he countered. "I was lying there, resting my poor exhausted body, and *you* had to come over, looking like another sun in the sky, and fondle me."

I gasped, sputtering, and he managed to look wounded and put upon. Deciding he'd only best me if I tried to deny it, I instead smoothed out the ground, laying the mapsticks in a row. "Look at this."

~ **15** ~

I WANTED TO strike out across the water, going at a diagonal, to locate the coastline the mapsticks revealed, but Zyr overruled me.

"It's faster," I protested. "If it's n'Andana, the sooner we find it, the sooner you can get back to Annfwn for the Gathering."

"First of all," he replied, chewing on the dried meat we'd brought along, "we don't know what landmass that mapstick represents. It could be a big island unrelated to n'Andana. Second, each mapstick doesn't always represent the same distance. Especially where the coastline has fewer features, one mapstick might cover twice the distance that another does."

"I didn't realize," I said, chagrined. Though I should have. I thought maybe I just got bored sometimes, the way some stretches seemed longer than others.

He shrugged, helping himself to some fruit. "How could you? It's not something you notice unless you're the one flying. But that means I want to fly to this point." He tapped the mapstick with the landmark notch that fit into the spread of the next few that led to my island. "We'll rest there, then strike out across the water."

"But we won't get there until tomorrow most likely," I pointed out with dismay. That notched mapstick was three up from our current location.

"Probably. But we can get there early in the day, get plenty of sleep, and I can hunt for more food." He frowned at the several blank mapsticks representing open water, dragging a finger over their smooth surfaces. "I'd be a lot happier if these showed some stops along the way. That could be a long way to fly. I'd like to be at my top strength, just in case."

That didn't sound comforting. "I thought you said you could heal from shapeshifting back and forth."

He raised a brow at me. "I can, but recovering strength is different. Only food and rest cures that."

"Why?"

He cocked his head, brow falling into a quirked frown. "I don't know. It just is."

"The way of things?" I nodded sagely.

"Clever minx." He took another piece of fruit. "I'll hunt tonight, too. Fresh meat will help. I just need to build up my endurance again."

"Maybe you should leave me behind."

"Why would I do that?"

"I've outlived my usefulness," I pointed out. "You don't need me to read the mapsticks anymore. You'll have a long way to fly across water and I'll just be dead weight."

He winced. "That sounds worse than I meant it to. I said you'd be dead weight if you didn't help fight if we get attacked."

"I still might not be able to fight."

"Regardless, I wouldn't abandon you in the wilderness, even if Queen Andromeda hadn't made it very clear you needed to come along. I trust her advice, even if you don't."

My turn to wince. "I didn't mean it like that. You just seemed worn out before and I don't want to make this journey more difficult for you."

"You aren't. You're making it more fun." He finished the fruit and stood. "Let's get going. I'd like to make it another stick and a half at least today if we can." He surveyed the blue sky, pausing on the low clouds scudding over the sea in the distance. "Storm is coming. We'll need shelter tonight."

"How can you tell?" I began putting the mapsticks away in their pouches.

He cast me a preoccupied glance. "Experience?"

"Hmm."

"All right, I don't know. I can just…feel it."

"Maybe you should rest more now," I said, not liking the idea of flying through a storm. "We could camp here."

"I feel totally restored, thanks to you, gréine." He grinned when I gave him a jaundiced look. "Nothing like a shot of sexual frustration to fuel a long flight," he added.

"Good to know. Then I shall have to make sure you stay that way for the long trip across the water."

He laughed at my sally. "I chased my tail right into that one," he admitted. "Ready?"

"Yes," I replied, waiting for him to shift. This time I'd made a pad of one of my shifts to put between us. No sense creating more temptation, for either of us.

NOW THAT I'D solved the puzzle of the mapsticks, time passed slowly as Zyr flew. And I kept watching the gathering clouds, worrying about the impending storm. Not that my fretting changed anything.

It would be good if I could practice aiming around his wings in flight, but I'd have to loose my arrows—which would mean losing them entirely—and I had nothing in particular to aim at.

Occasionally we passed flocks of birds, but it seemed wrong to knock them out of the sky just for practice, not to mention losing arrows, and they could be shapeshifters for all I knew. I played with the empty bow some, finding better angles to shoot from a sitting position. Really, this size of bow was best used standing, and once again I wished for a smaller, lighter recurve to use from Zyr's back.

Or a lovely, compact crossbow like my brothers used and let me try a few times in secret. My father had declared it a weapon for killing people and thus unsuitable for me. But, oh, how those arrows flew!

Pretending to have arrows doesn't do much, but I tried, sighting in on various gulls and other seabirds and songbirds we flew past, learning the timing of Zyr's wings. Over a long distance like this, he kept the beat steady and predictable. I imagined sighting, wait for the downstroke, draw and release. Upstroke, notch an arrow, wait for a target. Downstroke. Sight, draw, release.

It worked well enough in smooth air—in theory, at least—but gusting winds arrived ahead of the storm. Chill and tumultuous, they buffeted us, forcing Zyr to vary his flight to compensate, sometimes gliding through a sudden drop, then pumping his wings furiously to regain altitude or cut through a blustery patch.

Being in the sky like this as a storm arrived felt like nothing I'd experienced. I'd always rather liked storms. Or, rather, I'd liked to watch their wild fury from safely behind the tower windows in the Hardie manse. Probably a metaphor for my whole life, right there.

So, though the twisting, rollicking flight made my stomach flip and roil, I tried to find the joy in being part of the storm, as I had in observing them from behind glass and stone. The chill wind whipped my hair against my cheeks, and occasional raindrops stung still more. But there was an exhilaration to it.

And Zyr's erratic wing patterns presented a new challenge to distract myself with. It might be like this in a pitched fight, where he'd have to dip and dive, wheel and turn to avoid an enemy. I practiced trying to feel his adjustments before he made them, anticipating changes in the wing amplitude and frequency.

I had my eye on a flock of birds arrowing out of the thunderheads, picturing picking them off one by one with imaginary arrows, when something about them scraped across my nerves. They headed straight for us with an unnatural determination, ignoring the encroaching storm with a singlemindedness I'd only seen in the creatures of Deyrr.

"Zyr!" I shouted. He couldn't hear me over that blasted wind, head down as he concentrated on keeping us in the air. I thumped a fist on his shoulder near my leg and his head jerked up. I leaned forward into his field of vision and pointed at the birds.

He caught on immediately, handing the mapstick back to me. I tucked it safe in its pouch, just as Zyr took us in a steep dive that would've unseated me the day before. As it was I had to cling to the straps holding our packs to his back, squinting against the wind of our rapid descent that ripped tears from my eyes. Zyr reversed into a spiral and pumped up beneath the flock.

As if he shouted instructions in my head, I understood his intent. With an overhead field clear of his wings, I nocked an arrow and loosed it at the nearest bird. Not a great hit, as I didn't compensate entirely for the wind and my pitching seat, but I hit it. And with enough force to hamper the bird. It still gamely flew toward us, but lost altitude as it did, weighted down by the arrow piercing it clean through its body.

No time to see if it hit the sea. Zyr would watch to see if it came back upon us from below. He'd dropped and turned again, remarkably agile in the air, positioning me for another shot. Better this time. I got the next bird through the head, exploding it in a burst of oily black fluid. The body went on, still flapping its wings, but without direction.

Zyr roared, catching an undead bird in his curved beak, slicing it in half. As wicked sharp as I'd guessed. Two more birds dove for his head, and Zyr snapped his wings, jerking us backward and him into a rearing position that made me grab for the harness again—sending my next shot wild. He snatched one of the birds in his claws, ripping it to pieces, but the other made it past, piercing my shoulder with its beak and grappling my arm with its talons. I screamed, more in surprise at the sudden injury than actual pain, and Zyr's tail snapped past my cheek, decapitating the bird and taking off one of its wings. So fast I heard the crack of sound from it a moment later.

The talons still dug into my arm muscle, scrabbling and tearing at me. Hooking my other arm through my bow so I wouldn't drop it, I drew a dagger and sawed at the skinny, scaled legs. The body fell away in a one-winged bobbling flight, spiraling to its doom all unawares. The talons embedded in my arm still flexed, but without muscles to power them, they couldn't do more damage.

Doing my best to ignore the monstrous things, and gritting my teeth against the fiery pain, I nocked another arrow and looked for my next target. And realized we'd dropped so low we skimmed the white-capped waves. Spray dashed me, even colder against my face and exposed skin than the rain.

And Zyr labored beneath me, sides heaving and wings barely keeping us above water. Something caught my hair and I flailed in a panic, knocking it aside with my bow. Should've had my dagger, but I didn't know how to grapple both at once. Rocks loomed ahead and I realized Zyr headed straight for a patch of beach.

I held on, praying to any god or goddess who would listen. Moranu, Zyr's goddess. I prayed to Her to help Her favored son. *Just let him live through this.*

We hit the beach at high speed, Zyr folding his wings and tumbling across the small patch of gravelly sand. I hit the ground with a thud that knocked the wind out of me and made my vision whorl with black and silver stars. Dimly I heard the strange avian-feline roar of gríobhth as I tried to suck air into my lungs. It would come back in a moment, if I relaxed.

When I was a little girl, I fell out of a tree—well, my little brother pushed me, but I never told—and I lay there on the ground, panicked that I couldn't breathe. After an endless space of time, my lungs moved, grabbed at the air, and I breathed it in with desperation. I needed to get up, to help Zyr.

My head spun with sickening nausea, but I forced myself up, the wounded arm buckling. Zyr, still in gríobhth form, reared between me and the flock of birds. With talon, beak and whipping tail, he held them off, though one wing hung limply broken and he bled bright blood from numerous wounds.

I had to help him. Scrabbling for my bow and reaching for an arrow, I found the bow snapped in half and the quiver empty, the last of my arrows no doubt scattered across beach and sea. Growling in impotent fury, I flung the useless bow aside, and drew my dagger. Charging up on the broken-wing side, I slashed at a bird coming at Zyr.

And missed entirely.

Fiercely, I wished for some of Jepp's skill with daggers. Tays had a point about my miserable hand-to-hand skills. But I never thought I'd be in a place like this, on a lonely beach with only a shapeshifted gríobhth and rocks for company. Rocks. Shifting the dagger to my nearly useless left hand, I picked up a fist-sized rock, sighted, and hurled it.

The power fell sadly short of what I could do with a bow, but my marksmanship remained deadly accurate. The bird dropped to the beach, flopping toward Zyr's paw. Grimly, I dropped to my hands and knees and pounded it to a useless pulp. It kept pulsating, but at least it couldn't harm us.

Zyr swatted a bird toward me, and I caught on, pouncing on the thing before it could rise again, taking savage satisfaction in pounding it with the rock. Rain fell, washing the ooze into the gravel. Another bird flung my way—this one I had to grapple with both hands, barely jerking my face back from its snapping beak, putting my foot on its neck to hold the flapping thing immobile while I pounded its undead brain into useless mush.

A wave dashed over me, startlingly cold, dragging me off balance, and I clutched at the slippery rocks with both hands, gasping at the shock. Nearby, a bird dragged itself along the gravel toward Zyr and I lunged, snarling, pinning it with the dagger and dispatching its unnatural life with a rock.

I looked wildly about for more targets, and saw Zyr grab the last one from the sky with both front paws, stretching it between his claws and biting it in half. He threw the two halves in opposite directions, fell to all fours, and spun in a circle, wing dragging, scanning for his next victim.

"That's all," I said, my voice coming out a harsh croak from the scour of salt water and my shrieking. Zyr couldn't hear me, I thought, over the crash of the surf. But his head swiveled to me, his crest dripping with rain and black blood. He came to me, shifting as he did. In that in-between moment, I almost saw him as both at once. Man and gríobhth, two faces of a spinning coin.

He seized me, eyes still the wild blaze of the gríobhth. "Are you hurt?"

Mutely, I thrust my arm at him, the writhing talons embedded there a horror I could no longer bear. "Get them out," I demanded.

With a snarl, he grabbed one set, his fingers becoming sharp claws that sliced the talons into pieces separate from each other. He did the same to the other set, while I tried to focus. Maybe the blow to my head made me think he had the panther's claws on a man's hand. That must be it, because when I blinked, clearing the muck from my vision, he had human fingers again, plucking the talons out one by one. Then he dashed seawater over the wounds, sluicing them until they ran only red with my own blood.

Grasping my head in both hands, he stared at me. "Where else?"

I pointed to my shoulder, feeling too weak to articulate. He cursed, ripping my gown away from the shoulder wound, batting at my hand when I tried to cover my breast. "Be still," he growled, sluicing more seawater over the deep puncture wound. The salt burrowed into me and I screamed, but faintly, aware that meant I'd lost the last of my endurance.

The blackness rolled up and dragged me under.

I OPENED MY eyes to dimness and a roaring, pounding sound. A shrouded, low ceiling, the shadows dancing with firelight, the scent of smoke, and under it, things damp and musty, old tidepools and rotting sea creatures. Turning my head, I saw Zyr on the other side of the fire, asleep sitting up, head bent to the side and chin nearly to his chest, as if he'd succumbed to sleep without meaning to. He looked utterly unkempt, hair loose and snarled with rain and wind, his shirt torn open, mud on the skin beneath.

Something had happened to keep him from shifting back and forth to his usual impeccable presentation. I shivered violently, chilled, though Zyr had put two blankets on me and I was coated in sweat. The smoke stung my eyes and burned my throat, still wretchedly sore and tasting of salt. I coughed against the dryness, and my shoulder bloomed with a fiery, spreading pain that it shouldn't have been possible to miss before this moment.

My head felt too heavy to lift, so I reached up to the wound with my other hand, finding my shoulder bare and a hole above my breast oozing liquid—and another like it in the meat of my upper arm. Blood—or worse? I held my fingers up to the light, finding them covered with slick, pink fluid, like watery blood, none of the oily black ooze of Deyrr.

"I didn't bandage them because they need to drain," Zyr said, and I looked to find him staring at me, his eyes catching the firelight in a blue-gold shimmer. "How do you feel?"

"Cold," I said, my voice hoarse. I coughed again. "Thirsty."

With his mouth flattened to an unhappy line, he thrust a piece of wood onto the fire and crawled over to me with one of our water flasks. I tried to lever myself up and hissed at the spike of pain. Weakness washed over me in a wave of heat, leaving chill behind. The shivers turned to racking shudders.

"Don't do that," Zyr snapped. "Let me help you."

"Yes, Lord Zyr," I whispered, but he didn't smile. He slipped an arm behind my shoulders from the good side, and eased me up, holding the flask to my lips. I drank the cool sweetness, wanting to gulp it, but he held it at such an angle that

I could only sip. Reaching for the flask so I could adjust the angle, my left arm simply refused, howling with such pain that I choked on the water.

Muttering viciously in Tala—which still sounded pretty, despite the angry tone—Zyr clasped the flask between his knees and levered me over him, patting my back as I coughed.

"I'm fine," I managed, embarrassed to be essentially draped over his lap. Wearing nothing, I realized, under the blankets. "Why am I naked—where are my clothes?"

"Now there's a sign she's more herself," he declared, sounding still terse. But his hands were gentle as he returned me to my back, adjusting the blankets to cover me and holding the flask to my mouth again. "Be a good girl, lie still, and sip carefully. Too much and you'll puke it up and mess up our dry, cozy nest."

I took a sip, glaring at him. He returned it in equal measure, but this close I could see the lines around his mouth and one between his brows. Worry, not anger. The firelight danced with unusual brightness, and I still shivered. Fever. Which meant infection. Wonderful.

"It doesn't *smell* dry," I observed during one of the long, enforced pauses between sips.

His mouth quirked in a half smile—at last, as an unsmiling Zyr means the world has turned the wrong direction—and he glanced around. "Relatively so. Compared to the pouring rain outside, not to mention the stormy surf that would like to join us in our cave."

"We're in a *cave*?" Silly question, but now the low, shadowed and rough ceiling made sense.

"Yes. You're welcome. If you'd been conscious while I dragged you around the beach in the rain, looking for some shelter, any shelter, then you wouldn't sound so disdainful. It's a lovely cave, its best feature being that it's not under water."

"Sorry," I said, before I remembered not to apologize. That explained why he looked so bedraggled. And tired. He looked purely exhausted. "I'm sure it's a wonderful cave."

"Well, once I pitched out the dead seal and other decaying matter stranded by storms and tides, it improved considerably. The fire is helping to dry it out."

"Is that wise, with the smoke?"

He shrugged a little, giving me more water, expression stony. "Our domicile *is* lacking a chimney, it's true. But the smoke is going somewhere because it's been a full day and we haven't suffocated yet."

"A day?" I couldn't imagine it.

"Besides," he continued as if I hadn't spoken, "you're burning up with fever and needed the warmth. Practically everything we had was soaked. That's why you're naked, by the way, as I couldn't leave you in wet clothes. You also had several other injuries that you either didn't notice or didn't mention. They had to be cleaned and tended."

Oh. "Thank you," I tendered, trying to sound grateful, though it bothered me greatly that he'd examined me while I was naked and unconscious.

"You're welcome, again." He smiled wider, a hint of his former mischief in it. "I tried very hard not to look at the nicest bits."

"Then how do you know they're nice?" I retorted, but I'd gone muzzy, not sounding as sharp as I'd wanted to.

His fingers feathered over my face, soothing, calming. "I have a vivid imagination. Go back to sleep, gréine. You're safe with me and you need rest."

"So do you," I replied, though my eyes had drifted closed and my words sounded very far away.

He chuckled. "Always deferring. I'm going to lie down and

sleep next to you. That way I'll know if you wake. Will that satisfy you?"

"No sex," I cautioned, and he snickered.

His weight settled down on my good side, a surprising comfort. "I may have had many lovers, of all stripes and spots, but even I draw the line at corpses."

"Hey…" I protested, but I wasn't sure the sound came out at all.

~ 16 ~

I TOSSED THROUGH dreams. Birds chewing off my fingers and hands, and I couldn't move to stop them. Drowning in the ocean, a huge monster wrapping rotting tentacles around me, dragging me under, no matter how I flailed and fought. The gríobhth, beak clacking, speaking with Zyr's voice telling me I was only dreaming.

"I never dream," I kept telling him, trying to explain, but he only laughed. And the birds pecked at my eyes, no matter how I wept and begged them to stop. "I want to go home," I sobbed, and my mother placed a wet cloth on my brow, shushing me, telling me I was home.

"I'm home?" I couldn't believe it. Could it be true? Maybe I smelled the fruit orchards in bloom, so flagrantly redolent of spring.

"I'm your home and you are mine. Stay with me, gréine."

"I don't know that word." I focused on Zyr's face. His long, black hair fell around me, gleaming like night, the firelight gilding it. So beautiful. It was him that smelled of flowers, like the sweet air of Annfwn, with its tumbling blossoms and gentle warmth. "Kiss me."

He brushed my lips with a kiss, but pulled back when I tried to deepen it. "It means a burst of sunshine," he said, kissing my cheekbones and brow instead. Light, butterfly wing kisses like soft rain on my face. "Like when it's been cloudy and all of a sudden, the sun breaks through. You're that to me."

"That's pretty," I mused. "You're pretty, too. So wild and sensual and just… so beautiful. I want you, Zyr. Please. I want to—" I cried out as I tried to lift my arm. "It hurts."

He took the cloth from my forehead, dipped it in a bowl, and washed my arm with it. I hissed at the pain, and his face creased.

"Am I dying?" I wondered. I felt so weak, as if my life drained away by the moment.

"I need to open up the wounds," he told me. "Drain the infection."

"All right." My words came dully, the ceiling already swimming again.

"It will hurt," he cautioned me.

"Your hand is full of claws," I said, and giggled at the sight. "Cat paw claws."

"Mrow." He rumbled the cat's purring sound and I laughed again. "Pretty kitty cat."

"Brace yourself," he warned, leaning his weight on me and pinning me down. Excruciating agony rolled over me and my giggles turned to tears. "Karyn?"

"Do it," I said, the pain making me abruptly, brutally alert. "It can't hurt more than this."

But I was wrong.

WHEN I WOKE again I'd fought off the blankets, certain the sea monster had returned, but it drowned me in fire. So hot. I was burning alive. "No!" I cried, trying to escape the tentacles.

"Shh. It's good for you. You need to cool off."

I opened my eyes, the light hurting them. Every part of me bloomed with agony. I lay naked on the blankets, Zyr wiping me with a cool cloth. He saw me looking at him and laid a hand on my cheek. "You're so hot, love."

I could only whimper. "Then don't cook and eat me."

That seemed to decide something, because next I knew, I was in his arms, being carried outside. Water misted on my skin, blessedly cool. Then a wave of salt water crashed over me, freezing and shattering. My wounds stung like broken glass grinding into them. I wailed and thrashed, but Zyr held on, wading into the waves. "I won't let you drown," he said. He cupped my head, holding my face above water, the rest of me submerged, both of us floating.

The night sky soared above, the stars dancing in all colors. "So pretty," I whispered. I lifted my good arm, trying to pluck one.

"What are you doing?"

"I want to give you a star." I reached again. "Too far. Will you fly me there?"

"Anywhere you want to go, gréine."

I giggled and snuggled against him. "I changed my mind. Let's stay here forever. It's cool here."

This time the sea monsters didn't chase me.

I WOKE AT one point, curled up again in the blankets. A large dog, golden-furred with floppy ears, licked my face, making me smile, and I drifted off again.

WHEN I NEXT woke, I stretched, the immediate rush of pain reminding me of where I was and all that had happened. But it hurt nothing like I remembered. I lifted my injured arm—and could, so that was a good sign?—and held it up to the weak light. A bandage I recognized as a piece of one of my shifts covered the wound now. Black stripes like the tributaries of a river crept out from under it and traveled toward my hand, and up the other direction, spreading over my shoulder like a spiderweb. By tilting my chin and craning my neck, I could make out a similar starburst of black radiating out from another bandage just over my left breast.

It looked really horrible. But I wasn't dead. At least, I didn't think so. How did the dead know? Did the Deyrr-animated creatures retain their thoughts? Trapped inside those blindly, soundlessly trudging bodies. I shuddered at the notion. I should've told Zyr to kill me instead of trying to save me if I was to become that.

Moving slowly, bracing on my good arm, I sat up and looked around. The fire had gone out and the light came entirely from the mouth of the cave, tumbled black rocks beyond, shining in bright day. The sea churned, but not so furiously, and the pounding of rain had gone.

So had Zyr.

That familiar panic rose up, the certainty that I'd been abandoned completely and at last. No reason for him to stay, especially when he had a mission to fulfill, a responsibility to his people. I wouldn't blame him for leaving me. I'd even told him to. And yet my heart pounded, fresh sweat breaking out in runnels between my breasts.

Breathe, I instructed myself. *All the stuff is here.*

Maybe he'd gone hunting. But what if he'd run into more of Deyrr's creatures? He might be dead, or alone and injured.

A shadow swept over the cave mouth and I froze.

Then Zyr walked in and I nearly collapsed with relief. He was his post-shift self, hair perfectly smooth and tied back, blue shirt laced and incongruously unwrinkled given the surroundings. He grinned, scanning me. "You're awake. How do you feel?"

Hastily, I gathered the blanket to cover my breasts, and when I met his gaze again, his smile had gone crooked with mischief. "I feel much better, thank you," I replied with considerable dignity, especially taking into account my undignified state. But I couldn't help glancing at my arm. "How bad of a sign is all of … this?"

Zyr crouched as he made the rest of the way to me under the low ceiling, then sat beside me, setting a bowl down. The scent of roasted meat filled the air and my hollow stomach growled. He chuckled and handed me a leg of something. I didn't even care what it was as I bit in with a complete lack of manners, the hot fat trickling down my chin.

"Slowly," Zyr advised. "Remember the puking thing. If you can," he amended.

I chewed and swallowed. "I remember." One memory surfaced. "Were you a floppy-eared dog at one point?"

He smiled—self-consciously?—and nodded. "I needed to keep you warm and calm, and get some sleep myself. I thought if you woke up, that form would scare you less than some of the others." Then his smile widened to a grin. "I thought about being a nice fuzzy bunny for you, but I was afraid you'd shoot me with your bow."

"My bow broke," I said, feeling its loss again.

"I know—I found the pieces. Was it special?"

"No. Kral took it from an Imperial Palace guard for me."

"Then why so sad, gréine?" He touched my cheek, fleetingly, and I recalled the way he'd rained kisses on my face. And how I'd said he was beautiful and begged him to kiss me for real. Said I'd wanted him. How humiliating. I didn't recognize myself anymore. Looking away from him, I stared at the cave entrance, willing the tears to stay back.

"I'm even less useful than before," I said, my voice small. "I have no bow, no way to help or defend myself. You should've left me here. You still should. Go on without me."

"This again?" He shook his head in disgust.

"I'm weak, and there's this *stuff* in me. It's Deyrr, isn't it? I'm going to become one of those monsters, aren't I?"

"We don't know that," Zyr replied, wrapping his arms around his knees. "You've fought off the worst of—"

"Don't lie to me," I bit out, interrupting his soothing words.

He raised one brow. "Maybe you *have* been corrupted, interrupting a man while he's talking and all."

"Oh, fuck off." I said it in Dasnarian, but the tone must've gotten through, because he looked shocked, then burst out laughing.

"You're definitely doing better. No, listen to me," he ordered sternly when I opened my mouth. "Yes, you got that Deyrr filth in you, mainly from those talons being in your arm so long, I think. The chest wound is much cleaner. You're lucky because I'm pretty sure that if you'd gotten that poisonous crap that close to your heart, then you would've died. You very nearly did, so be happy that you're alive. I know I am."

He gave me such a fierce look that I decided not to say anything to that just yet.

"We don't know what that stuff will do to you, it's true," he continued more gently. "But it's going to do it whether you're in this cave or not, alone or with me. So it only makes sense that you come with me and continue our mission."

"All of that is true," I replied, choosing my words carefully, "but we can't make decisions based on sentiment. If I continue with you, I'll be a liability. I'm weak. I can't draw a bow, even if I had one. You don't need me to read the mapsticks. You all said it before—they're designed for a shapeshifter in animal form to use. I'm extra weight and you have a long distance to fly. Without me, you don't have to take such a large form, so you won't be such a target."

"Are you done?" he inquired, all politeness except for the hardness in his eyes.

"You know I'm right. This is the logical thing to do. You're at war and there's no room for liabilities in a fight like that."

He leaned back on one elbow, apparently casual, stretching out his long legs and chewing on a piece of meat. "I'm betting this is the way of things in Dasnaria."

"It's the way of things everywhere," I snapped at him. I really wanted to eat more, but he had a point that my stomach needed time. Its churning could be either hunger or nausea—hard to tell which yet.

"Hmm. No. I don't believe you're correct in that, my lovely Dasnarian warrior." He tipped his head to look at me, expression full of some emotion I couldn't read. "Where I come from, people aren't categorized as either assets or liabilities. We are friends, partners, lovers, family—possibly enemies, though we're honest about that, too—and we don't decide who is useful or worthwhile. I'm never going to leave you behind. Every. Single. Time you suggest I'd even contemplate it, you insult me." He bit out each word so distinctly that I could hear the sharp clacking of the gríobhth's beak.

"I apologize," I replied stiffly. "I did not intend insult."

"You know what—this time I'll accept the apology." But he didn't look forgiving. "What do you take me for, Karyn? I wonder if you even see me as a man, one who might care about you. What am I in your world view—an asset or a liability? Maybe I'm like a puppy to you, nice to pet, but not someone with thoughts and feelings of his own. I've been taking care of you for four days, praying every moment that you wouldn't die, and you seem to think I'll just flit off now and leave you. No wonder you don't want me as a lover. Who'd want to be involved with someone like that?"

Stricken, I stared at the no longer appetizing food. Nausea seemed to have won the day, though not for the reasons I'd thought. "I…" I didn't know what to say.

"Something else you don't seem to have gotten through your thick skull is that this is *your* mission, too. You might not recognize the King and Queen of the Tala as yours, but they charged you to do this, not me. We all took you in and you're supposed to be helping fight this war, but you're too busy trying to find excuses to duck out of it. You don't fool me for a moment, with all your 'I'm useless' whining. You're not even trying. Maybe you *should* have stayed in Dasnaria and lived the life they planned for you. You sure aren't doing anything with the freedom you sacrificed so much to get."

I gaped at him, remembering to close my mouth. He sat up and scrubbed his hands over his face.

"I'm going for a swim. See if I can catch us some fish. The oils will be good for you. Eat some more when you're ready, and there's water beside you, and an empty bowl, in case you puke. I figure you can wipe your own ass now." He became the black panther and stalked out, the shimmering fury somehow perfectly part of his sleek and sinuous exit.

Leaving me alone with my puke bowl and the even more sour taste of regret.

NOTHING LIKE SITTING alone in a dank cave—it was definitely dank, no matter how Zyr talked it up—to make you tired of your own dismal thoughts. Taking my restlessness as a hint that I should move around, I found my clothes. Clean and dry. I sniffed them and they smelled of fresh water and grass. More of Zyr's thoughtfulness. And I'd been so horribly ungrateful.

Two of my shifts had disappeared, likely to make bandages and the cloths he'd used to cool my fevered skin. The image rushed back of me lying naked in the firelight, his face intent and haggard as he bathed me. I put only one shift on, saving the three remaining ones, then my dress. It seemed silly all of a sudden, to put on so many layers.

Nothing much made sense anymore. Zyr had seen me naked, had touched me everywhere, but he hadn't lost control of his lust. He'd kissed me, and wanted more, but stopped when I would've kept going. None of those rules I'd been taught had applied.

Heroes don't follow other people's rules.

I wonder if you even see me as a man.

Maybe I'm like a puppy to you, nice to pet, but not someone with thoughts and feelings of his own.

You're not even trying. Maybe you should have stayed in Dasnaria and lived the life they planned for you.

I wanted to shake those words out of my brain. Instead I made my way out of the cave, my body groaning in protest, stiff from lying still for so long. *Four days.* The light on the beach made me squint, but not painfully like the fever-induced sensitivity. Zyr had made another campfire out there, neatly dug in the gravel, with a spit for roasting.

I felt grimy and stinking, my hair greasy with old sweat. It was in a clumsy braid, tied off with my ribbon fashioned in a neat bow, and I realized Zyr must've done that, too, knowing I liked to keep it out of my face. Untying it, I laid the ribbon on a rock, then undressed again and carefully put my clean clothes on a dry boulder well above the tideline.

Determined not to be self-conscious or ashamed, I walked naked into the water. I would've said I'd never been naked outside before, but that would be deceiving myself, because I remembered in sharp, starlit fragments how Zyr had carried me into the water to cool me off. And purge the wounds he'd reopened. Almost certainly saving my life.

I'd wanted to give him a star and he'd promised to carry me anywhere I wanted to go.

Tears stung my eyes and I dove into the next wave, the cool shock familiar and cleansing. I swam a little, letting my body loosen and warm. I had no idea how to make amends with Zyr. It might well be too late, but I could at least embrace this mission. He'd been right that I'd behaved as if none of the responsibility fell to me. I'd been living with one foot still in Dasnaria, even to the point of thinking of selling information to get back to where I'd been.

To a life I'd come to loathe.

So easy to forget that, in my fear. Whining and finding excuses why I couldn't do the things people asked of me. Well, that would change. Zyr might never forgive me—I wouldn't blame him—but I could at least begin repaying the kindness people had shown me. And not to cozen them into taking care of me, but because they deserved more from me.

Something bumped me in the water, and I shrieked, losing my stroke and going under. The something nosed me, pushing me up, and I surfaced, sputtering out salt water. A porpoise surfaced next to me, tossing its nose in the air, making a laughing sound, the blue eyes full of familiar mischief.

He turned, nudging his dorsal fin into my good hand. I closed on it reflexively and he began swimming away—so I let go. He circled back, nudging his fin into my hand again. This time I grabbed on and held tight, the water streaming over me as he swam, faster and faster. I aligned my body closer to his, and he surged through the swells, never going all that deep or too far from the beach, but speeding up so it felt like a kind of flying.

Laughter pealed out of me, the sheer joy of swimming with him unlike anything I'd ever felt. He was right. I was alive and I should relish that.

~ 17 ~

I STIRRED THE fire, dispersing the flames to distribute the heat so the fish would cook more evenly. After I'd tired of swimming—which happened pretty quickly, even with Zyr doing all the work—he'd taken me back to the shallows, pointing me to a big fish he'd apparently left stranded in a tide pool. He took off again, presumably to find another. So I gutted and cleaned it, still naked, since it made no sense to dirty my gown for a modesty that felt increasingly false by the moment. Maybe it had been the swimming with him, but I hadn't been self-conscious when he was a porpoise. For someone like him, clothing was just a weird thing you did in human form and not otherwise. After I had it clean, I dressed, then mounted the fish whole on the spit over the smoldering coals.

It was restful enough, sitting in the sun, letting my hair dry and monitoring the fish. A splash in the surf caught my attention, and I saw porpoise-Zyr in the shallows, another big fish in his mouth. Tucking my skirts up high to keep them out of the water, I waded in and took the still wriggling fish from him.

As soon as I did, Zyr became a man, clean and dry, but for where the water surged around his knees. "Thank you," he said with a smile, taking the catch back from me. "Shifting back without bobbling the fish isn't easy."

Feeling shy for no good reason, I bent to rinse the fish slime off my hands in the surf, my unbound hair shifting and sliding like heavy, coiling threads of silk on my bare arms. Zyr deposited the new fish in the same tide pool he'd put the other in, then sniffed the air. "Smells good?"

He seemed tentative, too. Maybe we'd kind of made up during the swim, but the harsh human words we'd exchanged still hung in the air between us.

"Yes, this one should be about done. Shall I, I mean, we could cook this one, too?"

"Later. I thought we could eat the first and smoke this other for the journey across the water." He frowned a little, maybe thinking that had been a bad reference to make. "It was very nice of you to clean and cook the fish," he offered. "I hope you're not too tired."

"I'm tired, yes, but not too much. It feels good to move around."

"Good." He seemed to be casting about for something else to say.

"I liked the swim, too," I said, wondering if maybe I shouldn't have mentioned that, but he smiled broadly.

"Yes?"

"Yes. Very much."

We stood there, smiling at each other like idiots.

"Shall we eat?" I ventured.

"I'd like that," he answered, and it seemed he said something else under the words.

We worked together, easing the fish off the spit and onto a makeshift platter of driftwood, not easy with the skin cooked crisp and the meat meltingly soft and flaking. Because it was easier, we ended up simply putting the meal between us, plucking out tidbits with our fingers.

It tasted fresh as the ocean and full of delicious oils, something my body craved, as Zyr had accurately predicted. It might've been the best meal of my life, on the otherwise deserted beach in the sun, in the company of a man who'd cared enough to save my life. He'd protected and fed me, I realized, taken care of me in intimate ways my own husband never had, exhausting himself to do it. I'd been a fool, and now it might be too late.

I eyed him, wishing I looked prettier. Now that I wanted to attract him, I had no way to fix myself up.

"What's that look?" he asked, raising a brow. "Did I do something wrong?"

"It's not fair that you can shapeshift and have combed hair and neat clothing," I complained.

"If it were up to me, I'd teach you to shapeshift so you could do it to heal," he replied grimly.

I blushed, abashed that my sally had landed poorly. But I choked back the apology that wanted to spring to my lips. He wouldn't want to hear me apologize for him having to tend me while I was hurt. "I really appreciate that you saved my life," I said instead, hoping it was more the right thing. "You were amazing. I would've died if you hadn't thought to open and cleanse the wounds, to cool my fever in the ocean."

He gave me a crooked smile, then sobered. "I wasn't sure you'd remember that night. You were kind of out of your head. Scarily so."

"If I could give you a star, I would," I told him, meaning it—and hoping he could hear the words I was still too much of a coward to say.

"I'll just have to fly you high enough to pluck one," he replied, meeting my gaze, eyes full of emotion.

I took a breath. "I'm very sorry that I treated you badly. I was thoughtless."

He was already shaking his head. "No—I should apologize to you. I had no business taking your head off when you were barely awake and recovered. It was just…" He blew out a breath. "It was a long few days. I didn't handle it well."

"You did. You took care of me."

Tilting his head, he got a funny expression. "I've never had to do that, you know. When my sister Anya nearly died in childbirth—several times, as she insists on getting pregnant again and again—it was always Zynda who went to help. She was there when our mother died, too. You're right to think of me as flighty."

"I never said that."

His mouth twisted in a wry, rueful grimace. "Karyn, gréine, you didn't have to. It was clear in every argument you posed against having sex with me. Besides, it's true. You're looking for permanence. A real life with babies and someone to take care of you. I came right out and told you I'm not that man."

"You have a right to not want that kind of life."

"You don't understand," he replied with bitterness. "If I've fathered children, I don't know about them, because their mothers knew they couldn't count on me. I've never been the one people could depend on like that. I'm not… good at it."

I needed to handle this very carefully. "I think… I'm discovering that I should be thinking about taking care of myself. When I can. And I have to point out that you've been taking very good care of me when I couldn't."

He studied me, smiling more, though crookedly. "I suppose that's true."

"Though I suppose your ethics—the values you spoke of— wouldn't let you do otherwise, when there was no one else here to help me."

His smile faded. "I took care of you because I wanted to, not because of some set of ethics."

I held out a hand to him, nervous that he'd refuse, but he took it in both of his, folding his long fingers around mine, keeping me close. "I do want babies," I told him. "Someday. But I think that maybe permanence is an illusion. With this war, everything we face, I'd like to try relishing the moment. Being happy to be alive." I looked at him meaningfully, willing him to receive my unspoken message.

He lifted one hand and tucked a strand of hair behind my ear. "You didn't braid your hair."

"No." I tugged away from our joined hands to snag the ribbon nearby. He watched, bemused, as I tied it around his wrist. "I'd like you to have this, as a memento of sorts. And I'll leave my hair loose, since you like it that way. Though it would be prettier if I could truly wash and comb it."

"You've never looked more beautiful," he said, his voice hoarse, and he cleared his throat. Holding his wrist out, he examined the bow, touching the silken ribbon with a strange expression.

"It's silly, I know," I said in a rush. I'd overstepped and done a foolishly sentimental thing. "It will disappear the next time you shift."

"No, it won't." He took my hands again, his gaze fierce on mine. "Zynda has precious things she's learned to keep with her when she shifts and comes back. If she can, I can."

Impossibly moved, torn between laughing and tearing up, I smiled. "You referred to a *thing* without sounding disgusted by it."

He blinked, then burst out laughing. "So I did. Apparently this is what comes of keeping company with mossbacks."

I made a face. "I probably do have moss on my back, being laid up for so many days and bathing only in seawater."

He gave me a very serious look. "I've examined every bit of your soft, lovely skin and I can vouch that it's perfect and flawless."

Yes, I blushed. But I also didn't mind so much. "You promised you wouldn't look," I pointed out, in my most prim tone.

"I didn't!" he protested, sounding injured and falsely accused, but his eyes sparkled with mischief. "I verified entirely by touch, keeping my eyes closed the whole time."

"Zyr!" I yanked my hands away, and he let me go, instead slipping close to me so fast that I gasped, his hands cupping my face. His eyes blazing and intent, he kissed me, lightly and almost chastely—if not for the burning desire so evident in his expression. I waited for him to deepen the kiss, but he didn't. Instead he moved away again. "You should rest," he told me. "You're still recovering."

I wanted to protest that I was fine, but I did feel unbearably drowsy. "I'm not sure I can bear to go back in the cave," I said, then yawned.

He chuckled. "It *is* pretty dank, I'll admit. Sleep here. I'll watch over you."

Because I trusted that he would, I laid down on the sun-warmed gravel and sank into healing sleep.

WE BUILT UP the campfire as evening fell. While I slept, Zyr had cleaned the other fish, sliced it into strips and smoked them over a low fire. He left me to keep an eye on it when I awoke, and took off in the form of an eagle, returning with another creature, already skinned so I couldn't tell what it had been.

"How did you skin it in eagle form?" I asked.

He gave me a sideways look. "My beak?"

I laughed, shaking my head. "I bet you did that thing where you shifted your fingers into sharp claws and used them like a knife. That's how you sliced up the fish, too, isn't it?"

He looked at the skinned animal, as if it might have an answer, then shook his head. "Do you remember *everything* from when you were fevered?"

"Yes," I said firmly. He gave me an opaque glance and I became suspicious. "Not really. Only flashes of things. Why—is there something you're not telling me?"

"Of course not," he replied too easily. He held up one hand and the fingers extended into long, razor sharp claws. He began neatly carving up the meat, handing the pieces to me to put on the spit. "My being able to shift selectively is generally considered a secret," he said, mentioning it oh-so-casually.

"Is it?" I recalled Andi's remarks about Tala secrets and her surprise that Zyr had told me as much as he had already. "You didn't seem to be hiding it from me. I figured it's a shapeshifter thing."

"My sexiest talent, and she takes it for granted," he lamented, shaking his head, then grinned at me. "Zynda can do it. A few others, but it's one of our more powerful skills. Most of the time we keep it subtle—make our eyes more like a long-sighted raptor's to see a far distance. Make our nose inside more like a hound's to better discern scent."

"Make your voice all growly to scare mossbacks," I added.

He had the grace to look abashed. "Yes, well, sometimes it's not an entirely controlled thing. Emotions can make it get away from us, which is one reason we keep the ability quiet, even among shapeshifting brethren."

"What are other reasons?"

He shrugged a little, concentrating on his carving, but I

thought he seemed… embarrassed? "It's monstrous," he admitted. "Becoming an animal is one thing—they're a natural part of the world—but being only part human is unnatural." He still didn't look at me.

"You showed me the gríobhth form and that's not exactly a natural animal."

"True." He shook his head at some thought. "That was an impulse of the moment."

"Why did you?" I asked softly.

He finally looked at me, bringing me the rest of the meat and tossing the remnants into the waves. "I wanted to impress the pretty girl, of course."

"There are lots of pretty girls," I said, carefully threading the meat onto the spit.

"Also true."

"So why am I different?"

He didn't reply immediately, so I glanced up at him. He was studying me, as if searching for the answer. "An excellent question," he finally said. "I think the bits on this end are done." He plucked them off, put them in a bowl and handed it to me. "Do you think you'll have the strength to ride tomorrow to at least the point where we'll head across the water? I don't think it's too far."

"Yes." I'd make sure I did. "All I have to do is sit there, after all."

"If only. The real trick will be getting off this beach and in the air again."

Oh. I hadn't thought of that. In the press of escaping the Deyrr birds, he hadn't landed on a high place to take off from again. "Is it even possible?"

"Yes." He sounded like I had, also grimly determined.

I bit my tongue on the impulse to point out he'd have an

easier time without me on his back. I wouldn't be so careless with him again. It made me think, though. "What if more Deyrr creatures find us?"

"I'll outfly them," he said with confidence, making himself comfortable on a log. "If I start to speed up, just lie flat and hold on."

"I wish I had a bow," I fretted. "Even that one was better than nothing."

"You didn't like it?"

"Well, it was a man's bow and standard Imperial issue, so decent enough, but not special. Not like the one I left at home."

"I didn't know it mattered. I thought they were all the same."

"Oh no. Mine was carved from a very expensive and rare wood that's both tough and flexible, and made just for me—so the length and draw suited me perfectly. I could hit anything with that bow," I said wistfully. "Best gift I ever received."

"Did Kral give it to you?" Zyr sounded idly curious, the way he did when he really wanted to know something. Surely he wasn't jealous.

I laughed, though, at the very notion. "Kral would *never* have given me such a gift. It would be highly inappropriate, possibly even something the emperor could interpret as treason, arming a woman. No, Kral always sent me perfectly appropriate gifts of clothing and jewelry, all selected by his mother, Her Imperial Majesty. And she loathed me, so she made sure none of them suited me." I hadn't thought of those off-handedly cruel gifts in a long time. The empress could easily have delegated that task to one of her servants, but the specific wrongness of everything she sent me had been a malicious reminder of her lack of regard. If nothing else, the empress was a master of the subtle art of delivering insult, and some of those gifts had spoken so eloquently of her opinion of me that I'd had to burn them. They'd conveyed a warning, too, that Kral would never truly be my husband, even if the emperor lifted his edict.

And that I'd never be empress. I supposed I'd understood that on some level, that Empress Hulda would've seen me dead before I took her place.

"How could anyone hate you?" Zyr asked, cocking his head and studying me, as if searching for the reason.

"Very easily, I'm sure." I wrinkled a nose for his flattery. "But as we only ever met a few times, it was really a matter of principle." I could see that more clearly now, too, that her hatred and relentless campaign to undermine my confidence had nothing to do with me personally. "You know—she's the sort of mother who treats her son like a substitute husband, doting on him and wanting his love and attention all to herself."

"Hmm." Zyr sounded like he didn't know.

"How long ago did your mother pass away?" I asked, trying to find gentle phrasing while desperately wanting to change the subject.

"Oh, a while now, but not that long. I haven't counted the years," he replied carelessly, but he stirred the gravel at his feet with a stick, making circles. "But she wasn't like Kral's mother at all. She didn't want my love and attention. Not from a boy who became a gríobhth in the cradle."

That still unsettled me, the idea of an infant shapeshifting— and yet, how adorable would a baby gríobhth be? All kitten fur, fuzzy down, and big blue eyes. "I don't understand why that's bad," I ventured.

He flashed me a wry smile. "I suppose you wouldn't. It's a complicated history."

I gestured to the campfire, the still light sky. "We have time, and you said you'd tell me more of your story."

"Teach me to make glib promises," he muttered, but he scooted off the log and settled on the gravel, stretching out his long legs and crossing them at the ankle, leaning back with his hands folded comfortably over his belly. "My mother was the Sorceress Queen Salena's sister—the Salena who was mother to Queen Andromeda, and the others."

"I remember. That's why you call them cousins."

"Yes, the Tala aren't so much for royalty, not like Dasnarians, apparently." He slid me a wicked smile, but I didn't take the bait. "But we are about power. The more magic we can do, the more forms we can take, the more... rank we have. Salena—she had it all. Magic, foresight, an incredible range of forms. That's part of how she became queen. With us, the most powerful become our rulers. My mother, well, she didn't have much ability. No magic, a few forms, nothing like her sister."

"Ah." I understood that kind of jealousy.

He nodded. "So she devoted herself to producing powerful babies. She mated with the most powerful sorcerers and prolific shapeshifters. But compatibility is an issue. We've all lived inside the magic barrier for so long that we're terribly inbred."

"That's why the babies don't thrive," I commented. When he raised a brow at me, I explained. "It happens in some of the Dasnarian ruling families—they're so intent on keeping their lands and power within the family that they marry brothers to sisters. After a few generations, the babies are born dead, or twisted, or both."

He stared at me a moment, lip curling. "Now I have an image in my head of bedding my sisters and... eh." He shuddered. "Thanks a lot for that. Anyway, my mother endured a lot of miscarriages—and babies that didn't survive long—before she bore Anya, my older sister. Anya was born healthy and lived to adulthood, but she's, if anything, even less powerful than my mother was. But my mother stuck with the same mate—since at least they were compatible enough to produce a healthy baby, and the magic isn't predictable, who it settles on and who it doesn't—and she conceived Zynda and me."

I blinked. "You're twins?"

"You didn't know? No reason you would," he mused before I could answer. "Yes, a miracle in our small world, healthy twins, and both of us born with indications that we'd have magic aplenty. Zynda shapeshifted first—she always has to be the best at everything—and became a baby hummingbird. You can imagine the trouble that caused."

I could. "How do you manage a baby like that?" I asked, fascinated.

He smiled, a fondly nostalgic curve to it. "We slept and played inside gauze nets. Some of my first memories are watching those white curtains blow in the breeze." His smile faded. "Then my own First Form manifested and my mother gave up on me."

"But why?"

"I could never be King of the Tala. Not with a First Form like that. The Tala would never accept me. Not like King Rayfe with his noble wolf First Form. A born leader, as it were." He didn't sound bitter about it, though, just amused. He cocked a brow at me. "You've seen for yourself. The gríobhth is… not easily controlled. I can lose myself to it."

"I think you control it and yourself just fine," I said staunchly.

He smiled a little, but sadly. "Zynda… My mother held out hope for her to be queen, but even when we were children, Zynda wasn't interested. She loves to be best, but she also loves the freedom of shapeshifting. She never wanted to rule. When Salena left us, my mother and Zynda had a terrible fight about it. It drove Zynda to the shamans, for which I've never forgiven my mother."

"The shamans are bad?" I asked.

"They're the ones who cooked her brain into thinking taking Final Form is a good idea." He shook his head. "She categorically refused to consider competing for the crown, but she'll sacrifice her freedom to be locked in a dragon's body for all time. Thick-skulled heroic idiot."

I didn't know what to say to that. He didn't seem to need me to.

"Then my mother kept trying and trying for new and better children, and ultimately died for it. There's a waste of a life for you."

"What about your father?"

"Him?" Zyr shrugged, elaborately. "Never knew him. Mother wouldn't say, and he wasn't interested in being more involved than depositing his seed. Like father, like son, eh?"

I didn't return the smile, fake as it was. "It's a sad story. My father is the one who gave me the bow, and taught me to shoot. Not common in Dasnaria, but he loved me and wanted me happy. My mother, too."

"Except they sold you into a sexless, loveless marriage."

I nearly asked which aspect bothered him more. Instead, I pondered the truth of his words. "I know that it's as hard for you to understand what my parents wanted for me as it is for me to understand how your parents treated you. In Dasnaria, there aren't a lot of options for girls. Among the small array of finite futures for me, being married in name only to the brother of the emperor was truly one of the best. I lived at home, with my family, and never had to live full-time in a seraglio with, for example, a mother-in-law who loathed me and had a reputation for skill with poison. I'm not at all sure that's worse than growing up feeling like my parents didn't love me enough to even care what happened to me."

Zyr considered me for a long moment, then looked away. "The meat looks ready," he said and dished it out into bowls. We ate in silence, he sunk in his thoughts and me turning over what he'd told me, wondering if I'd been too harsh. Feeling like I needed to say something more.

"No wonder you don't want babies," I finally said. "Or to know about them, if you have fathered any." He raised a brow at me, so I went on doggedly. "Who could blame you, with so much pressure? So much potential for sorrow. Maybe Zynda wants to take Final Form to do her part to make up for all those lost children."

"And I scatter my seed to the wind, making sure I don't have to witness the results?" He tried to sound mocking, but I heard the old grief beneath.

"I think you'd make an excellent father," I said. "If you decided you wanted to."

He took a deep breath and leveled a long look at me. "I…" He seemed to think better of whatever he'd been about to say. "We should get some sleep. It's a warm night—shall we sleep out here? I can take panther form."

"I don't want you to drain your energy before the long flight." He seemed like he'd been in other forms a lot the last few days. How much was too much?

He smiled, somewhat grim. "It will be all right. Sleeping beside you as an animal removes… certain temptations."

My turn to take a deep breath. "Maybe we should change that."

He eyed me. "What are you saying?"

Now or never. He wasn't taking my hints, so I'd have to be brave and just say it.

"I'm saying I want you to take my virginity. I want it to be you."

~ 18 ~

THE LOOK HE gave me wasn't pleased. It had a hint of sharpness in it, the way he'd looked when he said I'd given him insult. "You make me sound like a thief poised to rob you."

"I didn't mean it that way. The translation is bad—I don't know how else to phrase it," Why did this have to be so difficult? After all his flirtation and efforts to seduce me, he should simply take this out of my hands. I tried again. "I mean I want to be your lover. I'm accepting your offer."

He'd already started shaking his head, one hand straying to the ribbon I'd tied onto his wrist, plucking at it as if he'd like to get it off. "That's not a good idea."

The beach seemed to drop a little beneath me, humiliation staining my cheeks hot. "I see." No doubt my being so unkempt and unlovely repelled him. And seeing me so ill, having to—how had he put it? Wipe my ass—had destroyed all attraction. It was one reason women kept to the seraglio, so the men only saw them perfectly and beautifully presented. "I understand," I said, then realized I'd repeated myself.

"Get some sleep, gréine," he said gently. "I'll clean things up."

I wrapped myself in the blankets he brought and lay there with my eyes closed.

But it was a long time before I could sleep.

AT ONE POINT during the night, something woke me, and I startled at the feel of velvety fur under my hand. A familiar purr welled up, the big cat stretching and curling into me, cupping my hand in his curled paws, only a hint of the prick of claws carefully sheathed. The night had cooled, but his heat warmed me. I snuggled closer, musing vaguely how much the purr of the panther sounded like the gríobhth's.

IN THE MORNING, Zyr was back in human form before I woke, making me wonder if I'd dreamed of cuddling with him as the panther. But I never dreamed, so I didn't think so. A mist had come in during the night, making everything cool and gray.

"Good morning." Zyr smiled at me with his usual charm, as if he hadn't rejected me the night before. Though I supposed I'd managed to be polite to him after rejecting his advances so many times. Had he felt this crushed? He hadn't seemed like it, but if I'd learned anything about Zyr, it was that his mischievous carelessness covered quite a lot of pain. Maybe he'd just meant that sex last night wasn't a good idea and hadn't meant *never*. My eyes fell to his wrist, where I'd tied my ribbon in such a ridiculous burst of sentiment—and it was gone. I shouldn't feel so bruised. After all, it was only a silly bit of ribbon, without any real value.

"How do you feel?" Zyr asked. His smile had dimmed at whatever of my thoughts showed in my face.

"I feel good," I answered with forced cheer. No mooning

like a heartsick maiden. "Rested and ready for our adventure."

Fortunately, he accepted that at face value, handing me a bowl of leftover fish, and indicating the mapsticks he'd laid out where he'd been dragging the stick through the gravel the night before. Fog shrouded the beach, obscuring everything beyond a few arms' lengths, and brought a bit of chill with it. It seemed like a bad omen to me, but I didn't say so.

"Come look at this," he said, and I obliged, studying what he'd done. They hadn't been random circles at all, but some sort of map of his own. "I've been thinking about this. The departure point isn't all that far beyond where we are now, and from what I recall of flying over this area, we're not going to find another high point for me to take off from. Getting off the ground here will be effort enough that I'd rather not try it more than once. Do you have any objection to us simply striking out across the water once we reach this point?" He poked at it with the stick, and it did indeed seem relatively close.

"I thought you wanted a full night of rest before heading across the water," I ventured with some hesitation.

He shook that off as unimportant. "We've lost so much time here that I don't think I'd rest well anyway. Who knows what's going on back at Annfwn?" He gazed down the coast, as if he could see through the morning mists to the cliff city. "I don't think we're going to find much of anything in n'Andana, if that's even where these mapsticks lead."

"How will you know it's n'Andana if there's nothing there?"

"An excellent question. I suppose it would be too much to hope it's got a big sign saying so, hmm?" He grinned at me, though it lacked his usual humor.

"And I still don't understand how we can find it if it's been hidden all this time."

He shrugged. "Well, the sorcerers and scholars have worked

this out and understand it better than I do, but the way some enchantments work is you have to approach from a particular direction." He tapped the mapsticks. "Which is what these tell us. Also, the thinking goes like this. Deyrr and n'Andana were at war for a very long time, and the ancients of n'Andana implemented a last-ditch solution—they took all the magic in the world and condensed it in a place that's now Annfwn. So they could starve Deyrr of the magic that made them such a terrible enemy."

That kind of extreme solution sounded like something out of a Dasnarian tale, so I could believe it. "So n'Andana starved of magic, too?"

He nodded. "Exactly. And dragons are magic, so the people who'd taken Final Form couldn't shift back to human, so they either died or hibernated beneath the volcanoes."

That explained a great deal. "But there was still magic in Annfwn."

"Well, yes—but likely that was a mistake. It seems the Tala were probably n'Andanans who didn't want to live without magic, so they manipulated the rules and lived within a very small dome of magic."

Lawless and wild. I'd known it all along. But I didn't say so to Zyr. "So, if n'Andana was outside that dome of magic, why didn't anyone find it?"

"There are ways of making spells that last forever, by embedding them in objects—or in the land itself—so that they're self-sustaining. They can't be changed or made to do more than that, but they can keep going forever."

I thought of the Imperial Seraglio and how it stayed warm and green forever. Magic from a time when it was everywhere, perhaps.

"So it could be n'Andana was cloaked in some spell that

made everyone forget it existed, and didn't notice it when they did see it. Then that changed when the barrier around Annfwn expanded outward, bringing magic to everything inside again," Zyr continued.

"Like putting a spark to a pile of kindling," I ventured.

"Good analogy." He poked at his map in speculation. "It could be they forgot about us, too—or didn't know—so our arrival will be a big surprise. Still, best case scenario, if we do lead back a league of reinforcements, they'll do Annfwn no good if Deyrr has already overtaken it."

"Do you have a bad feeling?" I asked, mirroring his worried frown.

Giving me a half smile, he shrugged, but only a little. "I told you, foresight is not one of my gifts."

"But something is bothering you."

"Yes." His frown drowned out what little smile he'd managed. "Not about this, though. I dreamed of being a dragon."

I didn't quite follow his concern at first, then I understood. "Zynda?"

He started to nod, then stopped, scrubbing hands over his face. "I don't know. We've never been twins like that, and yet… You dreamed, too. What were yours?"

"I don't dream," I replied automatically.

He produced a knowing grin. "So you claim, but I know you do. Maybe you just don't remember them."

I decided not to argue about that. If I had dreams, I'd remember them, so for him to claim otherwise was silliness. I could at least be agreeable—and keep my insecurities to myself. After all, I had been the cause of the delay, and he clearly didn't want to spend any more time alone with me than he had to. I'd refused him—multiple times—so I could hardly assume the tragic role of the heartbroken maiden. I'd see this mission through, make my attempt to do something worthwhile, and then… go on with my life somehow.

Surely I'd find a man who wanted me, out there somewhere. The idea that I couldn't picture anyone but Zyr touching me was a temporary one, born of my own infantile attachment to the first man who'd put himself out to care for me.

"I'm fine with your plan," I told him. The sooner we left, the sooner we'd be done.

WE LEFT EVERYTHING we didn't absolutely need behind in the cave, nestled in a cache above the tideline. That included the extra blankets, changes of clothes for me, my useless quiver, and all but one flask of water. The dried fish fortunately weighed very little—which, upon reflection, must've been Zyr's clever foresight. His apparently carefree ways seemed to be anything but.

"Just enough fresh water for you," Zyr said. "I can go a while without it."

"We're crossing salt water. What if you do need it and we've run out?"

He gave me a cocky grin that didn't reach his eyes, the blue still muddied with worry. "There's ways around that."

"Such as?" I persisted, feeling mulish, but his tendency to leave out details couldn't be good.

"Same solution to if I tire before we reach land—I'll have to land on the water and shift to porpoise form. I can sleep in that form—and keep swimming—as well as drink and eat. If that happens, you know now how to hold on, yes?"

Oh. That swim I'd thought so spontaneous—even a joyful

connecting—had been simply another lesson. I'd very badly misinterpreted everything about Zyr. *This* was the reason for rules and etiquette. If I'd stayed within propriety, I wouldn't have made any of these blunders, wouldn't be so knotted up in my heart and mind…

"Karyn?" Zyr frowned.

"Sorry—I mean, yes, I can do that." I didn't ask my myriad questions: what happened when my strength gave out, how I would sleep in the middle of the ocean while holding onto a porpoise. More than ever it made more sense for him to leave me behind. And I felt compelled to say so. "But I want to say something. Hear me out and don't be angry as I truly mean no insult. You should go across the water as the porpoise. Then you don't have to worry about food and water, or having the strength to take flight from this beach. I'll be fine here and you can come back for me. I don't see how this doesn't make the most sense."

His eyes glittered with irritation, but he kept his reply deliberately reasonable. "You're forgetting two things. In porpoise form I can't read the mapsticks, so I won't be able to course-correct. And second, you're needed on this mission. Queen Andromeda said so. You're supposed to be with me, wherever we end up."

"You believe in her that much?" I replied, with some impatience. So much to stake on magical visions of a future that didn't exist because it hadn't occurred yet.

"I do. If you don't trust me to take care of you—and I don't blame you for that—trust in her multiple visions of the future in which you play a critical role."

Stricken, I knotted my hands together, wishing I had something to do with them, wanting most to reach out and touch him, to soothe the hurt he didn't show. "I do trust you," I told him as earnestly as I could.

He snorted, something between a huff and a growl. "Are you ready?" he asked.

I checked all the things hanging from my belt. If Zyr had to change form, I'd be the one to keep our supplies. "Yes."

HE'D WARNED ME it would be a rough start, but I still wasn't prepared. It didn't help that the fog hadn't burned off. To get the lift he needed, Zyr picked a clear stretch of beach and started running. At first, he kept his wings swept back, half-mantled and streamlined against the wind of our passage as he galloped faster and faster. As he'd bid me, I lay flat and low against his neck, the feathers sleek against my skin, and it seemed we ran through nothingness. The lion's body ran faster than I could've imagined, and seeing the ground rush past seemed so much worse than flight. If I tumbled off at this speed, I'd surely break my neck.

Finally I closed my eyes to it, beseeching Moranu to assist Her shapeshifting son, and tried to imagine myself as light as possible. I felt the wind resistance change as Zyr spread his wings, the gradual lift as he poured on speed. Then, as the tumbling thud of his paws against the gravel ceased, the massive surge of his shoulder muscles beneath me as his great wings labored to gain the altitude we needed.

We skimmed over the water, his chest heaving to draw breath to fuel his muscles. Zyr had warned me about this, too, that he'd go for the water because if we crashed, it would be a softer landing. And that he'd take his time to gain height as he felt he could. Still, the spray of mist against my face reminded me of that other flight when the Deyrr creatures drove us to the beach, and my heart hammered in remembered fear.

At any moment, I expected Zyr to falter, for him to drop—gradually or abruptly—into the hungry, misty waves. But, so infinitesimally that I didn't perceive the change for quite some time, he left the water behind, and had turned so that we paced the coast. I'd expected a more stark moment of relief than that—a sudden realization that we'd made it—instead of the gradual relaxation and alleviation of the fear of immediate crashing.

Remembering my one job, I pulled out the relevant mapstick, watching for the landmark we'd identified. Zyr had told me to keep it and let him know, mostly so I'd feel useful, I rather thought.

We came upon it much sooner than I expected, a spur of rocks into the water that wasn't quite as dramatic as the mapstick depicted, even with the wood rounded from all the hands, claws, and talons that had held it. In fact, I almost doubted, thinking maybe we should go on a bit to see if there might be a bigger one. Though that would add on to Zyr's time in the air. It would've been much easier if the sun had burned off the fog and given me a better view of the rest of the coastline.

But Zyr had left it up to me to decide—and this long line of jagged boulders seemed to be pointing in the right direction. A strange landscape feature along the otherwise smooth and curving stretch of beach. Hoping I wasn't making a mistake, I tapped Zyr on his furry shoulder and pointed at the line of rocks. He nodded, oriented his flight to the direction they seemed to point, and headed out over the open sea.

WE FLEW FOR hours. When the sun burned off the fog sufficiently—or Zyr flew high enough to leave the fog behind, as
tendrils of it still swooped and swirled below us—I soon
regretted wishing for it. The rays seemed to beat down on us
with greater intensity than I'd remembered. Zyr's body grew wet
with sweat, especially where I sat or lay against him, so I tried to
adjust my riding position to give airflow to different places.

As hot as I felt, I could only imagine how it was for him,
doing all the work. Occasionally I ate a bite of fish, sipping at the
water judiciously. I needed to make the water last, yes, but I also
had absolutely no intention of peeing on Zyr's back. One
humiliation—and insult to my host—that I could avoid with a
bit of planning. Occasionally he ate some fish, too, turning his
head to take a piece from me, remarkably careful with that sharp
beak that could easily sever my fingers.

Perhaps I felt the heat so because of remaining dregs of the
fever. Weariness plagued me, and I fought to stay awake. All we
needed was for me to drift off and plunge into the ocean. Then
we'd be forced to travel porpoise-style and I didn't relish that
prospect a bit. As the sun crossed the sky, we seemingly stayed
at the same fixed point, with no sign of land in any direction,
and only endless water beneath. I knew it had to be an illusion.
I'd been out of sight of land before on the *Hákyrling*. Something
about being on the sailing ship, however, had given me a sense
of forward momentum. And my traveling companions had been
able to point to maps and say where we were.

Here the mapsticks failed me. They had no features to reveal. Perhaps the number of them indicated the relative distance,
but we had no way of knowing what. I fervently wished Zyr
hadn't told me the ones we'd identified so far hadn't been
directly proportional to our distance traveled. What if we had to
fly for days? Even if Zyr's strength held out, it seemed it would

corrupt his mind to stay in gríobhth form so long.

By midafternoon, a headache formed behind my eyes and at the base of my skull. I tried to ignore it, but the one thing that helped, closing my eyes against the burning sun and glittering sea, dragged me down into beckoning sleep. So I forced my lids open, counting Zyr's wingbeats, matching them to my pulse, and relentlessly revisiting every bad decision I'd ever made—beginning with agreeing to go on this mission in the first place.

Who was I kidding? I wasn't made of heroic material. I'd been born to be an ornament and I should've stuck to my strengths.

Zyr flew on tirelessly, so I tried to emulate his determination. All I had to do was sit there. It shouldn't be all that difficult. As the sun set, however, with no sign of land, I began to seriously fret. I wouldn't be able to stay awake. And Zyr had accelerated. At first I hadn't been sure of my senses, but counting his wingbeats against my heartbeats confirmed it. He'd sped up because he, too, worried that we wouldn't make land.

After a while, well after full night had fallen, he did begin to tire. I could feel it in him. His breathing had grown labored and his head drooped from time to time.

Now would be the perfect opportunity for an attack, if the agents of Deyrr had some way to track us, although the previous attack had seemed a matter of opportunity on their part and bad luck on ours. Dinner conversations between my brothers and father came back to me, how they chortled over running some enemy troops ragged, staying just close enough to keep them from pausing to eat or rest. Then, when their opponents could go no longer, our side would swoop in on them and dispatch them all. The despair of exhaustion, my father had said, did more to defeat an enemy army than any weapon.

I finally understood, deep in my weary bones, exactly what

they meant.

Zyr faltered under me—not hugely, but just enough to bobble in the air and shock me to full alertness.

"It's time to take porpoise form," I shouted. In the moonless night, illuminated only by the fantastic wheel of stars above, I could see only the silhouette of his head as he shook it, refusing me. At least he understood my words. I'd worried maybe he'd become all beast. But a wise beast would stop flying, wouldn't it? I didn't know if the gríobhth would think of becoming a porpoise. "Zyr," I wheedled, trying another tactic, "can't we go down to the water? I'm afraid I'll fall."

But he ignored me.

Sighing to myself, I gave up counting and looked at the stars. Up in the sky like this, it seemed as if we flew through a globe of stars. Once I'd seen a crystal globe with glittering flakes of mineral floating in the fluid inside, like gold and silver snowfall around a fairytale castle. This could be like that, only the stars came in every color. I'd always thought of them as a pure white, but they weren't. The more I looked, the more I perceived their jeweled array of light. They even twinkled in reflection off the sea below, as if we flew through an endless night sky.

I'd never seen anything more beautiful. And it was me, foolish Karyn, riding on a mythical beast through a sky no one else had ever seen like this. A feeling of joyful peace settled over me. Even if I didn't survive, I'd at least lived long enough to see this.

DESPITE MY BEST efforts, I must've dozed off, because I jerked awake when Zyr dropped sharply. I cried out, grabbing ahold of him, and he rebalanced enough that I didn't fall. He breathed heavily, and his great heart pounded so hard that it seemed to throb against my calves where I clasped his sweat-soaked torso.

"Zyr, you *have* to rest," I begged.

He shook his head again, sharply, then seemed to be pointing his beak. I couldn't see anything different… But wait. There—was that darkness among the stars? Land. And then I smelled it. I never knew what the stories meant about the scent of land, but after so long with only the sea-salt saturated air around us, the scent of earth and green leaves stood out like beacons.

"Land!" I shouted, as if I'd been the one to discover it. Zyr wheezed out a sound of agreement, clearly all he could muster from an exhausted body. "You can make it," I told him, patting his shoulder. Silly of me, because of course he'd know that better than I, but I felt I had to contribute something. "You're incredible. So strong and brave, the most beautiful creature I've ever seen. No one else could've made this journey."

Perhaps it was my imagination, but he seemed to fly faster, gradually descending, his breathing still labored, but his flight smooth and steady once again.

At the end, though, it seemed to my admittedly lean experience that we came in too fast. I couldn't see the ground well in the darkness with my human eyes and only hoped the gríobhth had sharper night vision. There were rocks, for sure, because I could hear surf crashing against them.

Zyr came in hot, mostly gliding on arched wings, only closing them in a downstroke occasionally, mostly to slow us, I thought. Still too fast, though, like when the Deyrr birds had chased us, not his artful, graceful landings at other times.

I braced myself to tumble, angling for my uninjured side so I could maybe avoid reopening those wounds, if I didn't crack my head open.

We hit ground with a mighty thump, Zyr trying to run to scrub off the speed, wings flapping and arched forward, but he stumbled. Caught himself. Not enough. He stumbled again, then went head down, almost somersaulting with a great crack of something. I went flying—but did manage to land on my good side, rolling several times on something blissfully soft.

I hadn't quite gathered my wits or my breath, but I struggled to hands and knees, driven by concern for Zyr. He should've been in man-shape by now, coming to haul me to my feet and tease me about being worried.

Wherever we were, it was pitch black, the kind of matte darkness of trees around us, blotting out the glitter of starlight. Listening, I made out the pained wheeze of Zyr's breathing and crawled toward it. That way I'd at least be less likely to stumble and fall. My hands found his wing first, and he gave a harsh cry, half raptor, half lion. Gentling my hands, I traced my way along the big, feather-covered bone, gasping when I hit spiky shards, and he cried again, piteously this time. He'd shattered it—and bent it backward, because I had to reverse direction to make my way to his body. My eyes must've been adjusting to the darkness as I could make him out better. Being able to see didn't help, however. In fact, despair rushed back in at the sight of him twisted back against those beautiful wings, his long neck at a wrong angle. He hissed at me, clacking his beak—so I stayed carefully clear of it.

"Zyr, you have to shift back to human," I told him. "You'll heal. Just shift and it will be fine."

His eyes rolled, showing the white, and his head dropped to the ground. Heedless of being bit, I rushed to his head, lifting it and laying the surprisingly heavy weight in my lap. Feeling useless, I patted what would be cheeks on a human, as if I could revive him. Nothing. How did one save a dying gríobhth? The question sounded like a riddle from a terrible myth.

Fortunately, the water flask secured to my belt had survived the fall, the metal only a little dented. I still had half left, so I dribbled some into the crack of his beak. He didn't move, and I was afraid to pour so much in that I made him choke. Why didn't I at least have some healing skills?

All right, think, I instructed myself. No brilliant ideas came to me. I looked around, as if some sort of miraculous cure would present itself, then realized—my exhaustion-muddled brain finally catching up—that I could see better because dawn approached. We'd flown all day and nearly all night. We'd made it to land, only to have Zyr be hurt so badly he couldn't shift back.

What had he said about Zynda becoming the hummingbird to save her life? Marskal had fed her sugar water and she'd eventually shifted back to human, but she'd almost been a bird too long. But she'd at least been a healthy hummingbird, right? Not the broken thing wheezing in my lap. I needed help and there was none to be had.

Zyr had saved my life, but I wouldn't be able to return the great gift. I cursed myself in Dasnarian, disgusted with yet another failure to be even remotely useful.

"I'm pretty sure the lap of the virgin thing only works with unicorns," an amused voice said, also in Dasnarian. "Though stranger things have happened."

~ 19 ~

A GROUP OF armored Dasnarian soldiers surrounded us, somehow having snuck up on me in the pre-dawn dimness. Lowered helms obscured their faces, broadswords drawn and leveled at me and Zyr made their intentions clear. I knew that well-trained Dasnarian warriors could move silent as the grave when the situation called for it, but I should've been more alert.

Twice, thrice the fool me, for being so distracted, so distraught—and so certain we'd be alone in the midst of nowhere. This couldn't be mythical n'Andana, not with Dasnarians present. Though surely we couldn't have flown all the way to Dasnaria. I didn't have much sense of distance—especially measured by gríobhth wing—but it had taken us days to sail from Jofarrstyr to the barrier. Then more days upon days around the Nahanaun Archipelago, let alone the trip to Annfwn.

"What's the matter—cat got your tongue?" The lone woman with them—the one who'd spoken before—cackled at her own wit. "Though it's not exactly a cat, is it?"

She walked around us in a leisurely stroll, the ring of soldiers rippling as they stepped back to allow her circuit, then closed in again. Crouching close to me, she peered at Zyr's head thoughtfully. Her fair hair shone in the rising light, Dasnarian blond. She clucked her tongue and *looked* at me. A dread chill ran down my spine at the sight of her dark eyes, the matte black that came to the highest magic practitioners of Deyrr. Not that I'd ever met one to speak to or look into their eyes, but the stories were all clear—and the evocation of the dead gaze of Deyrr often used to caution ill-behaved children.

I may never have met one, or spoken to her, but this close I recognized the High Priestess, the very one who'd chased the *Hákyrling* from Jofarrstyr and attempted to kill Her Majesty High Queen Ursula. They'd all been on the Tala ship while I, often forgotten, stayed on the *Hákyrling*. But I'd seen the brief, intense battle from my hiding place—how she'd used her magic to freeze them and casually gutted the warrior queen while they all stood by helpless to prevent it. I'd been certain they'd all die, and myself, too, if only because I'd be taken back to Dasnaria to face execution.

Somehow, though, they'd defeated her. The High Priestess had taken something from the queen, from her entrails, a jewel that shone like the sun itself—before Zynda, in the form of a seabird, grabbed it back, and Jepp had somehow shaken the spell and they'd blinded the High Priestess and defeated her.

Sadly, it seemed the blinding hadn't taken, for she stared at me with intact globes of inky black, swirling with the oily dark fluid of Deyrr. There were scars, though—both eye orbits showed scarring from Zynda's talons on the one side and the bisecting line of Jepp's thrown dagger on the other. The High Priestess had lived through it somehow, and must've gotten the eyes themselves from …somewhere else. My stomach heaved at the possibilities.

"I do believe it's a gryphon!" she proclaimed, with a certain glee, and using an old Dasnarian word I'd forgotten—and never connected with the Tala "gríobhth." "I haven't seen one of these for nearly a thousand years. And here you have one, Daughter.

How clever of you."

"I'm not your daughter," I said, slowly and clearly in Dasnarian. I might've chosen to remain silent, but the tales all cautioned against allowing yourself to be claimed by Deyrr. Only those who refused their dark gifts, who fought to repudiate the God of Eternal Hunger could free themselves.

She smiled, radiantly beautiful, except for those pits of her gaze. "Silly duck. I already have my claws in you." Putting a hand on my arm, directly over the barely healed injury, she squeezed—making me gasp with pain and reflexively shrink away. Uncannily strong, she held me in place, her smile so sweet and lovely. "Don't be afraid, Daughter. I've been watching you and you're one of mine—that's a good thing. Especially as you've brought me such a gorgeous gift, such a unique pet. When you tell me everything you know of our enemy, I'll love you even more. You can have power, more than you ever dreamed of, and eternal life. Don't you want that?"

"No," I said as firmly as I could. "And the gryphon is a man, not a pet."

She laughed, the melodious tinkling of bells. "Do you think I don't know a Tala beast when I see one? Or that I don't know who you are, Karyn? Once the fourth highest ranked woman in Dasnaria, destined to be empress until that fool Kral threw it all away. Don't you hate him for that?"

"Of course not," I replied, but I didn't sound as certain as I'd wanted to.

She knew it, too, giving me a sad, sympathetic smile and stroking my arm as if to soothe it. Miraculously, the pain vanished, even the deep ache that had persisted since I'd awakened from the fever. "There. All better. Girls like us have to stick together," she said. "The men will run our lives if we don't. Buying and selling us like property, dictating who we'll marry, taking our children and locking us in jeweled cages and telling us it's for our safety. Of course you hate them." She'd lowered her voice conspiratorially. "We all hate them. And we'll all rise up and take our revenge. You can be in the vanguard, my lieutenant. Second most powerful *person* in all Dasnaria. Doesn't that sound attractive?"

"I don't want that," I said, but part of me did and she knew it, because she nodded knowingly.

"I can give you some time to decide." She smiled as if we'd become best friends. "The last thing I want to do is push you into something you don't want. Then I'd be just like the men, wouldn't I? I have some ideas of some treats you might enjoy, however. I'll give you the former Empress Hulda as a handmaiden—wouldn't that be lovely?"

It would be lovely, having power over my former mother-in-law, the torment of so many.

"I have the power to do it." The High Priestess lowered her gaze to Zyr, unconscious in my lap. "Or to heal this one. Would you like me to do that, as I healed your arm?"

My heart thudded with hope. If she healed Zyr, he could fly away, warn the others so they could attack the High Priestess and end all of this. He might even love me for it, for saving the people and land he held so dear. Most of all, he'd be alive. I owed him. More, I couldn't bear for him to die.

The High Priestess knew she had me. "Yes to that?" She stroked Zyr's head, an almost loving caress. "It would be the work of a moment and I'd be happy to do that favor for you. A shame, really, to let such a magnificent creature die. I wouldn't hesitate too long, however. It seems it broke its neck in the terrible landing. Trying to protect you. The loyalty of a devoted pet should be rewarded, don't you think?"

Then he had landed so badly to save me, not just out of

exhaustion. I couldn't let him die. What happened to me didn't matter. I'd never been more than a bynd in these games of more important people. This, at least, I could do.

"Karyn," the High Priestess coaxed, "don't you agree that I should heal the gryphon and save his life?"

Fully aware that I opened my soul to the dark god, I nodded. "Yes, I agree."

I WOKE IN a beautiful bedchamber, more lavish than my mother's back at home, or even the Imperial Seraglio. Blinking at the ceiling, painted to look like a summer sky, but with dragons detailed in gold leaf flying in flocks like birds, I tried to remember what had happened after I agreed to the High Priestess's terms.

She'd smiled with such genuine pleasure, stroked a hand over my forehead, whispering a maternal endearment… and I'd awakened here.

Where was Zyr?

I sat bolt upright, looking wildly around—and startling a girl who'd clearly been set to watch for me to wake. She squeaked in momentary alarm, then laughed, patting a hand over her heart. With dark hair, golden skin and deep blue eyes, she looked Tala—though no Tala girl that I'd seen wore her hair in elaborate braids like that. Heavy, velvety curtains had been drawn back from glassed-in windows, revealing a view of high, snow-capped mountains. This couldn't be Annfwn. Not any part I'd seen, anyway.

"Where am I?" I asked the girl, who'd gotten up to busy herself with a tray.

She brought it to me with a smile, setting it on my lap. Then she held up her hands and said something in a language I didn't know, sounding apologetic. She couldn't be more than twelve or thirteen, with her dewy skin and slight body showing only the first signs of budding womanhood. Gesturing to the tray, she smiled encouragingly.

I wanted to say I wasn't hungry, to demand to see Zyr, but in truth I felt weak to the point of dizziness from hunger and thirst. It wouldn't do any good to charge out of this room—wearing nothing but a silk shift so sheer it was transparent, I noticed—only to faint in the hallway.

Besides, I'd made an agreement with the High Priestess, and she was treating me like a guest so far, instead of a prisoner. Maybe she'd healed Zyr and let him go. That would be everything.

The girl gestured again to the tray, asking a worried question. A traditional Dasnarian breakfast lay before me, including an enameled pot I might have seen at home with a warming candle. Pouring a little into a matching cup, I sniffed it, then tasted. Tea from the Hardie estates. I couldn't mistake it.

Pouring more, I drank deeply, savoring the flavor of home, something I'd thought I'd never taste again. Biting into the pastries, I found them buttery, flaky and perfect, the fruit inside melting blissfully into a harmony of sweet with the hint of salt. I ate and drank it all, devouring everything on the tray. A true heroine—like the youngest princess in the tale I'd told on the beach forever ago—would've refused to eat and drink the food provided by Deyrr. But this wasn't a tale, and real people needed to eat. Really, that princess could never have survived that journey, let alone turned around and walked home on bleeding feet through the snow.

The story was symbolic, of course. And probably the food

and drink aspect cautioned against poison. That, however, is the weapon of a woman who dares not act openly.

The High Priestess of Deyrr, a sorceress who could recruit Emperor Hestar to her cause and promise the empress as a handmaiden, had no fear of acting openly.

Once I finished eating, my handmaiden rewarded me with a delighted smile, took the tray and helped me from the bed. Leading me into the next chamber, she showed me what she'd been busy doing in there. A tub of water steamed, mist rising from it in the cooler air, the scent of jasmine wafting to me. I'd always used jasmine-scented soaps and oils—at my mother's insistence—because the imperial princesses did, and I should never be less than they, if I wanted to maintain my rank.

Though I sank into the water gratefully, more than willing to finally get clean, the heady jasmine brought back *too* much of home. Those daily baths, grooming myself to perfection, on the remote chance that my lord and husband might suddenly arrive for a visit. Even though he never did without due notice, and even when all in the empire knew him to be traveling the seas, or waging war as His Imperial Majesty's general. Being constantly ready for the husband who never saw me had been my one responsibility. It had served me well when his sudden summons to the Imperial Palace arrived—though that memory, too, made me sick with regret.

The handmaiden soaped my hair with yet more jasmine, and I gritted my teeth against it, telling myself I'd at least be clean. I scrubbed myself with a rough cloth, glad to do it myself as I buffed my skin as hard as I could stand it, removing old skin and embedded dirt. The wound on my breast had disappeared, the skin as unflawed as before.

On my left arm, however, an inky mark wound all the way around in a circle, a menacing line of linked talons. I scrubbed at it, but it went more than skin deep. Very likely all the way to my soul. I belonged to Deyrr now, and the High Priestess had marked me with her design.

The handmaiden—who acted as if she didn't understand when I asked her name—rinsed my hair repeatedly with jasmine-infused water, wrapped my hair in a cloth, and helped me out, then toweled me dry and oiled my skin. She helped me into a robe made of more of the sumptuous velvet material so prevalent everywhere, as soft inside as out. Seating me in a chair by a window where hot sunshine streamed in, she combed my hair with the skill of the servants in the Imperial Seraglio.

As it dried in the sun, she switched to a brush, patiently and deftly coaxing my hair into shimmering waves—while I fought my sizzling impatience. Finally satisfied with my hair, she applied cosmetics to my face with the same skill, then at last took my robe so I could dress.

I'd expected a klút, given everything else Dasnarian, but she instead helped me into slim silk trousers and a close-fitting halter that hugged my breasts comfortably but left my belly bare. A flowing shirt went over the top of those, as sheer as the sleeping shift I'd awakened in, and draping dramatically down my back, cut high in front. All in varying shades of gold. Indeed, I suspected the cloth had been woven with threads spun of pure gold, the way they glittered in the sun.

As a final touch, the maid laced golden slippers on my feet—surprisingly sturdy—again going against the Dasnarian tradition where women went barefoot. When she showed me my image in a full-length mirror, I first hesitated to look, afraid to see the blue of my eyes replaced with the death-black of Deyrr's hold on me. So far I looked the same. A small relief. The gauzy shirt showed off the sinister black tracery around my upper arm, however, a mark I knew I'd bear the rest of my life.

I held my breath, long past done with the lengthy delay, ready to demand to see at least the High Priestess if my handmaiden fussed any longer. To my relief, she instead led me to the opulent doors of the room, opening them for me, and guiding me into a long hall. Guards in Dasnarian armor stood at attention outside my bedchamber and were posted at regular intervals along the hall.

I still didn't recognize the place. Not that I'd traveled much through the Empire of Dasnaria and its many kingdoms, territories, and protectorates. Still, the architecture didn't look like anything I'd seen. It reminded me of Annfwn, if I had to pick an influence, though the view out every window we passed showed more staggeringly high peaks and deep valleys all around. The palace must've been sitting on one of the highest peaks, to command such a view.

At least it would provide Zyr with an excellent take-off point. Or had already. *Please let him be healed and gone*, I prayed, maybe to Moranu, though I seriously doubted any god or goddess was listening—except perhaps Deyrr Himself. The thought made my stomach turn and I shuddered, but I managed a politely serene smile when my maid gave me a questioning look.

It took some time to wend our way through the great, sprawling palace—and the only other people I saw were the armored guards, all with helms lowered, who all stood at attention and never spoke, not even to throw out ribald remarks at my scantily clad form. Not at all normal behavior. Even if they regarded me as a woman of rank—doubtful, as the emperor had stripped me of rank along with my marital status and life expectancy—Dasnarian warriors saw no reason not to comment on a woman's charms and speculate on the pleasure she might bring them in bed. That's what a woman who left the protection of her father, brothers, and husband could expect.

I'd never thought I'd miss those uncomfortable catcalls, but their silence was eerie. They might be the undead people that my new friends had talked about having to dispatch at Ordnung. Once we descended a level, we passed others who weren't guards. Men and women strolled past, alone or in small groups, all silent—and all scrutinizing me with the blank coal-dark eyes of sorcerers and sorceresses of Deyrr. I counted at least two dozen, none of them acknowledging me beyond their dead and somehow mocking stares.

By the time my escort gestured me into a large atrium filled with flowers and blooming trees, I almost welcomed the sight of the High Priestess. At least she seemed to be mostly alive. She lolled on a dark blue chaise in the sun wearing a gauzy gown like my overshirt, and nothing else. Her bone-straight blond hair fell over the contrasting velvet like a waterfall of sunlight, and a slim gold chain with a glowing topaz rested in the hollow of her throat. A very young man, who looked to be from the same people as my handmaiden, knelt on the floor beside the High Priestess, holding a cluster of grapes, one poised to pop in her mouth.

She smiled at me, looked utterly delighted to see me—the expression disconcerting with those lightless eyes. "Karyn, how lovely you look. I didn't want to upset you before, but you were quite bedraggled when I found you. I knew you'd be so embarrassed for anyone to see you that way. And now you're all cleaned up and fit for the emperor's court."

"His Imperial Majesty would not appreciate me entering his court in this outfit," I replied, scanning the room for signs of Zyr. I don't know why *that* was the point I argued, except that it was so clearly an outrageous lie, among the many sugared untruths she spewed.

She seemed unoffended, even laughing as if I'd made a fine joke. "So true, so true. I didn't think you'd care to dress in a klút after all this time though, now that you've experienced freedom." She waved a hand in disgust. "They dressed us in those things to hobble us—did you ever realize that? They provide no warmth, no protection, and one wrong move and the layers unravel, leaving you exposed. We could only mince gracefully, or pose and be ornamental. Horrid things. What you're wearing is so much better."

"Still, I'd prefer my own clothing." I really wanted to ask what she'd done with the mapsticks, but I didn't want to draw attention to them. They might seem only like sticks to her. "And my other possessions."

"Soon enough. Come and sit with me. It's been so long since I chatted with a sister countrywoman."

"What part of the empire are you from?" I asked, full of curiosity. She spoke Dasnarian with a slight accent I couldn't place—and she spoke with a blunt disgust for our customs I couldn't imagine from any gently raised woman. And yet she seemed familiar with court etiquette and the manners of noble ladies. Then again, she'd made reference to being alive for centuries. She hardly looked to be more than twenty, but some tales said the sorceresses of Deyrr gained immortal youth in return for their service to the dark god.

She waved that hand again, still negligently dangling in the air from a swanlike arm draped over the back of the chaise. "It hardly matters. My past is firmly in the past and that's where it shall stay. You and I, Karyn, we are sisters under the skin, both of us repudiating our families, the men who strove to contain us. We recreated ourselves to be who *we* choose to be."

It sounded so like what Zyr and I had talked about—but slid sideways of that heroic ideal, falling into a slime pit of evil. Yet I didn't dare call her on it. So, I simply returned her smile. "Where is Zyr?" I asked. "Were you able to heal him?"

A look of irritation glanced over her face and vanished just as quickly. "Of course I was able to heal your pet. You must understand that such a minor act of healing is well within the powers of even a first-level sorceress, let alone myself. Deyrr is a benevolent master and His gifts lavishly bestowed. The god will love you because you're still a virgin, and a pure vessel for his magic. You'll see."

"I look forward to it," I replied with as much sincere enthusiasm as I could muster, resisting the urge to scratch at the crawling feel of the talon markings on my arm. My thrice-cursed virginity again. If only I'd gone to Zyr's bed when he first asked, I might've avoided this. All of this. But no time or room for regret. I needed to find him, as the High Priestess didn't speak as if she'd let him go—and set him free. If she killed me for it, that would be less of my life spent as her slave. "I'd love to see your work for myself."

She pouted, thrusting out her lip like a surly adolescent. "Later. I want to chat with you, get to know each other. I haven't had another woman to be my friend in so long." She sat up, clapping her hands together with enthusiasm. "We could begin your first lesson—wouldn't you like that?"

I had to agree that I would. I could hardly say otherwise. And yet, every time I agreed with her, the talons wound tighter, a feeling of chill running down to the fingers of my left hand, and up over my shoulder. *If you'd gotten that poisonous crap that close to your heart, then you would've died.* Zyr's terse observation came back to me.

Dead—or more possessed by Deyrr. Those lessons might inform me about that process, which would be good to know, but first Zyr.

"I'm so fond of my pet gryphon," I said, as if confessing reluctantly. "Now that you've cured him, I'd like to be certain he can't run away. Those shapeshifters can be so naughty."

"Yes," she breathed, saying it as if I'd spoken a great truth that few understood. "I just *knew* we'd be great friends, both with our affection for our pets. But you don't have to worry for a moment. I have the gryphon confined. It can neither shapeshift nor fly away from you. Something else I can teach you. Let's start our first lesson right now."

It took everything in me not to groan aloud, to keep a pleasant smile fixed to my face. Only my etiquette teacher's relentless training allowed me to keep a polite and happy expression. "Can my first lesson be learning that? I'd dearly love to know how to keep him from being so ornery."

Her delighted expression clouded, and I fully expected she'd seen through me. "It's really not the thing, Karyn, to start there. It's far too advanced for you. There's an order to these things and you must respect that."

"Oh." Nothing could keep my disappointment from showing, so I didn't try. Zyr had been in gryphon form so long, and now the High Priestess had fixed him there, and held him captive, a repetition of his worst nightmare.

"Tsk," the High Priestess tutted, her face full of compassion for my misery. "You really shouldn't get so attached to your pets, Karyn. Your heart is so soft. When you've lived for hundreds and hundreds of years, you'll learn better. Caring only brings pain." She brightened. "Especially when I can make you all the pets you want. There are ways and ways of binding them so they can never leave—or have power over you. They will always cleave to you."

Because they'd have no choice. Her unspoken words hung in the air, making me want to sob from despair or vomit from the horror. What had she done to Zyr? I almost couldn't face knowing—but I also couldn't allow myself to run away from this.

"You're so wise," I choked out. "I'll try to do better." That last came from habit, a promise that had always appeased the most strict of my tutors.

"There, there, darling girl." She rose from her chaise, ignoring the young man on the floor, who could have been a statue since he hadn't yet moved, and came to embrace me. Touching a sack of ice-hardened slime might feel similar. I shuddered at the contact, utterly revolted, and allowed some tears to escape in the hope she might think I trembled from weeping. Indeed, she let me go, smiled softly, and used her thumbs to wipe my tears away. They were smooth and soft—and might as well have been sharp as knives the way they scraped my skin.

But I worked up a watery smile for her, and told her what she wanted to hear. "You're so kind to me. I've never had a friend like you." Not a lie.

She looked so pleased I began to wonder if I'd mistaken her nature. What I knew to be true had already started to blur, just as in the tales. A fragment of ice in my eye, the promise of friendship and belonging, of power… Soon I'd lose myself. But I had to free Zyr first.

"If it means so much to you, my friend"—she cupped my cheeks in her hands—"then we can go see your pet now. You can reassure yourself that it's hale and healthy, and still all yours. I wouldn't take it from you. My first gift to you. The first of many." She smiled with such generous warmth I nearly believed Zyr had been hers to give me in the first place. "Good, yes?"

"Yes, very good," I agreed, handing her another sliver of my soul.

She giggled merrily and took my hand as if we were girls and best friends, indeed. We walked along a long arcade of more floor-to-ceiling glass windows showcasing the spectacular view, she with a bounce in her step. I marveled at the expense of so much glass in huge sheets. Though it still felt vaguely traitorous to think it, even the Imperial Palace had nothing like it.

"Did you build this place?" I asked, suddenly aware of how many pressing questions I hadn't thought to ask.

"Oh no!" She tipped her chin back, gazing up at the expanse of glass. "This is the nicest house I've ever had. Let's just say an old friend left it to me." She winked—so uncanny, with her golden lashes sweeping over the lightless pit of her eye—squeezing my hand lightly. "The zoo facility is quite nice, too. I just know you'll be pleased."

There was no mistaking that Dasnarian word. My heart sank further into despair. Not even a prison for a man, but one for animals.

Something buzzed over my skin as we passed through an open arched doorway to a short hall. Something that felt much like crossing the magic barrier that protected the Thirteen kingdoms from the rest of the world. The High Priestess slid me a curious glance. "Did you feel it? Those ancients wove such deft spells, to last so long."

"Which ancients?" I asked.

She laughed and swung our joined hands. "Don't play stupid. You wanted to find n'Andana and you found it, silly." She gave me another saucy and horrible wink. "But I found it *first.*"

I had no time to mull the implications, as we stepped through a second buzzing barrier into another atrium echoing with cacophonous sound. Birds sang from trees while others flapped through the air above, cawing and screeching. Some kind of animal howled and more sent up various growls. At least that meant they weren't possessed by Deyrr, as those were always deathly silent.

Large animals paced in niches, some of them extensively and exotically landscaped, presumably reflecting their native territories. Others had only bare cells, lying in them despondently, not even marking our passage.

In one like that I found Zyr, trapped and in chains.

~ 20 ~

MAJESTIC AS EVER, still in gríobhth form, he stood tall and proud in his cell. One with stone walls that bore deep gouges, clearly scored by his claws, blood oozing from them and decorating the walls, spattering the polished floor beneath his sleek black paws. A heavy metal collar encircled his neck, resting on his shoulders, and chains made of huge links bigger around than my forearm draped from there to rings in the floor. They had to be massively heavy, but he didn't sag under their weight. His beak hung open, parted with stress, and I imagined his breath panting hot and angry. Those deep blue eyes stared unseeing through me, feral, with intelligence, but showing no sign of *him*.

I'd lost him. I'd been resigned to that. The true horror was that he'd lost himself.

Without thinking I lifted a hand toward him, but the High Priestess yanked me back. I'd forgotten she still held my hand. "Oops," she chirped. "Don't do that. There's another barrier on its little house. All of these will burn your flesh off if you touch them without my assistance. It's settled down a bit—and can't see or hear you through it—so no need to agitate it again."

"He's bleeding," I pointed out, making sure to sound puzzled and perhaps as dim as she seemed to assume. "I though you healed him."

She huffed in exasperation, dropping my hand. "I *did*, silly bean. It did that to itself, clawing to get out."

I drew my brows together in a puzzled frown. "I don't understand—I thought you said you could control him, that he'd be my pet and would love me forever." A risk, to accuse her this way, to undermine my obsequious flattery, but I had to know what hold she had. "Why is he chained and locked in a cell if you control him?"

"Karyn, sweetling, you have to understand that these things take time." She waved a hand at Zyr. "It's confined until I release it. The chains are for its own good, so it will stop trying to claw its way out."

"So clever," I made sure to sound admiring instead of outraged. "However did you get them on him?"

"I have my ways." She lifted a shoulder and let it fall. From that gesture alone I'd have known her as Dasnarian, if a very old one. A thousand years old or older, she'd implied. Unless she'd lied about that. She probably lied as easily as breathing. Or maybe they didn't feel like lies to her. She talked to me with every evidence of sincerity—so either she lied brilliantly to draw me into her web, or she truly believed what she said.

Either way, I knew she didn't exaggerate her powers. I recalled how she froze everyone on the Tala ship while she gutted the high queen, and I considered asking some naïve questions, but that might be too dangerous if the High Priestess knew I'd been present for that. She knew so much about me—had said she'd been watching me—so it seemed likely she knew I'd been there. In which case, I shouldn't dissemble.

"With your great power," I said, before I could lose courage, "I'm surprised you need chains at all. After all, you've held a ship's deck full of warriors frozen with only the power of your mind."

She slid me a narrow look, but laughed, glowing with pleasure. "A mere trick. A smidge of the power Deyrr has granted me in His generosity and wisdom. All of which I'm offering to *you*. Do you understand now why I haven't taken your gryphon for myself yet?"

I didn't, and I really needed to. "I don't understand—will you explain? I apologize for my stupidity." An almost ritual apology in Dasnaria, that one, spoken by a lower rank female to a higher one. A calculated gambit on my part, and one that worked, because she smiled knowingly and patted my cheek.

"You will learn, Daughter. You see, I could bind it to me with the powers of Deyrr, make its will entirely subject to mine, but I was trying to be considerate of *you*." She gave me a reproving look. "If I bind it, the gryphon will be my pet, not yours. As much as I'd love to add a gryphon to my collection, I was being generous and saving it for you. My gift to you, remember? Your reward, if you learn your lessons well."

"Oh, I understand!" I exclaimed, clasping my hands together and giving her a formal bow. I allowed relieved gratitude to flood my face, while my thoughts flew.

What I understood was that her "gift" would function as a bribe and a lure. So be it. I memorized every bit of information she'd fed me. If she controlled the barriers on the cells, and the barriers were the same as the one controlled by Andi in Annfwn, then perhaps Andi could… no, no, no. How could I possibly get a message to Andi, let alone guide her here to do it? But the High Priestess hadn't been born to magic any more than I had. She'd acquired it through Deyrr, which meant I could, too.

Though that might take a long time—and it might be already too late for Zyr to be anything but what I saw before me.

Still, if he had to remain a gríobhth, then he could at least live free and not in this horrible cell that would drive him slowly mad.

Zyr's head jerked up, eyes bright with predatory fury, and a small trap opened in the ceiling. He launched himself at it, but a haunch of meat fell through, nearly hitting him on the head, and the door shut as fast as it had opened. Revenge and escape forgotten, Zyr seized the meat and began tearing at it, ripping off slices with his sharp beak and swallowing them whole.

"It's feeding very well," the High Priestess said, sounding pleased and reassuring. She slipped her arm through mine and tilted her head toward me companionably. "You needn't fear it will waste away."

Only that he'd lose himself to the gríobhth, eating in that form, too. "Has he had many meals then?" I asked, trying to sound happy, also, instead of appalled.

"Four meals, yes. I've been taking very good care of your pet while you slept." She hugged my arm. "You were so tired, poor thing. You slept all day yesterday, all night and well into the morning. And it did you so much good, don't you agree?" She waited expectantly.

"Yes, I do feel so much better," I said, trying to agree with the content and not her. To no avail, because she clucked her tongue in merry reprimand.

"You haven't thanked me," she said, with a hint of petulance. "For all I've done for you."

"You've been so wonderful to me," I hedged, gushing as I said it, to cover my fear. Using the excuse to move away from her disturbingly chill body, I extracted my arm and executed a deep, formal court curtsey, holding it. "I don't know *how* to thank you."

Giving her my thanks would only tie me deeper to her. It wouldn't matter after a point, but I had to retain enough autonomy to thwart her with Zyr. She considered me for a long moment, much as Empress Hulda would, letting my legs tire in the deep knee bend, testing my submission.

Zyr still devoured the meat, tearing into it with bestial ferocity, tail waving in apparent delight. My position near the floor put our heads nearly on a level as he fed and I watched him with my peripheral vision, quite practiced from keeping my gaze averted during interesting events.

And he caught my eye.

He'd turned his head, his crest of glossy black feathers pointing at the High Priestess, and his blue eye glinted with such expression that he might as well have been rolling his eyes at her. I nearly gasped with relief to know his personality survived. He'd told me the gríobhth brain was big enough for him to think like a man, but so clever of him to pretend otherwise.

Also, he clearly *could* see us, though the High Priestess believed otherwise.

I gave him a worried frown, and he narrowed his eye, shaking his head slightly and turning it into a movement that drove his sharp beak into the meat. Delicately and precisely placing a paw on the haunch, he extended his claws in a slow arc, demonstrating his control—then tearing out a slice of meat with savagery. I gave a slight nod.

Oh yes, we would have our vengeance.

I wished I could talk to him. Zyr would know what to do. This was his mission to begin with—his war, really—and I'd been literally along for the ride. My leg muscles began to tremble from the strain, which the High Priestess must've been waiting for, because she finally released me.

"You may rise." She didn't sound completely mollified, however. I straightened and she held out her hands to me, a clear invitation I didn't dare refuse. Placing my hands in hers, I kept my gaze submissively averted. From the corner of my eye, I noted that Zyr had reverted to blank animal behavior, no glimmer of human intellect in him. "Karyn, sweetling," the High Priestess said, squeezing my hands gently, "I know you're concerned for your pet, but you really must learn detachment. Don't tell me you've fallen in love with its man form."

I glanced up, startled and abashed.

She tsked. "Oh, you *have*. It's written all over your face."

I didn't know whether to deny or admit it. Mostly I wished Zyr couldn't see and hear us. What must he think? My face grew unbearably hot.

"I want you to listen to me." The High Priestess turned me to face the cage, where Zyr, apparently mindless, now cracked the big leg bone into splinters. She slid an arm around my waist and snuggled me to her. "It is a beautiful specimen in man form, it's true, but you must remember this," she said, very seriously. "These shapeshifters, they aren't really people at all. They're monsters—a whole other species of being—that happen to be able to take human form, too. Did it explain to you about First Form?"

I couldn't help another start of surprise. How did she know so much? She hugged me a little, as if reassuring me. "Don't be surprised. I've been studying these shapeshifters—first the n'Andanan ancestors, then their Tala descendants, for centuries. I was there when my sister sorceress Moranu created them."

"I thought Moranu is a goddess?"

The High Priestess laughed gaily. Zyr showed no sign of listening, cracking the bones and eating those pieces too. "Isn't it rich that they think so? Moranu, may She rest in Deyrr's embrace, would be so very amused by that. No, She was a woman, like you and I, but a powerful High Priestess of Deyrr. She wove the magic that made the first shapeshifters, teaching the animals She chose to take human form, to speak and behave as we do. That's what this place is."

At last she let me go, the side where her oddly chill body touched mine crawling cold from the contact. Turning to face the bigger room, she gestured grandly. "This was Her library, if you will. She collected animals from all over the world and brought them here, then worked Her magic to teach them to take other forms, too. Including humans. A combination of forced interbreeding and the grace of Deyrr. Those were the grand days, when magic ran thick and hot in the world, radiating from everything like the sun." She sounded wistful, nostalgic.

"She bred animals with humans?" I asked, fighting to sound neutral.

"Well, slaves," she answered. "Not people like you and me. Sometimes She let us watch, and those were spectacles, indeed. The proof is in their precious First Forms." She glanced at me, full of merry mischief. "That always indicates which animal they came from, long ago."

"That makes sense," I said, since she seemed to expect an answer.

"Of course it does, because you have an affinity for them, these shapeshifters—and they for you. That's no doubt why this one wanted to mate with you. They have this instinct to return to the human strain, compulsively chasing after women of our line. Still, you must be smarter. Don't be taken in by their clever imitations of people. They can be seductive and charming. Bed your pet, if you like, once you've bent it to your will. Let it take the form of a man if that's what pleasures you in bed. I've done that myself many times and they make such wonderful, ferocious lovers. It's not only men who can keep rekjabrel. Wouldn't you love to have a bed slave of your own?" Her smile took on such a lasciviously cruel bent that I had to look away. "But don't ever forget that it's a talking animal, and the beast is never far beneath that handsome face."

It made too much sense. And fit so neatly with what Zyr himself had explained to me, what Andi had warned me about. I'd seen the magic of Deyrr and never any sign that the gods or goddesses existed. That a High Priestess of Deyrr could've used magic to create the shapeshifters—however abhorrent her methods—made so much more rational sense than to imagine magical beings somehow springing up from nothing. And Zyr had pursued me with a single-minded obsessiveness that defied explanation.

I frowned, uncertain of what I believed anymore. Glancing back at Zyr, I saw no evidence of his human self. If I could talk to him, that would help. "You said he can't shapeshift?"

"The gryphon? No. I've locked it in that form for now." She waggled a finger at me. "I don't want you to be swayed by its silver tongue and charming games. Not until I've had a chance to open your eyes to the truth."

"Can you teach me how to do that, too?" I made sure to sound eager. If I could learn how she locked him into one form, it followed that I could unlock him.

"I can teach you everything," she promised. "If you're a good girl and learn your lessons. You have the native gifts. You've obeyed the laws and maintained your chastity for Deyrr, and He is well pleased with you. In time, you could be almost as powerful as I am. You can take over Moranu's library here, and play with your shapeshifters all you like."

"You are too generous," I averred, bowing to her yet again.

"I am, aren't I?" She laughed. "And I'll ask very little of you in return."

And here we were, at the crux. I widened my eyes, looking as confused as possible. *You look so sweet and innocent, asking me that with your pretty blue eyes wide.* "But you're so powerful. How can I possibly be of help to you?"

She gave me a narrow look. "Well, that's another conversation. One that must take place after your first lesson, so I know you can be trusted. Come along, Daughter. You've seen your pet now, and we have much to accomplish." She hooked her arm through mine, to lead me away.

Somehow, I found it in me to resist. "But can't we bring him with us? We could keep the chains on him. He can stay in my bedroom."

She smiled knowingly and tapped me on the nose. Even her fingertip left a chill behind. "Perhaps. If you are a good girl, and commit whole-heartedly to your lesson, then I shall let you keep the gryphon in your bedchamber. But no man form. Not yet! You've been so obedient and chaste that we mustn't risk spoiling that. Not until you've wedded Deyrr. Once the god has your maidenhead, you may indulge yourself with all the beasts you like."

She led me away, and I looked over my shoulder at Zyr. He had his head raised, the glittering hatred clear in his eyes as he stared daggers at the High Priestess's back.

Then we turned a corner and I lost sight of him.

THE HIGH PRIESTESS led me down many layers of stairs, deeper inside the mountain. The word "dungeon" kept coming back to mind, and I found it in me to be grateful that at least she hadn't put Zyr in this place. Yet.

For it quickly became clear that other shapeshifters had been imprisoned in this labyrinth. We passed cell after cell of pacing animals, all behind barriers, some from the natural world and others fantastic. They watched as we passed with more than animal intelligence—and also cringing with fearful obedience when the High Priestess glanced their way.

"You like my collection, don't you?" she asked, giving me a sly smile. "You can say so. It's polite to compliment your hostess, after all."

"There are so many!" I gushed instead of agreeing, though I doubted much could stop the momentum of my increasing slide under her control. "Where did you get them all?"

"Silly. This is n'Andana, origin and ancestral home of the shapeshifters. They were all just living in ignorance, abandoned long ago by their leaders, waiting for someone to come and take the reins, show them a purpose for their useless lives. Besides," she hugged my arm, then tickled the inked-on scars her creatures had given me. "Once you have some, it's easy to recruit more, hmm?"

"I'm not a shapeshifter," I said, trying not to sound as horrified as I felt.

"No, no. You're so much better than they are—pure human, not animal. And born to rule. Here is what I want to show you."

We walked onto a balcony into apparent sunlight, overlooking a sort of indoor landscape. Lush and warm, flowering plants and tropical trees decorated a series of lakes and streams that went on as far as the eye could see. And everywhere I looked, animals and people roamed, swam or lolled on the velvety green verges.

"Look familiar?" She dimpled with her twinkling smile, knowing my answer.

"Just like the Imperial Seraglio," I replied numbly. The same magically created sunshine and warmth. I'd never thought of that place as a prison, but this surely was.

"Old magic," she said with reverence. "Magic that was ours

to begin with, before Moranu's children stole it and escaped to here. They tried to starve us of it, but we're taking our own back now. This is your birthright, Daughter. Witness the power you could possess."

She swept a hand, as if gathering something—and every creature, animal or human, looked her way, and stood at attention. They poked heads out of the surface of the water, flew from the trees, ambled out of caves and dwellings. More appearing every moment, they amassed below, obeying the unspoken command of the High Priestess.

"Shall I have them do something for you?" Her eyes glittered with joyful madness, the power making her giddy. "How about *jump*."

Every one of them jumped, in the air, in the water, on land. Precisely once. And went still again.

I fought the rising nausea, and she patted my cheek sympathetically.

"Don't be afraid. It's wise of you to recognize the power I hold. You see now that I will win this war. We shall descend on Annfwn and take back what they stole—and you will be on the side of good and right." She giggled. "And on the side of the winners, which is most important. You understand my point, don't you?"

Dully, despairing, I agreed that I did.

THOUGH I FELT I'd eaten breakfast only a few hours before, the High Priestess insisted on a lavish luncheon, this time in a grand interior hall, illuminated by a miraculous arched ceiling made entirely of glass. Silk banners draped from airy upper balconies, hanging nearly to the floor. As someone who'd spent an extensive part of her life on embroidery, I recognized the exquisite skill that had gone into the needlework images on each banner.

Each depicted an animal, many far larger than life size. There were dozens, but I picked out many familiar animals—wolf, tiger, black panther, hummingbird, horse—and other mythological ones, too. At the far end, on an ocean-blue silk, a mermaid stared out. On a flaming red banner, a dragon flew. And rendered in gleaming black on shimmering silver, a gríobhth that might've used Zyr as the model.

The High Priestess caught me staring at it. "Your pet's ancestor, no doubt. That *is* its First Form, isn't it?" She asked it far too casually, so I did what I did best: played dumb.

"He wouldn't tell me," I confided. "I think he didn't trust me."

She patted my arm, reaching only a short way to do so, as she'd seated me at her left hand while she presided at the head of the long table. Other priests and priestesses of Deyrr had joined us for the elaborate feast. All gorgeously dressed, youthful in their beauty, they ignored me entirely, talking quietly amongst themselves in Dasnarian. The few conversations I could pick out revealed nothing of interest. They spoke of the weather, the meal, and other innocuous topics. It would've been like many feasts my family had hosted for special events and holidays, except for those dead, dark eyes they all had—looking like eyeless sockets in their comely faces.

"Don't be distressed about not knowing its First Form. They place such a superstitiously high importance on it, but it truly doesn't matter. Because of their mutable nature, the cleverest among them can learn to ape any form, even the extinct ones. So even if they claim one as their First, they might be lying." She wrinkled her nose playfully, as if discussing capricious children.

"Why lie about it if it doesn't matter?"

She snorted and waved a careless hand. "Who knows? Really, Karyn." She squeezed my forearm, sounding terribly earnest. "You must learn not to ascribe higher thought to the beasts. They do what they do, when they feel like it, with no more intellect than that."

"The shapeshifters have been left alone and ungoverned for far too long," the man opposite me spoke up. He was one of the few who looked older; deep grooves carved his handsome face, giving him a chiseled look. He spoke to the High Priestess, still ignoring me, though he'd clearly been listening to the conversation.

"We're working on changing that," the High Priestess replied sweetly. "Don't lose patience when the prize is within our reach."

He grunted and returned to his meal.

"What is the prize?" I asked, hoping for wide-eyed and innocent again.

The High Priestess considered me, then held up a finger, waving it slowly. "You mustn't always play so dumb. We know the shapeshifters and their allies attempted to recruit you to their cause. You can't be faulted for that. What choice did you have, exiled by that idiot Hestar and left to your own devices? It was clever of you to pretend to go along with their plans, but now you're back among your own people. Your true family."

"Unless you work for them," the woman to my left suddenly said. I might've been an empty chair until that moment, but now she stared at me. I avoided her awful gaze, looking at her strangely girlish face, round with full cheeks, surrounded by ringlets of rose-gold hair. "Are you a spy?" she asked, pursing her petal-pink mouth.

I nearly laughed—and was glad I couldn't, as it would have come out hysterical. Everyone accused me of being a spy. I only wished I was. Then I might understand all of these layers of politics and battling going on around me. *All I wanted was a normal life.* The protest ran around my mind. *Love. Children,* Andi had clarified. They seemed like such…frivolous desires now, as I sat at this table dredged from nightmares, with people who could snap my mind like the fragile teacups of my nursery days. And the only man I'd ever loved was chained in a cell, unable to even be a man.

This war will engulf us all. All the people who just want a normal, peaceful life will have to fight anyway. The point is to act despite that, to fight instead of cringing and hiding.

No matter how much I longed to be able to cringe and hide, I couldn't. I suppose that had been Zyr's point when he said that to me. Dredging up my courage, I met the pretty priestess's horrible gaze. "I am not a spy," I said in formal, court Dasnarian. "I was the fourth highest ranked woman in Dasnaria, destined to be empress, and I outrank you. You will address me accordingly."

Her soft mouth fell open, then curled into a snarl, but the pealing laughter of the High Priestess shocked her into silence. The High Priestess sat back in her grand chair—a throne, by many standards—and clapped her hands, laughing in apparent delight.

"Well played, Daughter. You are all I hoped. Now, we all know Hestar stripped you of that rank you just boldly claimed, but never mind that. I shall give it back to you. You *will* be empress, Karyn, mark my words. Our empress. By the time this war is done, no one will stand between you and the Imperial Throne of Dasnaria."

"She'll need an emperor," said the man across from me, as if pointing out a future business item, not arguing my ascension to the throne in the least.

"No, she won't," the High Priestess snapped back, a look of fierce displeasure on her face. "We've been through this. The era of the male fist holding the empire is over. I won't allow it. Our Karyn will rule alone." She reached over again and squeezed my hand, giving me that delighted smile. "Of course," she added, in a conspiratorial tone, "you can have all the, erm, *ferocious* lovers you like."

I smiled back, hoping it didn't look like I fought not to puke in her lap. "How will you raise me to the throne? It seems impossible, even with your great power."

She smiled secretively. "All right, I'll tell you. You deserve to know. Once we've captured Annfwn, the Heart, and the Star—and all those associated kingdoms—then we'll dispose of Hestar and his sons, in the grand Dasnarian tradition. That leaves your husband, Kral, heir to the throne, as he's unequivocally the next in line."

"Except for the firstborn," the priestess beside me pointed out. "Princess Jenna."

"Dead," the High Priestess declared with complete certainty. "Perished over two decades ago. I've seen it in the mists. Kral's claim is undeniable. With Hestar and his line dispatched, and Kral in turn, as soon as he's ratified, that leaves you. Simple."

"That's treason," I managed. Oddly, it saddened me to hear Jenna had perished. As if I'd lost another friend.

Laughter rippled down the table, broad grins and shaking heads for my foolish innocence. The High Priestess gave them a reproving frown and they quieted. "Deyrr existed before the upstart Konyngrrs seized the throne. You could say we outrank them."

"Kral won't want the throne," I persisted. "He gave it up

for—" For love, I didn't say. It sounded too silly, too weak a word in this gathering of power and horror.

"He gave it up for that chit. I *know*." The High Priestess made a moue of disbelieving disgust. "Don't worry there. A man raised to lust for power will always lust for power. We'll bring him along easily enough—and you'll be ready to take your place at his side again."

"Except our marriage was annulled by His Imperial Majesty," I ventured, not sure I should, but I thought she knew that.

She put her fingers over her mouth, pretending to hold back a secret, then giggled. "But was it?" Popping her hands apart, she smiled widely. "Did you know—I was there that night." She gave a little squeal of excitement.

I hadn't known. How… creepy to think of that. "Then you saw His Imperial Majesty grant me an annulment—and then sentence me to death." I said it accusingly, feeling I'd gained some ground against her sweetly manipulative clutches that muddled my thinking so much. "What friend stands by and allows that?"

She waved that off with a dismissive poof of her lips. "I would've rescued you before they torched you at dawn. It's not my fault that Kral's mannish rekjabrel interfered. In fact, they very nearly ruined things, being so impulsive. *I* was the one looking after your best interests and *I* was the one who made sure Hestar's stupid decision wasn't recorded. He knew better than to thwart my wishes." A growl crept into her voice, a glimpse of her true self. Then she went all sunny again. "I'll prove it. Girl!"

A handmaiden who looked very like the one who'd tended me that morning ran up with a sealed metal tube. Clearly she'd been poised with it nearby, to deliver it so quickly. I could barely absorb the implications of that, so astonished was I by the sight of that particular tube.

I knew it well. My mother and father had picked it out for me. My wedding decorations had been designed along the same theme.

Delighted by my astonishment, the High Priestess flipped the catch on the tube and opened the lid, then slid out the parchment inside. My wedding contract, sealed with the emperor's own hand.

She handed it to me, trilling happily, "Congratulations, sweet Karyn af Hardie. You're still married! I hereby restore your rank—and your glorious future."

~ 21 ~

THE HIGH PRIESTESS kept it for me, my cursed undying wedding certificate, "for safekeeping" she declared—and sent it off in its tube with the handmaiden.

My mind reeling, unable to muster much appetite, I picked at my meal, until the High Priestess chided me for it. "You'll need your strength for the ritual consecration," she promised. "Eat. Drink. You'll thank me for it." And she pressed a goblet into my hand with the sweetest of smiles.

Those ominous words did nothing to stimulate my lagging appetite, so I sipped the wine. An excellent vintage and one I'd been barely allowed to taste as it had been from our own Hardie vineyards, but destined for the Imperial Palace. The smoothly rounded taste of home helped to ease my incipient panic. I did my best to eat, too, spurred on by the High Priestess's command.

No matter what happened tonight, I certainly would need my strength. If I behaved well, she'd let me have Zyr in my bedchamber. Perhaps he could fly away out one of the windows.

A good reason to obey the High Priestess's suggestions, her voice a melodious running brook, speaking to me of all manner of things while I ate and drank. Her cheerful conversation required nothing of me, so I could sit quietly, appear to listen, and turn over my thoughts. She seemed happy with that arrangement, too, which made me happy in turn.

I'd never been particularly strong-willed—and I'd never wanted to be. My parents had praised me for my sweetness and obedience. Kral had found my softly yielding nature bewitching.

Only Zyr had ever chided me for it—and then only because he found my submissiveness so arousing.

I already had such a difficult time resisting the High Priestess—all of her arguments made so much sense that it became easier and easier to agree with the truth of them—that I worried that after this consecration, I'd do whatever she wanted with a smile on my face. What if I didn't *want* to free Zyr after that? I might become what she moment by moment molded me into, another version of herself. I might remove Zyr's chains only to replace them with my own, making him my pet indeed.

If his intellect truly rotted away while I trained to be a priestess, he could indeed become my cheerful rekjabrel, happy to service me however I asked.

And I might be empress. The first of the Hardie dynasty. How thrilled my parents would be with me. I'd deliver on their most ambitious dreams and more, far more than they ever hoped for. Wealth and power would be mine. I'd never again have to worry about who would take care of me.

Other Dasnarian women will tell tales of you. You'll be their hero. I'd be the first female ruler of the Dasnarian Empire. Zyr's words would come true.

Just not exactly how he'd envisioned.

But then, his ideals didn't necessarily have to be mine. I owed him and the Tala no loyalty, nothing beyond the services I'd already rendered. I'd found n'Andana for them, hadn't I? I was Dasnarian, born and bred. In retrospect, it seemed impossible that I had considered turning my back on my people—on my own *family*—to fight in a war against them. What had I been thinking? All because Jepp had pretended to be my friend and Kral had rescued me. Though he wouldn't have had to rescue me if he hadn't treated me so terribly in the first place. In fact, Jepp and Kral had interfered with my true rescue. If they hadn't, I would've found my destiny with the High Priestess and Deyrr so much sooner.

And Zyr. So charming and flirtatious. The High Priestess had a point there. I'd known all along that he must want me for some reason other than what he so glibly professed. To think I'd nearly given him my virginity instead of saving it for Deyrr as I was destined to do.

The High Priestess smiled at me, patting my hand gently. We sat alone at the great table. All the others gone. My plate and goblet stood empty.

I blinked, my eyes bleary, and the silk banners seemed to ripple, their animals prancing to life. "This is the Imperial Palace of n'Andana," I said, the realization coming to me from nowhere at all.

"More or less," the High Priestess agreed. She sat sideways in her large chair, bare legs draped over one velvet-padded arm, back against the other as she sipped from her goblet and watched me, a smile playing on her lips as she toyed with the glowing orb of her pendant. "They didn't call it that, of course. They had odd ideas about councils and consensus." She tipped her head back, gazing at the banners, her lovely hair falling in a golden sheet behind her. "They had clans, each represented by an animal—those you see here—and they'd meet in this very room to discuss issues and vote on decisions. They'd deliberate *forever* and it made them weak. They're still weak—and they're nearly extinct on top of it. We've outlasted them."

I'd been about to ask a question, but it fled my mind. "Is it time for my first lesson?" I asked. I wanted that. I couldn't quite remember why, but I'd very much wanted to learn… something.

"You've already had it, sweetling." She smiled in sympathy. "The first lesson isn't an easy one, so I did what I could to smooth the way for you. Discovering that the people around you have lied to you, then opening your eyes to the truth—that's one of the most difficult journeys we have to make in our lives. But everyone here understands. We've all gone through it, too. Rejecting those who'd control our lives and choosing our own path."

My eyes filled with tears, my heart feeling like a throbbing, tender thing in my chest, my left arm prickling in tandem, as if the inked-on talons danced their way around my upper arm. "I always followed the rules. I should've had a good life. I never disobeyed, not once in all those years. The only time—" I choked a little on it and she shared a sad smile with me, handing me her goblet. I drank the delicious wine my parents had barely let me taste.

"The only time?" she prompted.

"The only time I didn't follow the rules was when Kral offered the annulment. I should never have requested it. I didn't even want it."

"Of course you didn't. He manipulated you into it. Him and that foreign rekjabrel slut who seduced him to be a traitor to his people." She was all sympathy. "Kral should've controlled her, kept her in her place. Or killed her once he'd had his pleasure. You're his first wife. He had no business putting his rekjabrel before you—or any woman before you. That is not the way of things."

"You're so right." Understanding seemed to dawn, clearing away the clouds of doubt. "That was never supposed to be how my life went. I was supposed to be empress. *That* is the way of things."

"And now you will be. Because we love you. You will always know who your true family is because we have your back. We want you to succeed, to rule as you were born to do."

I clasped her hand, letting the grateful tears flow. "Thank you so much. I don't know what I would've done if you hadn't rescued me."

She held on, gaze on our joined hands. "We are stronger together, you and I, along with your brothers and sisters in Deyrr. You never have to be alone again. We all want only the best for you."

"I know. And I'm so grateful."

We sat there a moment, reveling in the closeness of our friendship. I'd been searching all my life for a friend like her, and I'd finally found her. I'd found my best friend and my god, both at once. I'd never felt happier or more at peace.

"The consecration ceremony is tonight at midnight," she told me. "You're excited, aren't you?"

"So much," I gushed. "But will Deyrr accept me—will I be worthy?"

"Deyrr already loves you. He simply waits for you to join him in His bed. Once He makes you His bride, you'll find perfect happiness. You will never doubt again."

Something not quite right. I narrowed my eyes, the animals dancing on their banners as I tried to focus on her words. "But I'm married to Kral. You have my wedding contract."

She jiggled our joined hands, her silver-bell laugh tinkling. "In the spiritual world, silly. Kral is your mortal husband—and only for a little while longer—and Deyrr will be the husband of your immortal soul."

"Oh," I breathed. She always explained everything so clearly.

"Now, you should go rest. Have a nice long nap, and your maid will prepare you for the consecration. I'm so very happy for you, my friend."

"Thank you." I stood, and found my handmaiden waiting nearby, with her serene smile. She led me back to the beautiful bedroom, now filled with golden sunset light. It gilded the peaks with pinks and violets, the clear sky beyond deepening into a blue that reminded me of … something.

Unable to stay upright a moment longer, I lay down on the bed.

Unable to keep my eyes open, I fell into a blissful sleep.

And I dreamed wonderful dreams.

I was a fish. No—a mermaid, my upper body mine, my hair streaming behind me, but with a strong fish tail propelling through crystal blue waters. Deeper and deeper I swam, certain of my destination, even as I had no idea what it might be.

And I recognized it when I saw it, a sparkling sphere at the bottom of the ocean, like the most beautiful jewel imaginable. I swam closer, drawn to it irresistibly. For a moment I caught a curious vision of blue crabs bright and glittering as sapphires, crawling over the surface, before they drew away like a parted curtain and I popped through the globe into thin air—landing ignominiously on my behind.

Queen Andromeda sat on a throne before me.

This woman was all Sorceress Andromeda, Queen of the Tala—with only hints of the woman who'd walked on a beach with me and asked me to call her Andi. Her hair, shining bloodred over deepest black seemed to float around her as if we were in water instead of air. And her eyes gleamed luminescent silver. She studied me intently, fingers weaving as if to braid strands that drew me to her. Indeed, I found myself standing on human feet and walking toward her.

Those feet dragged, though, as I tried to resist. She frowned, tugging—and I cried out at the sudden pain.

Then I stood before her, and she put a hand on my forehead, another over my heart. Though she didn't grip me, I couldn't pull away. Her luminous eyes stared into mine, seeming to fill the entirety of my vision like a full moon's bright light.

"I'm afraid this will hurt," she murmured, her voice sonorous as the sea, echoing through me. My left arm began to throb, then burn with agonizing fire.

I threw my head back and screamed, arching in place until it felt my back might break. But I stayed connected to the open palms of her hands as if welded there, she the blacksmith to my melting iron. My heart tore open, bleeding away the peaceful joy the High Priestess had given me. My mind cracked, emptying until only I remained inside, alone. Even more alone than I'd been before.

Forever and heart-breakingly alone.

I came back to myself in a sobbing heap, crumpled at the foot of the throne of the cruel sorceress. "Why?" I whimpered.

"Karyn," she called, like the sound of distant thunder over the ocean. Like the pounding of the rain and surf outside the cave I'd shared with Zyr.

"Karyn. Hear me."

Zyr. Where was he?

"Karyn. Listen to me."

Where was I?

I lifted my face to find Andromeda reaching a hand down to me, tears pouring down from her silver moon eyes. "I'm so sorry I had to hurt you," she said, "but I had to give you the choice."

"What choice?" I asked, my voice broken from the screaming. "Where am I?"

"You are in the Heart of Annfwn." She smiled sadly. "I've taken a grave risk in bringing you here."

"I thought you couldn't go to the Heart while you're pregnant."

She cocked her head. "You pay more attention than it seems you do. Well done. That was true before, but Zynda has returned in Final Form as a dragon. This pregnancy, at least, is one less worry."

"Oh." I absorbed that. Zyr would be so upset to hear this news, though I forgot exactly why.

"I'm going to ask you not to tell the High Priestess about Zynda, and not to tell anyone what the Heart looks like or where it is."

"I don't know where or even what it is," I argued, looking around at the crystal globe, the cobalt crabs shining and the sea beyond full of bright fish.

"You know enough, even if this may seem like a dream."

"I never dream," I said, remembering Zyr laughing at me for it. Zyr. I needed to remember something about him.

"Call it what you like. Your body is asleep, far away in n'Andana. I reached out to you in dreams and brought your consciousness here."

I contemplated her. My mind remained curiously empty, wiped clean of recent events, but I remembered enough of myself and my life to know how improbable that claim was. "I find that very difficult to believe."

She raised a brow, laughing without mirth. "You are so strong-willed and stubborn. I understand now why it's you at the center of this."

"You're wrong. I've never had a strong will. Zyr even chided me for apologizing and deferring all the time."

She was shaking her head. "Those are learned behaviors. That's why he chided you. Under it all, you have a will of steel. Who else could defy an emperor, an entire society, to request an annulment of her royal marriage?"

"That was a foolish mistake," I replied automatically, then paused. But had it been a mistake? At the moment of that decision, I'd experienced a kind of clarity of purpose I'd never known before. I'd been utterly certain of my choice, as I'd rarely been about anything in my entire life. For that crystal instant, it seemed as if a fog had lifted and I'd known—with an almost prescient understanding—what I wanted for me. Not for anyone else. For *me*.

"Regardless of the past," Queen Andromeda said, "you have a choice to make, and that's why I took the risk of bringing you here."

"What choice? I don't understand."

"Then listen. Do you remember the tale you told us on the beach in Annfwn, about the three princesses and the witch?"

"Everyone knows that tale."

She offered a gentle smile, still holding out her hand. I stared at her pale fingers with suspicion, unwilling to have her inflict that agony on me again. "Thanks to you, now we know it, too. Think of me as the princess come to retrieve you from the witch's castle. The High Priestess, she has put her mark on you—do you remember?"

Oh yes. Yes, I did. And there were other things I should remember to say, but I couldn't think of them. "She's my friend."

"I won't argue otherwise," Andromeda said, holding my gaze. "I've done all I can to tilt the balance back. I've cleared your mind and heart and soul of her taint, but if you welcome her back, if you agree with her, accept her gifts, drink of her wine and eat of her food again, then she'll have you as tightly as before and I won't be able to bring you back from it a second time. Do you understand?"

"No." My empty head pounded and my left arm itched. I

looked at it and the inked-on talons flexed, scrabbling for a hold on my skin.

"I can't erase it completely," Andromeda said, "because she'd notice. Unfortunately, leaving even this much intact gives her a hold on you. I had to leave just enough for her to believe she has you in her power still, and because you will need it. But she doesn't own your will anymore. And she can't again, not if you don't let her."

"How do you know all of this?" I demanded, some of my thoughts returning. "You're far away. How do you even know we found n'Andana, that I'm there sleeping?" I was sleeping. I remembered that part, being so drowsy and the High Priestess suggesting I rest. Perhaps all of this was a dream and I hadn't known it because I didn't recognize my dreams—which would make Zyr right about yet another thing.

Queen Andromeda winced, a glint of regret in her luminous eyes. "I… planted a seed in you, when we talked, so I could follow. You know I have visions of the future? Some events are more inevitable than others. You and Zyr in the High Priestess's hold was an inescapable event. And it's pivotal. You must understand that. The choice you make will tip how things fall out afterward one direction or another."

"Zyr is locked in gríobhth form," I told her, the memory of him in that cage coming back with searing intensity. "He's in chains."

"I know." She sounded infinitely sad.

"You set us up!" The anger burned bright and hot with the realization.

"No," she replied carefully. "That would imply I created the situation. The inevitability of pivotal events means I can't alter them, not without worse consequences."

"Why didn't you warn us?" I demanded, surging to my feet,

fisting my hands, wanting nothing more than to tear into her.

"Because it would've changed things for the worse," she replied evenly. "I can't prove that to you. I know you have no reason to trust me. But I promise you I saw no way around this eventuality. And I *looked*, tracing alternate timelines to exhaustion. You and Zyr had to pass through this nexus. What happens to us all after this depends on you."

"Zyr can't do anything," I spat with bitter anger. "He's trapped in a cell."

Andromeda's silvery eyes dimmed as she pressed her lips together. "I know. When I said what happens next depends on you, I meant you alone, Karyn."

"Me? I'm not even supposed to be here. I'm not on your side of this war—I'm a Dasnarian!"

"To be Dasnarian does not mean Deyrr," Andromeda said with insistence. "You know this. Aren't you an honorable woman from an honorable family?"

"Hardie honor has never been questioned," I asserted with stiff pride.

She smiled. "I don't question that. But you told me that no honorable family associates with Deyrr, or even acknowledges the existence of the Temple of Deyrr."

That was true. How could I have forgotten that? "I don't know what to do," I whispered.

"Deyrr is a poison that threatens Dasnaria, too," Andromeda said. "We are not enemies. We share an enemy. Fight with us against Deyrr. That's all I ask of you."

"I'm only a woman," I protested.

"So am I," she retorted.

I snorted, making a derisive comment in Dasnarian, which she apparently understood because she arched her brows at me.

"Calling *me* a liar? That's rich after you've been lapping up every lie the High Priestess fed you."

"You understood that?"

"You're not really here, remember? Only your consciousness is, so though we seem to be talking, we're more…thinking at each other."

"And you claim you're only a woman."

"I am a woman," she replied in a tone that allowed for no argument. "I am flesh and blood and female, just like you."

"And a sorceress with eyes like the full moon."

Her lips quirked in a wry smile. "I also act as a kind of portal for Moranu, especially when I call on Her for deep magic. The goddess is here, guiding us in this."

"Moranu was a Dasnarian woman, an acolyte of Deyrr."

"Are you sure?"

"The High Priestess told me."

"As I said, the High Priestess spins a web of lies to wrap the path she intends for you in pretty threads of silk."

"She opened my eyes to the truth. Maybe it's you who is lying to me."

"Would I have shown you the Heart or told you about Zynda if I could lie to you? I asked you to keep those secrets close because I couldn't hide them from you. We are in each other's minds. We cannot lie to each other. If you choose to betray me, I can't stop you."

"Then why risk this at all?" Confusion made my head ache. Could one feel pain in dreams? I didn't know.

"Because the risk is worth the gain," she replied, very seriously. "And because we've called you friend and the Tala don't abandon their friends. We don't leave anyone behind."

Zyr had said the same thing. If I did dream, my mind might be just churning up that memory. "I can't leave Zyr behind."

"Then don't. Look for something like this." She lifted her

other hand, showing me a glowing deep golden jewel cupped in her palm, a perfectly smooth sphere.

"What is that?" I breathed in wonder.

"It's the Star of Annfwn. The prize the High Priestess has sought, so she can control the barrier."

"She's already inside," I said without thinking, then realized it must be true.

Andromeda nodded seriously. "So she has something like this. Likely a similar jewel but smaller. She might use it in controlling things."

"Oh." That tickled a memory that wouldn't quite connect to my thoughts. "If she has one, why does she want yours?"

"Smaller is less powerful," Andromeda replied with patience. "If she had one like the Star, she'd have won already. That's why she wants this—having it would increase her powers exponentially."

"Like yours."

She smiled sadly. "Unfortunately, magic requires both the focus jewel and the wielder's ability. I have the Star and the Heart, but she greatly outmatches my abilities."

"I don't know what's real anymore. My head aches." I felt like I was splintering into tiny shards of myself.

Andromeda sighed, putting the Star away again, her image dimming. "I can't keep you here much longer. All I can tell you is to remember your own tale and safeguard yourself against the witch. Whatever she tells you, ask yourself what purpose it might serve her for you to believe her."

"Even if I do those things, I can't escape her," I protested, feeling the panic rise again. "I'm trapped. This place is an isolated fortress. And I'm no fighter. There's nothing I can do."

"There is." Andromeda gazed at me fiercely. "Remember that. The choice is yours."

"But I don't even know what choice you mean."

She faded into shadows, only the silver spheres of her eyes remaining, sliding together into a single full moon.

"Remember." The wind soughed her words in a thousand whispers. "The choice is yours."

~ 22 ~

I AWOKE TO my darkened bedchamber. Outside my windows, the full moon sailed high and bright, filling the sky with silver radiance that illuminated the snow-capped peaks. One of the windows must've been left ajar, because chill wind whistled through it.

Remember, it whispered.

I sat bolt upright. The whole strange dream flooded back to me. It couldn't have been real. Magic of that sort simply wasn't possible. That full moon shining through my window, on top of all the wine at lunch, had given me flights of fancy. And a headache. My eyes felt gritty and my temples throbbed. What had possessed me to drink so much wine?

That's what had made me think I spoke with Queen Andromeda. Certainly it hadn't been real. It had to have been a dream.

"I never dream," I said aloud, my voice hushed by the velvet-draped room. *Remember*, the wind whispered back. *The choice is yours.*

The doors to my bedchamber flew open and golden torchlight flooded the room, banishing the moon's silver glow. My handmaiden made an exclamation of dismay and hurried to the open window, shutting it firmly, and latching it—extinguishing the voice of the wind also.

Just as well. I didn't want the choice to be mine. I'd never asked for any of this. Jepp had said almost those very same words to me on that long-ago day in the Imperial Seraglio. *It will be your choice. The freedom to decide.* I wanted to burst into tears just as I had on that day.

I shouldn't have to make these choices. I'd done what was asked of me. I'd made one terrible decision. Wasn't that enough?

My handmaiden had been lighting all the torches and lanterns in the room, and now came to me, hands extended in invitation to rise. Because it was easier—and I needed the time to think—I went with her to the bathing chamber, where apparently I was meant to take a hot bath again. At least this time she pinned my hair up to keep it from getting wet. Otherwise, she soaped and oiled me with the same thoroughness as earlier in the day. And, in a further violation, she oiled my sex, too, using her fingers to push the unguent well inside of me, a clear indication of what lay ahead. I bore it all with apparent meekness, awaiting my opportunity.

Layers of jasmine later, she dressed me in a gown of sheer white lace. Spun of translucent silk and worked in an open pattern it would take me years to learn, the lace revealed more of my body than it hid. I kept expecting more layers of overdress, but my handmaiden sat me in a chair, working assiduously with fire-warmed rods to iron my hair again into a smooth gleam, coaxing it into orderly waves.

My habit of obedience had me sitting still for it, but I kept thinking about Zyr and how he'd liked the wildness of my hair. He'd liked all the spirit and disobedience in me, as no one else ever had. He must be prowling his bare cell, as best he could in those chains, wondering when I'd free him. Or *if* I'd free him.

If he could think at all.

I'd lost the will to fret about his captivity sometime during the long afternoon of wine and conversation. Though… maybe it hadn't been a conversation at all. I mostly remembered the voice of the High Priestess, not even her words, but the melody of it, like listening to lovely music.

Looking back at those hours, they seemed as if they'd happened to someone else. Like a tale I'd heard and vividly imagined. Except I recalled the taste of the wine and all the feelings the High Priestess had evoked in me. I'd been so happy. Happier than I'd ever been in my life. I'd belonged.

And Andi had taken it away from me. She'd taken that sense of belonging and ripped it clean away. I could hate her for that.

My handmaiden finished with my hair and applied more cosmetics. She did so artfully, but far more heavily than my mother would approve of. I looked more like a rekjabrel than a virginal maid and honorable wife.

But then, the High Priestess had said the god would divest me of my virginity at midnight, hadn't she? It seemed impossible that I'd greeted *that* news gladly. How did a god take a human woman to his bed?

One thing was certain: I didn't want to find out.

The choice is yours.

But how could it be my choice? I couldn't break Zyr out of those chains or fight the mind magic of the High Priestess. It still made no sense to refuse to eat or drink. I'd die of thirst within days.

And yet… wasn't that a choice?

Maybe I couldn't fight, but I could choose not to cooperate. *Don't agree. Don't offer gratitude. Don't accept her gifts.*

Though she'd claimed she wasn't, Andromeda must be a sorceress as powerful as the High Priestess the way she'd wiped my mind, heart, and soul clean of Deyrr's influence so I could decide again with my eyes open. To give me a second chance.

The choice is yours. Maybe the choice not to make the same mistakes again.

My handmaiden tugged me to my feet, showing me my image in the mirror again. If I hadn't become accustomed to going without clothing in the last days, my near nudity in the revealing gown would have scandalized me into paralysis. As it was, I could see that I looked beautiful, but not at all like myself.

The tale I'd told them back in Annfwn had always been one of my favorites, mostly for the heroine and that one line—*for beauty can be measured in many ways and no kind is better than any other.*

I'd never told anyone that was my favorite part. It had seemed silly and a minor piece of the tale. Even so, as much as I'd always loved those words, I hadn't truly understood them until this moment. Now I could see how everything I knew about myself—and those parts of me I had yet to discover—could be measured in many ways. And while no quality in myself was better than any other, I could choose which I preferred. *The choice is yours.*

I'd never really considered, either, how the heroine had died at the end. Zyr had been so incensed, insistent that the ending should be different. I'd always accepted that tragic endings were inevitable.

Perhaps not.

What if the tale *had* gone differently, and the youngest princess had outwitted the witch? She could've reclaimed her sisters' minds, saved the kingdom and lived. Then she might've married for love and had children instead of perishing at the wolf's teeth. That was Zyr's point all along. You fight when you have to, so that you can have a normal life afterward.

I'd chosen life back at the lake, when I foolishly—maybe innocently, as Zyr had called me—thought my greatest battle would be enduring Zyr's sexual attentions. If only my eyes had been open then, we could've enjoyed each other. Instead, my eyes had been so focused on some happy ending for some ideal of myself that no longer existed that I'd lost the happiness I could've held in my hands right then.

That was past and I couldn't change it. I *could* change what I did next. I'd fight this battle, and whether I lived or died, I'd at least know I'd done it on my own terms.

The choice is yours. So be it.

"I'm not going," I told the handmaiden, digging in my heels as she tugged me toward the door. She looked confused, then determined, and tugged at me again. "No." I used my best regal command voice, feeling as strong-willed as Andi had named me. Never mind that I was almost naked. My will came from inside, not from rank someone gave me or the rich gowns I wore. Not from following the rules. "I will not go."

She looked afraid and spoke to me in a rush of pleading words. I felt bad for her, clearly a servant in thrall to the priests and priestesses of Deyrr, but I wouldn't sacrifice myself to their god—and take Zyr down with me—to protect this girl. I couldn't protect anyone if I gave my will over to them again.

When she couldn't move me, she gave up and left, closing the doors behind her. Feeling the crawl of disobedience, I slipped up to the doors and tested the handles. Locked. I don't know what I would've done if they hadn't been—there'd been guards posted outside before and I doubted that had changed—but it seemed like the first step in fighting this cage. How could I know how strong the bars were that held me until I measured my strength against theirs?

Following that vein, I prowled through my chambers, checking the windows and other doors. The doors all led to closets, sitting rooms, and a servant's room. The windows all opened easily enough—to a brutally cold wind and a sheer drop that even the bright moon didn't illuminate. I listened for that voice in the wind, but it only howled of freezing death.

Andromeda, if she had indeed ever been present in my mind, had left entirely. I was on my own. I'd known that—had known it since that moment I broke all the rules and requested that annulment—but now I embraced that truth. The High Priestess had seen the gaping hole in me, had felt the wind of loneliness in me, and used that to offer the first of her gifts that I'd accepted. I'd been bought for the offer of belonging. And it had made me happy, for those short few hours, but it hadn't been real. I couldn't blame Andromeda for taking it from me. That happiness, that feeling of kinship, had been yet another veil over my eyes, just as my marriage to Kral had been.

None of that had been real. I supposed Jepp had seen that, had tried to explain it to me. I'd seen it, too, in that brief moment of clarity.

Oddly enough, the only parts of my life that seemed vividly real were those moments with Zyr. Flying on his back—even in my terror, I'd been wholly myself. Arguing with him. Laughing at his mischief. Kissing him.

I checked the drawers and wardrobes, looking for more clothes, not surprised to find nothing. Dasnarian to the core, the High Priestess employed the same familiar tricks. Deprive your captive of outdoor clothing in a harsh climate and she's as good as chained.

But not chained in actuality, not like Zyr. I needed to remember that.

The doors flew open and, as I'd expected, the High Priestess strode in. She wore a flowing golden gown, opulent and ornate, with matching jewelry, and an equally elaborate expression of concern. The teardrop pendant, a deep amber color like the Star, nestled at the hollow of her throat.

Rushing up to me, she took my hands, studying my face with her lightless eyes.

I had to leave just enough for her to believe she has you in her power still, Andromeda had said. That meant I should pretend to be as I was before. A dangerous line to dance, as agreeing too much with her would open the door to losing my will to her again. I didn't kid myself that I had the ability to keep her out. I'd fallen easily before and I could again.

So I smiled back, tremulously, letting her see my fear.

"Your maid says you refused to leave your bedchamber. Is that true?"

Don't agree. Now that Andromeda had cleared my mind, I could feel the snaky tendrils of the High Priestess's magic caressing my thoughts, testing them as I'd tested the bars on the doors. "I'm afraid of this ceremony," I told her. Absolutely true.

"Oh, no, there's nothing to fear, my friend. You know I only want the best for you, yes?" She squeezed my hands, the sticky web of her control sliding over my skin, climbing to the inky band of talons, making them constrict. With effort, I hid my reaction, dropping my gaze. How had I not felt it before? A great gift Andi had given me, this sensitivity, but I suspected it wouldn't last long under the onslaught of Deyrr's cloying touch. With my eyes lowered, I studied the topaz pendant dangling from the delicate gold chain around her swanlike throat. The key to the barriers between me and Zyr's cell. It took everything I had not to grab it and yank it from her neck.

"I think I'm not ready for the god's touch," I replied carefully, my mental feet firmly in my own truth, and pulled my hands out of her grasp, making a pretense of fussing with my hair.

"Yes, you are," the High Priestess replied firmly, the command in her voice bubbling through my blood, seeking a grip in my will. It slid away again, but I realized that refusing her would reveal my independence. Curse it all. I stared at her blankly. She smiled warmly, then slipped her arm through mine. "Come with me, Karyn. I'll be with you the whole time."

The way she spoke my name evoked how Andromeda had called me through sleep and dreams to speak with her. No wonder the old tales spoke of the power of names and how practitioners of black magic could use your name to command you. I shivered at the thought—and at the clammy feel of the High Priestess's body touching mine—and she patted my hand. Fortunately she seemed confident in her power over my will, because those seeking threads of magic withdrew as I walked obediently along with her. For the first time, it occurred to me that she might be physically dead. That would explain her unchanging youth, her apparent immortality, and the relative chill of her body. She wasn't cold, exactly, but rather the same temperature as everything around us, utterly lacking the warmth of a living body.

Only the dead never age, we said in Dasnaria, and I fully understood the truth of that now. Was this what they planned for me, an eternal, living death?

The High Priestess chatted amiably as we went through the winding halls, speaking of my future and how I'd be. Instructing me, I realized. I did my best not to listen, the magic in her musical voice palpable now.

That was a choice, too. I didn't have to listen to her. Instead, I thought furiously of how to escape, focusing all my attention on that. There had to be a way in, which meant a way out. Zyr could fly and I could ride him. I'd worry about freezing later. Getting us out was all that mattered.

The High Priestess led me into a temple that made my heart stutter and drop chill and already lifeless in my chest. I'd never seen a Temple of Deyrr, of course, but I would've recognized it regardless.

Made entirely of gold, every surface gleamed with metallic light. Shuttered lanterns of gold scattered candlelight through pinprick holes, and flaming torches reeked of some scented oil that reminded me of old blood. Images chased each other over the walls—gaunt figures fleeing through bare and wintry forests, skeletons scattered over the ground, and towering over them all, the giant figure of Deyrr. The god had been rendered in loving detail, robust and with a gentle smile as his great hands reached down to scoop up the people.

A basket hung over his arm, spilling with food and coins, traditional symbols of Dasnarian plenty. Behind him, people danced, these figures silvery, their eyes picked out with glittering black stone. I nearly laughed at that, wondering if the practitioners of Deyrr believed that lie, too, that they didn't see their own gazes looked as dead as the rotting corpses they disdained.

I couldn't laugh, or point this out to the gathered priests and priestesses, not only for fear of revealing I again possessed my own will—but because the sight of the statue of Deyrr filled me with such nauseating terror that it stole all laughter away. To think I'd been afraid of flying. Truly I had been innocent, not to understand the world held things far more worthy of my fear.

Garbed in golden robes, the priests and priestesses formed a narrowing path to the idol. Formed of gold, larger than even the biggest Dasnarian man, the god appeared to sit in a chair, grinning with sharp teeth, arms held wide as if to embrace his followers. Or a reluctant bride, as between his spread and massive thighs an enormous, rampant, metal cock reared up from his groin. A bowl situated beneath his artistically rendered scrotum, also exaggerated in size—or so I believed, from what little I knew of male genitalia—seemed perfectly placed to capture my virgin blood.

They might be disappointed there as my country-girl life of climbing trees and riding horses had likely left little of my hymen intact. Dasnarians relied far more on a protective family ensuring the chastity of their daughters, rather than something as prosaic as wedding-night blood. Though the size of the thing might do it. And as the smiling High Priestess led me closer to my leering, inanimate bridegroom, I perceived that the god's metal cock had been shaped with sharp edges that would draw copious blood indeed.

It made me wonder why my maidservant had bothered with the oil. Surely I wouldn't survive such a sundering. Or perhaps I wasn't meant to. I could be intended to bleed to death in the god's cold embrace, awaking again forever young and eternal in my clammy waking death.

I balked. I couldn't help it, my feet stumbling in the sheer horror of the prospect ahead of me. I'd waited too long. I should've escaped when I could, for there was no avoiding this fate. The High Priestess gripped my arm with her unnatural strength, crooning reassurance. At least my fear didn't seem unexpected, even if she believed me still under her spell.

Briefly, I wished I was. With the veil of false happiness and belonging, I might've gone to this lethal bedding with joy in my heart. It would have been a lie, but a restful one. I supposed most lies were meant to be soothing, so much easier than brutal truth.

Restful lies were a luxury of someone without the burden of choice, however. I'd spent too much of my life taking comfort in numb acceptance and easy obedience.

Though I still had no idea how I'd escape this fate. I wasn't Jepp to quickly draw hidden daggers and slice my way free in a whirlwind of merciless vengeance. Nor could I shapeshift to escape like Zynda would, or work magic like the Tala sorceresses. I had nothing, not even my bow and arrows. I'd been an easy bynd to take in Deyrr's game with more powerful pieces, and from what Andromeda had said, I'd be used to topple them.

We'd come to stand before the god, the High Priestess asking me something. I'd been so determinedly not listening to her that I didn't know what she'd said. The whine of terror filled my mind, keeping me from making any plan, my gaze helplessly riveted to that unholy cock.

"Karyn." The High Priestess spoke my name sternly, the magical command in it coiling around me like the blood-scented burning torch oil. The priests and priestesses chanted, I noticed now, a thrumming, low, and driving heartbeat of sound. "Raise your eyes to the loving face of your husband."

I obeyed, to preserve appearances and for lack of any alternative plan. The god had been sculpted so he appeared to be looking down at me. His eyes were made of inset jewels, glittering black beneath heavy golden lids, so lifelike I imagined he studied me. Andromeda's eyes had looked full of light—Moranu's presence, she'd said—and for the first time I believed in Deyrr. I believe the god existed and used this obscene idol as a vessel to work his foulness upon the world.

From my peripheral vision, I observed the High Priestess, who looked up at the god's face, her own a study in wonder and terror, a mirror of my heart. Had she been initiated this way, too?

"I'm afraid," I whispered to her, and her expression when she turned her face to me was filled with sympathy.

"It won't hurt long," she murmured, and kissed me on the cheek with her cold lips, her breath a waft of damp grave. "A moment of pain, and then you'll be filled with the joy of Deyrr. You'll be with me. With all of us, bathed in our love. You'll never be alone again."

"Do you promise?" I asked. "Have you been through this, that you know?"

She smiled, but the sweet curve of her mouth held ageless grief, finally matching her depthless eyes. "I have. We all have. Once your blood joins ours, you will be part of our family, one you can never lose. Now, look on the face of your husband, climb up, upon his thighs, and speak your vows."

Vows. *The choice is yours.* I looked up at that terrible, mocking face, those eerily living eyes—and saw that beyond, outside a high window, Moranu's moon shone full and bright. *She guides us both in this.* Moonlight glinted off the idol's teeth, each a lethal blade in its own right. The male priest who'd sat across from me at lunch stepped up on my other side, taking my arm in a firm grip.

"Do you, Karyn af Hardie," the assembly chanted, still in that thudding heartbeat rhythm, "accept Deyrr as your god, as your eternal husband?"

The High Priestess and the priest urged me to climb up, he lifting me and she raising my diaphanous gown as I straddled the metal thighs that spread me wide over that instrument of torture. The position of the metal arms made me slide in close against the statue's chest, the shape of it and the angle of the god's head making me arch back, exposing my throat to those blades of teeth. Blades. The moonlight shone on one tooth in particular, on the strangely alive eyes in the grinning metal head.

"Do you offer your loins, your throat, your life blood to Deyrr?" The assembly chanted. "Speak your vows and accept the great gift of eternal life."

I hung there, poised, my mind gone clear and bright as the moon, sharp as those teeth. Once again I stood in the emperor's painfully bright throne room, certain I'd refuse Kral's offer of annulment, determined to continue on my path of obedience.

"You know you want this," the High Priestess cajoled. "Say yes and start your new life."

So much easier to go along with this.

I made my choice.

~ 23 ~

"**N**O," I SAID.

I said it quietly, so under the thundering chanting no one could hear me. That didn't matter, because I knew the choice, the truth in my heart.

And the god heard. Those uncannily living eyes burned with fury. Wrapping a length of my lace sleeve around my hand, I seized the blade of tooth the moon had highlighted for me. It came loose, and I turned it, anchoring the blunt end against the heel of my hand. And I drove it into the god's eye.

It gave, like living flesh, black-oil blood squirting out to spatter my white gown. The world screamed, frantic magic coursing through me as if I burned alive. For a nightmarish moment, I fancied that I'd dreamed all of this in that cell in the Imperial Palace, that I'd been tied to Hestar's stake and now burned as he'd sentenced me to do. But the moon cut through the burning-blood smoke and I seized the second tooth it showed me.

I plucked that, too, and drove it into the god's other eye.

The screaming cut short—the silence enough to stun me. I knew I couldn't fail to act, so I extricated myself from the unmoving grip of the idol. It burned with fury, magic boiling from it, but finding no purchase in my mind, or heart. Only in my arm, where the inked-on talons sang with searing agony.

Ignoring it to the best of my ability, I swung one leg over, to remove my vulnerable sex from that angry and bloodthirsty cock. The metal thighs seemed to vibrate beneath me, as if some creature trapped inside sought to break free of its casing. A creaking sound filled the silent temple, metal grating against metal. Revolted, terrified, I scramble to escape.

A sharp pain lanced my thigh, opening a bleeding slice from just grazing the edges of the god's cock. I managed to get down, belatedly wishing I'd thought to grab one more tooth to defend myself with—but all the priests and priestesses lay collapsed on the floor.

Not dead, or even unconscious, they writhed in silent misery, clutching at their eye sockets. I wouldn't miss another opportunity to escape, but I forced myself to crouch at the High Priestess's side. Black tears poured down her face and I made sure to avoid them as I curled my fingers around her pendant and yanked hard enough to break the chain.

I fled, picking my way through them, holding the dripping lace high in case any retained enough wit to grab at me. Once clear of them, I ran out the doors of the temple, as fast as my bare feet could carry me.

At first I ran blindly, intent on getting as far from that horrible temple as possible. The lights of the palace had all been doused, the halls silent—the servants likely all asleep or wisely hiding–but my guiding moon shone brightly through the many windows. She seemed to make a silver path for me and I followed it for want of a better plan.

After a few turns, the hallways began to look familiar. And it occurred to me that the moon couldn't possibly be shining in every window I passed. Magic. *She guides us in this.* Fine—I'd take whatever help presented itself and save trying to figure it all out later. Perhaps this place had been Moranu's home, in some incarnation. *Let's just say an old friend left it to me*, the High Priestess had said. I'd known that tone well—from my mother and her friends, from the women of the Imperial Seraglio, from my hateful mother-in-law—that sugary voice that covered poisonous spite.

I felt sure that, whatever Moranu and the High Priestess had been to each other, they hadn't been friends.

When I reached that long gallery with the immense windows, I breathed a prayer of thanks to Moranu, whoever She might be. The moon rode lower in the sky, a shining beacon, and I ran with renewed vigor. Toward Zyr.

When I reached the first barrier, I held out the pendant and hurled myself through, as if speed would help. It buzzed as I crossed it, the same as it had that morning, but I made it through. The second barrier burned, but nothing like the clawing agony in my arm. The noise of the animals greeted me, a welcome cacophony of natural sound, so unlike the chanting and screaming of Deyrr. Even the scent of wet earth and excrement, of animal bodies, filled me with reassuring comfort.

Life smelled like this—full, rich, dirty, and warm. Deyrr offered nothing more than the cold facsimile of living.

Zyr waited for me in his cell, crest full and alert, his gaze sharp and predatory. I skidded to a stop, gazing at him and his chains in dismay. I'd have to go in his cell, but all of this would be for naught if I couldn't cross back. Even if I could get the chains off of him, the jewel might not let us both back out again. What was the point of having a choice if I'd only end up with no way to bring Zyr with me?

They'd be coming for me. I knew it in my bones, maybe in the shiver of moonlight. I had no time to dither. I'd always detested dithering in others and now I found myself doing far too much of it. An archer learns that early. You never draw the bow then aim. You aim, then draw and release in one movement. Hesitation is the enemy. *Think*, I commanded myself.

The High Priestess had said the barrier on the cell would burn my flesh off if I touched it, but she'd also said Zyr couldn't see through it and he had. *Whatever she tells you, ask yourself what purpose it might serve her for you to believe her.* Tentatively, refusing to be afraid, I bent my left arm and nudged my elbow against the cell barrier. That arm already hurt so much as to be useless, anyway, and searing that elbow wouldn't change that significantly.

It burned, yes—more than the other barriers—but when I pulled back my elbow to check, it looked the same. Zyr watched, head cocked. All right then. I could go in, but what if it only worked one way? We'd be trapped inside together.

I didn't see a way to test that, so I concentrated on his chains. What had the High Priestess said about those? She said they were to keep him from hurting himself. That wasn't useful. She'd said, too, that she hadn't taken him as a pet because she was saving him for me. That seemed highly unlikely. Maybe she couldn't. There'd been longing in her voice when she spoke of not seeing a gryphon in so long. And Zyr had said his gríobhth form was inherently magical, like Zynda's dragon.

Maybe the barrier couldn't truly hold him in and if I removed his chains, he could leave. Zyr was watching me, gaze intense, communicating something. "Is there a key to your chains?" I asked.

He fluffed his wings and shook his head. Curse it. But he continued to gaze at me meaningfully. I had no idea what to do. The chains, the chains… the High Priestess had said something about how I'd be able to take them after my first lesson, yes? And I'd had that lesson. Even though Andromeda had ripped the taint from me, I'd been through that conditioning, that so sweet absorption into their fold. *I had to leave just enough for her to believe she has you in her power still, and because you will need it.*

Perhaps the chains would answer to me, to the bit of power she'd given me, that still coiled into my blood through the scar on my arm, seeking its way to my heart.

But I couldn't know unless I went into the cell and tried. It could be I'd go in there and be unable to move the chains and be unable to exit again. *The choice is yours.* And it was an easy one this time. What point in escaping if I left Zyr behind? I'd rather die with him—my true friend, the one man I'd ever loved, however misguided I'd been in offering him my heart—than live without him.

Taking a deep breath, holding out the pendant, I flung myself through the barrier.

It burned. Oh, how it burned! It seared the breath from my lungs and made me briefly dizzy. I fell to my knees, staring at the smooth floor, bemused by the spattering of fresh blood. Had Zyr hurt himself again?

No, I realized, as his beak lowered, caressing my cheek with the rounded curve of it—the blood came from my hands, lacerated from those blades, and from the bleeding wound on my thigh. Zyr made a sound of distress, soft and trilling, surprisingly gentle from such a ferocious looking raptor. The purr welled up beneath it. The gríobhth, neither bird nor cat, yet somehow both. He seemed to match me in that way, neither Dasnarian nor Tala, yet somehow belonging to both.

I managed to sit up despite the dizziness and grasped his head in my hands, smoothing the fine feathers at his beak and around his bright eyes. "I'm all right," I told him. "And I'm getting us out of here. You didn't think I'd leave you behind, did you?"

His beak parted slightly, and his eyes sparkled. In my mind, I heard the man laughing at my joke. The High Priestess had twisted that truth, too. Zyr was the gríobhth, but he was also a person as much as anyone. How did one parse such things anyway? We all had bodies of flesh and blood, of relative intelligence. *For beauty can be measured in many ways and no kind is better than any other.*

He slowly raised his head and I held on, letting him draw me to my feet. Waiting patiently, he let me recover my balance. I clung to him for a moment longer than I strictly needed to—or could afford, with the priests and priestesses likely to come after me far too soon—but the living creature comfort of his warmth and strength, even his animal scent, made me unwilling to let go.

But I made myself do it. *Fight now so you can be happy later.* I let go and stood on my own two feet, willing the dizziness away. Zyr cocked his head, making that distressed sound, but I shook my head. "Small wounds. A bit of blood loss is all. Now hold still so I can see if I can remove these chains. Unless you know how I can do it, what she did?"

He wagged his beak back and forth in despondent negation, and once again I remembered how much this imprisonment must grate on him. I caught his head again in my hands. "We *will* get you out of here."

I examined the chains—they all attached to the collar around his neck to the various bolts in the floor. The simplest solution would be to remove the collar. Anything else would require multiple steps and possibly leaving the heavy chains dangling on him, dragging him down. No good if we had to fly and I saw no way around that.

The collar, though, was seamless—no lock or hinge present-ed itself. It ringed his neck at the joining of bird to cat, sitting on his shoulders, not constricting, but too small to go over his head. "How did she get this on you?" I muttered.

Zyr lifted his wings, half-mantled, in his gríobhth shrug. I studied him. "Were you unconscious?"

He nodded, clacking his beak in irritation.

I wondered though… "You definitely can't shapeshift?"

He gave me a *look* and I fisted my hands on hips in the same aggravation. "Work with me here—I'm trying to problem solve. I know that if you could shapeshift, you would, so you could at least talk to me, but I'm working backwards through this. The High Priestess has you locked in this form, yes?"

With a heavy sigh he nodded, then nosed his beak through my hair in apology. "It's all right. We're both on edge. Do you know *how* she locked you in this form?"

He cocked his head, giving me an intent stare with one blue eye, then waggled his head ambivalently.

"Yes and no?" I guessed, and he affirmed that. "I remember you saying that a punishment for criminal Tala is to lock them in their forms, so that means *you* know how to do it."

Eyes bright, he nodded vigorously. "So maybe you don't know exactly how the High Priestess did it, but it's probably a similar mechanism." Maybe to do with the jewel.

He nodded slowly, then caressed my cheek with the round of his beak. My reward, I supposed. "What I'm thinking is, what if she can also force you to shift? If she can lock you in this form, it seems she could also work it the other direction. So what if she healed you by forcing you to shift, put the collar on you, then made you shift back again?"

Zyr lifted his head and gave me a long and penetrating look, then nodded reluctantly. I kissed his beak, smoothing the small feathers around it the way he liked, the only comfort I could offer him regarding what must feel like a profound violation.

"If you can't shift, and if I can find a way to do what she did and shift you out long enough to take the collar off, do you think you could shift back to gríobhth again and fly us out of here?"

His crest rose in question. I wasn't sure to which piece, so I took a guess. "I don't know if I can, but I'd like to try. But I do think we have to fly out. We're in high mountains and it's very cold outside. I'm not sure there's a better way."

He nodded, then shrugged his wings and folded them again. Might as well try. I still had my hands on his head, so I closed my eyes, focusing on the magical crawl of the mark of Deyrr on my arm. I thought about that feeling of togetherness the High Priestess had infused in me, about the luminosity of Andromeda's eyes and how she'd spoken to me mind-to-mind. She'd taken a risk in showing me the Heart, in telling me that we couldn't lie, because the gain would be worth it.

Truth and lies. Beauty comes in many forms. I teased at the threads of it.

And I said a prayer to Moranu.

I imagined the moonlight of the many-faced goddess of shapeshifting flowing into me. Zynda claimed the goddess had sent her back from death, so I appealed to Her to guide me. I imagined Zyr as I'd known him, a long-limbed man with flowing black hair and penetrating blue eyes. I pictured him teasing me mercilessly, kicking back in his chair with restless grace, telling me stories by the campfire, caring for me with exacting tenderness, enticing me into a kiss that had devastated my heart.

My fingers tingled, my left arm burning with the bite of Deyrr. Then emptiness.

I gasped, my eyes flying open. And Zyr stood before me. Zyr the man.

Not his perfectly groomed self, but naked and rumpled, his hair hanging in ragged tendrils, circles of exhaustion under his eyes, lines of strain around his mouth. In distress, I clapped my hands over my mouth to suppress the cry that might alarm him. He didn't look right at all. I'd brought him back, but not fully.

The toll of remaining in gríobhth form too long.

Then he pulled the collar over his head, dashing it to the floor, and smiled at me—and though it was a shadow of his cocky grin, I could see *him* in it—and I dropped my hands to smile back.

"We have to—" I started, but that was all I got out before he seized me, mouth descending on mine in a kiss so ferocious it wiped my mind as clean as Andromeda had done. He kissed me like a starving man, making low sounds in his throat, desperate, full of need. I opened to him, wanting, *needing* to give him everything. Taking what I offered, his tongue plumbed my mouth, his hands roving over my body. I became crucially aware of my near nudity—of his obvious excitement in his unclothed state—how my skin responded to his touch through the sheer openwork lace. Arousal flooded me.

I moaned, and he growled, gripping me tighter, his hand suddenly under my gown, sliding up my thigh…

"No!" I managed, wrenching myself out of his grip. He made a move to reclaim me, his gaze as wildly glittering as the predatory gríobhth, and I put my palm on his chest, holding him away. "No," I repeated, firmly, quelling my own longing to have him hold me again. "We're not safe," I told him slowly.

His nostrils flared and his lip curled in a snarl, fingers twitching as if he might extend claws. Indeed his nails looked long and far too pointed. And he hadn't yet spoken. My heart sank.

"Zyr, can you speak?"

He cocked his head, so like the gríobhth.

"Zyr, I—" I stopped, aware of a change in the noise level outside the cell. The barrier on it suppressed some sound, but not all. Someone was coming. "We have to go."

Taking no chances that the gríobhth form might not be able to pass through the barrier, I held out the pendant to lead the way, and grabbed Zyr's hand and pulled. He came willingly—though maybe largely so he could put his hands on me again—and he moved through the searing force better than I did. Good thing he had a hold of me, because I sagged and nearly fell.

He caught me, holding me upright, but lifted his head, sniffing the air. A low, ominous growl rolled out of him, one I'd never heard from him before, and that made my hairs stand on end. "Can you shift back to gríobhth?" I hissed at him, and began tugging him toward a window, praying one of these would open like the ones in my chambers—and widely enough to let us through. "It's a sheer drop. You'll have to shift, let me get on, then leap out."

He scanned the room with feline intensity, still sniffing, fingers even more clawed now, showing no sign of understanding me. Despair dragged at me. We couldn't fail now. Not when I'd come so far. Zyr came along more reluctantly as I dragged him toward the towering windows, his attention focused on the far side of the room. Near the entrance.

"Karyn!" The High Priestess called in her over-sweet fake voice. "You have something of mine. I should've known you'd come to find your pet."

Zyr lunged in that direction, the growl rising into a keening snarl, but I kept his hand with all the strength in me, pulling him in the other direction along the windows. They shone in the moonlight, the glass clear, the panels soaring overhead, the seams between showing no latches. Curse it.

"I'm not angry," she sing-songed. "All great transformations can be frightening. Deyrr forgives you, and I forgive you. Just—" Her mellow voice curled into a snarl of rage. She'd found the empty cell. "Where are you, you conniving thief!" she screeched.

Truth.

Other voices joined hers now, calling out a search pattern. With one hand, I fought Zyr, who tried to pull me toward our enemy, strangling back a sob of frustration and terror as I scanned the windows, hoping against hope. If he'd had a running start, we could've maybe broken through them, but it was too late to try that with the High Priestess and the others searching for us, even if there'd been enough room.

And if Zyr had understood me.

A sparkle of moonlight caught my eye and I stumbled toward it, pulling the reluctant Zyr with me. At least he did follow. I had no illusions that if he'd truly tried to break free of my grip, with his superior strength he could've done so easily. Andi had told me I had an influence on Zyr she didn't quite understand, so I used it. I pointed at the latch above my head. "Open that," I commanded in a low voice, but with all the regal certainty I could put into it.

I could reach it, but I didn't want him running off to fight when I turned my back. Indeed, he glanced longingly in the direction of the nearest voices. I grabbed his chin, making him look at me. "Open the latch, Zyr. Do it for me."

His eyes lit with a fierce fire of lust, and he grinned, a salacious and sensual smile. Fine then. Better than the alternatives. He reached up, flipped the latch, and the window swung wide, icy wind pouring through. Zyr smiled at me hopefully and I imagined him wagging his tail, so I gave him a sound but brief kiss, pushing him back when he tried to prolong it.

"Thank you," I told him fervently. "Now shift. Become the gríobhth and take us out of here."

He frowned, the invisible tail lashing now, and looked back toward the calling voices. Near, so near.

"Zyr," I begged him, "please, in the name of anything you

ever loved, please please please take me out of here."

"Well, what have we here?" The High Priestess crooned, then tsked. "Thinking you can escape me so easily? Is that what you thought, my precious princess?"

I wrapped my arms around Zyr, keeping him from lunging at the lovely blonde. She emerged from the shadows, her gown in tatters, her face spattered with the oily black blood of Deyrr. Hers or someone else's, I didn't care to know. She'd draped a heavy medallion around her neck—one I recalled from the priest—the glowing center another, smaller jewel like hers and the Star. Did they all have them?

Zyr wriggled against my hold, trying to get free—blessedly aware of not hurting me, though. I thought fiercely of him becoming the gríobhth, but I couldn't concentrate as I had before, couldn't form that image as surely as I had of him as a man.

"So clever, though," the High Priestess sounded admiring, coming still closer. "You're a natural, my friend, just as I knew you would be. See how easily the jewel responds to you? Deyrr chooses wisely. Give up this silliness now and come with me. The rite is not so terrible and you'll love how you feel after—and you'll have a jewel of your very own. You can even keep your pet and have it after your husband takes his due. I can see the appeal of your Tala pet, however. It's quite the fine figure of a man. You'll have to share. Come, pet, come to me."

Zyr quieted, and though I couldn't see her around his body, I knew she pulled on his strings. I glanced desperately at the open window. I could fling us out of it. We'd fall and die almost certainly, but better that than slavery. Zyr had said he'd rather be dead than a captive. So would I.

The choice is yours.

Maybe Andromeda had meant this all along.

So be it.

That cool clarity descended on me, the certainty of knowing. I eased Zyr backward. He'd gone eerily compliant, following my lead. My bare heel hit the low threshold of the window frame, howling wind freezing my back.

"Karyn." The High Priestess sounded stern—and alarmed. "What are you doing?"

She lunged toward us and I threw her pendant at her. As I hoped, she leapt to catch it. Just enough to keep her from catching hold of us.

"I'm choosing," I said, and fell back, taking Zyr with me.

~ 24 ~

WE PLUMMETED THROUGH the icy air, my mind still clear and calm, time slowing to stretch out the extended seconds. I had long moments to think about what I'd done—and to reflect that I understood now why Zyr had mocked me for calling his controlled drop "plummeting." They weren't the same at all.

This was so much worse. And lasted forever.

I braced for the crash against rock, aware of the wind of our descent pulling tears from my eyes, of Zyr against me.

I'd killed us both, and I sent a fervent prayer for forgiveness. Especially for my petty joy that we'd at least die together.

Then even that was ripped from me, as Zyr disappeared. I cried out, reaching for him, finding nothing. I would die alone.

As I no doubt deserved.

A *whoomf* of sound. The cry of an eagle.

No—the gríobhth!

And he caught me, gathering me in his front paws as if I weighed no more than one of the mapsticks. I dug my fingers into his silky fur, holding on with all the tenacity in me, burrowing into his warmth.

He flew, and I clung like a burr, tucking up my legs and feet to warm against him. I'd had some vague idea of me directing him, of spotting some shelter, but none of that mattered now.

We were alive. We were escaping.

To where didn't matter so much.

After a while—I had no idea how long, as time had yet to regain its usual shape—he slowed, then circled. I craned to look, but saw only a chasm disappearing into lightless depths below. It gave me a sudden vertigo and I buried my face in Zyr's fur, forcing myself to take even breaths.

Then he touched down, landing on hindlegs, wings working furiously to keep himself reared up as he opened his forelegs to ease me off him and set me down. My fingers cramped as I made myself let go, half-frozen, half-constricted from holding on so tight. I hoped I hadn't hurt him, digging in so hard.

He set me on my rear end, because I couldn't make my legs work. Snow and freezing stone beneath immediately penetrated the fragile lace, and I squealed, the shock doing what my mind couldn't and making me crawl to my feet. The cold lanced through me, and I shivered violently. The moon must've set—or returned to Her usual course instead of following me—and the black of deep night shrouded everything. My bare feet were so numb I didn't even feel the snow, and blasts of snowflakes hit my face.

Where on earth had Zyr taken us?

I turned my face from the biting wind—and saw a darker shadow against the night. A house? Taking a cautious step toward it, I slid on the ice, and Zyr caught my arm. Back in human form, and on his own, thank Moranu, but still naked, his skin bare under my hands. Before I knew it, he'd picked me up, carrying me in his arms and toward the house.

He knew enough to recognize a good place, dark as it was, and to find the front door—but he paused there, thwarted and uncertain. I reached for the latch, praying it wasn't locked, and the door swung open. Zyr prowled in immediately, kicking the door closed, and blessed warmth enveloped me. I hadn't expected it to be warm, and wondered if someone lived here, asleep somewhere.

Sconces around the room flared into light, and a fire in a huge fireplace roared to life. Zyr could still work his magic then. He carried me across the room to the fire and knelt, laying me on a thick, furry rug there.

"Zyr?" I asked. His face looked remote, feral, that animal ferocity in it. He looked at me, those hot blue eyes traveling to my scantily clad body and firing with lust. Lifting a hand, he touched my cheek, surprising tenderness in the gesture, then pushed his splayed fingers into my hair and following with his greedy mouth.

His body fell on mine, hot and heavy, his mouth urgent, and he gripped my hair, holding me there while he kissed me with fevered intensity. This wasn't how I'd imagined it between us— or at all, as I thought he'd resigned himself to not wanting me. This Zyr, however, this gríobhth in a man's body did want me with a consuming passion. He'd forgotten whatever qualms had made him refuse me, and I responded to his fierce sexuality with a furious desire of my own.

I wouldn't have to talk him into taking my virginity. He wouldn't balk now, and I'd both have him, at least for this one night, and the unwholesome god wouldn't be able to take me.

The lace ripped, giving way as his urgently roving hands shredded it off me. With a distant thought, I hoped that if the house was occupied, they wouldn't hear us. It didn't seem possible to stop either of us now. I yielded to him utterly, giving voice to my moans and whispered encouragement. Not that he needed it.

His hands roamed over my bared skin, rough and delightful, his mouth following after to lick and nip at me. I writhed under him, lifting each part of me to him in offering, in whole-hearted surrender, giving myself as I'd longed to give my body to my husband. To my one true love.

For no matter what happened after this night, Zyr would be that to me forever. He didn't need to marry me in some ceremony. We did this between us, in fire and glory, in a profound celebration of the most primal acts of life. I loved him and would give him everything in me.

When his hand cupped the slick and swollen flesh of my sex, I orgasmed, the pleasure ripping through me unlike anything I'd experienced at my own hands. The oils they'd prepared me with helped, but so did my own fluids, opening the way for him.

Before the spasms left me, Zyr pushed back my thighs and slid between them, the head of his cock pressing against my virgin passage. I lifted my hips, begging with voice and body, and his wild blue eyes met mine. His teeth had gone sharp, the shape of his pupils feline, but I saw him inside. I reached up to frame his face, beloved in all its angles and shades of beauty.

"I love you, Zyr," I told him. "Take me now."

He hesitated an endless moment, a glimmer of something in his eyes, a shadow of uncertainty. I slid my hands down his back, grasping his magnificent buttocks, and lifted my hips, pushing myself against him. He shuddered, the tension in his body enough to snap.

"Now, Zyr!" I commanded. "Do it!"

He thrust into me, the force of it making me skid across the fur. But he had a fist in my hair still, so I bowed up with a cry of agonizing pleasure. The orgasm returned as if it had never ceased, racking me with convulsions as Zyr thrust into my body, filling me unimaginably. His mouth fit over mine, drinking in my cries and I gave them to him with willing delight.

My love. My husband.

He wrenched his mouth away, rearing back and crying out in a great snarling cry, like no animal and all beasts in one. His pelvis ground against mine, sending a fresh wave of pleasure through me as he buried himself to the hilt, so deep inside me I knew I'd feel him there forever.

Then he collapsed over me, a heavy, hot blanket, his skin touching me inside and out. With a sigh, I kissed the salty, soft hollow at the curve of his collarbone, then let the sweet release and exhaustion take me.

WHEN I AWOKE, the fire still blazed, but milky daylight glowed through the many small, square panes of the large windows, a blizzard raging outside. A fluffy blanket of silk and down covered me.

And Zyr was gone.

I sat up, the blanket falling away and my hair sliding soft and heavy over my naked back, the skin there sensitive as sunburn. I ached all over, my fingers and toes tingling, my sex deliciously sore. I'd well and truly lost my virginity. The sheer happiness of that—and how incredible the sex had been—curled through me with warm satisfaction.

Almost enough that my worry over Zyr dimmed. It rushed right back, however. He'd still never spoken to me, though I felt his essence, his mischievous personality, his intelligence, still inside. Perhaps he just needed time as a man to regain himself. Zynda had, so he could, too.

We'd been blessed with so much luck—or the beneficence of his goddess—that I refused to believe he couldn't come back from this. There must be a way. We could fly to Annfwn and perhaps Zynda could help him. If a dragon could make babies live, she could surely help a grown man. I'd carve out a happy ending for us, no matter what it took.

Extracting myself from my furry nest, I stood and examined the remnants of the lace gown. Never sturdy to begin with, it had been reduced to a pile of mere scraps of tangled threads at Zyr's demanding hands. The memory of his ferocity made me shiver, and my sex clenched, craving more. A clinking sound came from the other room, so I walked in there clad only in my wild cloud of hair.

Surely if anyone lived here they would've shown themselves by now. We'd hardly been quiet in our lovemaking.

Zyr stood in the kitchen, his back to me, and my heart relaxed to see him in human form and healthy. He, too, was naked, his black hair snarled and hanging down his back nearly to his masculine buttocks. I admired that sight—all mine, at least for the moment—along with his long and spectacularly muscled legs. He heard me and turned, giving me a view of the glorious front of him. He was as well-endowed as my sex remembered, and another wave of yearning rolled through me.

His face looked more normal, though he wore a wary expression that was not at all like his usual mischievous and confident self. The toll of captivity showed in the haunted shadows of his eyes, and I wanted to find a way to soothe that pain.

"Good morning," I said, tentatively, as if I might spook him by speaking too loudly.

He only watched me, though I thought he'd understood me.

"Are we alone here—and safe?" I asked. Even if he remained the gríobhth in his mind, I knew he'd have patrolled his territory.

He nodded once, a shadow of beak slicing through the air.

His gaze drifted over me, head to toe and back up again, and his face creased with concern. I walked slowly toward him, and he visibly braced himself. Stopping in front of him, I raised my hands to frame his face, as it seemed to calm him, and he flinched away. I paused, astonished, hands hanging empty.

He shook himself, that gesture of ridding himself of something unpleasant, and gazed at me steadily. Tension rippled through him, and his face showed deep unhappiness. With me.

I dropped my hands. He regretted what had happened between us. Oh, how that stung. A little piece of my heart broke off.

He said something to me in Tala. I recognized a few words, but struggled to make sense of it. I smiled anyway, glad at least for this much. It made sense that he'd regain his native language first. "You can talk again. Oh, Zyr, I'm so relieved. So happy for you, but I don't understand."

His brow furrowed, the frown daunting. My smile faded.

"I said," he tried again, in halting Common Tongue, "that you should go ahead and hit me. I deserve that and worse. I deserve to be castrated."

My mouth fell open, no words rushing to fill the space. "I don't understand." I'd repeated myself, but this went beyond language. "Can you explain?"

"Don't you dare defer to me now," he said in a rush, the words coming more easily, his face darkening with building fury. Not at me though, I decided. At himself. "You should hate me for what happened."

"You were injured," I said, shaking my head. "We were both taken captive. What the High Priestess did to me wasn't your fault."

He looked bewildered, then fury returned, though his face crumpled with it. Lifting his hands, he seemed about to take ahold of me, but he curled his fingers into helpless fists, shoving them down by his sides. "What did she do to you?" he growled, sounding exactly as he had in that night and moonlight-drenched solarium.

"It's a long story," I said, slowly and firmly, as I'd spoken to him then, "and what's important is that I'm all right. And so are you. We are alive and whole and together. I know being imprisoned is the worst thing that could happen to you, but you're free now."

He clapped his teeth together with a click, reminding me of the gríobhth's clacking beak, and his jaw bulged with tension. "It's not what happened to me, it's what I did to you. Don't play stupid," he grated out.

"Don't call me stupid," I replied, my own ire rising. "What are you talking about?"

"I raped you, Karyn. Don't try to deny it. I see my marks all over you—scratches and bites—I mauled you like an animal. There's blood all over the furs. I was brutal to you, I forced you, which is criminally wrong in any circumstance, but you were a virgin. You were saving yourself for your husband. That makes it so much worse." He scrubbed his hands over his face, his body sagging as he leaned back against the counter.

If he hadn't looked so broken by guilt, I might've held on to my anger—and the hurt that he, even now, didn't see a future for us. I'd known that, but somehow I kept forgetting to inure myself to that particular truth.

I extended a leg, showing the long, scabbed over slice, and held out my hands, covered with more cuts, large and small. "I think most of the blood is from these," I explained. "I really doubt I shed much virgin blood."

He dropped his hands, his face a picture of bewilderment. "You weren't a virgin anymore." His expression darkened, fingers curling into fists again. "Did they—"

"No," I told him firmly, taking his wrists in my hands, holding him steady. "I was a virgin last night—or earlier this morning, more likely—but the whole virgin blood thing is mostly a myth. I'm surprised you don't know that."

He glared at me balefully. "What do I know about virgins?"

"Well, it's true, especially for grown women who are physically active." I was rattling on, but talking seemed to make him focus on thought, not emotional reaction. "With younger brides, especially those girls barely into adolescence, then yes, there's a lot more blood. Which makes sense since they're much smaller than their adult lovers." Sometimes the women got to telling those stories, topping each other with a tale more gruesome than the last.

"That's horrifying," he whispered. "How can you speak so matter-of-factly of such a terrible practice?"

"That's the way of—" I caught myself lifting my shoulder in that fatalistic shrug and reconsidered. "No, you're right. It's a terrible practice. Dasnaria can be a cold and cruel place, especially to its women."

He regarded me for a long moment, then grimaced, a bare twitch of his sensual mouth, full of self-loathing. "As I was to you."

I was shaking my head before he finished. "No, I gave myself to you willingly, with all the desire and delight I'd hoped for. More, truly. Last night was incredible for me, so don't *you* diminish the sweetness of that memory by coloring it as rape."

"I don't really remember it," he admitted. "I don't remember much at all—just fragments. How long was I in gríobhth form?"

"I'm not entirely certain. I think the High Priestess shifted you out of it at least once, but overall… two days, maybe three."

"Too long," he said, more reflectively than to me. "No wonder nothing makes sense."

"It will. You're already much more…" *human*, I decided not to say. "You're more yourself. You're talking again."

"I wasn't able to talk?" He asked it carefully, but he'd paled.

Easy stepping needed here. "We didn't have a lot of time for conversation."

"Don't make excuses for me," he snapped.

"I'm not. You were disoriented. You mostly growled and snarled. But you also flew us out of there and brought me to safety. To this safe place, for which I'm so grateful. Thank you."

"Don't *thank* me," he hissed. He seemed to realize I held his wrists still, and tugged them away in a sharp twist. He stared at his hands as if he didn't recognize them. Took a deep, shuddering breath. "I'm so sorry I hurt you, gréine. Even if you say you were willing, I wanted so much more for your first time."

"It was perfect," I insisted. "I'm only sorry you don't remember it."

His gaze returned to my face, and he grimaced ruefully. "I'm glad I don't."

Another strike to my tattered heart. "I know you'd decided you didn't want me, and I understand that last night you weren't yourself, but I don't regret it. I am glad, so thankful it was you." My voice choked up, and I fought back the tears, lowering my face so he couldn't see. The last thing he needed was a weepy, clinging female thinking she had a right to his bed because he'd dallied with her.

"Wait." At last he touched me, placing gentle hands on my arms. "Why do you say that? I wanted you from the first moment I saw you. I never made a secret of it."

"On the beach," I said, still looking down. I'd fought the High Priestess, I should be able to control myself enough not to sniffle. "When I offered you my virginity, you said it…" I had to take a deep breath. "It wasn't a good idea." That last came out weakly. How I hated that phrase now.

"Oh, my gréine." He rubbed his hands on my arms, then gently pushed back my hair. "Don't weep."

"I'm not," I replied defiantly. How ridiculous that I'd cry over this, after all we'd been through.

"I said that because I know—knew—how important your virginity was to you, to your future. And I'd realized... I'm not good enough for you. I can never be the man to give you the life you want."

"Wanted," I corrected miserably.

"What was that? Please look at me, Karyn."

I lifted my face, my vision watery. "I only thought I wanted those things. You were right all along. I was a silly girl drowning in the wreckage of my former life, clinging to those rules of honor as if they'd keep me afloat. But none of that was real. *My only regret is that I didn't say yes to you long ago.*"

He let go of me to rake his hair back, scrubbing his scalp in frustration. "I explained this to you—I can't be the man you want."

"Then don't," I replied, a bit sharply. "If right now is all I can have, then I want to have it. I want to have you while I can." Deliberately I laid my hands on his chest, scraping lightly with my nails. He hissed, eyes deepening in color, his cock thickening.

"Karyn..." He said my name on a moan. "Don't do this."

I paused, studying his face. "You don't want to?"

He laughed, raggedly, gesturing to his rising erection, but holding his hands out and away from me again. "Obviously I desire you... but I don't want to hurt you again."

"You didn't hurt me before," I replied, laying my lips on his skin and tasting him. Salt and sweet, a hint of musk.

He groaned, his body thrumming under my hands and

mouth. "I was rough."

I looked up at him through my lashes. "I liked it."

His face sharpened, getting that predatory glint in his eyes, and I shivered with arousal, my sex flooding with welcoming fluids, my nipples peaking hard. I moved closer and rubbed them against him, loving the way he shuddered at the touch. "I warned you about this," he ground out.

Oh, yes—and by doing so, he'd handed me the exact weapon to use against him. "I'm sorry, my lord," I said meekly, casting my gaze down. "I only want to please you."

He growled, low and deep, something I felt more than heard. I slid down his body to my knees, caressing him with mouth and hands as I went, and his growl became a sound of despair. He fisted his hands beside his straining thighs.

I took him into my mouth, and he convulsed. "Moranu save me!" he snarled.

Looking up at him through my lashes, I let his cock slide slowly from my mouth, then delicately circled the tip with my tongue, teasing him. He gazed down at me, threading his fingers into my hair, touch gentle, eyes hot with demanding lust. "I think She already saved us," I murmured, "and this is how we celebrate."

"Is that so?" he replied silkily, his tone the only warning I got. Seizing me, he picked me up easily with his shapeshifter strength and deposited me on the counter. He'd been cutting up vegetables and meat, I saw, making us a meal.

I barely had a moment to note that—and be warmed by this considerate man I'd found—before his mouth took mine. Wrapping his hands in my hair, he tugged my head back, making me arch, and kissing me in that voracious way of his. His hair fell around me like a veil of black silk, sliding against my bare skin teasingly. I squirmed, panting, and he pushed between my spread thighs, lightly caressing my open sex with the shaft of his upthrust cock. I held onto his shoulders and wrapped my legs around his lean waist, trying to pull him closer, desperate to have him inside me again, but he held himself just far enough away that I couldn't quite get the friction I craved.

"Oh, no, gréine," he muttered in my mouth. "I'm going to take my time with you, make this something we'll *both* remember. Do you know what happens when you tease a predator?"

My mouth had gone dry, the rest of me drenched with need. "No," I managed to say.

He smiled. Slow, sensual, and full of wicked mischief. My heart tumbled with joy to see it, to see the trickster emerge in him again.

"My sweet, innocent almost-virgin," he said, his voice caressing, full of cruel promise. "Tease a predator, get the claws."

~ 25 ~

HE LAUGHED SOFTLY at whatever he saw in my face, and broke free of my clasping legs with effortless strength. With one hand, he lifted my thigh so my foot rested on the counter, and he anchored it there, holding me open with a firm clasp on my ankle, then leaned his hip against my other knee, pinning it in place. The other hand moved in my hair, gathering it, then winding with steady pressure, making me arch more, leaving my throat and body open and vulnerable.

Pausing, holding me at his mercy, he looked into my face. "Are you sure you want this?"

I licked my lips, drawing his hungry gaze there. "More than anything I've ever wanted in my life."

"So be it then. I'm taking my time with you. I've fantasized about this and by Moranu, I'm going to remember every moment." His mouth found my throat and I moaned, shuddering at the hot clasp of his lips, the sensuous stroke of his tongue tracing the tender skin, finding out the most sensitive spots— where he bit me lightly.

"Zyr," I gasped, unable to hold still, digging my nails into his muscular shoulders. "Please…"

"Please torment you more?" He inquired in that falsely polite way of his. "I do believe I will, my delicious Dasnarian princess. I think I might just devour you." His teeth closed over the juncture of my neck and shoulder and I cried out, unable to assimilate the extraordinary sensation. "So hot," he murmured, easing off and licking the throbbing spot. "So sweet."

His mouth trailed down the midline of my chest, where my breasts heaved with my frantic panting. Taking his time, he meticulously circled each breast with his tongue, carefully avoiding my nipples. I let go of his shoulders, threading my fingers into his silky hair, and clasping his skull, trying to pull his mouth to my taut nipple. To no avail. I couldn't move him—and he only chuckled at my efforts. "So impatient," he purred, and I felt the vibration through his tongue. "When I've barely even started on you."

He returned to his careful exploration of my breasts, finding that stroking the tender undersides drove me wild. I thrashed so much that he let go of my ankle and hair, stopping to kiss me fiercely. I clung to him, frantically rubbing against him as he held me. When he came up for air, he smiled, though his gaze remained ruthlessly predatory, and he kissed me on the nose.

"Naughty," he said, and unwound my arms from around his neck, taking my wrists in a firm grip, and moving them behind my back, standing between my spread knees so I couldn't close them. He grasped both my wrists in one hand, holding them easily against the small of my back, pushing them in to make me arch again, lifting my breasts. "Remember about the claws?" he asked softly.

I shuddered, unable to tear my gaze away, as he held up his free hand for me to see, his long fingers extending into silvery sharp claws. He flexed them, watching my face. "Do you trust me?"

I did. He'd caught me when I fell. He always kept his promises. "Yes."

He rewarded me with a kiss, sweet and lingering. "Watch."

Helplessly, I did, as he lowered his hand to my vulnerable breast, lightly tracing the shivering skin with his claws. A moan tore out of me, guttural, animal, and his lips tugged into a smile. He traced slow circles on my goose-pimpled skin, my nipple crimson and tight. I couldn't look away, nor would he let me move.

He left a faint red line behind, perfectly concentric despite my shivering response, a demonstration of his control. The light scratch built on itself, so that what started as a tickle intensified into an itch, then began to sting, the sparks of sensation making my breast seem to swell, the skin growing unbearably tight. I kept holding my breath, until I couldn't stand it anymore, sobbing it out and desperately drawing in air.

Still he tormented me, drawing closer and closer to the tightly pebbled areola.

When he flicked my nipple with his claw, I screamed, convulsing into orgasm, my sex opening and closing on nothing.

He bent over me as I undulated, taking my nipple and part of my swollen breast in his mouth, flicking his tongue against the turgid, sensitized flesh. I sobbed with the excruciating pleasure, and he licked the sting away, soothing me. Gradually I calmed. Until he nipped my nipple, making me gasp and squeal. Smiling at me with delight, he kissed me, still not letting me go.

"That was fun," he purred against my lips, the sweet rumble of it shredding me. "Let's do the other side."

I moaned in despair. "Zyr, please," I begged him.

He gave me a politely attentive look, retracting his claws and transferring his grip on my wrists, then lifting his other hand and slowly extending claws from it. I watched with fascinated trepidation and anticipation. "Please what, my helpless prey?"

"I can't take any more," I said, groaning as he pressed my wrists into the small of my back, my breast rising.

"Am I hurting you?" he asked with smooth concern that didn't fool me for a moment.

I narrowed my eyes at him. "You know you aren't. It's just too much."

"Now there you're wrong. It's not nearly enough." He caressed my cheek with the claw, a light scratch that shivered straight to my sex. "Remember—you wanted this."

"I want you to just fuck me already," I snarled, struggling against his implacable grip.

"Oh, I will," he promised with dark menace. "I will fuck you senseless once you're properly tenderized. Now be a good tidbit, hold still, and watch."

I sagged with despair—not that it made any difference, as he held me exactly as he wanted me no matter what I did. He began his slow tracing on the other breast, attentively following the same meticulous pattern. I'd thought maybe I could stand it better, knowing what was coming, but if anything, the anticipation made it worse.

I began to unravel, coming apart and losing all control. Whimpering, pleading, mewling, I writhed under his merciless teasing. He never stopped in his slow trail, watching my skin redden from his attentions, then devouring me with his wild blue gaze. Closer and closer he came to my trembling nipple. I froze, straining, waiting for that final bright caress that would undo me.

He paused. "Look at me."

I dragged my eyes up to his face. He smiled, wicked, and slowly licked his lips.

The tip of his claw flicked my nipple and I fell apart entirely, screaming my release and shuddering capitulation.

Again he took most of my breast into his mouth, but also finally let go of my wrists, gathering me close as he licked and laved the throbbing, tingling skin. I clung to him, wrapping my hands in his long hair and holding on, gulping and crying with the keenness of the collapse.

He eased me into a semblance of calm, then pressed my hips forward, to the very edge of the counter, trailing kisses up my body until our mouths met. This kiss poured into me. Instead of feeding on me, he filled me with a sweet tenderness, like a cool draught of water.

When he lifted his head, he rained kisses on my face—and lifted both of my thighs so my feet settled once again on the counter. I held on to his shoulders, watching him, uncertain what he planned next.

"The look on your face," he said with a smile. His fingers brushed down my inner thighs, making me tremble violently in reaction. "I'd planned to show you two can play your game, to feed on your sweet sex until you were a quivering mass of need."

"I'm already there," I whispered, half-hoping, half-dreading that he'd do it.

"So am I," he answered. "And I don't think I can wait for you any longer."

"Oh, thank Moranu," I breathed.

He laughed softly, and slipped soft fingertips through my slick folds.

My eyes rolled back in my head, and I lost all breath.

"My darling gréine," Zyr murmured, stroking me still as he positioned himself. "Open your eyes and look at me."

Blearily, I did, our gazes locked as he slowly entered me. He groaned low and long, taking his time still, his face contorting with the effort. I clasped him with my internal muscles, drawing him in, and he shuddered, gripping my thighs, and finally seated himself deeply within me. Deeper than I'd known I could feel. He watched my face intently, a curious half smile on his lips. Adjusting his hold on me, he slid his hands behind my back, wedging his upper arms against my knees, opening me even wider… and *pressed* me onto him.

The deep penetration fogged my mind, robbing me of what little reserve I'd retained, and I began to climax in slow rolling unstoppable waves. He rocked inside me, not thrusting in and out, but working us together in a building harmony that intensified unbearably with each flex of his hips and hands. I couldn't seem to find any purchase, each fresh wave of orgasm stronger than the last, the boundaries of myself blurring, our slick skin sliding together, his hair in my mouth and wound around my fingers. How I loved him.

He let out a guttural cry, and fastened his mouth on mine, his body finally giving up control, shuddering and shaking as he poured his pleasure into me, and I balanced on that ultimate peak.

And finally fell.

A LONG TIME later, he moved—only to brace one hand on the counter behind me. He still held me sealed against him, still buried to the hilt in me, but he sagged, bending heavily over me.

"You should sit," I murmured in his ear, then kissing it, and tracing the erotically curled and delicate lines, feeling him quake with reaction.

He laughed, shakily, and picked me up. Still buried in me, one hand against my sadly human tailbone to keep me there, he snagged a stool with his foot and sat on it. His long legs let him brace against the floor and he kept me straddling his lap, my legs dangling on either side of him, my oversensitized nipples brushing his chest. A small aftershock ran through me, echoed in him.

He studied me somberly, some deep emotion in his eyes, and I pressed my palms to his cheeks, studying him in turn. He looked much better, some of those haunted shadows had faded, the lines of strain softening. "How are you feeling?" he asked.

It made me laugh a little, mostly at the impossibility of answering that. "Rattled. Sated. Hungry."

His lips quirked in a wicked turn. "Still?" He flexed his hips, rocking inside me, and I clutched at him. "No," I groaned. "For food. No more, please."

Stilling, he kissed me. "I'm rattled, too," he whispered against my lips, then leaned his forehead against mine, sliding the fingers of one hand through the long fall of my hair. "Did you mean it?" he asked, eyes closed.

"Mean what—when I said no more? Just for now. Some food, a nap, then you can torment me again however you like."

He lifted his head, giving me a burning look. "I will. I'd like to put my tongue inside you and hold you down while I purr and you—" He groaned as I clenched around him, impossibly aroused again just by the thought. "I'll take that as a yes."

"Yes," I replied shakily. "Oh yes."

Meeting my eyes again, he sobered. "You said you loved me. Was that sex or did you mean it?"

Oh. That. "I meant it. I said so before."

He shook his head slowly, then smiled with a rueful half-shrug. "Not that I remember."

"I meant it," I repeated, letting him see the truth of it. "I love you, with everything in me."

He gazed at me for a long moment. "Karyn, I don't—"

I put my fingers over his lips to stop the words I didn't want to hear. "I don't need you to love me back, Zyr. I went into this with open eyes. But I won't lie about how I feel, and neither should you."

"I'd never lie to you, gréine." His low words held the intensity of a vow, and I smiled, smoothing my fingertips over the sharp stubble on his jaw, realizing I'd never felt any hint of beard on him before.

"I never thought about you growing a beard," I commented, scraping my nails lightly over it.

His lips quirked in a wry smile. "I always take care of that when I shift back to human form. This might be the longest I've gone without shifting since I was a kid."

It seemed odd to have a conversation like this, with our bodies still joined. Maybe all lovers did this, or maybe it was a Tala thing. Either way, I liked being physically connected to him. Indulging myself, I traced the lines of his face, his arching brows, finger-combing the tangled hair back from his brow. I'd never seen him so unkempt, not even after nursing me for days on end. "Why haven't you?" I asked softly.

He cocked his head, turned his face to brush a kiss against my wandering fingers. "You know, when Zynda came to me and told me what happened to her, she asked for my help because she hadn't been able to shapeshift since she came back to human form."

"Did you help her?"

A frown drew his brows together and I rubbed it away with my thumb. "At first I teased her. My prodigy of a sister, unable to shift. Then I told her it was all in her head, that she was letting fear get in the way. I wasn't...as kind to her as I might've been."

I considered him. "I wouldn't say my brothers were ever 'kind' to me, but I always knew they loved me. Besides, you did try to help her."

"I didn't succeed. All those children I've taught, and she

went away no better off than before. I don't know if she regained the ability or not. On one level, I didn't want her to. If she can't shift, she can't take Final Form and I wouldn't lose her forever."

A jolt of memory stirred remorse in my heart. He didn't know yet that Zynda had returned to Annfwn as a dragon. I'd have to be the one to tell him—and how I hated to have to layer on more pain when he already bore so much.

"The funny thing is—" He broke off, cleared his throat. "The irony of it all, is that now I understand exactly how she felt. It's as if I… strained something fundamental in myself. I feel hollow inside. I'm not sure I'll ever be able to shapeshift again. I wish I could tell her that I understand now."

"You will be able to shapeshift again. You've already recovered so much."

He shook his head, grief stark in his gaze. "I don't think so. Zynda warned me that we could be broken and I didn't listen to her."

"But Zynda did shift again," I reassured him, then closed my lips over my hasty words.

Too late, because he frowned at me. "What are you talking about?"

I sighed. "It's a long story. And I'm hungry. Can I tell you everything as we eat?"

Grudgingly, he stood, sliding out of me and setting me on my feet, searching my face. "I don't like secrets," he said. "They're just as bad as lies."

I nearly kicked him. "I'm not keeping secrets. We haven't had much opportunity for conversation, if you hadn't noticed."

He gave me a black look. "Because you seduced me."

Nearly choking on my outrage, I sputtered. "It wasn't difficult. I hate to inform you that your leash is quite short and I only had to give it a little yank and—" I squealed as he lifted me off my feet, kissing me soundly and spinning me in a circle until I grew dizzy from both, melting against him.

Finally he set me down, laughing, and kissed me on the nose. "You can tug my leash any time, gréine." He turned me toward the counter and patted my bottom. "But you're hungry—and so am I—so if you'll finish making the meal, I'll see what I can find for us to wash up with."

"Clothing would be nice, too," I said, surveying what he'd started.

"As my lady commands," he replied from right behind me. He slid his hands around my waist, then up to cup my still sensitive breasts, lightly brushing my nipples with his thumbs, as his cock rose hard against my bottom. I sagged back against him, food forgotten, and he nuzzled through my hair to kiss the side of my neck. "Though I like you naked," he murmured, one hand drifting down to cup my mound, his fingers easily parting my slick folds, caressing me and making me moan. "Hot, wet, and available to me."

I tilted my head to the side, giving him better access to work his erotic magic on my throat. "I am," I agreed. "Naked or not."

"Oh, Karyn," he breathed. "I think I must have you again. Will you indulge me? I promise to be quick."

I laughed at that, as I found it hard to imagine. Women gossiped about men being too quick, in and out and gone again, leaving them to finish off their own pleasure. Zyr would never be that man, if only because he reveled so much in every sensual moment. I pressed my bottom against his hard cock, already halfway to orgasm again, his clever fingers stoking me into mindless need. "Yes," I said on a low moan and started to turn.

"No, like this," he said, his voice low and urgent. He abandoned his teasing caresses to guide my hand to the counter, pulling my hips back. Gathering my hair, he draped it to fall all to one side, then put a firm hand on the back of my neck, pressing me down, then stroking his hands down my spine, before caressing my bottom. "Spread those gorgeous thighs for me," he demanded in a hoarse whisper, then groaned, sliding his fingers along my open folds, and into my slick passage. "Ah, Karyn, you are so beautiful. So pink and wanting. I can't get enough. I promised to be quick, I know, but I have to taste you."

Grasping my thighs, he spread them even wider, then put his mouth on me. I gripped the counter, my forehead falling against it. He lapped at me, long, luscious strokes—and his tongue became raspy, like a cat's, scraping over my pearl, and making me moan uncontrollably. Purring, he added a deeper harmony to my sobs of pleasure, the vibration driving me as wild as he'd promised. My thighs quaking, I lost myself yet again, falling into a sea of rolling waves that blurred into a slow and lovely climax. As I orgasmed, he thrust himself into me, raising me onto my toes, and holding my hips.

Not so controlled this time, he took me as he had the first time, with fierce intensity, his purrs melding into growls. I writhed in place, gasping with the overwhelming pleasure. As he reached his peak, he bent over me, whispering something in his language, pinching my nipple in one hand and my pearl in the other.

The acute shock sent me spinning, and my vision went black, sprinkled with stars like the night sky of n'Andana.

WE ENDED UP coming back to ourselves tangled on the warm

stone floor, and it occurred to me vaguely that the heat came from there. Remarkable. And lovely.

Turning in Zyr's embrace, I snuggled against him, kissing that sweet spot in the hollow of his collarbone, and savoring the slide of his skin against mine. He chuckled deep in his chest, hands moving under my hair. "You know," he said softly, "I didn't expect you to be so…enthusiastic about sex."

I tipped my head back to look at him, wondering what word he'd chosen not to say. "What do you mean?"

He shrugged a little, his arm muscle flexing under my cheek. "I had imagined slow seductions and lots of gentle reassurances."

"Ah. I tried to tell you that being a virgin didn't mean I was innocent."

"Yes." He drew out the word, considering me. "Yes, you did. But I still don't understand how you can be so passionate and have held that in all those years. How did you stand it?" He sounded honestly bewildered.

"It was my duty," I replied. "You may have seen my honor as a silly, meaningless set of rules, but it wasn't to me. I held firm to my vows."

"Until I forced you."

"No," I said firmly. "Until I decided they no longer applied, that I wasn't the same person who'd made those promises. Remember, I offered long before this. I meant that, too."

"I remember," he replied with a faint frown. *Not a good idea.* "You have so much more character than I do, such strength of will. If someone asked me to promise to be celibate, I'd have broken my vow before the end of the day." He said it lightly, mocking himself, the pain and self-doubt clear beneath.

I framed his face in my hands and kissed him. "I don't believe that. You nearly killed yourself carrying us across the water, and nursing me back to health, and so many countless small ways that you demonstrate your devotion to your people and your sister. Maybe nothing ever mattered enough to you to make and keep a difficult promise."

"Maybe not," he breathed, rolling onto his back and draping me over him, spreading my hair into a cape over us as he drew me into a long, almost shockingly tender kiss. "Are you too sore?"

"No," I answered. I didn't need to think about it. Even if I had been, I wouldn't give up any of this.

That time, we made love with heart-breaking sweetness, a storm of unspoken emotion swirling between us. And afterward I fell asleep on the bed of his body.

~ 26 ~

I DRIFTED BACK to consciousness with him carrying me down some stairs. "Where are we going?" I asked, my voice throaty.

He glanced down, giving me a cocky grin. "Surprise."

"Zyr." I tried to wriggle free, to at least sit up, but he tightened his hold.

"Since you so gratifyingly passed out from my attentions," he continued cheerfully, "I decided to reward you for the compliment." He entered a room of polished stone and past a warm fireplace. "Ta da," he proclaimed with a flourish and set me on my feet. A steaming pool of water lay before me and I sighed with delight. "Naturally heated by the earth," he informed me. "That's what keeps the house so warm, too, despite being abandoned."

"Oh, I wondered about that."

He patted me on the bottom. "Get in. I'll go fetch the food."

Needing no further urging, I stepped onto the first shallow step, moaning at the feel of the hot water, and waded the rest of the way in, sinking to cover my head and surfacing to slick my hair back. Despite what he'd said, Zyr lingered there, watching me with an intent expression.

"Something wrong?" I asked.

He shook himself and smiled. "Now that I know your sex

noises, I hear them in all your little sighs and sounds. It makes me want you."

I glanced pointedly at his lax cock. "I suspect even your notoriously lustful self needs some recovery time."

He grinned, that cocky and confident smile of old. "Not necessarily," he said, glancing down at himself. His cock lengthened and swelled, rising to full erection. "There are good reasons to take a talented shapeshifter as a lover," he assured me.

I raised an eyebrow, deciding not to point out that he clearly retained at least some of his shapeshifting abilities, despite his fears to the contrary. The claws he'd used on me, the purring and the raspy tongue—that memory filling me with liquid desire—not to mention this display. Better for him not to overthink it just yet. "I thought you promised me food," I said instead.

"True. And you must be sore. Remind me of these things." He frowned, his cock relaxing again. "I must learn to be considerate of you."

"I'm fine," I promised. "And I will tell you if I'm not. Right now, I'm really hungry."

"Aha." He bowed. "Excellent reminding."

He turned and strode out of the room with feline grace, and I sighed, enjoying the play of muscles as he moved. Such a beautiful man. All mine, at least for now. In truth, I didn't want this idyll to ever end. It seemed we could simply stay in this isolated house, sleeping by the fire and making love. Let the world and its wars go on without us, and have the normal life I'd longed for. Surely that could be one of those many futures Andi had seen, in her exploring of the paths of fate as hlyti wove them to its amusement.

The choice is yours. Her words echoed in my mind, and it seemed to me that perhaps I hadn't finished choosing. Soon we'd have to leave this place. The High Priestess and her horrible cadre had to be searching for us. This idyll had to end.

But not just yet. Until it did, I intended to savor every moment.

I found some soap—that thankfully smelled of a spicy wood and not like jasmine—and took the opportunity of his absence to thoroughly scrub my skin and hair clean of the last vestiges of Deyrr. I rinsed and soaped again, finally satisfied by the time Zyr returned.

He set a tray with the food, two mugs, and a pitcher of something cool on it, judging by the condensation beading on the metal. "Wine. Some meat. Some vegetables," he declared, then slipped into the water with the grace of his porpoise self, dunking entirely as I had.

"I'm surprised you found all this here," I said, pouring us wine and handing him a mug. "If it's been abandoned."

"Well, it has and it hasn't." He frowned thoughtfully, sipping. I plucked a cube of meat and chewing eagerly. Plain, but delicious. "Someone has been here—and they laid in supplies in a clever box out in the snow—but no one has been here in years."

"How do you know?"

"By the smell," he replied, as if that had been obvious. I suppose it was, and that was how he'd found the cache of food. "Where *are* we, Karyn—do you know?"

I kept forgetting how much he'd missed. "We're in n'Andana," I told him.

"Then we did find it!" He grinned in triumph. "I knew we could do it."

"We did," I smiled back. "Unfortunately, Deyrr was here first."

He sobered. "Maybe you should start from when I crashed."

So I told him the whole tale, giving him every detail I could recall, so he'd have my memories, at least. When I got to the part about Andromeda summoning me, he raised his brows in astonishment.

"My clever cousin," he mused. "I didn't know she could work such magics. She's growing more powerful every day. Tell me more about the Heart—what did it look like?"

"Don't you know?"

He made a face. "Of course not. The females of the family guard that secret like you protected your virginity, zealously and to an unreasonable extent." He ducked, grinning, when I splashed water at him.

"Well, I can't tell you," I said primly. "Andi asked me not to."

"Figures," he grumbled good naturedly, then quieted, his gaze dark and speculative. "Andi couldn't go to the Heart unless she shapeshifted—I know that much about how its kept hidden, that it takes a shapeshifter capable of multiple forms to get there—and she wouldn't have risked her pregnancy unless Zynda had returned in Final Form. That's how you know Zynda could shapeshift again. Andi told you."

I moved over to him, framing his face with my hands. "I'm so sorry, my love. I wish I could spare you this truth."

He smiled, sorrow in it, and put his hands over mine. "I knew it already, from that dream. And I knew she'd find a way. She's always been like that. Nothing could ever stop her. Now she's a dragon in truth, and not just in her fiery and arrogant heart." He said it lightly, making it a joke, but I knew he grieved the loss of his twin.

"I knew you," I told him, "even when you'd been the gríobhth for days and couldn't talk to me. You were still yourself inside. You haven't lost your sister. She will just look different on the outside." Beauty in its many forms.

He kissed me, then set me away from him. "No distracting me. Finish the story. All of it, including every detail of this 'ritual' they put you through."

I'd intended to gloss over some of that, but he watched me keenly, stopping me from time to time to probe for more information. So I told him everything. Partway through my description of the horrid idol, he picked me up and set me sideways across his lap, wrapping his arms around me and holding me tight.

It helped, and I hadn't known I needed that. I told him all of it, trembling with the memory. He ran his hands over me, as if checking for injuries I hadn't mentioned. "I really hate—with a vicious consuming hatred—that I wasn't there to protect you," he said in a low voice that grated with the force of his emotion. The gríobhth. Close to the surface.

"I'm all right," I promised.

His fingers lingered over the inked-on talons circling my left arm. It had gone quiet, no longer gripping me or sending its insidious whispers to my heart. "Is this forever then?" he asked.

"I don't know. I'm sorry it's so ugly."

His stricken gaze flew up to mine. "It's not. In fact, it's oddly beautiful and I don't know how to feel about that. I don't want them in you."

"Maybe Andi can remove it when we get back."

"Yes." He frowned a little and I could follow that thought. *If* we got back.

"Do you think you can find the way back without the map-sticks?" I asked, knowing I had to bring it up.

He sighed. "Then you don't have them?"

"No. They took everything."

"I'm thinking the answer is no. That was a long journey even knowing the way—and I barely made it—even if I can shift again, there's no room for mistakes. I'd have to know at least the landmarks for the launch point and direction."

I nodded, unsurprised.

"Finish the story—how did you get us out?" He didn't stop me again, letting me continue all the way to reaching our sanctuary. Then he picked up my foot, holding it out of the water and examining my toes.

"You could've gotten frostbite," he said in an eerily calm tone. "You could've lost your fingers and toes because I carried you virtually naked through freezing air, and all I did was rut at you like a beast."

I rolled my eyes at him, pushing away so he'd see. "This again?"

He regarded me grimly. "Still."

"I'm perfectly capable of stopping you if I need to. I did in the cell, like I told you. You asked me to trust you—well, you should trust me."

Relenting, he smiled a little, though his jaw remained set. "I want to rend them all to pieces for what they did to you."

"You may yet get your opportunity," I replied.

"We have to go back," he agreed. "We need the mapsticks. Even if they're already inside the barrier, the High Priestess and her minions having those jewels gives them too much power. And we're here—we should get as much information as we can. Or kill them all and stop this now."

"Yes." That had occurred to me, too. I'd told Zyr all about Andi's nexus, and the implications had laid a weight of responsibility on him, as well. "Or set her army free."

He gave me a smile and touched my cheek, but didn't voice the thought in his saddened eyes that likely none of those under her control could ever be freed. "It would've been lovely of my cousin," he commented, somewhat caustically, "if she'd given you some hints about the ideal steps for us to take."

"I don't think she could."

He snorted in annoyance. "All right, we'll go when the weather clears. And if I can shapeshift again. By the look of the landscape, walking isn't an option."

I thought of the youngest princess, walking to the witch's palace on the mountain. "No, it's all high snowy peaks and deep valleys."

"I can't believe you threw us out the window to die."

"You would've made the same choice."

"Yes." He coiled a strand of my hair around his finger, holding it up to the light, turning it so the shades of gold glimmered. "We also need that marriage certificate."

I paused. "That's hardly important."

"It is," he insisted. "It's a binding contract among your people. We destroy it and we remove their ability to use you as their tool. Besides, you're not married to *him*. I won't have something out there saying you are."

I gazed at him, taken aback by his vehemence. The gríobhth in him looked back, possessive and protective. With a sigh, I settled against him. "Have it your way."

"Ah, I love to hear that," he purred. "Come. Let's get out and dry off. I want to have you in a proper bed. In *my* bed," he added with particular emphasis.

I closed my eyes against the surge of emotion. He might not mean those words exactly as I heard them, but it was enough. "Yes, Lord Zyr," I replied meekly, and his hands tightened on me.

He stood, water sheeting off of us, and he carried me out of the pool.

It took us some time to reach an actual bed, however.

THE FOLLOWING MORNING dawned bright and clear, the storm having cleared off. If the High Priestess had been delayed in searching for us by the weather, nothing would hinder her now. Zyr stood naked before the windows, scowling at the clear skies, and turned at my disappointed sigh.

"I never thought I'd pray for snow," he commented, then came over and tugged the covers off of me, looking at my naked body intently.

"I'm fine," I told him, and he glanced up, smiling wickedly.

"I know. You're just so beautiful I want to look at you while I can. I imagine you'll insist on wearing clothes once we leave here."

I giggled, stretching, reveling in his admiring regard. "I think that would be the wise choice. If there *are* clothes. We never did look."

"I did," he admitted. He gestured to a pile of clothing on a nearby chest, including a pair of leather boots on the floor, and what looked like a furry cloak. "Those should fit you. And I found this." He reached to a table beside the bed and, sitting beside me, set it down.

Curious, I sat up. "A bow!" And a quiver of excellent arrows. "Where did you find this?"

"There's a whole armory," he explained. "With several other bows, if you don't like this one, but this seemed like the right size for you."

Eagerly, I slid off the bed, taking the bow with me. Shaking back my hair, I strung the bow and drew, testing it and myself. My left arm throbbed, weaker than it used to be, but the bow responded as sweetly as my own back home. I gave Zyr a radiant smile. "It's perfect. Thank you."

"You're perfect," he replied, watching me with an odd expression, which he turned into a cocky grin when he caught me studying him. "From now on you should practice naked. Just to please me."

I wrinkled my nose at him and went to the clothes, putting my new bow down and taking those up. "I want to bathe once more before we leave. And maybe have another meal, if there's enough food."

"There is, enough for a few more days, in case I can't shapeshift."

I set the clothes down and went to sit beside him on the bed, taking his hand in mine. He regarded me seriously, the uncertainty clear in his eyes. "Zyr, you can shapeshift," I told him.

"You don't know—" he started, but I interrupted him.

"I do know. I think you're so accustomed to life as a shapeshifter that you don't realize all the little ways you do it," I told him. When he frowned at me, I added, "The claws? The raspy tongue and purring. Your… other tricks." I gave his cock a significant glance.

His face cleared. "I hadn't thought of that."

"You would have, eventually," I teased, and stood again to retrieve my clothes. "I'm going to bathe and give you some privacy to practice."

He caught my hand. "Karyn… thank you."

"I didn't do anything," I said, giving him a curious smile.

"Yes, you did. More than you know." He squeezed my hand and let it go. "Go bathe and dress or I'll have to drag you back to bed yet again."

Because I could, I washed my hair again, drying it before the fire before braiding it. I didn't have any ribbons anymore, so I used a piece of lace from that misbegotten white garment. I didn't go back upstairs to the bedroom we used, giving Zyr his space, and instead tromped out into the snow in my new boots to find this food storage chest and put together a meal.

There weren't a lot of options, but there was enough to make a hearty stew. By the time Zyr wandered into the kitchen, it was ready to eat. "These n'Andanans are clever," I said to him over my shoulder. "This cooking setup is excellently thought out."

I turned, taking in his immaculate appearance—the familiar black pants and blue silk shirt, his hair once again sleek and tied back. For some reason I felt a pang of sorrow. Selfish, when I should be happy for him. "It worked."

When he returned my smile, his seemed a little sad, too. He drew my braid over my shoulder, running his fingers down the winding bumps. "Back to the real world for us."

Ah, that explained my sadness at seeing him back to his usual self. "You look good though."

"As do you." He took my hand and twirled me in a slow circle, rounding a hand over my leather-clad bottom as he did. "If I can't have you naked, then these pants are the next best thing."

I warmed with pleased embarrassment. What my mother would think to see this outfit. "Maybe we can come back here sometime, and stay naked and unkempt for a week."

"If we live through this," he muttered. "Did my cousin indicate any hope of that?"

I shook my head, dishing up the stew. "She said she couldn't tell me much, or it would change things and imperil us more."

"This is why I hate foresight," he complained, taking the

bowls from me. "It's not useful."

I followed him to the little table. "I don't think that's true. I wouldn't have had the courage to resist the High Priestess and get us out if Andi hadn't told me it was possible."

"I'm not sure I believe that." He extended his arm across the table to set the bowl in front of me. "You are—"

I gasped, and he broke off, going alert. "What's wrong?"

Reaching over, I touched my ribbon around his wrist, revealed when his sleeve had slid back. "You still have it."

He turned his hand to hold mine. "Of course I do. I told you I'd keep it."

"You didn't have it before," I countered. "That next morning on the beach. I thought you forgot about it." Or threw it away.

"I…didn't feel right wearing it," he explained slowly, studying our joined hands. "I knew you had a lot of expectations of me and I seemed certain to fail them."

"But you're wearing it now," I pointed out, feeling breathless, maybe even hopeful.

His eyes met mine and he grimaced ruefully. "Well, I figure that we're pretty certain to die today, so I thought I could probably make it a few hours without letting you down."

"Zyr," I said, very seriously. "You have never once let me down. You're the best man I've ever known and I'll love you until my dying breath."

He lifted my hand and kissed it, eyes full of emotion. Then he gave me a cocky grin. "Also easy to say if that's only a few hours away."

I laughed. "True."

And even though we might not survive the day, and though he hadn't made me any promises—that required believing in a future—I let myself revel in the hope that we'd have one.

~ **27** ~

WE ATE, CLEANED up the house and set it to rights again. It seemed empty and expectant as I stepped outside, bundled in my new fur cloak, and I made a mental promise to come back. If we survived, we should replace at least the food, in case other travelers needed the refuge.

It occurred to me that the former occupants might be living in that dreadful landscape beneath the palace. I knew Zyr didn't want to dash my hopes, but I still nursed the idea that they might return.

Zyr, in gríobhth form, turned his head to look at me expectantly. He'd shifted a bit ago and taken a test flight, to be sure he could. Something else he hadn't spoken aloud, how his confidence had been shaken, but he'd casually told me to wait inside and stay warm while he stretched his wings, and I knew he'd wanted me to be safe if he failed.

But he'd returned, black fur and feathers gleaming with blue highlights in the frosty sunshine. The chill wind off the high peaks ruffled his crest, and his gaze glittered with some of his old fire. I buckled a harness onto him that he'd found, suggesting that I could use it to anchor myself to his back. In case of another aerial battle.

Climbing on, I fastened the straps around my calves and thighs. The fur-lined leather pants Zyr had found for me were ideal for this arrangement. I threaded the final buckle around my waist. As Zyr had said when he found the harness—in the same armory where he'd gotten the bow and where I dug out more arrows and, bless Moranu, a crossbow, too!—with the smallest adjustment, the harness seemed perfectly designed for this purpose: to allow a rider on the back of a flying animal to stay secure and hands free for fighting.

I couldn't decide if that was a good omen or bad, that we followed in the footsteps of the disappeared or captive previous occupants of the well-fortified house. With my new bows at the ready and several quivers stowed in various places, I patted Zyr on the shoulder. He'd had his head turned around, watching with interest. "I'm ready if you are," I told him.

He nodded, giving me a long look, so much of him in it. Then he faced forward, his strong body gathering beneath me, and ran across the stone terrace, leaping off with wings spread. I let out a whoop of pure joy and triumph.

If we died today, it would be on our terms. On the wing and armed to the teeth.

FOR A WHILE we flew in circles. He felt sure that, despite his fragmented memories of our escape, that he hadn't flown more than an hour. It had seemed endless to me, but I believed him. Neither of us had any clue about the direction. Still, I'd assured him the palace had to be easily visible, high on that mountain and with all those shiny windows.

We'd debated approaching by night, but the gríobhth vision worked best in bright daylight and Zyr hadn't been confident of doing a partial shapeshift for night vision in that form. Besides, I had a feeling that Deyrr and his followers were no weaker at night and could be stronger, creatures of darkness that they were.

The vantage from Zyr's back at midday showed the sprawling landscape of n'Andana that we'd missed before. The high mountain peaks that surrounded the palace and that housed our temporary refuge did go for some distance, but then quickly fell away to lower, green and rounded hills. A blue glint in the distance showed the ocean not all that far away on some of our loops.

Spotting a tumble of white stone on the coast that looked more structured than most, I nudged Zyr to investigate. He obligingly flew in that direction, and it soon became clear it was indeed a city, and far more vast than the cliff city at Annfwn. Built partially into the hillsides, but also on top of them, the buildings stood in orderly tiers, as well maintained as our refuge had been.

And equally as empty.

Zyr landed on a parklike hillside above the city proper, and I unbuckled the straps so I could get down, taking my bow and quiver with me. I stared at the silent city with chill horror. "Did she take them all? Even the children, the eldsters, the sick and the weak?"

He nudged me, then took a few steps, settling his wings.

"If you're going to shift," I said to him, "I can take the harness off."

The look he gave me was pure gríobhth arrogance, and still shaped the expression on his face when he became a man, in his perfectly groomed mode. He held up his wrist, showing me the ribbon, as crisp and perfect as when I'd tied it on him. "I've been practicing keeping *things*," he replied, with that same sneer he'd used for the word in the past, but his eyes danced with mischief. "It's not as if it's difficult. Part and parcel of keeping company with mossbacks, I suppose."

I thumped him on the arm and he laughed, making me smile. Something he'd done on purpose, I knew, to help me feel better. He put me in front of him, wrapping his arms protectively around me, as we both surveyed the deathly still landscape.

"There aren't even any natural animals," he observed. "No songbirds. No sign of life in the sea."

"She took everything. Every one of them."

"Building her army."

"Yes."

We stood quietly a moment longer. "We can fly over the city, if you like," he offered. "Maybe some people are in hiding."

"If so, why would they reveal themselves for us? No." I very nearly told Zyr we should make a break for it, fly out over that deceptively tranquil ocean, that we could risk drowning rather than returning to the palace. But that would be the coward's way out.

I sighed, then squared my shoulders. "Let's go get that jewel, if we can't kill her. It will at least slow her down, rob her of some power."

"Dropping her from a high place would slow her down more," he observed with glittering relish.

"If you can make that happen, I'll love you forever."

He spun me around and kissed me. "You already promised that."

"I promised to love you to my dying breath—it's not the same thing."

"It is to me. Tell me again. Tell me as often as you like."

"Yes, well. It bears repeating." I kissed him back. "I'll love you forever, Zyr."

He held me very tightly, as if he'd never let me go.

WE FLEW INLAND again, taking up our previous search pattern. Zyr spotted the palace at the same time I did, swiveling his head to stare at the glittering point on one snow-covered peak. The spires rose high like crags of their own, and a darker road showed in places beneath it. "That's it," I shouted.

With a dip of his head in acknowledgement, he struck out at an oblique angle, powerful wings pouring on the speed. The only other time I'd felt him fly this fast was when we'd been trying to outrun those birds, and I'd been distracted then. Lying low on his body to lessen the resistance, I exulted in the sheer freedom of racing through the air like this. Expecting to die made everything—flying, sex, love, even laughter—all that much sweeter.

Zyr looped behind the peak, climbing as he did—then, coming around, he dove. We'd come in fast and hard, and hope to take them by surprise.

No such luck. A flight of birds rose from behind the castle towers, all sizes and varieties. They swarmed toward us and Zyr took evasive action, folding his wings in a searing dive, then cracking them open to bring us around nearly horizontal. If I hadn't been strapped on, I would've fallen. As it was, I took full advantage of having my hands free. And I knew Zyr's body as well as my own from having him moving inside me, knew the flex and play of his muscles, even his intentions, it seemed.

We moved as one being, the crossbow all I'd hoped, my arrows flying straight and true before I knew I'd aimed. I dropped the biggest from the sky, while Zyr used tail and claws to keep the smaller ones from harrying me. It helped to battle Deyrr's creatures in the air, because we didn't need to prevent them coming at us again in their eternal drive to reach us—only disable them so they couldn't stay aloft.

It would be different on the ground. A fast-approaching prospect as Zyr, with his trademark single-minded intensity, continued on to the castle, refusing to be distracted by our attackers.

He poured on the speed—enough so that he left the clumsy Deyrr undead behind—and drove straight for the palace.

The alert had gone out, clearly, as more fighters, human and animal, poured out of the gates, thronged the walls and crowded the turrets. Some of the humans fired arrows at us, but not well, and Zyr dodged the missiles easily. Shooting us out of the sky wasn't their primary objective anyway. We'd have the real trouble on our hands when we touched down and they mobbed us to take us captive—or we died stopping them.

Thus we wouldn't land. At least not where they expected.

Zyr folded his wings, tightening his profile, accelerating the dive, and protecting them from injury. I pulled the hood and cloak over my exposed skin, unstrung my recurve and put it in against the protection of my body, the crossbow ready in my lap, and buried my face against Zyr's silky fur. My part had finished. I'd described the position of the High Priestess's atrium and how it looked, next to the glassed-in arcade that led to the massive expanse of glass that was the zoo. The zoo would've been easier to hit but breaching that would sentence most of the animals and shapeshifters within to a wintry death.

But we both knew we'd take that if we had to.

Zyr purred in reassurance and warning, and I inhaled his scent. He'd tease me for being typically and tragically Dasnarian, but if I had to die, I viciously celebrated that I'd die bound to him. His plan might work or it might not.

Regardless, I'd made my choice and I regretted nothing.

We hit the glass and time slowed. The shattering, the scream of metal twisting under the impact of our mass hitting it at Zyr's maximum acceleration. A thousand stings made their way through the heavy cloak and we seemed to drift timelessly.

Bracing for impact, I felt Zyr disappear out from under me, tucked my head, and rolled. It still stunned me, slamming the breath from my body. Still dizzy, I fought my way free of the cloak, dropping my crossbow at my feet for backup, stringing my thankfully unbroken bow, and nocking an arrow—beyond glad for the long habit that let me do these things without thought.

Only then did I scan the room, searching out Zyr—who lay on his back, in human form, perfectly beautiful in his blue silk shirt, the High Priestess crouched over him. She bled black oil blood, her face contorted in a snarl of equally black rage as she held his skull, staring into Zyr's eyes, chanting as he convulsed.

I shot her through the neck. Not an ideal shot, but the closest I could without risking hitting Zyr. The force of it tipped her off him, and then I followed up with an arrow through her black heart.

She knelt there, looking up at me, golden hair spilling around her gold-clad body, and laughed at me.

"Oh, sweetling." She tsked, giving me a derisive smile. "Surely you didn't think I'd be that easy to kill?"

I shot an arrow through her mouth, sending her back to the floor with the force of it. "No," I replied evenly, "but I figure chopping you into pieces too small to move will accomplish the same thing."

I reached down and yanked the jewel from her neck, tossing it to Zyr, who'd climbed to his feet. He moved slowly, disoriented, but he caught it—and immediately swallowed the pendant. There'd be no easy reclaiming of the thing.

"Did you have to shoot her through the mouth?" he complained. "I want to hear her scream as I dismember her." His fingers lengthened into long, lethal claws as he stalked toward her. Then he froze, midstep.

I couldn't move either. The High Priestess yanked the arrow out of her throat and sat up, leaving the other two piercing her as if they were nothing more than decorations. "Oh, you silly bean," she hissed. "You stupid, stupid girl. Did you think I needed that paltry jewel to transmit the magic of Deyrr?"

She stood and prowled over to me, leaned in and sniffed. "And you wasted your maidenhead on this filthy beast. You could've had so much more. I offered you a place at my side and you scorned it. For shapeshifter cock." She shook her head in disgust, slipping my bow from my fingers and sending it skittering across the floor.

The doors flew open, soldiers streaming into the room, animals on leashes with them, snarling and slavering to reach us. Winged creatures poured in the broken windows, barring that escape, even if we could've moved.

"Did you think that would save you?" the High Priestess asked, her attention on me. "Deyrr is happy to take you on his lap, virgin or not. You'll just never reach the rank and power that you might have. But you will be his. And you will be mine." She squeezed my breast, then passed her hand between my legs, smiling sweetly, her eyes lightless pits. "You'll be my slave, which will be even more fun. Now watch while I cut my necklace out of your pet."

Against my will, my head turned, fully in her power, and I saw Zyr staring at me in helpless rage. Though I couldn't smile at him, or change my expression in any way, I did my best to show my love for him in my eyes. *I'll love you forever.*

He looked back at me, and I thought I saw the same in his

wild blue eyes.

"Hold still now," the High Priestess crooned, trailing a finger down his chest, parting the silk to bare him. "A pity to mar such a magnificent form. Maybe I'll heal you after. You and your slut can perform for me. Or I'll just have you fuck me while she watches. That would be a fitting punishment for her."

The scream nearly choked me as his flesh began to part, as easily as his shirt had. So loud it rang in my skull that I didn't realize the roaring came from outside. A searing blaze of heat washed over me, and I stumbled, nearly falling with the ability to move again.

Zyr recovered faster, seizing the High Priestess by the throat. And the mob of soldiers flew at him, covering him in a mass of bodies. I ran for my crossbow, and another roar and wash of heat had me spinning to the windows.

A dragon hovered outside. Enormous and blue-black in the sunshine, gleaming like a jewel. With a man riding on its back.

The dragon spouted flame, gentle as a blown kiss, melting away the twisted metal frame, clearing the Deyrr creatures from the area just inside the windows, and landed with a grating scrape of immense talons. The man slid down its leg, sword drawn and ran straight at me where I gaped in shock.

Lieutenant Marskal. "With me, Hawk!" he snapped as he ran past.

I spun to follow his charge. Zyr had become the gríobhth again, rearing up to use both sets of front claws and that whipping tail to decimate his enemies. I couldn't see the High Priestess anywhere. Marskal engaged his attackers with cool, calm decision, employing his sword as meticulously as he had in drills. The dragon—Zynda, surely—snaked her head on her long neck, plucking off a bear lumbering for Zyr's back. She didn't dare use her flame, I realized, with Zyr in the midst of the fray.

I shot a human soldier through the eye, knocking him back, and scanned for the High Priestess. Feeding her to Zynda's incinerating breath would be enough for me.

But I couldn't see her, and more soldiers poured in the doors. We'd be overwhelmed soon, even with our rescuers.

"Zyr!" I shouted, knowing he'd hear me.

His head swiveled my way, sharp beak dripping blood both red and black. Shaking off a wolf doggedly chewing his wing, Zyr seized Marskal and half-leapt, half-flew with him to me. Marskal vaulted to Zynda's back, reaching down a hand to me, to pull me up behind him. Zyr flew to her back and shifted into man form behind me.

Zynda roared, spewing flame across the gallery. But it seemed to hit an invisible wall, evaporating into nothing. Beyond that barrier, the fighters parted, allowing an enormous naked gold man to stride through, the High Priestess by his side. The golden idol of Deyrr, come to life.

"Go!" I screamed and Zynda backwinged off the terrace, dropping low, and angling through a narrow cleft to the far side of the mountain.

She put distance between us and the palace, then wheeled until the setting sun warmed our backs, and flew into the clear blue sky. Taking us home.

~ 28 ~

WE FLEW THROUGH the evening and all the night, Marskal passing back water and food once he'd made certain that we were mostly unharmed and not followed. He and I—the unfortunate mossbacks of the group—had some cuts and deep bruises, but nothing severe enough to keep us from going on.

He assured us that Zynda could fly easily to Annfwn, and knew the way—and that it wouldn't take that long at dragon speeds. We all preferred to get well away from n'Andana and safely home.

Home. Yes, I looked forward to returning to my adopted home.

Otherwise, flying on the dragon didn't allow for much conversation other than terse shouts. I even slept from time to time, warm and secure between the two men—though Zyr kept his arms wrapped around my waist, leaning me back against him so I wouldn't be too much in contact with Marskal. He needn't have been jealous, but the gríobhth nature is a possessive one, and I was fine with being possessed by this man I'd chosen.

I'd given myself to him in the way of my people, and that meant letting him have me in the way of his. Having him nuzzle my neck and press kisses to my temple made the journey that much sweeter.

WE MADE IT to Annfwn at dawn, the sky pink and gold with it. Several Hawks scouts on the backs of flying and swimming shapeshifters spotted us, hailing us with glad welcome. To my astonishment, hundreds—maybe thousands—of sailing ships anchored all around. A perimeter guard of more Hawks and Tala saluted as Zynda sailed through, landing on the beach.

"Yes, it's better," I heard Marskal observe, the wind no longer too loud to hear. "But far from ideal. What if a dragon approaches that isn't friendly?"

Zynda cocked her head, shrugging her wings, and it made me wonder if they'd been having a conversation. She crouched down on the sand, and Marskal slid down her leg with practiced agility, then held his arms up for me. Zyr landed on the sand, and shouldered him aside with a frown. "I'll do that."

To my surprise, Marskal, usually so serious, grinned and held up his hands, glancing at Zynda, who'd lowered her head to nuzzle him.

Zyr helped me down and held me a moment. "Are you good to stand?" he asked, looking me up and down.

"Yes. Go say a proper hello to your sister." I began plucking at the ties of the cloak, more than ready to get the sweltering thing off of me in the warmth of Annfwn.

Zyr nodded crisply, narrowing eyes, walked up to Zynda— and kicked her hard on the snout. "You fucking heroic idiot!" he shouted at her. "You just *had* to go and do it, didn't you?"

Marskal began laughing, silently, bending over with it. I frowned at him, bemused by the reaction. Then gasped when the dragon vanished and Zynda the woman stood in her place. She wore a pale blue wispy gown and her long hair whipped in the breeze. Putting her hands on an astonished Zyr, she pushed him on his ass in the sand.

"What about you?" she demanded. "What in Moranu were you thinking, storming that castle with only a mossback for help!"

"You… you can shapeshift back from Final Form," Zyr stammered, then scrambled to his feet.

"Brilliant observation." She threw up her hands. "Turns out Final Form isn't so final."

He leaned in. "Why didn't you tell me, you stupid harpy?"

She leaned in, too, eyes blazing with blue fire, just like his. How I'd missed their nearly identical appearance—and natures—I couldn't imagine.

"Oh, I don't know, you whining puppy," she snarled, "maybe because we were busy saving your miserable life."

Zyr blinked into the panther, tumbling her back into the sand. I started forward, but Marskal snagged my arm, and in that moment, Zynda became a tiger, rolling the black cat and pinning him with her great jaws.

I pulled at Marskal's grip. "They'll kill each other."

He shook his head, grinning widely. "Trust me. This is something they do. Let them work it out. How about us mossbacks leave them to their Tala games, get patched up and find something real to eat?"

I glanced dubiously at the squabbling siblings—Zyr now a large brown bear who, quite literally, had the snarling tiger by its tail. "If you're sure," I said.

He slung a companionable arm around my shoulders and pointed me at the cliff city. "I am. And perhaps you and I can swap some tales while we're at it."

A graceful blue heron swept down from the city, landing in front of us and becoming Queen Andromeda. Before I quite assimilated that, she'd seized me in a fierce hug. "You did it, you did it, you did it!" she chanted, rocking us both from side to side in her dance of joy.

I laughed, hugging her back, the feeling of embracing another woman—a living woman—reminding me of the sisters I'd left behind.

She set me away from her, holding my shoulders, eyes alight and glimmering with a hint of Moranu's silver. "I want to hear *everything*, but first tell me if you're hurt. I've got a healer waiting. What about you, Marskal?"

He huffed genially. "I'm clearly second-best to the hero of the hour, but I only have a few scratches."

"Knowing you Hawks that means just shy of a mortal injury." Andi took my left arm in her hands, sliding her fingers over the black markings of Deyrr. Her touch tingled, almost like sparks. "I'm removing the last of this taint immediately, however."

"Thank you," I replied fervently. The sparks penetrated, feeling uncomfortably like worms crawling under my skin—with something very like that moving in squirms. Marskal watched with interest, but I had to look away. Two raptors dive-bombed each other nearby, Zyr and Zynda, still at it. A huge shadow passed overhead and I squeaked in alarm.

"It's Kiraka," Andi murumured. "Hold still. She wanted to hear your report of n'Andana."

"Oh," I said, wondering how I was supposed to talk to the ancient dragon, one reported to be excessively cranky and inclined to incinerate people who annoyed her. "Ow!"

"Sorry." Andi didn't sound at all sorry and I glared at her intent face. The great bronze dragon alighted on the beach, folding her wings and lying flat in a sinuous curve. A petite figure on her back climbed down, rather awkwardly, then put her hands on the small of her back and arched, her very pregnant belly obvious in silhouette. Queen Dafne Nakoa Kau Po. This got better all the time. Marskal strode over to great her—probably the dragon, too, for all I knew.

Andi finally released my arm, and when she met my eyes, hers glowed with fulminous moonlight as in my vision. Andromeda the sorceress. "The taint is gone," she told me, echoes of that ocean sound in her voice.

I glanced at my arm, seeing the chain of black talons still chasing themselves around the curve of my muscle.

"I can't get rid of the mark entirely, not without abrading the skin, and then it would leave a scar," she told me with regret. "But we can do that if you want it gone."

"No," I said. "That's all right. It's a reminder that I'm not the same person I used to be."

Andi nodded gravely. "A badge of honor." Then she smiled, glancing at the still-battling Zynda and Zyr. "Come on, let's heal and feed you, then you can tell us all your tales."

IT ENDED UP being hours of tale-telling, especially as King Rayfe and Queen Andromeda declared we could eat in the council chambers and brief everyone relevant at once. Dafne sat with us, relating questions and details from Kiraka. They'd gotten the bones of our story out of me—over hot tea and a plate various people kept filling for me—before Zynda and Zyr joined us. They'd both shifted back to their cleaned-up versions of themselves, so showed no signs of their spontaneous battle—but also had their arms around the other's waist and heads tilted together in some quiet exchange.

They parted as they reached our gathering, Zynda giving me a warm smile that made her deep blue eyes sparkle, before she went to Marskal and slid into the seat next to him. Zyr simply picked me up, sat in my place, and settled me on his lap, oblivious to the interested looks around the table. I gestured to my plate and he helped himself to that, too.

Queen Andromeda—I could hardly call her Andi with all the Tala council present—explained to Zyr how Zynda had been able to magically follow the thread to our location, expressing again how sorry she was that it had taken so long. Zyr produced the pendant, handing it over to his queen, and she laid it on the table, regarding it thoughtfully from time to time.

Messengers had already gone out to High Queen Ursula, to Jepp and Kral out on the *Hákyrling*, and also to Windroven where Queen Amelia and Ash had started negotiations with another newly awakened dragon.

They talked on about strategy and defensive plans, but the long night on top of the battle soon took its toll on me. A full belly and the soothing comfort of Zyr's embrace lulled me into sleep.

I AWOKE SOMETIME later—a long time later, because night had fallen—in a big bed with open sky above me, and Moranu's bright moon shining in. Frowning at it in confusion, I wondered where I could be. Then Zyr's arms wound around me, drawing me against his naked body, his mouth nuzzling kisses on my neck.

"You're awake?" he murmured.

"Yes, I'm sorry I woke you." I was in his apartments in

Annfwn. I remembered that open ceiling for flying out of and wondered what he did when it rained.

He leaned up on one elbow, a candle beside the bed flaring to life. Brushing my hair back from my face—he must've taken it out of the braid when he put me to bed, stripping me naked, too—he studied my face. "You look better," he announced.

I scowled at him. "I didn't know I looked bad."

"You looked tired and beat up," he informed me. "The healer did wonderful work, but they should've let you sleep sooner rather than interrogating you."

"Maybe everyone was waiting for you and Zynda to finish beating each other up," I replied tartly.

He grinned, kissing me on the nose. "It's really good to fight with her again. Thank you for your patience."

I laid a hand on his cheek. "I'm so happy for you."

"Of course, she's even more insufferable now." He lay back with a sigh, gathering me against him. "All impressed with herself for being able to outdo my gríobhth form. She can fly incredibly fast in that form. Plus there's the breathing fire thing."

"Does this mean you want to learn to be a dragon, too?" I teased.

"Maybe." He rolled his head on the pillow to look at me. "Would you mind?"

"Why would I mind? You should do whatever makes you happy."

"It's not that—or not only that—but we'll need all the firepower we can muster to fight that army of Deyrr."

A sobering thought. "And the might of Dasnaria."

"Yes." He sounded more serious, too. "We got word back from the *Hákyrling*. The Dasnarian navy is amassing outside the barrier."

"Ah."

"But we have time enough to worry about that." He turned on his side, pillowing his head on his bent arm and gave me a long, somber look. "I won't try for dragon form, though, if it would bother you."

"I don't understand why you think it would," I replied cautiously.

He shrugged, playing with a lock of my hair, and I saw he had my ribbon around his wrist. "I don't know how to do this monogamy thing. Aren't I supposed to ask you about important life decisions?"

I caught my breath. "Monogamy thing?"

"Yes. See? Here you are, in *my* bed." He waggled his eyebrows meaningfully.

"So I see," I answered, a laugh welling up in me. "I'm happy to be here."

"Good. And I have it on excellent authority that, according to Dasnarian law, since the offer has been made and accepted, it can't be controverted."

"That's true," I breathed, surprised that I could with the hope in my chest crowding everything else out.

"Will you let me care for you for the rest of your life, Karyn?"

"Yes." I framed his beautiful, beloved face with my hands. "Will you let me care for you the rest of your life, Zyr?"

He turned his face to kiss my fingers. "Yes. You can tell me what else we need to do."

"To do?"

"To be married," he replied with some impatience. "Whatever rituals you mossback Dasnarians do, I'm doing them."

I couldn't breathe again. "You don't have to do that, Zyr."

"Oh yes, I do. You're mine. You said so. You promised to love me forever."

My heart flooded with love. "I am yours, yes. But I know the Tala are different, that they're not monogamous. I'll love you forever no matter what."

"Well…" He looked somewhat abashed. "I may have over-simplified. That depends a great deal on our First Form, and that fundamental nature."

"Oh yes?" I wound my arms around his neck, rubbing my nipples against him. "I think the gríobhth is lustful, fierce, and possessive."

His eyes glinted in the candlelight, hands sliding down to cup my bottom, and lift one of my legs over his hip. "Yes. And monogamous, did I mention?"

I gasped as his clever fingers stroked me, the heat rising between us. "I think you left that out."

"Hmm." He kissed me deeply. "I spent a lot of time in the gríobhth mind. And heart. Did I mention that I love you more than my own life?"

I laughed. "No, but I knew."

"Figures. The gríobhth knew, too. It just took me a while to catch up." He kissed me again, and then again, as if he couldn't stop. "We'll marry in the Tala way, too. That will convince you of how much I love you, gréine."

"I don't need convincing—but you can tell me as often as you like."

He rolled me onto my back and slid into me, long and slow and sweet, then brushed a kiss over my mouth, his wild blue eyes watching me. "Of course, the Tala way mostly involves a lot of sex," he murmured, raining kisses on my upturned face. "And a little blood."

I laughed. "Of course it does." I wound my fingers in his hair and dragged him down to cover me.

the saga of The Uncharted Realms continues in
The Dragons of Summer
part of the
Seasons of Sorcery fantasy anthology
available for preorder now:
https://www.jeffekennedy.com/seasons-of-sorcery/

TITLES BY JEFFE KENNEDY

OTHER FANTASY ROMANCES

A COVENANT OF THORNS

Rogue's Pawn
Rogue's Possession
Rogue's Paradise

THE TWELVE KINGDOMS

Negotiation
The Mark of the Tala
The Tears of the Rose
The Talon of the Hawk
Heart's Blood
For Crown and Kingdom

THE UNCHARTED REALMS

The Pages of the Mind
The Edge of the Blade
The Snows of Windroven
The Shift of the Tide
The Arrows of the Heart
The Dragons of Summer

THE CHRONICLES OF DASNARIA

Prisoner of the Crown
Exile of the Seas
Warrior of the World

SORCEROUS MOONS

Lonen's War
Oria's Gambit
The Tides of Bára
The Forests of Dru

THE FORGOTTEN EMPIRES

The Orchid Throne

CONTEMPORARY ROMANCES

Shooting Star

MISSED CONNECTIONS

Last Dance
With a Prince
Since Last Christmas

CONTEMPORARY EROTIC ROMANCES

Exact Warm Unholy
The Devil's Doorbell

FACETS OF PASSION

Sapphire
Platinum
Ruby
Five Golden Rings

FALLING UNDER

Going Under
Under His Touch
Under Contract

EROTIC PARANORMAL

MASTER OF THE OPERA E-SERIAL

Master of the Opera, Act 1: Passionate Overture
Master of the Opera, Act 2: Ghost Aria
Master of the Opera, Act 3: Phantom Serenade
Master of the Opera, Act 4: Dark Interlude
Master of the Opera, Act 5: A Haunting Duet
Master of the Opera, Act 6: Crescendo
Master of the Opera

BLOOD CURRENCY

Blood Currency

BDSM FAIRYTALE ROMANCE

Petals and Thorns

OTHER WORKS

Birdwoman
Hopeful Monsters
Teeth, Long and Sharp

Thank you for reading!

About Jeffe Kennedy

Jeffe Kennedy is an award-winning author whose works include novels, non-fiction, poetry, and short fiction. She has been a Ucross Foundation Fellow, received the Wyoming Arts Council Fellowship for Poetry, and was awarded a Frank Nelson Doubleday Memorial Award. She serves on the Board of Directors for the Science Fiction and Fantasy Writers of America (SFWA) as a Director at Large.

Her award-winning fantasy romance trilogy *The Twelve Kingdoms* hit the shelves starting in May 2014. Book 1, *The Mark of the Tala*, received a starred Library Journal review and was nominated for the RT Book of the Year while the sequel, *The Tears of the Rose* received a Top Pick Gold and was nominated for the RT Reviewers' Choice Best Fantasy Romance of 2014. The third book, *The Talon of the Hawk*, won the RT Reviewers' Choice Best Fantasy Romance of 2015. Two more books followed in this world, beginning the spin-off series *The Uncharted Realms*. Book one in that series, *The Pages of the Mind*, has also been nominated for the RT Reviewer's Choice Best Fantasy Romance of 2016 and won RWA's 2017 RITA® Award. The second book, *The Edge of the Blade*, released December 27, 2016, and is a PRISM finalist, along with *The Pages of the Mind*. The next in the series, *The Shift of the Tide*, came out in August, 2017. A high fantasy trilogy, The Chronicles of Dasnaria, taking place in *The Twelve Kingdoms* world began releasing from Rebel Base books in 2018.

She also introduced a new fantasy romance series, *Sorcerous*

Moons, which includes *Lonen's War*, *Oria's Gambit*, *The Tides of Bàra*, and *The Forests of Dru*. She's begun releasing a new contemporary erotic romance series, *Missed Connections*, which started with *Last Dance* and continues in *With a Prince* and *Since Last Christmas*.

In 2019, St. Martins Press will release the first book, *The Orchid Throne*, in a new fantasy romance series, *The Forgotten Empires*.

Her other works include a number of fiction series: the fantasy romance novels of *A Covenant of Thorns*; the contemporary BDSM novellas of the *Facets of Passion*; an erotic contemporary serial novel, *Master of the Opera*; and the erotic romance trilogy, *Falling Under*, which includes *Going Under*, *Under His Touch* and *Under Contract*.

She lives in Santa Fe, New Mexico, with two Maine coon cats, plentiful free-range lizards and a very handsome Doctor of Oriental Medicine.

Jeffe can be found online at her website: JeffeKennedy.com, every Sunday at the popular SFF Seven blog, on Facebook, on Goodreads and pretty much constantly on Twitter @jeffekennedy. She is represented by Sarah Younger of Nancy Yost Literary Agency.

jeffekennedy.com

facebook.com/Author.Jeffe.Kennedy

twitter.com/jeffekennedy

goodreads.com/author/show/1014374.Jeffe_Kennedy

Sign up for her newsletter here.

jeffekennedy.com/sign-up-for-my-newsletter